Vis Major

Railroad Men, an Act of God—White Death at Wellington

For Jim

Other books by Martin Burwash

Cascade Division, 1995, Fox Publication
The Great Adventure, 1998, Fox Publications

Vis Major

Railroad Men, an Act of God—White Death at Wellington

By

Martin Burwash

An Historical Novel

iUniverse, Inc.
New York Bloomington

Vis Major
Railroad Men, an Act of God—White Death at Wellington

iUniverse books may be ordered through booksellers or by contacting:

iUniverse
1663 Liberty Drive
Bloomington, IN 47403
www.iuniverse.com
1-800-Authors (1-800-288-4677)

ISBN: 978-1-4401-6177-3 (pbk)
ISBN: 978-1-4401-6179-7 (hc)
ISBN: 978-1-4401-6178-0 (ebk)

LCCN: 2009933020

Printed in the United States of America

iUniverse rev. date: 8/24/2009

To all the people of Wellington, both spirit and flesh, this book is dedicated.

Great Northern Rotary X-800 at Wellington, circa 1910. Engineer John Robert Meath standing lower left. Photo courtesy, Mrs. James Meath.

"It is plain from the evidence in the case and from the undisputed facts, that this avalanche was what is known in law as vis major, or an act of God ..." Chief Justice Judge Herman D. Crow, speaking for the Washington State Supreme Court in the case of Topping v. The Great Northern Railway, August, 1914.

A Note to the Reader

This text began in 1961, when, as an eight-year-old boy, I was sprawled across our living room floor, absorbed in the December issue of *Trains Magazine.* Contained within its pages was a three-paragraph reference to a tragic snow slide that occurred in the Cascade Mountains, just east of our house in Tacoma, Washington. A spark was ignited by that article, and a fire of interest in that event has burned inside of me ever since.

Although other accounts of the 1910 Wellington Avalanche have been published, none have been written strictly from the point of view of those who knew best what actually happened—the railroad men who battled the week-long storm that triggered the disaster. This book is an attempt to present the story from their perspective, and give the reader an appreciation for what those men experienced.

What was it like to operate a steam-driven snow plow day after day without food or rest? What effect did hours of exposure to blinding snow and bone-chilling wind have on the minds and bodies of the men? How did men, charged with the responsibility of keeping the railroad open, deal with the frustration, fatigue, loss of will, and spirit?

No facts have been consciously altered. All events described carry with them historical documentation. The dialogue is purely fictitious, but is based on actual spoken testimony and what is known to be true about the lives and backgrounds of the characters. If, in the process of bringing these men back to life, I have taken certain liberties in their speech and thoughts, I hope I will be forgiven. It was done in an effort to finally give voice to men long silenced by litigation and the dark void of eternity.

Martin Burwash

Part One

Wellington … "the end of the earth." – Basil Sherlock

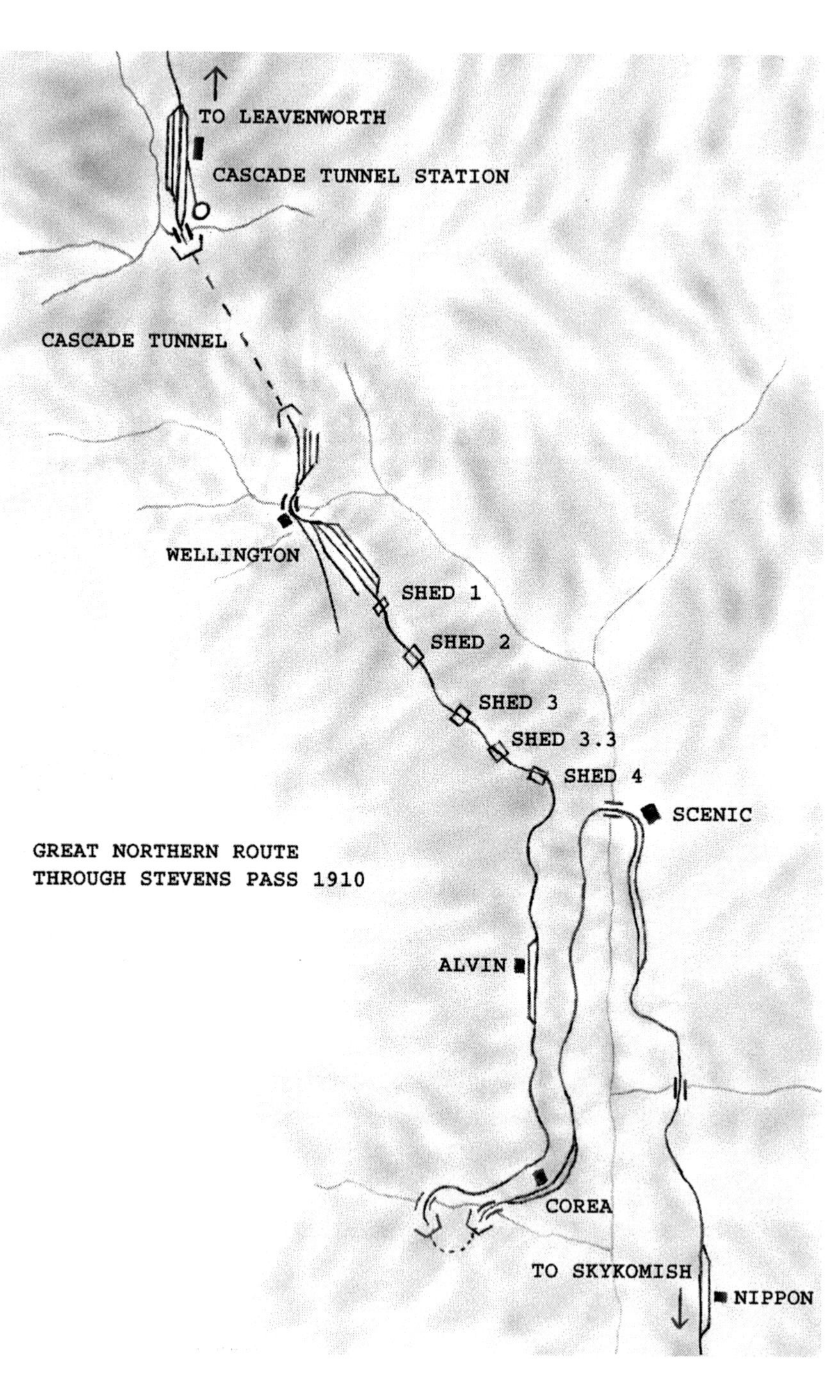
TO LEAVENWORTH
CASCADE TUNNEL STATION
CASCADE TUNNEL
WELLINGTON
SHED 1
SHED 2
SHED 3
SHED 3.3
SHED 4
SCENIC
GREAT NORTHERN ROUTE
THROUGH STEVENS PASS 1910
ALVIN
COREA
TO SKYKOMISH
NIPPON

September 6, 1909
William Harrington, Assistant Trainmaster

Harrington knew before he entered Superintendent O'Neill's office that afternoon why he had been summoned. He was there to tell the superintendent whether or not he was willing to assume the duties of the "Snow King" this coming winter. The offer would come, that he knew. The pride he took in being a good freight train conductor and his performance had landed him the position the previous two winters.

What do I tell him? Can't make up my mind, Harrington thought.

Harrington's battle with his own inability to decide began when he received the written notice from O'Neill that he was once again to be promoted to the Assistant Trainmaster in charge of snow removal.

Couldn't wait for the snow to fall last year. Can't shake the notion this one's gonna be a bad one. Lil wants me off the plows. Should never said I'd tell O'Neill "No." Need the money. Kids ain't cheap. Never good to thumb your nose at a job offered by the Super. Quick way to get on his shit list. Living with Lil, not O'Neill. Lil. Wants the money. Doesn't want me away earning it. Can't win with women.

It was hot and sticky outside, but Harrington's nerves caused him to perspire more than the weather.

Sweating like a pig. Jumpier than a frog with a lit match pinned to his ass. Got the door open waiting for me. Here goes.

Seeing Harrington, O'Neill motioned him to enter and sit in a chair placed at the left-front corner of the desk. The superintendent leaned back in his chair and stretched. Immediately a cigar went to his lips followed by a lit match. Harrington sat, said nothing, and watched O'Neill fold one arm across his chest, the other holding his cigar. The uncomfortable Harrington attempted to look casual as well.

Damned chair. Built for a backache.

Harrington crossed his legs, but could not find a natural position for his arms or hands. He knew O'Neill was eying him closely, all the while titled back slightly in his chair, calmly smoking.

Damn you, O'Neill. Know I'm on pins and needles.

"Care for a smoke, Mr. Harrington?" O'Neill offered. He took his cigar from his mouth and tipped the ashes into a full ashtray.

"No thanks, sir. Never took up the habit. My wife wouldn't have it if I did, I guess," Harrington admitted.

"Just off a run, eh?" O'Neill once again leaned back in his chair enjoying his smoke.

Christ, kill the chitchat. Harrington squirmed in the rigid wood chair, trying to clam his nerves. "Yes sir, had the 451 time freight. Heavy with wheat it was."

O'Neill nodded in silent agreement, blowing the smoke casually between his lips. "And the roadbed, the boys getting it ready for winter? I need to get up there and inspect it." O'Neill continued to make idle conversation.

"Mr. Harley is about done at Shed 3.3, sir. The track is in as good a shape as I've ever seen, and that's a damned fact."

If you don't get to it I will. Harrington was beginning to fume under the stress of his own anxiety.

"Sometimes I envy you boys out there on the road," O'Neill lamented. "Try staying cooped up in here shuffling papers for a couple of weeks straight."

There was another awkward silence. Letting out a slight sigh, O'Neill, grabbed a file from his desk. He rose from his chair, walked behind Harrington, and closed the office door before returning to his desk.

"I need you up there as the Snow King, Bill."

The almost pleading tone to O'Neill's voice and sudden informality caught Harrington totally off guard. *Jesus Christ, putting the squeeze on.*

"Well, I've given it a lot of thought, sir, no doubt about that. And I… well sir, you know I thank you for giving me first crack and all. Just hoping you're not overlooking a few of the other boys that might do a better job. I know Ira Clary sure can pilot a plow train."

It was a speech Harrington practiced any number of times over the past few weeks.

A slight sense of relief came across his body.

Spit it out. See how he takes it. Might let me off the hook.

For a moment it appeared that O'Neill was seriously considering what Harrington had just said. "Ira Clary is indeed a very capable conductor and knows the mountain," O'Neill allowed. "Still, he needs more time to learn to hold that Irish temper of his. No, it's you I need to take charge this winter. I need your experience. I don't want to break in a new man this winter."

O'Neill stood, file still in hand and walked around to the front of his desk. He pulled from it a letter from General Manager Gruber and handed it to Harrington.

"I'm sure you know about our contract with the Postal Service. We're going to be adding two new trains just to handle the mail." O'Neill paused to judge Harrington's reaction.

Harrington gazed at the letter not really reading it, all the while stroking his thick, black moustache. *Damn the luck. Brass putting the screws to O'Neill, he's puttin' the screws to me. Gotta keep the line open for the mail.*

"Been hearing talk of these mail trains," Harrington replied.

"The UP is coming on strong," O'Neill continued. "They're offering to haul for slightly less, but we still have a shorter route to Seattle."

O'Neill was now perched on the edge of his desk, just inches from Harrington. He finally got down to the point.

"Gruber is on my ass about this. The postal service is going to be watching our on-time performance real close this winter. Those sneaky bastards over at the UP … they've got the post office scared that we can't consistently deliver on time in the winter because of our route. UP is saying just because our route is shorter, doesn't mean it's faster."

O'Neill paused and took another couple of quick puffs from his cigar, exhaling the smoke while Harrington digested this information.

Wished to hell he'd blow that smoke out the window. Getting a headache. Got O'Neill, Lil, and now the goddamned UP ganged up against me.

"What it comes down to, Bill, we've got to keep the pass open this winter," O'Neill continued. "You see what I'm driving at here? Not the winter to be breaking in a new Snow King. I need your experience up there."

"So if we lose any mail to the UP this winter, I take the fall. Well, I got to hand it to you, Jim, that's one hell of a way to convince a man to take a job that's already a pain in the ass," Harrington said, shaking his head.

"Yeah, I know, but you need to know what we're up against. Besides, you won't be the only scapegoat. The three of us will be in the stew pot together. You, me, and Blackburn."

"Jim—" Harrington paused briefly, gauging his sudden informality, "—me and Blackburn don't get along so good. You know that. He's good at going against my calls and decisions. I mean, I understand I'm just a temporary assistant trainmaster, but as I see it, we need to know going into this who's doing what."

Returning to his chair, O'Neill leaned on the right armrest. It was Harrington's turn to eye his boss. He watched O'Neill attempt to rub the fatigue out of his eyes, then squeeze the bridge of his nose.

"Blackburn's a very good trainmaster, Bill. Wouldn't have him up there if he wasn't. He'll probably end up as a superintendent. He just needs some time to learn how to handle the men. I'll have a talk with him and see if we can't come to a clear understanding of duties."

Another silence found its way into the room.

What are you gonna do, sack him? Blackburn ain't gonna change.

"I know you don't want the job. Hell, I had that figured when you stalled off responding to my letter," O'Neill said, interrupting Harrington's thoughts. "But damn it, you're the only man on this division I can trust with this responsibility, Bill. Truth be known, if you were to say yes, well, I'd be personally grateful."

O'Neill spoke in a tone so gentle it reminded Harrington of a man courting a beautiful woman. The impulse to say no was still strong. He was torn between his sense of duty toward the railroad, towards

O'Neill, and the promise to his wife that he would turn the position down.

Need to get up. Walk around. Take a leak. Can't think clear.

Harrington again stroked his moustache, a habit he had when he was trying to make up his mind. He took a deep breath, just to calm down.

It was that voice. A man of O'Neill's strength and authority, talking to him as if he was in dire need of a personal favor, that tone of voice was enough to convince Harrington to again take charge of snow removal across the pass.

That son of a bitch. Probably never uses that tone on his own family, Harrington surmised. *Worked on me. Can't say no.* He dropped his chin to his chest and let out a long sigh. With the image of Lillian's stern look searing through his head, he made his decision.

"Okay, I'll do it. I'm your man for another winter."

"Well, I'm a little overwhelmed with your enthusiasm there, Bill, but I'm grateful. Really, I am. It takes a load off my mind knowing you will be up there when the snow starts flying."

Maybe for you. My troubles are just starting.

Harrington picked up his hat and stood up. O'Neill met him, stepping around from behind his desk extending his hand. Harrington grasped it and felt the power of O'Neill's grip. He countered by squeezing the superintendent's hand as tightly as he could. Releasing their near-death grip, they walked to the office door, O'Neill opening it and gesturing for Harrington to exit first.

Getting the royal treatment. Give the boss what he wants, you're the best damned guy on the block. Soon as something goes wrong on my watch, be the first one on my ass.

"Mr. Longcoy, Conductor Harrington has agreed to assume the duties of the Assistant Trainmaster again this winter," O'Neill announced. "Make sure the proper papers are drawn up and ready. Mr. Harrington, I will see you later this year, I'm sure."

"I'm sure we will meet up again soon enough, sir," Harrington replied, making certain the formality had returned now that they were speaking in front of O'Neill's clerk, Earl Longcoy. He watched O'Neill return to his office, closing the door behind him.

"Well, congratulations, Mr. Harrington," Longcoy said in a cheery voice.

Harrington just nodded at him, turned, and left.

Christ, kid. Haven't got a goddamned idea what this means. Just agreed to another winter of no sleep. Living in a damned snowbound hell. Get to go home and tell Lil I just broke my promise. Gonna have hell to pay.

November 13, 1909
Basil Sherlock, Telegrapher

Concentrating on the dots and dashes coming across the telegraph wire, Sherlock didn't even notice the stooped little man entering the Wellington station office. His headset on, the earpiece glued to his left ear, Sherlock was bent over the tabletop desk that filled the bay window of the depot. His pencil moved across the pad of thin paper used to transcribe train orders as the well-trained partnership of his ear, mind, and hand were translating tiny electric pulses coming from the dispatcher in Everett into the words that ran the railroad.

With snow falling all week from Scenic eastward, nearly to Merritt, Conductor Harrington assumed his duties as the Snow King. In as much as the day-to-day business of calling snow plow crews and communications was centered at Wellington, the workload of the operator on duty increased significantly.

"Harder the snow falls, harder the key rattles," Sherlock muttered. A plow train had been clearing the day's accumulation of snow along the line. Sherlock was engrossed in the task of issuing clearances so the plow and pusher locomotive could depart Cascade Tunnel Station and come west to Wellington where they would be serviced and spotted for the night.

"Hate to bother you, sir. Mind if I stand by your stove and warm up a bit?"

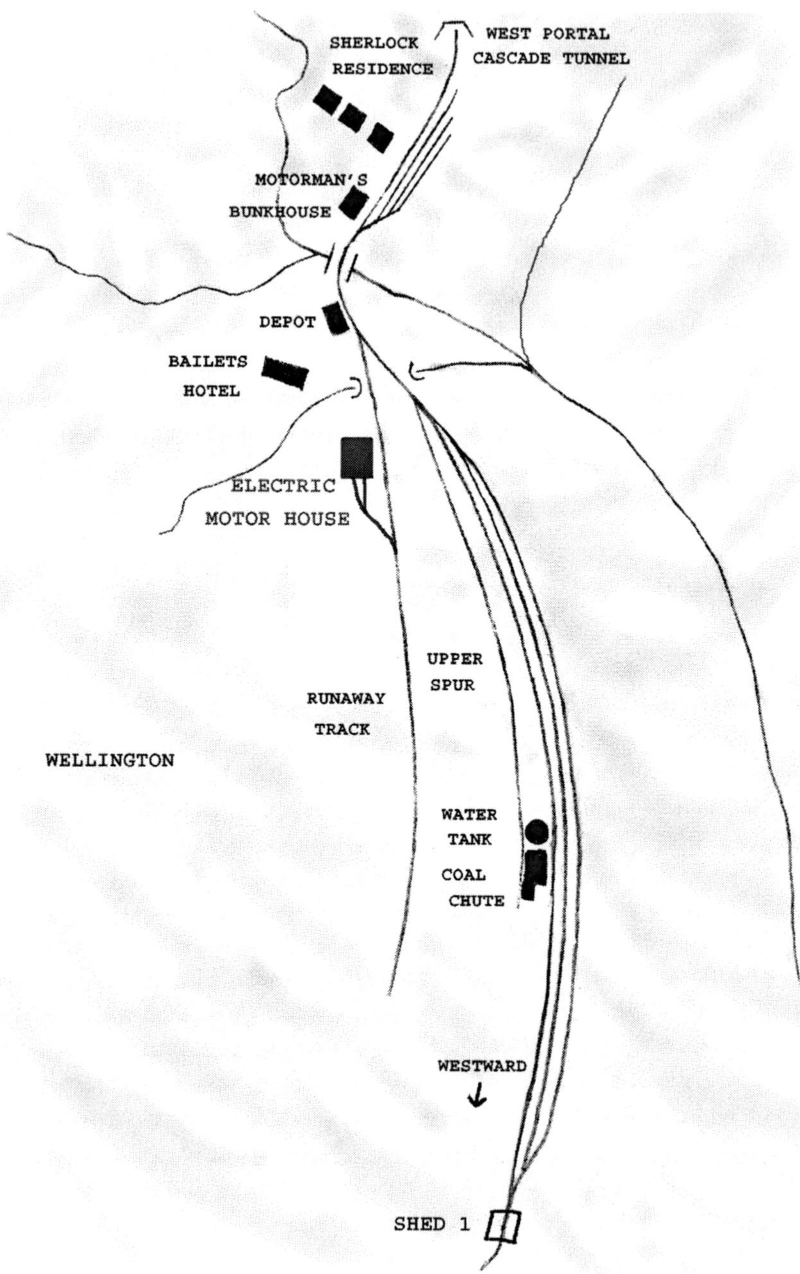
SHERLOCK
RESIDENCE
WEST PORTAL
CASCADE TUNNEL
MOTORMAN'S
BUNKHOUSE
DEPOT
BAILETS
HOTEL
ELECTRIC
MOTOR HOUSE
UPPER
SPUR
RUNAWAY
TRACK
WELLINGTON
WATER
TANK
COAL
CHUTE
WESTWARD
SHED 1

Sherlock's head bolted upright, his eyes wide.

"Good Lord, man!"

Quickly regaining his composure, Sherlock gave the man the once-over. The intruder was small, weighing barely 100 pounds. A heavy backpack and rifle were strapped to his back, causing him to stand slightly bent at the waist. A couple of days' sparse growth speckled his hollowed, red cheeks. The man wore a dirty coat and from under a drooping, wet hat he stared back at Sherlock.

Hunter. Too broke to stay in the hotel. Too wet to stay outside.

"No harm, I guess. Just keep to yourself and keep quiet," Sherlock snapped. "I'm busy here with railroad business."

The intruder said nothing, but lowered his rifle and pack to the floor. Facing away from Sherlock, he commenced to warm his hands over the top of the coal-fired pot-bellied stove in the back corner of the room.

Sherlock silently fumed, all the while tapping a confirmation of an order back to the dispatcher on his telegraph. *Busy? More like overwhelmed, Never dreamed the workload would be this heavy. Middle of nowhere. Snowbound hell. Telegraphers should band together. Demand a higher pay scale.*

Sherlock and his wife, Althea, came to Wellington in the late summer. A man with higher seniority "bumped" him from his previous position at the Great Northern station at New Westminster, British Columbia, just across the Washington boarder. Positions were often open at Wellington, where the turn-over of personnel was high. Will Flannery, the senior operator at the station held the day shift, "1st Trick." Sherlock was assigned "2nd" Trick, 4 p.m.-to-midnight. The isolation was wearing on Sherlock. In three months time, he had made few friends. His serious nature, often pouting attitude and lack of humor quickly alienated him from the other railroaders working at Wellington.

Althea thinks this is some kind of grand outing. More like a career breaker. Agent at New West had it in for me from the beginning. Might be young, but know more about running a station than him.

Although only 22 years old, Sherlock was an experienced telegraph operator. Even so, the complexities of the duties required at Wellington came as a surprise. It seemed to him that Wellington and

Cascade Tunnel Station were like the opposite bulbs of an hourglass. The Cascade Tunnel was its narrow neck. Unlike the sands flowing naturally through the neck, however, with the constant pressure of the dispatchers and Trainmaster Arthur Blackburn, Sherlock felt he was required to wade into the sand-filled chamber and push as many grains through the narrow passage as he possibly could. Snow just compounded the problem, adding to the flow the snow plow trains now operating across the pass.

Three quick strokes of a bell broke the silence of the room. The little man, still hovered over the stove, jumped and spun around.

"What was that?" came his anxious inquiry.

"Just never mind," Sherlock said, rising from his chair. "It's a signal telling me a train is ready to come through the tunnel."

From the corner of his eye, Sherlock could see that the hunter accepted the explanation, but kept watching, intrigued to see what would happen next.

Up and down. Inside one minute, outside the next. Don't see why they even bother giving us a chair. Never sit in it more than five minutes.

Sherlock walked over to the staff machine, a strange-looking mechanism mounted on the outside wall of the room. These machines hung in each station and were used to control the movements of trains across the pass. With the lock released by the station operator in Cascade Tunnel Station, Sherlock pulled a staff baton from the machine and prepared to hand it to the crew of the approaching train. Possession of the staff gave the train permission to proceed to the next station. It was a relay of sorts; a staff would be dropped off and reinserted into the machine at the same time the new staff was picked up as the train passed each station. Since only one staff could be removed from the machine at a time, this prevented two trains from occupying the same section of track at once.

Yet another bell rang. Sherlock, back at his desk, put on a single earphone and pulled a telephone mouthpiece mounted on an accordion frame towards his face.

Stepping on a foot treadle under his desk, he spoke into the mouthpiece, "Wellington." Sherlock strained to hear the crackling voice on the other end.

"This is Cascade Tunnel. Harrington's outfit is just leaving. He says he'll keep the staff until he's done servicing and tied down in the upper yard."

"I copy that Cascade Tunnel. I have his clearances ready."

Sherlock rolled up the orders he just received over the telegraph and tied together copies for both the engineer and the conductor. He took a bamboo hoop on a long handle from a rack on the wall and secured one set of orders to its frame. Still grumbling over the workload, Sherlock donned his heavy winter coat, stuffed the other set of orders in his pocket, and grabbed a lantern. It took a moment of searching, but he finally found a match from an inner vest pocket, and lit the lamp. Although it was barely 5:30, darkness was fast setting into the mountains.

Once outside, he leaned the order hoop against the wall. He carefully picked his way across the wood station platform and down the ramp to ground level.

Slick as snot out here. Shouldn't have cleaned off all the snow.

He approached the runaway switch then set lantern down in the snow next to the stand. Digging into his pants pocket he pulled out a set of keys. The cold mountain air numbed Sherlock's fingers. Twice he dropped the keys in the snow before he was able to release the lock on the runaway track switch-stand. Grabbing the hinged lever, Sherlock tugged on its handle as hard as he could, swinging his body clockwise at the same moment.

Going to break my back throwing this switch ten times a night.

Twice more he jerked on the lever before the switch points yielded to his strength and moved into position, aligning the runaway track. A light from the east and the shrill sound of a steam whistle echoing announced the plow train's arrival.

The size and width of the snow plow bearing down on him intimidated Sherlock. Instinctively he stepped back, away from the switch-stand. Slipping, he nearly fell over a small pile of snow mounded next to the track.

"Easy there, Sherlock," Harrington hollered, climbing down from the cab of the plow. "Might as well wait 'til the snow gets good and deep before you start falling on your ass."

Sherlock ignored the jab. "I have your clearances here, Mr. Harrington." He pulled the orders from his coat pocket.

"Hey Sherlock! You got the coffee pot drained already?"

Sherlock winced upon hearing the voice of Engineer Bob Meath calling out from the plow.

"I haven't had any, but there's a hunter in there warming up. He might have had a cup or two," Sherlock replied. *Just what I need, Meath in town. Should get double pay just for putting up with him.*

"A hunter you say. Well, well." Sherlock obviously caught Meath's attention with the announcement that a stranger was in the station.

"Be right back, Boss. I'm gonna get me a jolt of ol' Basil's special brew." With the agility of a cat, Meath sprang from the plow, landing on both feet on the station platform.

Wished he would've slipped and fallen on his ass.

"Make it quick, Meath, we need to get serviced and clear," Harrington warned.

"Feel free to water those tea pots without me. I can hold down the fort here," Meath replied over his shoulder.

"Just get your coffee and get your ass back out to the plow," Harrington snarled. His words fell on deaf ears, as Meath had already disappeared into the station. Turning to Sherlock, Harrington grabbed his orders. "You can head back in, Sherlock. Coal and water aren't bad off, so we should be clear in half an hour or so."

"As you wish, Mr. Harrington."

Sherlock picked up his lantern and had almost returned to the order hoop when Meath came bursting back outside, a steaming cup of coffee in his hand.

"Good God, man, watch where you're going," Sherlock scolded. *Can't imagine them trusting this man with something as important as a snow plow.*

"Easy, Basil, no harm done. Say, did you know that poor drowned rat in there only has a buck-fifty to his name? Kind of a sinister look about him, too. Might have to call in the sheriff to investigate."

"Goddamnit, Meath, get back on that plow! We're leaving!" Harrington roared.

How does Harrington put up with him? Beyond me. Sherlock shook his head in disgust. *Meath. Absolute imbecile.*

"Yes sir, Sherlock," Meath calmly continued, ignoring Harrington.

"Might have to bring the court into session this evening to take care of this matter. So you be ready."

Meath, careful not to spill his coffee, made his way back to the snow plow.

"Hey Al," he called into the plow, "grab this coffee. I gotta climb on before the Snow King leaves me behind …" and, looking right at Harrington, continued, " ...and wouldn't that be a shame."

Brakeman Al Dougherty appeared at the cab door and cradled Meath's coffee cup, taking a sip while Meath scampered up the ladder. Raising the battered tin cup in a toast, Dougherty looked at Sherlock, "Good cup of mud, Sherlock."

Sherlock pretended he was busy with the order hoop, ignoring Dougherty.

Harrington climbed on below Meath. Swinging his lantern, he gave the engineer of the pusher locomotive the "go-ahead." Two short blasts from the locomotive's whistle acknowledged Harrington's signal, and the outfit slowly moved past the depot.

As the locomotive clanked past, Sherlock held the hoop upright, which allowed the engineer to snag the orders and staff with his outstretched arm. Bob Ford leaned out the cab window, and as he grabbed his orders he shouted out to Sherlock to make sure Meath didn't take all the coffee. "Could be a long night," he said with a grin.

What does O'Neill see in that Harrington? Absolutely no control over those men. Going to be up to mischief all night.

Back in the office, Sherlock took off his coat, still agitated over the exchange with Meath. As he hung it on the rack he again eyed the hunter.

"You realize, sir, you can't stay here unless you have a ticket on one of the trains. Do you have a ticket, or are you planning to purchase one?"

"All's I got is a buck-fifty on me. That get me back to Seattle?"

"Hardly, sir. Well, if you're not going to be boarding a train tonight, it's best you leave and find accommodations elsewhere."

"Just let me stay a mite longer," the man pleaded. "Another hour or so and I'll head out and leave ya alone. I don't suppose you'd tell me when the next freight train is due through."

"Indeed I will not, sir. And if you're smart, you'll keep those thoughts to yourself. We don't take to hobos hopping our freight trains."

Got to get him out of here. Stay here too long they'll catch him and set-up that damnable court. Best to send him packing right now. Can't let anyone know I tipped him off.

"Sir, I must ask you to leave. You can go over to the hotel. $1.50 should get you a room or at least a hot meal to tide you over. But you can't stay here." Sherlock was trying his best to be firm with his words and display an air of authority.

"Well, alright, but I don't see what harm I'm causin' staying right here," the little man whined. He picked his pack up off the floor, and with what appeared to be his last ounce of strength, hoisted it over his shoulder.

"Good night to you, sir." And with that he stepped out the door.

Thank God he's gone.

Grabbing the line-up sheet, Sherlock studied the list of trains.

Quiet shift. I get that snow plow in the clear, be able to do a little housekeeping. Mr. O'Neill will be here more often now that it's snowing…

The station door flew open, interrupting Sherlock's thoughts. The little hunter came bolting through the doorway with brakeman James "Curly" Kerlee and "Wellington Town Sheriff," conductor Ed Lindsay close behind.

"Mr. Sherlock, as the duly appointed Sheriff of Wellington, I am placing this man under arrest. I need you to lock him in the back room until we can have a trial," Lindsay demanded.

"I ain't done nuthin! You ain't no sheriff!" The little hunter's eyes were wide with anger and fear.

"If I ain't no sheriff, why have I got this?"

Lindsay opened the lapel of his work coat. Pinned to the interior was a shiny, well-worn police badge.

"I'm tellin' ya sheriff, that's the guy," Kerlee interjected, pointing to the hunter. "Me and my friends heard him talking about puttin' a rail across the tracks and sending a train into the canyon. He said he was gonna collect all the loot off the dead people."

"He's lyin'!" the hunter shouted back. "I've never seen him before!"

"Oh really, this is just too much. Why you're no more a sheriff ..." Lindsay spun around and glared, cutting Sherlock off mid-sentence.

"You need to find your friends to backup your story," Lindsay instructed Kerlee. "Find them and report back here."

Kerlee nodded, winked at Sherlock, and disappeared into the night. Lindsay approached the hunter, grabbing the frightened man firmly by the upper arm.

"I have no choice but to arrest you for plotting a willful act of sabotage against the Great Northern Railway. Sherlock! Open up the back room."

"You can't do this! Dammit, man, I ain't done nuthin'! I came up here alone!"

Sherlock begrudgingly rose from his desk and walked across the room.

Have to go along with it. Life'll be a living hell around here if I don't.

Once again, Sherlock pulled his keys from his pocket. He unlocked the storage room and Lindsay ushered the little man inside.

"You can tell it all to the judge," Lindsay snarled and closed the door. "We're holding your pack and rifle for evidence."

"Better lock it, Sherlock," he hollered, making sure his prisoner heard. "Don't want him trying to escape. Might have to shoot him with his own gun if he does that."

"What the hell you blokes doing? You can't keep me here!"

Lindsay put a fist to the storeroom door. "Quiet! We can keep you there as long as we want. The judge is in town. We'll have the trial as soon as he gets here, so just settle down!"

The hunter fell quiet. Lindsay strolled across the room and rejoined Sherlock back at the desk, placing the prisoner's pack and rifle underneath.

"Really, Mr. Lindsay, that poor little beggar only has a buck-fifty on him," Sherlock scolded.

"Yeah, but that'll buy a round, won't it?"

November 13, 1909
Anthony John Dougherty, Brakeman

The heavy logging chain on his shoulder caused Dougherty to stumble slightly as he made his way to the front of the snow plow. Stopping next to the wheels, he let the chain slide into the snow.

Like back on the farm. Getting the plow stuck. Hauling that damned chain through the mud. Unhitch the team. Pull the whole mess out backwards. God, glad I'm railroading.

Six years had passed since Dougherty left his childhood home in Waverly, Minnesota. Being the middle son in a houseful of brothers and sisters, and not wanting to farm, there was nothing to keep him on the land. He hired out with the Great Northern, eventually becoming a brakeman. Given the nick name "Al," Dougherty worked his way west, and for the past three years was holding down regular runs between Everett and Leavenworth.

Dougherty took to the mountains right off, despite advice to the contrary from others. There was camaraderie amongst the men on the mountain like none other he ever experienced, especially during the winter plow runs. For the first time in his life he felt he belonged, his presence was important, that he was an equal.

Once spotted for the night on a spur track in the "upper yard," Dougherty's job was to chain the front wheels of the rotary to the rail. This ensured that the plow and its pusher engine would not accidentally wander down the track and out onto the adjacent main line if their brakes failed.

"Hey, Bobby, get your ass out here with a lantern so I can see what the hell I'm doing," Dougherty called out in the darkness.

Within seconds the area around the front of the snow plow was aglow with light. Their tattered grips sitting in the snow, Meath and Harrington stood over Dougherty with their lanterns. The young brakeman was on his hands and knees, using a short metal rod to dig out the snow between two wood ties. With the rock ballast exposed, Dougherty burrowed the rod underneath the rail, clearing a space between the bottom of the rail and the ties to each side.

"Here, hold my lantern, Bill and I'll give poor old Al a hand."

Free of his lamp, Meath joined Dougherty down in the snow, digging out a pathway for the chain. With each link rattling, Meath pulled the chain through the plow's wheel assembly and fed it down the back side. Dougherty reached under the rail, grabbed the hook and wormed it out through the pathway he had just dug in the ballast and snow. A grunt escaped his lips as he looped the chain around the frame surrounding the front wheels. Working together they completed the task by securing the hook onto the thick links.

"Let me make sure she's good and tight, Al," Meath offered, lying on his stomach. "Shine a light under the plow here."

Dougherty grabbed one of the lanterns from Harrington. As he leaned forward to shine the light under the plow, Meath spun around on his back and pelted the unsuspecting brakeman in the face with two loose-packed snowballs.

"Goddamnit, Meath!" Dougherty hollered. Meath scrambled to his feet and immediately took refuge next to Harrington, avoiding Dougherty's sure retaliation.

"You can't hide behind Bill all winter, Bobby. Just remember that."

"Oh for Christ's sake," Harrington moaned. "Let's call it a day."

Bobby. Best friend a fella could ever want to have. More like my big brother, Dougherty thought.

The two men made a good pair. Both were tall with a youthful look, although Dougherty's habitual smile contrasted with Meath's dead-pan expression and darting eyes. It was their sense of humor and talent for instigating elaborate practical jokes that made the two popular with the men working the mountain.

"We gonna have a trial for that hunter tonight, Bobby?" Dougherty asked, his voice obviously filled with excitement.

"Be a good night for it. Blackburn's down at Skykomish so he won't be around to bugger things up. That new assistant trainmaster will be around, but I hear he's a pushover."

"Up your ass with it, Meath," came Harrington's over-the-shoulder reply.

Passing the sectionmens' house adjoining the depot, Meath tapped his bag. "I'm headed in there so's I can become Judge Grogan. Get the courtroom ready, will ya, Al?"

"As you wish, Your Honor. What's gonna be the charge? Have you decided?"

"Yeah, Lindsay talked to me while we were watering the outfit. He arrested the poor little beggar on the old wreck-the-train scam."

"Alright. I like prosecuting that one. Who are my witnesses?"

"Lindsay's got Curly and Fred Allen in on it. Maybe we can get Bat to be a witness too. You get things going, I'll catch up with Bat and clue him in."

"You got it, Bobby."

Dougherty walked past the depot, extinguishing his lantern and leaving it on the platform. Harrington headed inside.

"Hey Bill, could you sign me and Bobby out? He's over in the sectionmens' house, and I'm headed straight up to Bailets on court business. You gonna stick around for the trial?"

"Yeah, I'll sign you two out. That way I'm not responsible for your antics after that," Harrington replied, his voice thick with sarcasm. "I got a few things to take care of this evening. I'll be in the side office. Be nice if you assholes keep your court proceedings down to a small riot."

Dougherty headed up the hill towards the Bailets Hotel. Spining through his head was all that needed to be done. Happy, excited to be a central part of the goings on, his hands were in the pockets of his wet, dirty coat. He whistled a jovial nondescript tune as he crunched through the snow on the well-worn path leading to the saloon.

Need a jury. Find Flannery. He'll be the clerk. Bobby'll probably make Sherlock defend the guy. That'll put ol' Basil in a fit.

The stuffy heat and smoke of the saloon nearly bowled Dougherty over when he strode through the door. Standing inside the doorway for an instant, he sized up who was in the room.

"Close the damned door, Al. Hasn't anybody explained to ya'all it's winter out thar?" Archie Dupy said in his southern drawl.

"Boys, we've got a big trial tonight. A very serious matter needs to come before the Honorable Judge Grogan. As the prosecutor, it's my civic duty to gather up a jury of upstanding citizens," Dougherty announced to the group.

"Hell, the only time we're upstanding is when we have to go out back and write our names in the snow," came the slightly slurred voice of electric motor conductor, John Scott. The room erupted in laughter.

"Boys, boys. We've got a trial to tend to. Will, can we count on you being Court Clerk?" Dougherty called out, seeing the first trick telegrapher at a back table. Flannery raised a glass of beer and nodded in the affirmative. "Okay then. Well, I count eight heads here, looks like I'm gonna have to swear all of you in for the jury. Mr. Scott, any objection to being the Jury Foreman?"

"Never let it be said the men of the Great Northern Railway shy away from their civic duties," came Scott's drunken reply. "Duty calls, boys! Drink up and pay up!"

Dougherty was about to leave, but paused. "Hey, anyone seen Lindsay? He's got the badge, don't he?"

"Eddie went down to the motor house, Al. Was a sayin' he needed to get Campbell and Strohmier in on this. Ain't no trains moving tonight, so them electric boys ain't got a thang to do. Hell, by now I'd say them two boys probably got ol' Lindsay about cleaned out in a game of whist," came Dupy's reply amid more laughter.

"Okay, head for the depot and get things set up. I'll go bail Ed out of trouble."

Back in the cold night air, Dougherty breathed deep, relishing the moment. He bounded down the trail and followed the tracks away from the station, then jogged up the runaway track to a large structure perched on the hill above the main line. The building housed the electric locomotives used to pull the steam-powered trains through the tunnel. Ed Campbell was the conductor in charge of the electric engines assigned to the 7 p.m.- to-7 a.m. shift, just as John Scott was the day-shift conductor. Andy Strohmier was the night-shift engineer and Dougherty was guessing another engineman, Charlie Andrews, was probably hanging around as well.

Get the motor boys in on this. Be about a dozen on the jury. Not bad. God, this is fun. Betcha there ain't another spot on the whole GN where they're havin' the kinda of fun we're havin' up here.

Dougherty burst through the door of the barn-like motor shed. Inside standing side-by-side on adjacent tracks were the shiny electric locomotives. In one corner, a couple of electric bulbs dimly lit a table next to a stove, where four men were gathered, cards in hand. The nose of one of the engines was parked so close to the card players it looked as though it had been dealt into the game as well.

"Lindsay, we need you over at the station, the trial's about to start," Dougherty hollered, his voice echoing in the cavernous room.

"Be right with ya, Al," Lindsay answered, his eyes never leaving the cards in his hand. "I'm down a few bucks to these boys, but I finally got my big hand of the night."

"Yeah, you've been saying that for an hour, Lindsay, and you've done nothing but lose," Ed Campbell replied.

"Gonna need you boys too," Dougherty interrupted. "Ed, Andy, Charlie, need all three of you for the jury."

Lindsay threw his cards down on the table. "Ah the hell with it. I'd probably lose this hand too. Seeing as how I'm the damned sheriff tonight, best not keep the Judge waiting."

By the time Dougherty and the others reached the depot, the transformation from railroad station to courtroom was nearly complete. The group from the saloon, all experienced in the ways of the Wellington Court, already commandeered the operator's room, over and above the loud protests of Sherlock. The "jury box" was set up along the back wall. It consisted of four chairs, stripped from adjoining rooms, and two ten-foot planks. Using the seats of two chairs to support each plank, two rows were constructed. This produced enough space for the jurors sit. An empty spike barrel was rolled in from the section house, and the end of a square crate was nailed to its top. The barrel, along with another chair, was elevated on two other crates, creating the judge's podium. To its left and below, another chair was positioned for the witness stand. These items were placed along the inside wall. Near the center of the room, two more crates were positioned about six feet apart with yet another plank between them. A single chair for the prosecuting attorney was on one end, with two chairs, one for the defendant and one for the attorney for the defense, on the other. Standing against the wall directly behind was the "gallery," composed of the witnesses and various onlookers gleaned from the Fogg Brother's saloon and the workers' shacks lining Haskell Creek.

Andy Strohmier and Ed Campbell strolled up the ramp onto the station platform and went inside. Dougherty and Lindsay walked across the front of the depot, over to where Meath was huddled with three other men: Fred Allen, Bat Nelson, and James "Curly" Kerlee.

"Okay, Bobby, give me the details so we can keep the story straight," Dougherty told Meath.

"We're gonna run the standard wreck-the-train scam," Meath instructed. "Fred, you and Bat will lead off. Curly, we'll finish up with you. You got it?"

All three men nodded.

"No problem, Bobby," Kerlee said. "We've run this story enough times. We got it inside and out."

"I'm gonna make Sherlock defend him. He'll be in such a damned hurry to get us out of the station, he won't say a thing. Be the easiest conviction you ever had, Al."

"Now remember, Curly, listen close to what Fred and Bat say, your stories have to mesh," Dougherty warned. "I can bail you out of a few minor flub-ups, but you boys have to agree on what you say."

"Don't worry, Al. Like Curly told the Judge here, we've got this story down," Nelson calmly offered.

Dougherty's mind was racing.

Boys know the story. Sherlock won't know what hit him. Have Bobby boot Sherlock on the grounds of incompetence. Damn, that would be funny.

"Ed, grab my coat, got a little surprise for the court tonight." Meath took off his work coat, and from it produced a long, black robe. Giving his coat to Lindsay, he slipped the robe on.

"Jesus, Bobby, where'd you get that?" Lindsay asked, obviously admiring the effect: all the while Dougherty and the "witnesses" were doing a poor job of choking back laughter.

"Never mind; let's head on in. Boys, I believe it's time to bring this court to order." Meath bent down, picked up a thick book that looked suspiciously like a dictionary, and produced a gavel from his hip pocket. "Time to announce the arrival of the Honorable Judge F. Stanley Grogan, Ed my boy."

Kerlee, Allen, and Nelson went into the depot, Dougherty following closely behind. Reaching over Sherlock's shoulder, he grabbed a blank Western Union tablet and pencil, then took his seat at the end of the "table" in the middle of the room.

Spinning around in his chair, Sherlock glared at Dougherty. "Give those back. I might need them at any moment!"

"Don't worry about it, Sherlock. I don't see anybody lined up wanting to send a wire," Dougherty replied. "Besides, court is about to start. If you want to be in contempt, just keep arguing."

Dougherty heard Sherlock mutter something as the telegrapher returned to his desk, his back to the room. He hunched over the train list and pretended to be engrossed in his work.

Dougherty continued to eye Sherlock. *When Bobby makes him the defense lawyer I'll offer him a few sheets off this pad. Really get his britches wedged up his ass.*

Dougherty's thoughts were interrupted with Lindsay's grand entrance into the room.

"Hear ye! Hear ye! This court in the town of Wellington, the County of King, the State of Washington and the Country of the United States of America is now in session! The Honorable F. Stanley Grogan presiding! All rise!"

There was a general scraping of furniture and a shuffle of heavy work boots as all in the room came to their feet, except Sherlock.

Meath swept into the room. With the oversized robe, it looked to Dougherty as though he was gliding on air. The baggy sleeves fluttered as he walked past the jury and assumed his position on the makeshift podium. The room was in absolute, shocked silence. Making a formal production out of positioning his robe, Meath sat down, looked about the room and proclaimed, "You may be seated."

The shock was quick to wear off.

"Jesus, Joseph, and Mary would you look at that, boys," came the voice of Ed Campbell from the back row of the jury.

"Sit down? Shouldn't we be kneeling?" asked Jury Forman Scott. "Here I thought I was a comin' to court, and I end up at evening mass."

Scott made the sign of the cross while laughter broke out in the room, along with a goodly number of whistles and catcalls.

Meath rapped his gavel on the top of his wood crate desk. "That'll be enough of that. There will be order in this court."

Not about to let Meath off quite so easily, Scott stood up. "Your Honor. As Jury Foreman, I've been instructed to ask you, where the hell did you get that robe?"

The noise level in the room continued to increase.

"Sit down, Scott, before ya'all gets us in contempt," drawled Archie Dupy, himself a juror. "Besides, didn't ya'all hear the news? Why, the good judge got that new preacher in Goldbar into a card game last week."

With that, the "small riot" Harrington had warned about earlier nearly erupted. Meath pounded his gavel so hard and so often the top of the crate nearly came off the barrel.

"I said there will be order in this court and I will have it!" he bellowed.

That robe's a bad idea. Going to be giving Bobby hell about it all night, Dougherty realized. He glanced to his left. Even Sherlock had turned in his chair and was watching the proceedings.

"Sheriff Lindsay, do you have business for the court?" Meath questioned.

"Indeed I do, Your Honor." Lindsay made his way forward from the back of the room. "We have a very serious matter. A man has been charged with attempting to commit an act of sabotage against the Great Northern Railway."

"Sheriff" Lindsay motioned to Sherlock, who tossed him his keys. Unlocking the storeroom door, Lindsay led the little man into the room and in front of the judge.

"What the hell is going on around here?" the "defendant" asked, obviously confused by the transformation that had taken place in the room.

Meath again rapped his gavel.

"Silence! I will be the one asking the questions, here. I'll give you time to tell your side of the story. Now then, please state your name, residence and occupation."

The little man looked around.

"I don't gotta tell you a thing," he snapped. Eyeing Meath closely he continued, "You ain't no judge. You come in off of that train and got some coffee a few hours ago. I seen ya."

"Well sir, if this is not a court, and I am not a judge, why am I wearing a black robe, why have these gentlemen been sworn in as a jury, and why is that gentleman behind you prepared to prosecute a case of sabotage against you?"

"I ain't done nothing, damn it!"

"Sir, I will ask you only once to hold you tongue, or be cited for contempt of court. Now, your name, your residence, and your occupation, if you please."

Better get on with it. He might bolt on us, Dougherty quietly fretted.

"I'm Franklin Jones," the little man sighed. "I live in Snohomish. In the summer I work on the farms down there, in the winter I come up here and hunt cougar. There, you happy?"

"Mr. Jones, you have been accused of plotting a willful act of sabotage against the Great Northern Railway. How do you plead? Guilty or not guilty?"

"I'm not guilty! How many times do I gotta tell you blokes that?"

"Have you a lawyer for your defense, Mr. Jones?"

"Oh sure, I carry a damned solicitor everywhere I go. I ain't got one and I don't need one. This ain't no damned court."

"Again, sir, I will ask you to watch your language." Meath warned the witness. Opening his "law book," he addressed the court. "According to section 6, paragraph 4, line 12 of the laws governing the great and sovereign State of Washington, and I quote, 'if a defendant has no attorney it shall be the duty of the presiding officer of the court to appoint one.' Sir, is there anyone present in this room you would care to have represent you?"

Jones looked about the room of strangers, until his eyes fell on Sherlock. Dougherty saw it happen.

Hot damn, going to finger Sherlock.

"How about the station man over there?" Jones said, pointing to Sherlock. "He's the only one here I've even talked to."

"So ruled. Mr. Sherlock, this court hereby appoints you as the lawyer for the defense." Meath rapped his gavel to make the ruling official.

Dougherty leaned back in his chair. *Ol' Basil's gonna bust a flue.*

"Lawyer for the defense! Why, that's absurd!" Sherlock had spun around in his chair, his face red with anger. "I refuse to be a part of any of this! Besides, the rules are quite specific, I'm on duty!"

"Your Honor!" Will Flannery stood up just as Sherlock was about to launch into another tirade.

"Yes, Mr. Flannery," Meath said, pointing to him with the handle of his gavel.

"As the senior telegrapher at this station, I hereby grant Mr. Sherlock a temporary leave for the purposes of acting as the lawyer for the defense of Mr. Jones. I can take over Mr. Sherlock's duties and still be the court recorder."

The gavel once again hit the top of the crate. "So ruled. Mr. Jones, you may join your attorney at the table."

Flannery nearly launched the reluctant Sherlock out of the operator's chair and over to the plank table in the middle of the room. Jones had already settled into the far chair, forcing Sherlock to sit next to Dougherty. The prosecutor wasted no time.

"Hey, Sherlock," Dougherty whispered, "if you need some paper I'll loan ya few sheets off this Western Union pad I got."

Sherlock glared at his "legal adversary," but said nothing.

"Is the prosecution ready?" Meath inquired.

Dougherty rose to his feet. "We're ready, Your Honor."

"Then call your first witness."

"The prosecution calls to the stand Julius Piedmont."

Fred Allen made his way towards the witness stand amid a few chuckles. Flannery stood up.

"Mr. Piedmont, do you solemnly swear to tell the truth, the whole truth and nothing but the truth, so help you God?"

Allen shrugged and looked at the jury. "Yeah, pretty much."

Again, it took Meath's gavel to bring the room back to order.

Dougherty approached the now sitting witness.

"Sir, for the record, would you please tell this court your name, where you live, and what you do."

"I'm Julius Piedmont. I mostly live around Everett, and let's just say I'm a professional traveler."

"Mr. Piedmont, how is it you came to be in Wellington?"

"Well, I come up here on a freight train last night."

"And were you alone?"

"No, I come up here with a couple of friends of mine, and a stranger."

"A stranger, you say. Is this stranger here in this room, and if he is, could you point him out?"

"Yeah, he's here. That guy sitting on the end of the table there."

"Let the record show the witness has pointed to the defendant," Meath interjected.

Jones leaped to his feet. "He's lying! I've never seen that man before in my life!"

Meath's gavel was pounding the top of the crate. "Mr. Sherlock, I must insist you control your client. He will have his say in due time."

Sherlock pulled Jones back down to his chair. Dougherty leaned against the table and caught part of what Sherlock was whispering.

Something about get it over with and it's all fake. Okay for you, Sherlock, time to turn up the heat. Starting to think Jones has fallen for this, Dougherty thought.

"Mr. Piedmont, can you tell this court about your trip to Wellington, especially anything that might have to do with the defendant?"

"Well, it was like this. Me and my two friends over there were making our way to Wenatchee. We're planning to head north to the Okanogan and do a little prospecting. Anyway, we stopped off at Skykomish to get warmed up a bit and get us some supper. We jumped the next freight out of town."

"And what time was that, Mr. Piedmont?" Dougherty interrupted.

"Oh, I'd say a little after seven. Had a hard time finding an empty boxcar, so the three of us jumped into the first open door we saw. No sooner do we get in, and we saw that feller in one corner."

"And did you speak to the defendant at any time?" Dougherty prompted.

"Sure we talked. The usual stuff. Where ya headed, whatcha up to. Asked about his rifle there." Allen pointed to the backpack now sitting at the feet of "Sheriff" Lindsay.

"And what did the defendant tell you?"

"Well, he talked some of hunting. We asked him what he was hunting for, and, well …"

"Go on, Mr. Piedmont, what did he tell you he was hunting for?"

"Well, it was the strangest thing. He tells us he's hunting for loot."

"Loot?" repeated Dougherty.

"Well, that's what he said. Couldn't figure out what he was talking about. That's when he tells us he's gonna go down to the station, find out when a passenger train is headed down the mountain. He tells us he's gonna lay a big piece of rail across the tracks and send the whole thing into the canyon. Then he's gonna go down and collect all the loot out of the mail cars and baggage cars. Maybe even off a few dead people if they're rich."

Shake Jones up a little, Dougherty thought. He spun around and faced the little man. Jones' eyes were wide, and Sherlock was physically restraining him, whispering madly into his ear not to pay the least bit of attention to what was being said.

"Mr. Piedmont, I gotta admit, I'm alarmed by your testimony, and a little confused. You say this happened shortly after 7 p.m. last night. Yet it wasn't until 5:30 this evening that anything of his terrible plot was told to the sheriff. Why is that?"

"Well, it did worry us some at the time. That's why we got off here at Wellington last night. We couldn't find the sheriff right off, and then we saw that little guy head off to the hotel, not the station, so we just figured he was pulling our leg."

"What changed your minds this evening?"

"We were working on a way out of town. Hadn't seen the guy all day, so we just sorta forgot about it. But then we walked by the station and saw him in here talking to the guy who's his lawyer there, and, well, that's when we got scared. No way did we want a train wreck hung around our necks. We split up and went looking for the sheriff. One of my friends was the one who run into the sheriff. They came and got me after he was arrested, so that's all I know."

"Thank you, Mr. Piedmont." Dougherty returned to his seat.

"Mr. Sherlock, your witness. Do you care to cross examine?" Meath asked.

"We have no questions for this so-called witness," Sherlock paused to clear his throat, "Your Honor."

"As you wish. You my step down, Mr. Piedmont."

"You may call your next witness, Mr. Prosecutor."

"The people call Mr. Hiram Magillacutty."

Bat Nelson approached the stand and was sworn in. Jones, in a loud raspy whisper was complaining to Sherlock over his lack of defense. Just as Meath had predicted, Sherlock was trying his best to convince his client the key was to end the trial as quickly as possible, vainly attempting to assure the man this court carried no authority.

Dougherty rose to his feet and approached the witness stand.

Get things going. Scribbled on the note pad were the words, "Jones chummy with Sherlock." He stood in front of Nelson, acting as if he were formulating his line of questioning, all the while giving his witness a chance to read the note. Nelson tipped his head slightly and ran his forefinger across his nose.

A veteran of the Wellington court, Nelson had no difficulty recounting the story already outlined by Allen. As the testimony was presented, Dougherty paced in front of the table, glancing at Sherlock.

"Is there anything you can add that we haven't already heard, Mr. Magillacutty?" Dougherty prompted.

"Well, sir, there is one thing. When we passed by the depot this afternoon, I kinda stayed back and looked in for a bit through the window there. And well, it sure looked to me like the defendant there and his lawyer were pretty chummy."

"Chummy? What do ya mean by that?" Dougherty probed.

"Well, you know. Like they were friends."

Sherlock was on his feet so fast that his chair fell backwards onto the floor.

"This is preposterous!" he shouted.

"You have an objection, Mr. Sherlock?" Meath calmly inquired.

"Do I have an objection!? I object to this entire silly charade!"

"I'm sorry, Mr. Sherlock, but your objection must be more specific in order for me to rule," Meath instructed in a thoroughly patronizing voice.

"Oh, all right," said Sherlock, completely exasperated.

Looks like Basil's getting caught in the net. Dougherty allowed a smug smile to cross his face.

"I object on the grounds that even if the witness was actually watching from outside, which I doubt, but if he was, there is no way he could know what was being said in the room. For all he knows I could have been trying to tell the man to leave. Which, indeed, I was."

Sherlock, red in the face, righted his chair and sat down hard.

Meath paused for a moment, acting as if he was giving Sherlock's point serious thought.

"Objection sustained," he finally allowed. "Mr. Flannery. You will strike from the record the last comments made by the witness."

"As you wish, Your Honor," Flannery answered, even though he had yet to write a single word.

Dougherty shrugged and sat down. Once again Sherlock refused to mount a cross examination.

Dougherty took the floor.

"The people call Casey McGirk."

James Kerlee made his way forward. By now, Harrington had come from the back room and joined the gallery. Dougherty approached the witness stand. As with Nelson, he had written a note on his pad. It read, "not afraid to use gun."

Kerlee, too, had no problem accurately recounting the details presented by the first two witnesses. It was a case that was tried often in Meath's kangaroo courtroom. Sherlock assumed an air of disinterest.

"You know, there is one thing that bothers me about the defendant," Kerlee offered, summarizing his testimony.

"And what is that, Mr. McGirk?" Dougherty asked.

"Well, you see, my friends had already got off the box car. I was alone with him for a bit. I told him that was a nice little rifle he had there. And, well, sir, he tells me it was a good gun and he wasn't afraid to use it, especially if someone was to get in the way of him looting a wrecked train."

"Are you sure, Mr. McGirk? Are you absolutely sure those were his words? If so, I'm going to have to expand the charges to include … attempted murder." Dougherty turned and stared solemnly at Jones who seemed to have grown slightly faint. The little man had slumped down in his chair with his head tilted back and his eyes closed.

"Oh, I'm sure."

"May the court assume you have no intent to cross examine, Mr. Sherlock?" Meath sighed.

"You assume correctly," came Sherlock's flat reply.

Okay Sherlock, I'll get ya to play ball. Dougherty was on his feet.

"Your Honor, may I address the court?"

Meath gave Dougherty a "give it a try" glance and voiced, "Proceed."

"Your Honor, the people of the state don't care whether we win or lose a case. No, we just want justice to be served. I'm afraid that justice isn't being done and that a mistrial might be declared. So I'm asking that Mr. Sherlock be removed on the grounds of complete incompetence."

Sherlock was on his feet, his face inches from Dougherty's.

"Incompetence! How dare you, sir! Fine, I'll play your silly little game and we'll just see who in this room is incompetent!"

Took it hook, line and sinker. Dougherty said nothing but sat back down, giving Meath a sly smile.

Sherlock approached Kerlee, who was now slightly slouched in the witness chair, his arms folded across his chest.

"Refresh my memory, Mr., ah, McGirk, is it?"

Kerlee nodded.

"Fine. What time did you and your friends board the train last night in Skykomish?"

"About 7:00."

"About 7:00. And at 7:00 p.m. was it daylight or dark at Skykomish?"

"As dark as a night can get."

"I see. And where were you and your friends situated in the box car in relation to the defendant?"

"We were in one corner of the car and he was in the other."

Damn it. If he's going where I think he is, we're in trouble here. Dougherty was seeing his case begin to unravel and Meath seemed to be in no hurry to stop it from happening.

"Objection, Your Honor!"

Meath gave Dougherty a quizzical look. "On what grounds?"

"I fail to see what any of this has to do with attempted sabotage."

"Your Honor," Sherlock interrupted, "Any competent person would realize proper identification is a core issue."

"Overruled." Meath gave Dougherty a slight shrug.

Okay, at least Curly knows what Sherlock's up to.

"Now," continued Sherlock, "by the other side do you mean he was nearly 40 feet away from you?"

"No, no. He was on the same end as us, just in the other corner."

Dougherty breathed a little easier. *Looks like Curly is gonna wiggle out of Sherlock's trap. Damn, underestimated ol' Basil.*

"So he was in a dark corner eight feet from you."

"Yeah, thereabouts."

"And so, Mr. McGirk, you are expecting this court to believe you were able to identify this man while sitting in a dark corner of a dark box car and, as you yourself said, on a night that was as dark as a night can get?"

Just let it ride Curly. Tell him yes, Dougherty subconsciously coached.

"Well, we all got a couple of good looks at him 'cause he kept lighting matches for that pipe he's got tucked there in his pack."

The quick sense of sweet elation running through Dougherty suddenly turned sour. Jones was on his feet and shouting.

"That's all a damned lie and I can prove it! I bought that pipe this afternoon from the lady up at the post office. Go ask her, she'll tell ya!"

Now Dougherty's chair hit the floor as he bolted upright, red in the face. "Objection, Your Honor!"

Meath's gavel again hit the top of the crate. "Order! Mr. Jones, sit down!" he demanded. "What are your grounds, Mr. Prosecutor?"

"There is no witness to backup the defendant's, claim, which, was made without being sworn in."

"Objection sustained. Have you any further questions, Mr. Sherlock?"

"No."

"Then the witness is dismissed. Have you any further witnesses, Mr. Prosecutor?"

"No, Your Honor, the prosecution rests."

"Very well. Mr. Sherlock, you may present your defense."

Gotta stay away from that pipe business, Dougherty thought, as Jones was being sworn in. *Damn it, Curly. Shoulda said you got a good look at him when you got off the train at Wellington.*

Jones told his story of arriving alone, hunting for cougar, and being short of money after buying the pipe at Bailets. He spoke of warming himself in the depot and of Sherlock telling him to leave.

"And that's the God's truth," he concluded. "I don't know who those three men are and I don't know why they want to get me in all this trouble. It ain't like I got any money."

"Thank you sir, and my sincerest apologies to you for becoming involved in this ridiculous trial." Sherlock looked at Dougherty, "Your witness."

Dougherty rose. "No reason to cross examine the witness. We are satisfied that the nearly uncontested testimony of three men will hold more weight than the unproved story of one."

"Thank you. You may step down, sir," Meath said. "Does the defense rest, Mr. Sherlock?"

"No, it does not, Your Honor. The defense requests that Mrs. Bailets be subpoenaed by the court to back up my client's purchase of that pipe."

Damn it! Sherlock's got us by the balls on this one. Think of something quick.

"Objection, Your Honor!"

"Yes, Mr. Prosecutor."

"Well, ah, well, since Mrs. Bailets is the postmistress and therefore a federal employee, she is exempt from subpoenas except from the feds."

Dougherty sat down, knowing his objection and logic were weak, at best.

Maybe this will give Meath some wiggle room. Sherlock said nothing, but out of the corner of his eye, Dougherty could tell that he also knew he had gotten the best of them.

Meath killed time by thumbing through the pages of his dictionary, acting as if he was searching for a legal precedence on which to base a ruling.

Dougherty looked over at the jury. To a man, all were smiling.

Damn, they know. Sherlock outfoxed us, Dougherty silently admitted.

Meath cleared his throat. "In accordance to the laws governing the great and sovereign State of Washington, it is indeed illegal for a lower court to issue subpoenas to federal employees. Objection sustained."

Not good, Bobby. All totaled, not that bad either. That should end it, Dougherty allowed.

"Fine, Your Honor." Sherlock was not about to give up. "Then I move these proceedings be moved to the Post Office where Mrs. Bailets can be questioned. And I would remind the court that even lower court proceedings are carried out on a routine basis in federal buildings." Sherlock stared straight at Dougherty with a wide grin on his face.

Slumped in his chair, Dougherty let his pencil drop.

"Your Honor," he said, not looking up from the table. "In the interest of quick and fair justice, the prosecution will let the defendant's testimony that the pipe was bought from Bailets' store this afternoon stand."

The summaries were quick and predictable. Dougherty did his best to patch the damage by interjecting the notion that identification was also made when all four jumped from the boxcar in Wellington. The cat was out of the bag, however, and Dougherty knew it.

Meath turned to the jury.

"Gentlemen, you have heard the evidence. You now have before you the grave responsibility of administering proper and fair justice. You may retire to the back room to consider your verdict."

"No need to hash this over, Your Honor," Jury Foreman Scott announced. "We're all in agreement. The defendant is not guilty!"

Laughs and cheers filled the room. Jones was wildly shaking Sherlock's hand and pounding him on the back.

Ah hell, Dougherty thought. Pulling Sherlock away from Jones, Dougherty grabbed the telegrapher's clammy hand and shook it as well.

"Well done, old man! You sure did get us on that pipe bit."

Dougherty could tell Sherlock was taken aback by his willingness to accept the outcome graciously. A "Well, thank you" is all Sherlock could mutter.

Meath, still rapping his gavel, shouted over the crowd. "You are a free man, Mr. Jones. This court is adjourned."

"I only got a buck-fifty, but I'll buy all of you a drink over at the saloon, at least 'til my money runs out," Jones offered exuberantly.

"Excellent, my good man," Meath answered. "Your hospitality will not be declined. We need to tidy this room up a bit, then we'll be right along."

Jones picked up his pack and rifle, shook Sherlock's hand a final time and disappeared out the door.

"Okay, boys," Meath continued. "Let's pass the hat and get our friend Mr. Jones some traveling money."

Ed Lindsay sent his derby around the room.

"Campbell will put in double since he's got all my money," Lindsay said, getting a good laugh from the group.

"Got $9.50," Meath counted. " I'll throw in four bits to make it an even ten bucks. Will, okay if he spends the night here? I'm sure Sherlock won't try and kick him out again."

"Sure," answered Flannery.

"Whadda say, boys. Let's go spend Mr. Jones' money before we give him ours."

The group quickly removed the barrels, chairs, and planks from the room. It was snowing again. The men hunched their shoulders against the wind-driven flakes as they made their way up the path to the Bailets Saloon.

Dougherty was still standing on the platform when Meath, his robe safely tucked away, walked out of the station.

"The son of a bitch got us, Bobby. I can't believe we let it happen."

Meath laid his arm across Dougherty's shoulder. He grabbed his neck and gave it a few good shakes, then patted him on the back.

"Not to worry, Al. Our day will come. Mr. Sherlock will take a good fall."

November 23, 1909
John Robert Meath, Engineer

A good-sized crowd was gathered in the Wellington depot when Ira Clary came bursting through the door in an absolute rage. His eyes were like lightning bolts flashing from man to man.

"Where's Meath and Dougherty?" he demanded.

"Probably with Harrington, tying down the rotary in the upper yard," replied Will Flannery, having just gone off duty.

"Good, because by damned we've got some work to do."

"What's all the fuss about, Ira? Looks like you've got yourself in one hell of a state," Harrington said, walking through the door. He dropped off his release forms and the staff to Sherlock, who had relieved Flannery.

"You're damned right I'm in a state," snapped Clary. "It's that goddamned turkey of Bailets. Something has to be done."

William Bailets, owner of the Bailets Hotel and Saloon, had stumbled onto what he decided was a real moneymaker. During the first week of November, he traveled to Snohomish, returning with a 27-pound, live turkey. Placing it in a cage on the bar, Bailets promptly began selling raffle tickets, giving each holder a chance at winning a fresh Thanksgiving feast. For the first few days, ticket sales were brisk, as the few married men in town each bought several chances at winning. However, sales soon began to lag, since the predominantly bachelor population could care less about winning the bird. In desperation, Bailets started making it clear to his patrons that the amount and quality of whiskey served depended directly on the purchase of a raffle ticket. Grumbling, most anteed up, and bought a ticket or two just to keep the spirits flowing.

However, by mid-month, the grumbling among Bailets' regulars slowly escalated into an out-and-out revolt. Bailets had gotten greedy. He already raffled the turkey off twice, each time to a bachelor on Foreman Robert Harley's section gang. Each time, Bailets offered to "buy" the bird back for the price of a bottle, and promptly began selling tickets again. The net result was a grin on Bailets' face. He was now receiving the majority of the payroll issued by the Great Northern Railway to the men at Wellington.

"I see what this is all about, boys. Poor ol' Ira had to settle up his bar tab tonight," chimed in Bat Nelson. "What's the matter Ira, you drink yourself into debt again?"

A knowing chuckle rose among the men.

"Hell, look on the bright side, Ira," Nelson continued, "you're bound to win that turkey this time around. You're well invested by now, I'd guess."

"Laugh all you want, Bat, but Bailets has your name on his ledger too!" Clary countered. "I'll tell ya boys, it's a damned sad day when a fella can't afford to get drunk in Wellington."

"Hell, Ira, why don't you join the dagos over at the Fogg Brothers," Harrington suggested. "They ain't proud. They'd sell a Mick a glass of whiskey."

"Very funny, Bill, you son of a bitch. Already been there. Those two bastards are charging about as much for their rot gut as Bailets is for his booze."

"Ya know, Ira, a good sharp knife could end all your troubles," section crew foreman Harley offered. Looking at a few of his crew scattered through the crowd he added, "Any you boys wanna help Ira out?"

"Who we gonna cut, Boss? Bailets, or the turkey?" came a voice amid more laughter.

Into this tempest wandered Al Dougherty and Bob Meath. They tossed their grips on top of those owned by rest of the plow crew that came off duty. Parting ways, Dougherty stood alongside Harrington next to Sherlock, who was busy receiving clearances and orders for a westbound freight. The crowd along the far wall made room as Meath approached. He took up his usual stance, leaning against the wall, his arms folded and feet crossed.

"So what's up, boys?" Dougherty asked with the innocence of a newborn child.

"That goddamned turkey of Bailets! That's what's up!" Clary shouted back.

"Owe the good barkeep a few dollars, do ya Ira?" Meath asked in his usual, calm voice.

"Who the hell doesn't? I say we go over there right now and string that damned bird up by the neck. Wouldn't bother me none to see Bailets swinging right along side of it, either," Clary added.

"Damn, Ira, calm down. We can't string a man up over a turkey, for chrissakes." Dougherty was doing his best to bring some order to the group that was fast becoming an angry mob.

"Why the hell not?" challenged Nelson. "Seems to me he's got us strung up by our you-know-whats right now."

Meath kept silent. The entire time he was eyeing Sherlock, hunched over the desk, his back to the crowd. *Getting the turkey out of town ain't the problem. Figure a way so Bailets can't finger us.*

"Well, before we hang the bastard, I want my money back," added one of Harley's broke sectionmen.

"Yeah, me too!" came another voice.

Have Sherlock take the fall. Get back at him for that trial. Ira's good and mad. Get him to stir up trouble in the bar. Keep Bailets busy. Al and me can boost the turkey out the door. Throw it onto that westbound. Then what?

Meath was in his element, plotting and scheming. He reached into the top pocket of his grimy overalls and produced a half-smoked cigar. Not bothering to light it, he placed it in the corner of his mouth and began to roll it side to side as he thought.

"Sounds like a damned good idea to me! What are we waiting for? Let's go, boys! We'll make like a lynch mob and scare the son of a bitch into giving us our money back. Then we'll hang that damned bird." Clary was turning for the door.

"Hold on! Hold on, boys!" Dougherty was standing in front of the door, blocking Clary's path. "We've got to come up with something here that won't put the lot of us in jail."

Can't talk here. Sherlock'll know every move. He never goes up to the bar. Convince Bailets Sherlock put somebody up to stealing that bird. Money. A phony reward. Make Bailets think Sherlock's behind a reward scheme. Poster on GN stationery. Can trick Sherlock into writing it. He's scared to death of Harrington. Get Bill in on this.

The entire time Meath was thinking, the unlit cigar kept rolling across his mouth. It was a habit he had when an idea was taking form. Dougherty noticed it first, and as his eyes fixed on Meath, the rest of the crowd became silent.

"You onto something, Bobby?" Dougherty asked.

"Well boys, as much as I hate to see such an injustice being done in the very jurisdiction presided over by the Honorable Judge Grogan ..."

"Oh, for chrissakes," Clary interrupted, "you got an idea or not?"

"Sure I do. Seems to me we need to hit Bailets where it'll hurt him the most. Right in his pocket book," Meath offered, pulling the wet stogie from his mouth and using it to point. "Just quit buying whiskey and raffle tickets from him. Let him eat that bird on turkey day. He's going to, anyway. I say a week's boycott of his place will teach him a good lesson."

For a moment there was stunned silence in the room.

"What the hell? You in with Bailets or something?" Clary pointed an accusing finger at Meath. "What the hell kind of a plan is that?"

Nodding his head towards Sherlock, who was still facing away from the crowd, Meath pointed to the door.

"Getting pretty stuffy in here. Besides, poor ol' Sherlock can't hear himself think with all your hollering. Let's step out onto the platform for a minute and I'll tell you boys all about the boycott. Just give me a listen, that's all I ask." Meath headed out the door, winking at Dougherty.

Oughta throw Sherlock off the trail. Passing Harrington Meath mouthed the words, "I need you."

Huddled in the cold out on the station platform did little to improve the mood of the crowd. Hands stuffed into the pockets of their coats, stamping their feet, a fog formed over the men from their breath hitting the frosty mountain air.

"Just what the hell you got in mind, Bobby?" Nelson asked.

"Come on Meath, a damned boycott, Christ-a-mighty you gotta do better than that!" Clary's ongoing rant had his entire head steaming.

Ignoring Clary, Meath turned to Harrington as he wandered out the door. In a low voice he asked, "I need to know where that westbound freight is and if Campbell and the motors are bringing it through. Don't tell Sherlock it's me that wants to know."

"I'll be right back," Harrington smiled. Turning on his heels, he went back into the station.

"Harley, I need a favor from a couple of your boys," Meath asked, in the same subdued tone. "I need them to be out at the runaway switch. When that westbound freight comes through, I don't want Sherlock anywhere around that switch or on the platform. After the switch is thrown, they need to be behind the section house so I can see them from the saloon. They'll need to signal me when the train stops."

"This don't sound like a boycott to me," Harley answered, with a high degree of suspicion. "Just what are you up to, Bobby?"

"Hold on just a sec, Harley," Meath turned his attention to Harrington, who had stepped outside. "Well?"

"Coming into Cascade now. Campbell is bringing them through. Should be here in about a half an hour or so."

"Okay boys, we ain't got much time. Here's what we're really gonna do."

The crowd that filtered into his bar over the past half hour pleasantly surprised Bailets. Whiskey sales were brisk and the men even seemed willing to buy a few raffle tickets as well. In a good mood, he whistled a tune while he kept the men's glasses full and his bar polished.

The last to enter were Harrington, Dougherty and Meath. Harrington strolled across the room and took up a station next to the turkey cage, covered for the night with one of Bailets' aprons. A table adjacent to a window and closest to the door was purposely kept open. Meath and Dougherty pulled the wood chairs from under it and settled in.

"A bottle of whiskey, barkeep!" Meath called out. "And if you keep those damned turkey tickets in your pocket I'll pay up my tab and pour all you boys a drink."

Amidst the cheers from the crowd, Bailets hustled out from behind the bar with a bottle, pouring a shot to each man gathered. Arriving at Meath's table, he topped off Dougherty's glass. Placing the nearly empty bottle on the table in front of Meath, Bailets pulled a group of folded papers from his shirt pocket and leafed through them.

"Counting this bottle, your current bill is $2.35, Mr. Meath. For an even $2.50 I'll throw in a ticket on my bird."

"I'll keep that fifteen cents," came Meath's reply. He glanced out the window and saw the glow of a headlight from the east. "Oh, and by the way, can I have a signed receipt showing full payment?"

"As you wish," said Bailets. He scribbled out a receipt and signed it. With the transaction complete, he returned to the bar, thinking nothing further of Meath's request.

With a drink poured, Meath lifted his glass and addressed the crowd. "Boys, to a late winter and early spring."

"To a late winter and early spring," came the loud reply and the clicking of glasses.

Meath took another look outside. He could see the two sectionmen that were acting as lookouts. The subtle waving of their lanterns told Meath that Sherlock had already come outside to align the runaway switch, and was now back inside the station. He could plainly see the westbound freight slowly approaching the station. *Get the show on the road. Time this just right. Be out and back so Bailets doesn't know I'm gone.*

"You ready?" Meath whispered to Dougherty.

Dougherty topped off his glass once more from Meath's bottle and casually nodded an affirmative.

Looking across the room where Clary and Nelson were sitting together, Meath brushed his right index finger across his nose. Both men returned the signal.

"Damn you, Ira!" It was the loud, piercing voice of Bat Nelson. "You drank my whiskey!"

"What the hell you talkin' about?" Clary bellowed back.

"That was my damned glass you just drank. It was fuller than yours!"

"The hell it was!"

"The hell it wasn't!"

Keep it hot, boys. Got Bailets' attention. Meath went back to looking out the window. The two sectionmen were behind the tool house on the east end of the station platform. With their lanterns shining, Meath could see a clear trail from the saloon stairs down to where the men were positioned. The freight train was already stopped.

"You thieving son of a bitch, Ira!" Nelson grabbed the nearly empty shot glass from Clary's hand and threw it, narrowly missing his ear. It shattered against the wall, raining glass down on Archie Dupy and Pattie Kelly, who sat at the table directly behind Clary.

Get to fighting, boys. Train ain't going sit there all night. Excitement was growing in Meath's stomach. He struggled to look calm.

"Alright Bat, you've been askin' for this!" Clary stood up and shoved the table to the side. Nelson leaped up as well, making sure his chair fell over backwards.

Bailets had witnessed enough. He came out from behind the bar, a wood club in his hand.

"Break it up, you two!" he demanded.

The moment Bailets tried to gain access to the fighting men, he was quickly cut off by the saloon patrons, who gathered in a tight circle. Some were telling Clary to teach Nelson a lesson, while others encouraged Nelson to put Clary to the floor.

Waving their lanterns. Damn train's moving. Meath looked back to the crowd and twirled his finger. A few men parted, swallowing Bailets into the mob.

"Okay Al, go," Meath whispered.

In a move quick enough to get the job done, but not enough to draw Bailets' attention from the fight, Dougherty moved over to the bar. He draped his coat over the turkey cage and removed the entire bundle. Hustling across the room, Dougherty handed his cargo to Meath, who by then had the saloon door open and was partially outside.

"He's all yours, Bobby," Dougherty said, and calmly returned to his seat.

Meath did not hear a word of it. On a full run, he bounded off the porch and raced down the snow-covered hill toward the tool house. *Get down there. Find an empty. Don't slip. Damn, bird's heavy.*

The cold air awakened the bird. Its loud gobbles pierced the still night. Far enough away from the saloon and behind the station, only Meath and the two section men heard the doomed bird's protests.

By circling around the backside of the tool house, Meath arrived trackside, out of view of Sherlock, who was back in the warmth of the station.

Made it. Here comes an empty. Door open. Going slow, one, two, three …

In a swift movement, Meath pulled off Dougherty's coat and Bailets' apron. With surprising ease he tossed the cage through the open door of the slowly passing car. It landed upright and skidded to a stop about midway across the floor. The bird fell quiet.

"The poor son of a bitch must either be froze already or in shock," Meath told the sectionmen as he ran past, headed back to the saloon.

Completely out of breath, his face red, Meath stumbled back into the bar and retook his seat. The "fight" between Nelson and Clary was still more than occupying Bailets.

Meath quickly looked around the saloon. His eyes immediately settled on the empty end of the bar. *Damn it. Can't let Bailets see the bird's gone.*

"Al," Meath urged, shoving the coat and apron towards him. "Quick, sneak behind the bar and put a whiskey case up where the turkey was. Throw the apron back over it."

Douhgerty kept one eye on Bailets while he took an empty box from the back corner. He quietly placed it on the spot once occupied by the turkey, and carefully covered it with the apron.

There was still plenty of noise coming from the center of the room when Dougherty returned, putting on his coat. Catching Harrington's eye, Meath gave him the "thumbs up."

Harrington was watching the entire process from the bar. Putting his whiskey glass down, he hollered over to Clary and Nelson, "Boys! Knock it off! No point in busting up the only decent bar in town and getting your heads busted in the process."

Like the parting of the Red Sea, the men pulled away and dispersed across the room. Bailets, Clary and Nelson were left standing alone.

Still in a rage, Bailets pointed his club at the two combatants, "Clean up this mess and get out!" he demanded.

Clary and Nelson looked at each other and shrugged. They righted the furniture and wandered out the door, smiling at Meath and Dougherty as they left. Seeing a good crowd gathered around the bar and that Harrington had Bailets occupied in a deep conversation, Meath and Dougherty left as well.

Once outside, Dougherty could not contain himself any longer.

"How'd it go?"

"About as good as it could," Meath allowed, without so much as a hint of a grin. "Got down to the track just in time for an empty to show up. I gave the cage a toss; it landed about mid-way in. Just about right, I'd say. Far enough in so it won't rattle out, close enough to the door so that bird will be froze stiff by Skykomish."

As the two men ambled towards the depot, Meath was still plotting. He rummaged for a cigar and lit it. *Sherlock take the fall. Figure out a reward poster. Got Bailets' "John Hancock" on this receipt.* Meath pulled the paper from his coat pocket and carefully ripped off the portion containing the saloon owner's signature.

"What are ya up to, Bobby?" Dougherty asked. Both men had come to a stop.

"I'm trying to figure a way to pin this business on Sherlock," Meath answered amid puffs, the cigar now placed in its usual position in the left corner of his mouth. "Let's go roust Harrington out of the saloon. I'm gonna need him."

"No need, Bobby. Here he comes now."

Harrington walked up to the two men; a smile was peering out from under his oversized moustache.

"Ol' Bailets still ain't seen the bird's gone," he chuckled. "I sent the boys home and I was the last one out. Hell, he won't notice until morning."

"You got a scrap piece of paper and a pencil, Bill?" Meath asked.

"Yeah, got one here someplace." Harrington began reaching into his pockets, finally retrieving a stub of a pencil and an annulled slow order.

Standing on the station platform, Meath put the order form against the sectionmens' tool house wall, and scribbled a few lines. He gave that and the paper containing Bailets' signature back to Harrington.

"I need one more favor of ya, Bill. Take this to Sherlock. Tell him that Bailets' turkey got swiped tonight. Hell, you can even tell him Bailets thinks I did it. Tell him that Bailets wants two reward posters made up. Have Sherlock write what I put down here, and tell him Bailets says he can carbon his signature from this paper. Bailets wants one posted on the saloon door and one down here at the depot. He'd like to have them up before morning. Give Sherlock some bullshit line about Bailets trusting only him. Ol' Basil will fall for that. You got all that, Bill?"

Harrington's shoulders were bouncing. One hand was covering his eyes as he shook his head.

"God help me if you ever get mad at me, Meath," Harrington blurted out amidst his fits of laughter. "Okay, I'll go put the noose around Sherlock's neck."

The next morning snow had resumed falling. Meath, Dougherty, and Nelson were getting the plow ready for another day's work. Harrington and Clary were in the station, receiving clearances to run west to Skykomish. Having greased and oiled the machine, Nelson returned to the fire deck. Dougherty had climbed back into the cab to check the wear on the clutch plates. Meath was in front, closely inspecting the stay bolts on each of the massive blades. Out of the corner of his eye he spotted Bailets approaching, red-faced, clutching a sheet of paper.

Here we go, he thought. *Give him the dumb ol' railroader act.*

"What do you know about this? My turkey's gone and now this!" Bailets shook the paper in Meath's face. "This was on my door this morning!"

"Well, let me see what's on that paper and maybe I can tell ya what I know," Meath said, pretending to be in a complete state of confusion. After reading the poster, he looked at Bailets, making sure he appeared to be even more perplexed. "You know, there's another one of these hanging up at the depot, too. Now ain't that odd."

"Theft and forgery! Someone's going to jail over this. And I'm not talking about your illegal kangaroo court either!" Bailets' temper was long past the boiling point.

"Hey, Al," Meath called up into the cab of the plow. "Jump down and take a look at this."

Dougherty dropped down from the rotary and stopped behind the two men, looking at the reward poster over Meath's shoulder.

"Damn, your bird get stolen? Hundred-buck reward! You must really want that bird back!" Dougherty exclaimed.

"You idiot! I didn't write this. It's a forgery."

"Now that you mention it, that is on GN stationary," observed Dougherty.

Meath continued to stare at the paper.

He's falling for it. He allowed himself to gloat ever so slightly. *Set the hook before he can think the whole thing out.*

"Ya know," Meath said, slowly and deliberately, "a guy could pay someone a few bucks to steal your turkey, fake a reward poster, magically find the bird, turn it in and collect the reward. And you'd have to cough up some money just to save face around town."

"Ya know, Al," Meath continued, nudging Dougherty, "that's damned good. Why the hell didn't we think of it?" Meath stopped and eyed Bailets.

His wheels are turning. Swallowed it hook, line and sinker. Time to haul him in. Meath put on his best poker face.

"Now, Mr. Bailets, ya know me and ol' Al here can barely write our own names. Why, this fancy of a reward poster musta come from an educated man."

"And a man that can lay his hands on GN stationery," added Dougherty.

"That's right," agreed Meath. "Never quite seen writing like that. Must be somebody pretty new in town, I'd say. Wouldn't you, Al?"

Dougherty, with a look of extreme seriousness, nodded in agreement.

"Most guys around here sign their bar tabs. You ever seen fancy writing like that Mr. Bailets?"

Just keep reeling him in, Meath thought.

"No, can't say as I have," Bailets said, as he scrutinized the poster even closer.

"Well then, must be someone who doesn't hang around your bar all that much, wouldn't you say?" *That'll send some suspicion Sherlock's way,* Meath hoped.

"Well, that could be the case," Bailets allowed.

"Why, I'd say if you could figure out who had the smarts to write this fancy poster, you'd find the man that swiped your bird."

"Gotta agree with that, Bobby." Dougherty had his arms folded, a large frown was painted across his face, his head still nodding up and down.

Both Meath and Dougherty saw Bailets' eyes narrow and look toward the depot.

"That Sherlock fellow is always bragging about how smart he is," Bailets mumbled as he turned and walked back towards his saloon.

Meath turned to Dougherty and calmly shook his hand.

"Nice bit of work, I'd say."

Harrington and Clary strolled up from the station and joined Meath and Dougherty. Clary broke out into gales of laughter, nearly doubling over. "Jesus, Joseph, and Mary! Did you see the look on Bailets' face?" he hooted.

"By damn, boys, you did it!" Harrington slapped both Meath and Dougherty on their backs. "You got Bailets and Sherlock in the same trap. Hell, let's celebrate and go plow some snow."

December 20, 1909
Arthur Reed Blackburn, Trainmaster

Blackburn trudged through the loose snow back towards his plow. Nothing of what he saw, nothing about what was being done, nothing at all set well with him. He paused to catch his breath. Digging inside his wet coat, he pulled his watch from his vest. The time did not set well either.

Time's a wasting. Trains stacking up. Gotta get things rolling damned fast.

All day a cold wind blew fog up from the Scenic Basin, blanketing the upper slopes of Windy Mountain. It laid a wet shroud across the tracks. Out of the gray gloom snow fell, adding to the raw dampness of the day. Above Blackburn the thick clouds completely obscured the mountainside—the very thing he needed to see clearly.

For the bulk of the afternoon, Blackburn and his plow crew were clearing a slide that had come down off the mountain and blocked the tracks just east of Snow Shed 3.3. The snow had packed hard, making it difficult for the blades of the plow to cut though. Only when the plow was backed away from slide, then rammed into the mass were they able to begin to buck through the obstruction.

It had come as somewhat of a surprise, because in years past, the snow shed had successfully guarded the tracks from just such an event. For some reason, though, high above Blackburn, lost in the fog, the snow came tumbling down the mountain by a slightly different route, missing the shed and sweeping across the right-of-way.

Shouldn't be this big a slide. Hasn't snowed that much. Damned forest fires. Completely change how the snow slides down off the hill. No trees or brush to hold it. Breaks off and comes straight down. Missed the damned shed altogether. Need to see the top of the damned mountain to know for sure what the hell's going on up there. Oh well, can't wait any longer. Make another run. Stick the mail trains behind this little slide, O'Neill's gonna have my ass. Damned mail contracts. All I hear about these days.

Blackburn turned and paced back to the slide, where Roadmaster Thomas McIntyre and his section foreman, Robert Harley, had their crew of Italians hand shoveling. Twice Blackburn had propelled his plow into the white mass, and twice he had to retreat. The snow bank was taller than the 13-foot fan of the plow, causing the machine to burrow inward, and eventually plugging the chute where the snow exited the fan chamber. Blackburn had no choice but to wait and allow the men to hand dig the slide down to a size the plow could handle. The crew had been working barely an hour, but Blackburn was exasperated with what he saw as a snail's pace.

"Let's clear these dagos off of here, Mr. Harrington. It's time we got busy and bucked this thing out of here," Blackburn announced, having come up alongside his newly appointed Assistant Trainmaster.

Earlier in the day, Harrington, having completed a plow run from Leavenworth, turned his plow and engine, and backed west from Wellington to double Blackburn's crew. They now had two plows facing in opposite directions, with two pusher locomotives sandwiched in between. It was the only aspect of the day that met with Blackburn's approval.

"The boys haven't had much of a chance to shave this thing down to where we can handle it," Harrington countered. "Mac and Harley just told me they need another hour or so."

"We haven't got another hour. Damned little slide's had us tied up most of the day. No excuse for it. Now find Harley and McIntyre and let's get moving!"

Can't get along with him. Argues every decision. I'm the damned trainmaster. He's my assistant, Blackburn thought as Harrington, offering no further argument, disappeared into the fog.

It was bad enough that the line had been closed for the better part of the day. Compounding Blackburn's anxiety was the knowledge that Superintendent O'Neill was on his way up from Everett. Blackburn wanted the line open before O'Neill arrived, if for no other reason than to satisfy his own sense of pride. As Skykomish Trainmaster, Blackburn answered directly to O'Neill and was in charge of the train crews and day to day movement of trains over the pass. It was a thankless position. Caught between the wishes of the Superintendent and keeping the men focused and disciplined, Blackburn often felt he was on a mid-evil rack being slowly stretched apart. It took an aggressive, hard-nosed attitude to be a trainmaster, which often did not set well with the men he supervised. He knew he was unpopular, but ultimately, it was O'Neill he wished to impress. *First slide of the year. Handled worse. Handle this without O'Neill.*

As the afternoon wore on, the snow lessened. Even so, dusk was coming early due to the heavy cloud cover. Ghostlike figures slowly appeared through the gloom as the sectionmen walked clear of the slide.

"Can we proceed?" Blackburn called out to no one in particular.

Getting dark. Will have to get lanterns lit.

"My boys are clear, Mr. Blackburn, but you're jumping the gun." It was Roadmaster McIntyre. As a roadmaster, he was equal in authority to Blackburn, but was responsible for the track maintenance crews while Blackburn over-saw the trainmen. "You try to buck straight through, you're gonna get her stuck as sure as I'm standing here."

"He's right," Harrington added, having joined the group. "That slide's still too tall and the snow along the upper bank's too loose. She'll slough in on the sides and bind the wheels."

"We've got two engines pushing. I'll take that chance, gentlemen," Blackburn countered. "We've got to get this railroad running. That bunch of dagos with shovels isn't going to do it. Mr. Harrington, man the plow, I'll stay out here and direct."

"I'll keep my boys ready," McIntyre said as he parted. "They ain't done shoveling yet."

Blackburn ignored the jab.

Onboard the plow, Harrington whistled off. Plow engineer Bob Meath returned the signal in kind, and was followed in succession by pusher engineers Ben Jarnigan and Pete Imberg. A final "all's clear" wave was relayed from McIntyre to Blackburn to Harrington. The brakes were released and the giant fan of the plow began to rotate as engineer Meath pulled out his throttle. Back on the pushers Jarnigan and Imberg put their engines in motion and began the charge.

Blackburn stationed himself clear of the fan's chute, but where he could get a good view of the both progress of the plow, and of Harrington, who was hanging from the left door. As the plow approached, the slow clanking sound of the blades heightened in pitch to a loud whine as the fan increased in speed. A knot of excitement formed in Blackburn's stomach.

Hit her hard, boys. Hit her hard!

He kept motioning Harrington forward as the plow collided with the wall of snow. Smoke erupted from the stack of the plow and those of the pushers. A torrent of snow shot from the chute and over the bank, disappearing into the fog.

The plow chewed away at the blockade. As the wall of snow got deeper, large packed chunks broke off and slid across the hood of the fan. Rolling off to the side, they slowly found their way alongside, and then eventually under the machine. So intent were both Blackburn and Harrington on the forward progress, neither noticed.

"Keep her coming! Keep her coming!" Blackburn yelled. "She's gonna take her!"

Suddenly, the plow stopped. The drive wheels of both pusher engines spun wildly, sending a shower of sparks out from the interface of steel wheel and iron rail.

"Keep coming, goddamn it!" Blackburn's face was red, from exposure to the weather and now anger at the sudden faltering of the plow.

By working together, the two engineers in the pushers put their locomotives back on firm footing. Yet no sooner did the outfit resume its attack on the slide when a large portion of the bank above the plow broke loose, causing snow to fall against the right side of the plow. As more snow slid off the bank, it began to accumulate under the machine, threatening to lift the wheels off the rail.

"All stop!" Blackburn hollered.

He need not have said a word. Reacting immediately to the crisis,

Harrington already gave the order to apply the brakes, and was madly whistling the stop signal to the engineers in the pushers.

For a moment, all was quiet. Blackburn hopped down from the bank. He crouched down and closely inspected the underside of the plow.

"We're still on the rail," he called out.

"Looks like you got your tits in the wringer this time, Art," McIntyre mumbled, having joined Blackburn. "Harley, get your boys down in there. Let's get Mr. Blackburn shoveled outta trouble."

Harrington, too, joined the group, a shovel in his hand.

"Never saw it coming. Sloughed off from the other side," Blackburn reasoned, more to himself than Harrington.

"Hit her too hard too quick," Harrington said. "Damned snow banks are just too unstable to buck this hard, seems to me."

"Seems to *me*, if we don't get this railroad running damned fast, it's our jobs that are going to be unstable, Mr. Harrington," Blackburn snapped.

"Gonna spend more time now shoveling us out than if we let them boys finish up on the slide to begin with," Harrington grumbled as he began to pitch snow away from the trapped machine.

"We damned near got it bucked out, just like I said we would," Blackburn countered.

Fifty damned feet left. Stuck. Back to waiting for a bunch of damned dagos to shovel me clear. Damn the luck.

Darkness was fast overcoming the mountains. Lanterns were lit, their little spheres of light combining to cast an almost eerie yellow glow over the scene. In the last gasp of daylight, Jarnigan and Imberg managed to pull the plow free. With the sectionmen shoveling from on top of the slide, the plow was once again slowly eased into the remaining mass.

It was 6 p.m. by Blackburn's watch when he rang up Wellington from the telephone inside Shed 3.3.

"Wellington" came the scratchy voice of Sherlock.

"Blackburn here. Inform the dispatcher the line is clear. We will release the staff at Alvin and protect trains through the slide area."

"I copy that, Mr. Blackburn. Oh, and I have a message from

Skykomish. Mr. O'Neill has arrived and expects a full report on why the long delay."

It was like someone sucker-punched Blackburn in the stomach.

"Do I need to repeat …"

"No, no. I copy," Blackburn hung up.

Goddamn it. Gonna catch hell for a slide that shouldn't have even been here.

December 21, 1909
James Henry O'Neill, Superintendent

Standing alongside Blackburn, O'Neill scanned the gully that lay before the two men. Snags, blackened by summer fires, protruded from the snow. The absence of needle-covered limbs laid the mountainside bare, giving it a totally different look. Without the usual layer of underbrush as well as the protective evergreen canopy, the dynamics of the hill was completely changed from previous years.

"So you can see, Mr. O'Neill, the forest fire last summer has changed this part of the hill. Instead of the snow sliding straight down and over the shed, it splits. Some comes down like before, but more of it ends up over here, coming down this little gully. It misses the shed all together, and ends up on the tracks."

O'Neill listened as Blackburn pointed out the problem at the east end of Snow Shed 3.3. Not happy about the line being closed for so long the day before, O'Neill hiked up the side of the mountain to have a firsthand look. He wanted to take his trainmasters to task for what he felt was a poor performance, but now he had no choice but to reconsider. Things were drastically changed on the mountain since the previous winter. The troubles here had little to do with Blackburn or Harrington.

He carefully surveyed the mountainside. His eyes slowly trailed from the top ridge down to the tracks below. *Major rebuild to stretch the shed. Have to extend the roof well up the hill for it to hold up.*

"The only way we can protect the line is to extend Shed 3.3," Blackburn paused, looking for some type of reaction from O'Neill.

"Yes, Art, I see your point."

"McIntyre and I have taken some measurements. I've got them written down right here." Blackburn produced a folded piece of Great Northern stationery from his coat pocket. Handing it to O'Neill, he continued his pitch. "We'll need to extend the shed no less than 200 feet, but 300 would be even better."

O'Neill looked at the crude map and numbers scribbled across the sheet of paper. *Don't need to sell me. Trouble is, I've got bosses too.*

O'Neill thought back to a recent meeting he'd had with Gruber, the General Manager of the Western Division. The very subject of additional snow sheds was discussed. Gruber was not in a spending mood. With the drilling of the summit tunnel and the installation of the electrification between Wellington and Cascade Tunnel Station, Gruber made it very clear to O'Neill he was satisfied that the railroad through the pass could be now operated at peak efficiency.

"So far the snows have come pretty evenly. It snows a little, it freezes, and sets up. But look what happened when this last little storm blew through. Right off it starts sliding here again. God help us if we get a heavy blast that lasts a day or so. Be tough to keep the line open."

"Yes. Indeed it would. Then again, that's why I have you and Harrington up here now, isn't it?"

O'Neill could tell Blackburn was taken aback a bit by the comment. "Ah, well yes, I guess it is," Blackburn stammered.

Onto something there, Art. Just don't know it. Be tough to keep it open through here. Big boys in a state over those mail contracts. On-time performance slipping. Be the wedge I need to pry some money out of them.

The two men took one last look around. The clouds that brought the most recent snowfall were thinning. The sun was slowly forcing its way through their gray exterior. Shafts of light began to stream down into the Scenic Basin far below. The wind blowing the clouds aside allowed the rays to engulf the mountainside where O'Neill and Blackburn stood. Reflecting off the snow, the sudden brilliance of the scene caused both men to squint as they eyed the white mountain peaks that were slowly appearing.

"Not hard to figure out why they named this area Scenic, eh, Art?"

A sudden gust of wind blowing down from the summit gap to the east momentarily shrouded the men in a swirling mass of powder snow.

"Or why they call this Windy Mountain," Blackburn added.

Although the situation at Shed 3.3 was serious, it was not the primary reason O'Neill decided to spend a few days at Wellington. It was nearly Christmas, and the first big snowfall of the year finally hit. O'Neill wanted to see firsthand how Blackburn and Harrington would respond to the challenge, knowing the heaviest snow would come in January and February. The long delay the day before did not set well with O'Neill. He still suspected part of the previous day's problems stemmed from Blackburn and Harrington not working well together.

"So how are you and Harrington getting along?" O'Neill asked, clearly on a bit of a fishing trip.

"He runs his plow crew and I run mine, I guess," Blackburn responded, still gazing out at the mountains.

"That's what I'm worried about. You two keep working your separate ways, we stand a good chance of the left hand not knowing what the right hand's doing. You two need to quit butting heads."

"He's my assistant, I'm not his," Blackburn snapped back.

"Listen to me, Art. You've got to let go a little. You've got your hands full just getting trains over the hill. Let Harrington worry more about the plow crews. That's why I've got him up here." O'Neill stopped himself. He did not want to launch into a lecture.

"The way I see it, if the line's blocked by a slide, I can't get the trains over the hill. I have to be where the trouble is and take charge," Blackburn replied, irritated.

"I'm not saying you shouldn't. What I'm saying," O'Neill paused to gather his thoughts. "Art, listen to Harrington and take his advice now and again. God knows I've taken your advice often enough."

"I'll keep that in mind, sir. We'd better get back—sounds like the boys are about done." Blackburn began to pick his way back down.

Stubborn sort. Don't think I did a bit of good, O'Neill silently fumed.

Arriving back trackside, O'Neill and Blackburn watched rotary X-801 make the final run. Conductor John Parzybok, whose plow was in the trailing position, stood on the snow bank, guiding his counterpart, Ed Lindsay, who was hanging from the door of the 801. The plow was eased into the mound of loose snow. The blades made quick work of the last of the obstruction.

"Well, that's that," Blackburn commented. "Sweep her clean coming the other way with the trailing plow and we can re-open the line. Now then, Mr. O'Neill. My plan is to break up the set right here. I'll take the westward-facing plow on down to Skykomish where we can service it and turn it. The eastward-facing plow can take you back up to Wellington. Mr. Harrington made a flip east to Leavenworth, but he should be back in Wellington by now. Parzybok can double with him." Blackburn glanced at O'Neill, afraid he had overstepped his bounds.

Calm down, O'Neill thought. *Giving orders. Taking charge. That's why you're here.* O'Neill simply nodded in agreement.

Within a half hour, the plows were separated and the line through the slide area plowed clean.

"I'll release the line for westward trains when I get to Wellington, Art. I'll do my best to get you a longer shed here. Be a nice Christmas present for you and the boys, now wouldn't it," O'Neill commented as he headed for the east facing plow. "If we don't see each other over the next week, Merry Christmas, Art. Do try to make it down to Everett and spend the holidays with Rose and your little daughter."

"And the same to you, sir. I'll do my best to spend Christmas at home," Blackburn admitted.

O'Neill smiled.

Nothing like a wife and family to settle a man down.

Once the plow arrived at Wellington, O'Neill wrote out an order re-opening the line west.

"Take this on to the depot, Mr. Parzybok," he said handing the order to the conductor. "I'm going to get a bite of supper."

Dropping down off the plow, O'Neill walked toward his private car, spotted on the upper spur, west of the station. *Tired, wet and hungry.*

Gruber won't give me the sheds. Don't see him up here bucking slides. Brass. Want everything done fast and for free. Luck's going to run out one day. As he stepped into his car, the welcome smell of hot food greeted his nose.

"What's in the oven, Lewis?" O'Neill called out. "If I didn't know better I'd swear you're cooking a ham."

Lewis Walker, O'Neill's Negro steward, stepped out from the kitchen.

"Ham it is, Mr. O'Neill. I talked my good friend Mr. Bailets into giving me one. Fixin' up some yams with candy to go with them. I got dry clothes laid out for you, so you go on and get ready for dinner."

"Well, I guess I got my orders. Yes sir, Mr. Walker!" O'Neill cracked a grin as he walked on past and into his sleeping compartment where he began to change into fresh clothes.

Not supposed to talk to a steward like I do. Especially a Negro. Plenty of folks hate us Irish, or so I've been told. Same with him. Respect Lewis. Damn good cook, good family man, always a grin.

O'Neill sat down at his table. Walker placed a plate before him with two thick slices of ham and mounded with candied yams.

"Now there's plenty more, so you just dig right in, Mr. O'Neill. If you don't eat it all I will," Walker said, patting his stomach, "and Lord knows I don't need it."

"Lewis, I'm afraid I'm going to have to fire you," O'Neill teased, his mouth already full. "It's my wife. She says if you weren't such a good cook, I'd stay to home more."

Walker laughed, waved his hand at his boss, and disappeared back into the kitchen.

After dinner, O'Neill gathered up a group of papers from his desk, as well as the snow shed measurements given to him earlier by Blackburn.

"I'm headed over to the station, Lewis," he said, leaning into the kitchen. "We're heading home tonight on 25. You better take a few days off and get ready for Christmas."

"Why, thank you sir. I'll have your bed turned and ready. Best you get some sleep while traveling. Your wife is gonna want you to fire me if you show up home looking the way you do."

"Lewis, your concern is touching, but I think you're just afraid another boss wouldn't put up with you the way I do." O'Neill strolled out the rear door onto the platform of his car. "Oh, by the way," he added, turning slightly, "that was one good supper."

O'Neill's heavy boots crunched through the hard, frozen snow as he walked toward the depot. The clouds had moved on. Above, the clear winter sky seemed to be a solid mass of stars. The peaks to the east were silhouetted against the glow of a rising moon. O'Neill paused to light a cigar.

Getting damned cold. Shoulda worn my heavy coat. Lewis is going to give me hell for not. Clear and cold. Could stay this way until spring. Good long cold snap. Just what the doctor ordered. Set up that snow pack good. Let all of us have a merry Christmas.

The rotary that brought him into town had been doubled with Harrington's outfit and was peacefully steaming on a sidetrack in the upper yard. Loud laughter from inside the station caught O'Neill's ear.

Yep, Harrington's boys are in town. Be a crowd at the station. So much for quiet. Better there than in the saloon, drunk.

O'Neill paused at the door while he stomped the snow off his boots. He read a mock reward poster that was pinned on the frame.

Bailets had a turkey stolen. One hundred dollar reward no less. Bet Meath's behind this somehow. No business of mine. Glad it isn't.

O'Neill opened the door and elbowed his way through the crowd of railroaders. The men were gathered in a tight circle, laughing at two men in the middle.

Looks like Clary and Nelson are faking a fight. Won't even ask why.

Harrington was first to notice the presence of the Superintendent and the difficulty he was having making progress through the crowd.

"Make way, boys! Make way! Mr. O'Neill is here!"

Clary and Nelson immediately ended their mock brawl and the center of the room quickly cleared. A dead silence fell over the men.

O'Neill cracked a grin and tipped his hat, taking his cigar from his mouth. "Thanks, boys. I've just got to drop off these wires and I'll be out of your hair."

"Well, you're sure welcome to hang around, Mr. O'Neill," offered Bob Meath. "You never know what fun we might hatch tonight."

"That's a tempting offer, Mr. Meath, but unfortunately, duty calls. I've got a snow drift of paper work yet to take care of."

Approaching Sherlock, he stumbled over his name. "Mr., ah …"

"Sherlock, sir, Basil Sherlock."

"Yes, yes, Sherlock. I need these sent off, and also inform Cascade Tunnel Station and the electric crew I want my car placed on the rear of number 25 tonight. Here are the required orders."

He removed yet another stack of papers from the corner of Sherlock's desk, again tipped his hat to the crowd, and disappeared into a room across the narrow hall beyond the telegraph office. Sitting alone at a small desk, O'Neill took a couple of quick puffs off his cigar.

Be fun just to be one of the boys again, he lamented. *Can't join them even if I had the time. Just ain't the same anymore. Being there would ruin their fun. Oh well. See about Mr. Blackburn's snow shed.*

O'Neill immersed himself in the paper work before him.

Back in the operator's room the crowd stayed silent for a moment while Sherlock tapped on his key, sending out the messages O'Neill had left.

"Hey Sherlock, mind if Pattie here sings a song or two?" Meath asked.

Sherlock spun around in his chair, his headset still on his ear. "Not at all, some music would do me just fine." He turned back around and resumed his keying.

"How about *The Wearin' O the Green' Pattie*?" Meath requested.

The suggestion struck a positive chord, and the crowd, of largely Irish lineage, ushered brakeman John "Pattie" Kelly to the middle of the room.

Looking straight at Alfred "Ole" Strandrud, Kelly began to sing in his clear Irish tenor voice.

Oh Molly dear did hear the news that's going 'round
They are hiring Norwegians from Saint Paul to Puget Sound.
And when an Irishman comes around and says he wants a job
They turn away and always say go away you Irish slob.

The room broke into fits of laughter, with a number of jabs and nudges aimed at Strandrud, who was nearly doubled over as well. Even before the laughter subsided, Kelly broke into another verse.

Oh Paddy dear did you hear the news that's going 'round

The shamrock is forbid by law to grow on Irish ground
And Saint Patrick's Day no more we'll keep, his color can't be seen
For there's a bloody law against the wearing of the green.

The crowd went quiet as Kelly sang. The words and notes floated about the room, echoing with a solemn resonance as he finished the last verse. For another moment the room remained silent.

It was Dougherty who finally spoke.

"Hey boys, have you heard the news that's goin' 'round? Why, I'm told Ole over there is about to tie the knot. Yes sir, his days as a free man are numbered."

"Holy hell, is that right, Ole?" Ira Clary asked. The rest of the group chimed in and gathered around the embarrassed Strandrud.

"Vell," he said with his heavy Scandinavian accent, "I yust tink it's time. Yah sure, da end of February is ven I'll go and get myself hitched."

Another round of laughter filled the room. Strandrud's ribs took a number of well-meaning jabs.

"Well then," Meath interrupted, "Pattie, maybe a song for Ole's impending doom is in order."

Kelly raised his finger in the air, "I've got just the tune."

He cleared his throat as the men settled down. Lining the perimeter of the room, each took his place. Kelly again stepped to the middle of the large office and began to sing.

As we gather in the chapel here in Old Kilmainham Jail
I think about these past few days, oh will they say we've failed.
From our school days they have told us, we must yearn for liberty
Yet all I want in this dark place is to have you here with me.
Oh Grace just hold me in your arms and let this moment linger
They'll take me out at dawn and I will die.
With all my love I place this wedding ring upon your finger
There won't be time to share our love for we must say goodbye.

The words of the first stanza and chorus drifted across the hall, breaking O'Neill's concentration. He paused in his reading and looked blankly out the window. The moon cast its bright light on the snow, outlining in surprising detail the surrounding mountains. And then the second verse rang in O'Neill's ears.

Now I know it's hard for you my love to ever understand

The love I bear for these brave men, my love for this dear land.
But when Padhraic called me to his side down in the GPO
I had to leave my own sick bed, to him I had to go.

Good God, the boys are really feeling the green tonight, "The Wearing of the Green" and now "Grace," O'Neill thought.

The clear, soulful notes of the chorus streamed from Kelly's throat and into O'Neill's ears. Quietly, he rose from his desk, left the little office and took a position out in the hall. He looked through the ticket window into the operator's room and saw the men gathered about. Most were staring down as if counting the cracks in the boards of the floor. Meath was next to his friend Dougherty. The husky brakeman was leaning against Meath, his arm resting on the rotary engineer's left shoulder. Ira Clary and Snow King Harrington were to either side of "Ole" Strandrud, each with an arm resting on the lanky Norwegian's shoulders. As the final verse filled the air, O'Neill's thoughts turned of his wife and daughter in Everett and those who came before him.

Miss my girls. Away too much. No way to treat a family. Tough life. Best damned division on the GN, toughest to run. Tough. Old folks say nothing's as tough as they had it over in the old country. Belfast, they say, was tough.

And as Kelly gained breath and began the final chorus, the men, at least those who knew the words, joined in. It was Kelly's voice that still pierced the air with its true tone, but the collection of tenors, baritones and basses in no way distracted. O'Neill was moved by the sincerity of the sound, the sincerity of the men. He had felt it before, but not quite as strong as he did that very moment. *Got the best-damned bunch of railroaders on any road, anywhere.*

Oh Grace just hold me in your arms and let this moment linger
They'll take me out at dawn and I will die.
With all my love I place this wedding ring upon your finger
There won't be time to share our love for we must say goodbye.

The music broke free from the walls of that little station deep in the Tye River canyon. It drifted out through the clear, cold night and engulfed the mountains.

Downgrade, Frank Martin pulled his head back into the warm engine cab and shouted at his fireman, Harry Partridge.

"Come over here Harry, you gotta see this!"

Partridge joined Martin on the right side of the cab. Together they looked down into the Scenic Basin. Far below were the lights of the station at Scenic and the Hot Springs Hotel. The light of the moon sparkled as it reflected off the ice-crusted snow and the twin ribbons of steel cutting across the valley. The entire scene was cast in a cold, but breathtaking blue glow.

"I gotta figure that's about the way the Almighty sees it from heaven, don't ya think Harry?"

Part Two

"We got no sleep." –John Robert Meath

Tuesday, February 22, 1910, 6:00 a.m.
James Henry O'Neill, Superintendent

Colder than a well digger's ass in the Klondike, O'Neill thought as he was about to board his private car. Now coupled to the rear of Train 4, it was ready to take him from his cozy home in Everett to the snow clogged Cascades a mere 40 miles to the east. The warm aroma of hot coffee and fried bacon drifted from its interior and pierced the predawn cold. The A-16 was O'Neill's home away from home. Indeed, with the time spent out along his division, the car seemed more like home than his own house. "You can't run a division from an office," he would say.

Smells like Lewis is cooking enough to feed the whole damned division, O'Neill surmised as he walked through the rear door.

At the far end of the car, the dining table was positioned alongside the window. On it, a cup of steaming coffee sat with an elegant table setting of Great Northern china and sterling silverware on a linen tablecloth.

More trouble on the mountain. O'Neill sighed, pulled up a chair and lit a cigar. He sat for a few minutes staring out at the nearly deserted station platform, alternating slurps of coffee and puffs on his cigar.

Mail trains arriving late day after day.

"And a good morning to you, Mr. O'Neill," greeted Walker.

"Morning, Lewis. I suppose you're going to stuff me so full of breakfast I won't be worth a damn for the rest of the day."

"Now Mr. O'Neill, you just hand me up your cup and let me worry about breakfast. Mr. Longcoy is getting things set up in your office and will be right out."

Earl Longcoy. O'Neill stared at the lit end of his cheroot. *Going to go a long way with this railroad. Nineteen-year-old kid. Making a damn sight more than I did at his age. Get him out on the road. Learn railroading from the bottom up. Good office boy. Need to make a railroader out of him.*

"Good morning, sir."

O'Neill turned from the window and looked into the boyish face of Longcoy. A tall, lanky young man, his sandy hair was always neatly combed, perfectly parted down the middle. The starch collar of his white shirt clung to his neck in a stranglehold and his tie was always straight.

"Hello, Earl, sit down and have some breakfast with me. I have a hunch Lewis cooked enough for the both of us."

"Thank you, sir. I have the latest telegrams from the mountain."

The car gave a slight lurch forward. The posts supporting the station platform roof began to glide slowly past the window. It seemed to O'Neill that it was the platform moving and the train standing still. Only the occasional thump of the car crossing a switch point, the gentle rocking, and the rhythmic vibration of the wheels on the jointed rail hinted motion.

"Care for a smoke, Earl?" O'Neill asked. *Tease him a bit. Make a man out of him yet.*

"No thank you, sir. Now, about these messages ..."

"How bad is it?" O'Neill resigned himself to the business at hand. "Did Blackburn and Harrington report?"

"Um. Let me see." Longcoy shuffled through a pile of telegrams.

"Here it is. The latest is from Mr. Blackburn. He left Scenic and is plowing west to Skykomish. Right now Skykomish is reporting calm winds and light snow; about four inches fell overnight," Longcoy continued. "Scenic reports wind, six inches new, the temperature at ten degrees. It seems the wind's kicking up pretty good, snow is blowing up at Alvin. Wellington reports wind as well. They're guessing they got about eight inches overnight. Cascade Tunnel Station also has eight inches of new snow, but only slight winds. On down the hill, things are calm and two to four inches of new."

"So what trains are up there now?" O'Neill asked.

"According to the messages, Mr. Blackburn left Cascade Tunnel Station earlier this morning coming west on plow X-801 ahead of number 25. The X-807 brought 3 and 27 up to Cascade Tunnel Station. By then they were close enough behind 25 they're coming down on their own with no rotary escort."

"Anything ahead of them?"

"Ah, not sure." Longcoy again flipped through the telegrams. "It looks like a First 451 was through Wellington ahead of all of those trains."

O'Neill snubbed out his cigar. A disgusted look crossed his face.

"Goddamn it. How far ahead of the mail train is that freight?"

"I'm not sure, other than the freight is supposed to hold at Scenic for 3 and 27 to run around it."

"And the rotary?"

"Ahead of the freight, sir."

"Christ. So the mail train is stuck behind two passengers and a goddamned freight. When we get up there I want to sit down with Blackburn and Harrington. We've got to maintain a clear track for that mail train, no matter what." *Gonna raise some hell with those two.*

"I'll make a note of that, sir."

"Damn it to hell, I thought we had that all ironed out long ago. Toughest part of running a division, Earl, keeping all of your men sharp and thinking the way they need to be thinking."

"I believe the idea was to have the rotary in Skykomish early enough so it could take us on up."

O'Neill ignored Longcoy's explanation of what was an obvious case of poor dispatching. Under the gun by his superiors, the on-time performance of mail trains 27 and 28 was in the forefront of O'Neill's mind. A good showing throughout the winter would solidify the U.S. Postal contract with the Great Northern, and ensure the railroad a substantial source of revenue. Thus far, their arrival times had been steadily slipping, and O'Neill was hearing about it.

"Where's Harrington?"

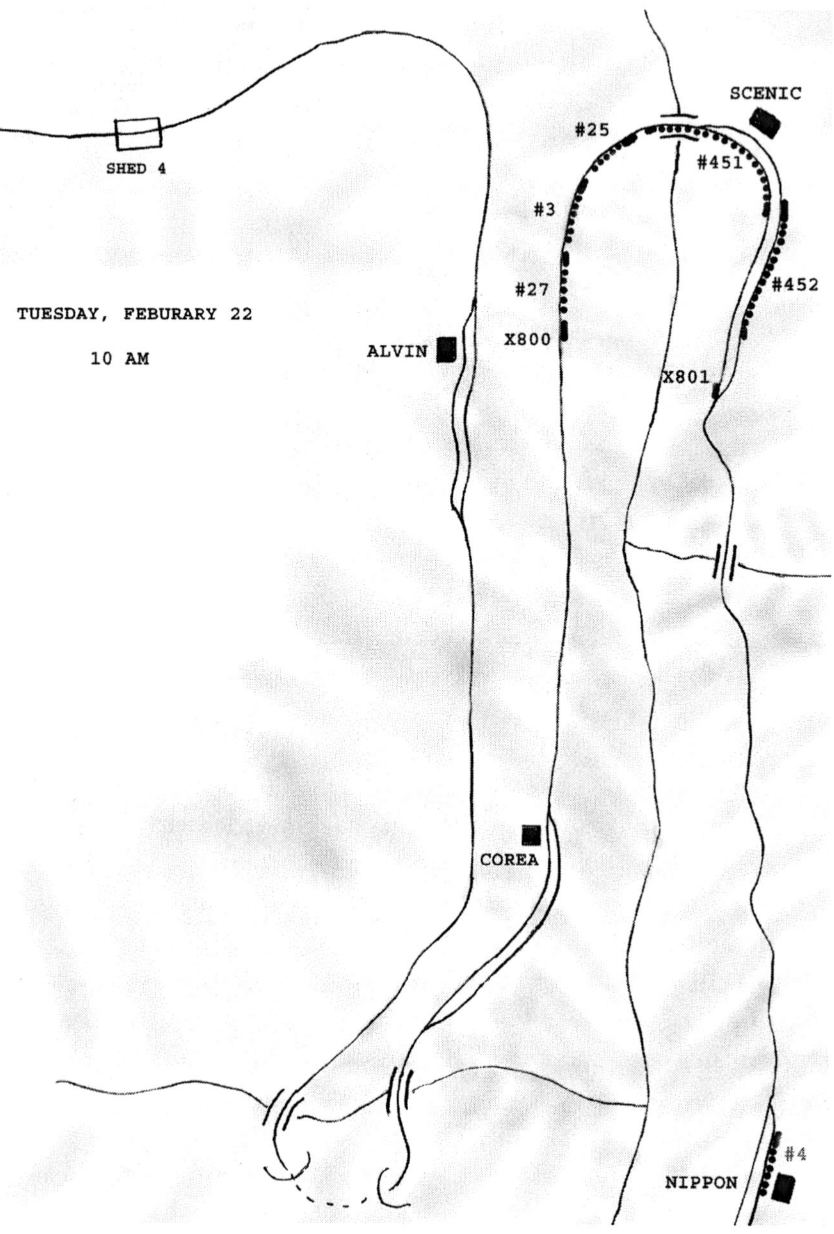
SHED 4
TUESDAY, FEBURARY 22
10 AM
ALVIN
#25
SCENIC
#451
#3
#27
X800
#452
X801
COREA
#4
NIPPON

"He has the X-800 and is still up at Cascade Tunnel Station along with the 807. He's going to clear the yard, then move over to clear the yard at Wellington while he's at it. He'll be on call to protect eastward movements from the top and anything coming west out of Leavenworth."

Lewis Walker emerged from the narrow passage leading to the kitchen with a tray balanced on his hand, slung high above his shoulder. On it were six china plates, each covered with a silver hood.

"Excuse me gentlemen, I didn't mean to bother you."

"Nonsense, Lewis. Mr. Longcoy has my head stuffed with railroad business; you might as well stuff my belly with food. So, what's for breakfast?"

Dawn revealed yet another dark, gray day. Moisture-laden clouds clogged the valley of the South Fork of the Skykomish River. Their formless fog lay like a funeral shroud over the mountain peaks, draping halfway down their snow-covered flanks. It was a colorless, dismal morning.

O'Neill was on the back platform of his car as Number 4 slowed to a stop at Skykomish. Feathers of snow floated harmlessly from the sky, more the products of a passing flurry than an organized storm. He swung down from the A-16 and headed straight for the depot with purposeful strides, his hands buried in the pockets of his overcoat. In the yard, a helper engine was being switched from the waiting track to be coupled to the point of number 4. On the siding was rotary plow X-801 with its pusher engine, serviced and ready to lead the train east. Stamping the snow off his heavy mountaineer's boots, O'Neill entered the station. He ignored the telegrapher in the operator's room to his left, and burst into the small roadmaster's office to the right. Inside were Trainmaster Arthur Blackburn and Traveling Engineer Duncan Tegtmeier.

Both men were leaning against the desk in the center of the room reading telegrams and spoke in near unison. "Good morning sir."

"Morning boys, what have we got? 27on its way down?"

The slight pause and uncomfortable looks on the faces of the two men told O'Neill all he needed to know. *Damn it, something's gone wrong.*

"We've got some problems up at Scenic, Mr. O'Neill," Blackburn admitted. He handed a telegram to O'Neill. "Here's the latest."

O'Neill ignored the paper and focused on Blackburn.

"Well, what the hell's the problem?" *Hold your temper, let the man explain himself.*

"Ah, well, sir, it all started with an eastbound freight," Blackburn offered. "It's this damnable cold weather. Their helper had boiler problems. By the time they got in the clear, 25 was stalled down at the West Scenic switch. Froze tight, what with the wind and all."

"Jesus." O'Neill lit another cigar. "So where's 27?"

"Behind 3. Sounds like the westbound freight, ah, First 451, ahead of them pulled a drawbar trying to move past the east switch. Their engine is running low on coal. I'm getting a relief engine ready right now over at the roundhouse."

"So the siding and main line are fouled by two freights? That First 451 can't move?"

"No sir. That's how they broke apart. He iced up while taking water, and broke in two when he was trying to buck his way out. Sounds like about midtrain. He can't back up to recouple. 3 tried to shove him back together, but even going downgrade, couldn't get enough footing."

"So the whole goddamned mess is just sitting up there right now? The line's blocked, is that what you're telling me, Mr. Blackburn?"

"Yes sir."

Calm down. 27's going to be later than hell again. Not a goddamned thing I can do about it. Need some extra power up there to shove that train back together. Better bring Harrington's outfit on down too.

"We have men digging out 25 and 451. Sounds like both 3 and 27 are able to bump back and forth enough to keep their trains loose," Blackburn added, obviously trying to placate O'Neill.

"Mr. Tegtmeier, is your plow ready?"

"Yes sir, just out of the shop and in fine shape."

"Good. Tell your boys we'll be heading out in fifteen minutes or so. I'll be going with you and Mr. Blackburn on the plow," O'Neill ordered.

Tegtmeier tipped his grease-soaked hat, and with an obvious sense of relief quickly strode from the office and out across the yard.

"Now, Art, it's time to get this railroad running again. Go over to the roundhouse and crew-up two of the 1900's. I want those big buggers coupled to the 801's pusher. We'll use one to start 25 and put 451 back together, and the other will replace the failed helper of that eastbound. At least get them out of the way. While you're doing that, I'll get word up to Harrington. I want his crew at Scenic to lead 3 and 27 on down. Now, let's get going. We'll talk more about this later. I don't know what the hell happened, but I'm tired of 27 getting stuck on my division."

O'Neill knew the cab of a working steam rotary snow plow was the last place to try and hold a lengthy conversation. The exhaust exploding through the stack directly behind the cab wall and the whine of the shaft spinning the giant fan, created a din that only hoarse-voiced hollering and shrill, piercing whistle blasts could penetrate. As much as O'Neill wanted to take his trainmaster to task for the hold-up at Scenic, the racket generated by the X-801 prevented him from doing so.

Each man stationed himself on opposite sides of the machine. Blackburn was hanging from the door on the downhill side, watching the fan hurl the light accumulation of snow far into the Tye River Canyon. O'Neill was leaning out the uphill side, studying the snow overhead, watching for signs of it sliding. His mind was further up the mountain however, planning to the slightest detail the job that lay ahead.

Ain't gonna be easy. Drop one of the mallets off at the west switch. Plow up to the engine on 25. Back out, run up the siding. Let the mallet back in and couple-up. O'Neill closed his eyes for a moment and tried to visualize the complex moves that needed to be accomplished.

"Mr. Tegtmeier, take my place!" O'Neill shouted.

Passing to the other side of the cab, O'Neill came up behind Blackburn and bellowed into his ear.

"Before this is over," O'Neill hollered, "I want to take a moment with both you and Harrington. Is that understood?"

Wedged between the door jam and Blackburn's back, O'Neill could feel the trainmaster's muscles stiffen. Blackburn nodded but did not voice a single word.

Got him thinking. These boys are going to have to learn—when it comes to these mail trains, I mean business.

An hour of intense railroading had passenger train 25 and the stalled freight train moving west. The troublesome eastbound freight had been backed down the siding far enough for the X-801 and trains 3 and 27 to enter, allowing Harrington, who had arrived with the X-800, to pass by.

Harrington brought his plow down the main line and was waiting for trains 3 and 27 to pull up behind him before proceeding down the hill to Skykomish. O'Neill saw the opportunity he had been waiting for. Standing ankle deep in the freshly fallen snow, he pointed first to his right at Blackburn and then to his left at Harrington.

"Gentlemen: a word, if you please."

Lay down the law. Don't get carried away. Men watching. Short. To the point. Not the best time to chew out my trainmasters.

"Yes sir, Mr. O'Neill." The barrel-chested Harrington, his face red and weathered, was at his side. Icicles produced by his heavy breathing hung from his mustache. Blackburn stood opposite, saying nothing.

"Now listen close, both of you. You are trainmasters. You have the authority, in fact, I fully expect both of you to manage the trains crossing this mountain. Trains 27 and 28 must be expedited across this division. No exceptions. If a dispatcher decides to try and run a slow-moving freight ahead of these trains, you've got to question it. Get the chief on the horn if you have to. You know this mountain and what it takes to keep trains moving. That's why I've got you here. I don't want any more of this damned sloppy railroading like we've seen this morning. Now, let's get things moving, boys."

O'Neill slapped each man on the back.

Sharp words. Don't beat the boys down. No sense kicking them in the teeth over this.

"Mr. Harrington, as much as I like keeping company with you, you'd best get your clearances. I want you to protect 3 and 27 on down the hill. Mr. Blackburn and I will help get that eastbound going. I'll hop back on 4 when it gets here. By then I'm sure Mr. Longcoy will have a mountain of paper work waiting for me."

Tuesday, February 22, 1910, 2nd Trick, Wellington
Basil Sherlock, Telegrapher

The strong winds that had been buffeting Sherlock's house all afternoon greeted him like a slap in the face when he finally ventured outside. He glanced at the thermometer on his porch; the mercury had not been able to struggle past 20 all day. Shoulders hunched, head turned to the side, he leaned forward to make any headway towards the depot against the gusts and blowing snow. *So much for an early spring.*

Sherlock had spent a restless afternoon. He stumbled home from his shift in the wee hours of the morning after making a rare appearance at Bailets Saloon to drink a toast to Alfred "Ole" Strandrud, who was leaving for Seattle to be married. Ever since the turkey incident, Sherlock and Bailets were not on the best of terms. In a town as small as Wellington, the only way to avoid the saloon owner and his accusations was to steer clear of his establishment. With the bar crowded with well-wishers, Sherlock kept himself surrounded by the hard-drinking railroaders and away from the icy glares of Bailets.

He awoke in the morning with his head aching from too much whiskey the night before. Seeing the A-16 being placed on the coal chute spur earlier that afternoon did not help. His stomach was tied in a knot.

Going to be a tough shift. O'Neill in town. Be watching every move. Not like I can't handle my own shift. He pulled out his watch. *Quarter to four. Second 452 must be on its way up. No sign of the snow plows. Blackburn must be with them over at Cascade.*

Stuffy, warm air mixed with tobacco smoke met Sherlock as he passed through the depot door. O'Neill was dictating yet another message to Flannery, so Sherlock quietly took off his coat and lingered at the back of the room.

While Flannery keyed, O'Neill turned. "Good afternoon, Mr. Sherlock."

"Good day to you, sir," Sherlock mumbled, still not approaching the desk.

"Well, I trust you're good and rested. I just put poor Mr. Flannery through the mill and by the looks of things, your shift isn't going to be much easier."

"I believe I'm up to the task, sir."

O'Neill grabbed a china cup that obviously came from his private car. He walked over to the potbelly stove. Setting the cup down, he threw another small shovel of coal into the firebox. He grabbed the filthy coffee pot from the stovetop and filled the delicate cup with thick, black brew. The contrast seemed almost funny to Sherlock—the refined lines of the china tea cup, the primitive crudeness of the coffee pot, and the rest of the station's environment, which by now he detested. O'Neill seemed to notice none of it. To Sherlock, O'Neill was far more interested in lighting another cigar.

"I have confirmation of that last message, Mr. O'Neill." In an often-practiced and well-choreographed move known to all telegraphers, Flannery spun around on the office chair, removed the headset, and hung it on the scissored frame of the telephone speaker.

"Very good, Mr. Flannery."

"Now, Mr. O'Neill, if you'll excuse us for a moment, I'll go over my transfer with Mr. Sherlock so he can take the chair."

O'Neill fell silent, content to stare out the window at the swirling snow. He drank his coffee and smoked while Flannery went over the specifics of the current locations of the various trains. Just as Sherlock suspected, his first task would be as it usually was; preparing clearances and the staff for eastbound freight Second 452.

"Okay, Basil, she's all yours. Now don't let Mr. O'Neill catch you in here asleep like I always do." Flannery gave Sherlock a slap on the back, and then slipped into his coat and hat. "Have a good evening, Mr. O'Neill."

"I'd say a good evening would mean this snow would let up, wouldn't you say? Oh, and not to worry—I believe I'll be able to keep Mr. Sherlock awake."

With a grin and a wave, Flannery was gone.

Flannery. Accuse me of sleeping on duty, Sherlock pouted. *Poor excuse for a joke.*

O'Neill strolled from the window and walked over to the wall opposite Sherlock, leaving a trail of cigar smoke behind him. He tapped the barometer that hung there and jotted down the reading. His forehead seemed noticeably furrowed as he returned to the desk.

"Are the orders for the freight ready, Mr. Sherlock?"

"Yes sir, all I need to do is clear the staff machine, but I'll wait until they're here and the helpers are coupled."

"Good. I want you to send the following message to J.C. Devery in Leavenworth. *Request weather conditions east slope. Report to Wellington.* And you may initial that JHO."

"February twenty-second, two, two, nineteen ten, one, nine, one, naught, to J. C. Devery, J as in James C as in Cat D-e-v-e-r-y at Leavenworth, L-e-a-v-e-n-w-o-r-t-h. Request weather conditions east slope. Report to Wellington, W-e-l-l-i-n-g-t-o-n, JHO."

"Very good, Mr. Sherlock."

"Issued at 4:23, four two three p.m. BWS."

"Correct. Send it."

Sherlock tapped out the message, glad to finally be doing something useful.

"Ring up the dispatcher in Everett and find out how soon he'll have his updated train list," O'Neill ordered, still looking blankly out the window.

Pulling the scissored mouthpiece to his lips, Sherlock plugged the small switchboard connection into the receptacle labeled "Everett Dispatch," and pressed the foot treadle under his desk.

"Dispatcher, Wellington," he said.

"Dispatcher, second sub Mountain, came the scratchy reply.

"Sherlock here, Mr. Johnson. Mr. O'Neill wants to know when your new train list will be ready."

"The chief and I are working on it now. Be ready in about thirty minutes. You can tell Mr. O'Neill it looks like all first class trains are running close to time, except 27. Reports are they still aren't into Spokane. Looks like they'll be behind 25 tonight. Running about six hours late."

"I copy. Wellington out."

"Dispatcher out."

Wonderful. Get to tell O'Neill his mail train is six hours late.

"Mr. Johnson will have the list in about half an hour, sir. From what they have been told, 25 will be ahead of 27. Right now the mail train is about six hours off time."

To Sherlock's surprise, O'Neill said nothing. He finished his coffee and carefully put the cup down on the edge of the operator's desk.

"Six hours late. Looks like you're about to learn how to run a railroad in a snow storm, Mr. Sherlock ," O'Neill finally said, with a slight smile.

"Can the lesson wait, sir?" Sherlock asked in an almost timid voice, fearful the superintendent would take offense. "Second 452 is approaching." Sherlock motioned out the window.

O'Neill chuckled. "Nothing worse than the damned boss underfoot, eh Sherlock? I'm going to grab a quick bite to eat. By the time I get back, we should have Devery's report and the train list. Then we'll get down to business."

With that, O'Neill was out the door.

Second 452 had arrived and was ready to proceed east. Two electric motors were coupled to the steam engine that brought the train upgrade from Skykomish. Two more electric locomotives were ready to begin pushing on the rear of the train.

Sherlock rang up the operator at Cascade Tunnel Station on his staff machine. With the lock released, he grabbed a single baton, unscrewed it and attached each half to a set of running orders.

Whistling off, the train began moving out of the lower yard towards the station. Sherlock hustled outside. As the lead engine rolled by, he handed up a set of orders and one half of the staff to the outstretched hand of Ed Campbell. Both crews of the steam engines, the road engine on the front of the train and the helper ahead of the caboose also received running orders, as did the train's conductor. When the last set of motors ground by, the other half of the staff was handed up.

The train past, Sherlock picked up a small square of paper stuffed in a weight dropped on to the station platform by the conductor. He hustled back inside, brushing the snow off his shoulders. The paper unwrapped, he sat back at his desk. Putting on the headset, Sherlock pulled the telephone mouthpiece to his face and pressed the foot treadle.

"OS Wellington." He paused, waited for the crackling voice of the dispatcher in Everett to fill his ear, and then began his report.

"Extra East, E-A-S-T, 1914, one, nine, one, four arrived Wellington at 4:40 p.m., four four naught p.m., by at 4:53, four five three p.m. with 28, two, eight loads and 12, one, two empties, 1523 one, five, two, three tons. Carrying helper 5000, five, naught, naught, naught, 1908, one, nine, naught, eight and 5003, five, naught, naught, three. BWS. OS."

As he spoke, Sherlock entered the numbers on the train register sheet that was sprawled across his desk. He listened as the dispatcher repeated the numbers.

"That is correct. Wellington out."

"No so fast, Mr. Sherlock. I've got the train list for you."

"One thing after another," Sherlock muttered grabbing a tablet. He rolled a blank train sheet and three carbons into the typewriter, and listened as Johnson read off each train number, the last recorded time, and the location. After typing each entry, Sherlock read back each item for verification. No sooner was that task complete, than the telegraph came to life with the report from Devery.

No end to it. Running a railroad from the middle of nowhere. Sherlock felt his shoulders tense and the beginnings of a headache as he transcribed the message. *Least O'Neill and that god awful cigar smoke's gone.*

Shortly, O'Neill burst through the door, finishing the last of a thick ham sandwich.

"So, any news, Sherlock?" he asked as he poured himself another cup of coffee.

"I have both the train list and a report from Mr. Devery, sir."

"Excellent! Now let's get down to business."

It seemed to Sherlock that the weather conditions on the east side of the mountain were to O'Neill's liking. The wind and snow battering the western slope had not made a major impact on the east side. The line-up of trains, however soon had him fuming. Two slow-moving freight trains had already left Leavenworth ahead of the passenger trains, and were climbing towards Wellington.

"Damn it to hell. Don't like those two freights ahead of number 1." O'Neill looked down at Sherlock, a lit cigar now in his hand. "Ring up Everett."

For Sherlock, it seemed like hours of non-stop work on the telegraph and phone. Slowly, however, an organized plan to keep the railroad running took form.

That man thinks faster than ten stenographers can write.

Orders were issued for eastbound train 2 to hold at Skykomish and wait for the arrival of East 26. Traveling one directly behind the other with a single, conditional staff, both would be escorted over the mountain by Harrington and rotary X-800.

Sherlock could see that the trains coming west posed a dilemma for O'Neill, however. He paced across the room, staring at the train list.

This is the clear thinker everyone tells me about?

The bell on the Wellington staff machine broke the tense silence.

"That must be that first freight at Cascade Tunnel Station, sir."

"Clear your machine, but ring up the operator. See if Blackburn is available. I need to talk to him," O'Neill ordered.

Doing as he was told, Sherlock relinquished the chair to his superior when Blackburn's voice came across the phone. He busied himself tending to the fire in the stove while keeping a close ear on the conversation.

"Who's running that First 401?" was O'Neill's immediate demand. He listened.

"I'm going to let him go ahead of 1, but you tell Mr. McFadgen, if he doesn't make track time to Nippon he'll be bumping cars in Everett the rest of his days on the GN. One more thing, 25 is running ahead of 27 tonight. The Kalispell boys didn't do us any favors. Giving 27 to us six hours late. I'm going to hold 25 at Leavenworth, then start it out behind the 802, maybe an hour or so ahead of 27. Devery says things aren't so bad over there. 27 should be able to damned near catch up with them at Cascade Tunnel. I want 27 to keep track time on our division. Keep our asses out of the firebox. Now get the operator back on, I'll give the desk back to Sherlock so we can get this show on the road."

Standing silent, Sherlock could not help but be impressed. *His brain and a train sheet. Laid out the whole division tonight.*

O'Neill swung around in the chair and vaulted to his feet. He tossed the headset onto the telephone mouthpiece..

I'm already beat and he's running around here like a schoolboy.

"It's all yours, Mr. Sherlock. Ring up Mr. Johnson in Everett. We've got orders to put out."

Tuesday, February 22, 1910, 7:00 p.m.
William Harrington, Assistant Trainmaster

Sitting at a large table in the dining room of the Skykomish Hotel with his rotary crew, Harrington reached for his cloth napkin and wiped off the thick gravy about to drip from his moustache. He liked gravy, especially roast beef gravy. Upon receiving his plate, Harrington went so far as to head back into the kitchen for an extra ladle.

"Why didn't you just put your dinner in a bowl and have Flo fill it up with gravy?" quizzed Ira Clary, the crew's conductor.

Harrington shrugged, then dipped a slice of boiled potato in the brown sauce and popped it in his mouth, only to again swipe his napkin across his upper lip. Bob Meath, sitting across the table, stared at Harrington for a long moment.

"What?" challenged the "Snow King," his mouth about ready to receive a gravy-soaked chunk of beef.

"You know, Bill, I think we can rig up a little trough. Hang it from your ears and slide it right under your moustache. You could catch all that gravy and re-use it instead of wasting it on your napkin."

Laughter erupted from the men sitting at the table. Even Harrington had to put down his fork and chuckle. He ran his now gravy-stained napkin over his mouth and grinned. *Like working this crew. Meath, best damned wheelman on the mountain. Ira, gonna be the next Snow King.*

"Yeah, well, I got thicker hair on my ass than you've got sprouting on that baby face of yours, Meath."

Again laughter filled the room, and this time it was Meath taking a napkin to his mouth, nearly choking.

"Jesus, Bill, warn me when you decide to crack a joke. Damned near choked," Meath sputtered between coughs. Regaining his composure, he went on the attack. "Gentlemen, poor Mr. Harrington is simply a 19th-century man getting shoved kicking and shouting into the 20th-century. If you'll take notice, Bill, the clean-shaven face is all the rage. Your moustache, on the other hand lost favor shortly after Custer met his demise. I don't mind telling you, Bill, with this smooth face, the women of Leavenworth have not given me a moment of rest."

"Trouble is, there's only three women in Leavenworth. One's blind and the other two run around town on four legs and go bow wow," Clary butted in, turning the groans rising from the table into more laughter.

"And what's this about the women not giving you any rest?" Clary continued. "From what I hear, you've got a stack of sweet-smelling letters for a certain lady back home."

Undaunted, Meath shrugged. "No secrets on a railroad, that's for damned sure. There might be a note or two from a certain Miss McCabe. Old family friend."

"Family friend my ass," Clary mumbled before resuming his meal.

Still chuckling, Harrington pulled his watch from his vest pocket and glanced at the time. It was a sobering move. The table fell silent except for sound of silverware against the plates.

"26 should be showing up pretty soon. They're gonna hold them here until 2 arrives and we'll take them both over."

"We're going off duty at Cascade," Clary added. "Gonna change engine crews too. Bobby Ford will shove us up the hill, and when Lindsay relieves me I think Imberg and Pettit stand to take you on down to Leavenworth."

"And that leaves just me and poor ol' Bat here to pull another double shift. Just ain't right, is it Bat?" Meath whined.

"Meath, you know as well as the rest of us you spend half your time back there sleeping, and Bat, I don't even want to know what you're doing back on the firing deck all by yourself," Harrington snarled.

"Besides, Meath, I figured you'd want to get to Leavenworth as soon as you can, so all the ladies can chase your 20th-century ass around town."

"Bat" Nelson, having ignored the conversation, concentrated solely on eating. He wiped his plate clean with his last bite of meat. He nudged Meath, and pointing to the carrots on his plate calmly asked, "You gonna eat those?"

The dinner-time chat put Harrington back into a good mood. For the bulk of the day he had been brooding over the little lecture delivered to he and Blackburn by O'Neill. The words "sloppy railroading" still stuck in Harrington's craw.

Got my ass chewed for decisions I wasn't even a part of. Can't overrule Blackburn if I want to. That bastard's the trainmaster, for Christ sakes.

Harrington managed to put all of that behind him by the time he walked towards the depot, still licking gravy from his moustache. Snow was falling out of the night sky in large, wet flakes with a purpose and intensity that was lacking earlier in the day. In the light of one of the station windows, he closely inspected the small accumulation of snow on his coat sleeve.

Late winter slush. Tough to blow. Sticks to everything. Slides before you know it. Be about it for the year.

Inside the station, a large crowd of railroaders was gathered. Number 2, the Oriental Limited, had just arrived from the west, joining 26, which had been sitting on the siding for about an hour. Even though the crews of both passenger trains and their helpers were veterans, Harrington wanted a meeting to spell out the procedure they would be following for the overnight run across the pass.

Harrington entered the telegraph office and was greeted with a half dozen mumbled versions of "Evening, Bill." He acknowledged them with a nod of his head. For the next few minutes, he went over in the run east in meticulous detail. By the looks on the faces of the experienced trainmen gathered, he knew none needed to hear his lecture.

"Jesus, Bill, take it easy, we ain't gonna plow into you." Even-tempered John Glouser, engineer of Number 2's helper, was beginning to get a little irritated at Harrington's sudden urge to spell out every detail.

Acting like an old lady, but after this morning and O'Neill up at Wellington, last thing I need is a calamity. Blackburn ain't calling the shots tonight, I am. My ass is in the sling.

"Just making sure we all know what's going on, that's all. We'll probably meet 25 and 27 over on the east side somewhere. I guess 27 is running late. Understand he's behind 25 tonight. Everybody clear?"

There was a general agreement among the men. With the usual pats on the back and bets on making running time to Wellington, losing crew to buy breakfast in Leavenworth, they filed out of the station and boarded their trains.

On his way out of the station, Harrington grabbed a car inspection lantern off one of the pegs on the wall. The operator looked up from his desk, but before he could say a word, Harrington cracked a grin and held up his hand.

"I know, I know. I promise to bring a bunch of them back next time I'm down." He reached into his coat and fumbled through his vest pocket. He dropped a silver dollar on the desk alongside the telegraph key. "Here. If I don't bring back a couple of lanterns next time I'm here, this is yours. Fair enough?"

"You're on, Mr. Harrington." The operator dropped the coin into the top drawer. "Here's the latest telegrams. Looks like it's getting a little nasty up at Wellington, starting to blow pretty good."

Using a match given to him by the operator, Harrington lit the lantern, grabbed the messages and staff, then headed out the door. Over his shoulder he called back, "Better nail up a few extra pegs, you're gonna need 'em for all those lanterns I'm bringing back."

Back into the biting cold of the snowy night, Harrington trudged down the tracks towards his outfit. Passing under the cab of pusher engine 1154, he noticed fireman Earl Fisher was leaning out the window, catching snowflakes in his gloved hand.

"Cascade cement, eh Bill?"

"Sure is, Earl, good sign that spring's about here. Maybe this is the last good snow. Wouldn't hurt my feelings if we're about done for the year."

"Ain't gonna fight ya on that, Bill. A little sick of these long winter runs myself."

Continuing on toward the cab of the rotary, Harrington hollered up to the fire deck of his plow, which was already enclosed by the thick canvas curtain.

"We ready to roll, Bat?"

"You bet, Bill." Nelson's head popped out from behind the curtain. He paused for a moment and looked at the lights of the town diffused through the falling snow. "Goddamn it, Bill, now don't the town look pretty tonight. Like a Currier and Ives Christmas picture, I'd say."

"You just keep thinking that, Bat. I'm thinking a warm bed in Leavenworth is gonna look a damn sight better to me. Figure on taking water at Scenic."

"See ya up there, Bill."

With his lantern slung on his arm, Harrington climbed into the small cab of the X-800. He paused before entering the cab and looked up at Pattie Kelly who sat on the plow's roof. He was bundled up tight in a heavy coat, a scarf wrapped around his face so only his eyes were peaking out.

"Ready to roll, Pattie?" Harrington asked.

Not even trying to answer, Kelly gave his lantern a slight swing and nodded his head. Even though the plows were originally equipped with headlights, they had long since shattered off their mountings by the jarring action of bucking slides. It was left up to brakemen like Kelly to withstand the elements and watch the track ahead.

Inside, Charlie Smart was filling his lantern with kerosene while Ira Clary checked the flanger hoist. Clary's responsibilities were divided: he operated the flanger, a blade that removed snow from between the rails, and relayed Harrington's orders to the plow's engineer, known as the "wheelman," as well as the engineer the of pusher engine by way of the whistle. He also lent his eyes to the difficult task of plowing at night. Harrington glanced behind him down the narrow passage between the boiler and the wood cabin. Bob Meath, the plow's wheelman, was in his usual position, leaned back in his small seat box, his back against the boiler, arms crossed, legs stretched out across the passage, and his feet propped up against the wall.

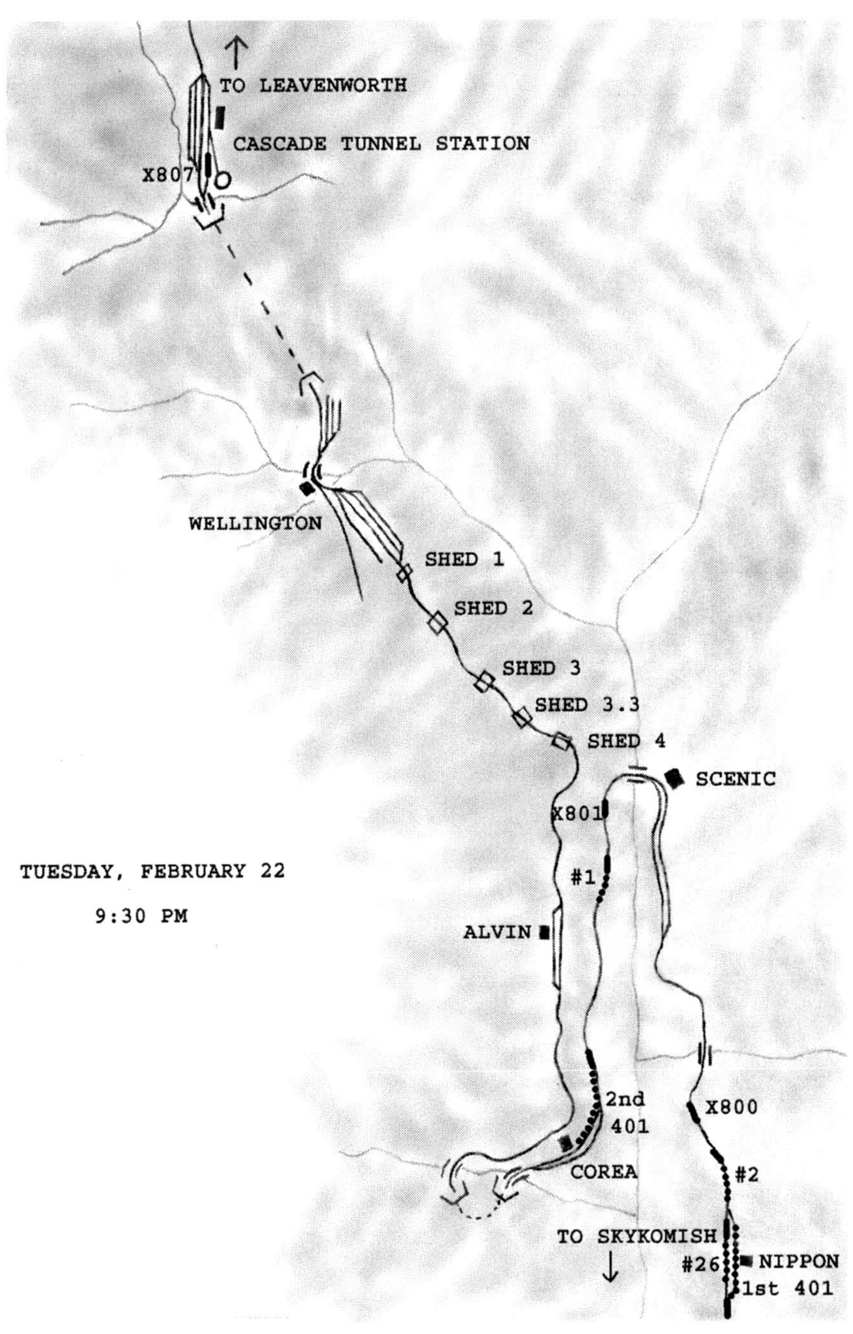
TO LEAVENWORTH
CASCADE TUNNEL STATION
X807
WELLINGTON
SHED 1
SHED 2
SHED 3
SHED 3.3
SHED 4
SCENIC
X801
#1
TUESDAY, FEBRUARY 22
9:30 PM
ALVIN
2nd
401
X800
COREA
#2
TO SKYKOMISH
#26
NIPPON
1st 401

Harrington poked his head into the passage and loudly cleared his throat.

"Mr. Meath, beggin' your pardon, sir, you being a 20th-century man and all, but Mr. Hill would greatly appreciate it if you would get off your goddamned ass and get this thing turning!"

Undaunted by Harrington's remarks, Meath yawned, stretched, and positioned himself behind the large reverser lever alongside his left leg. He grabbed onto the throttle that hung down from the boiler to his left, and gave it a few tugs.

"You know, Mr. Harrington, two whistle blasts would have accomplished the same thing without the profanities. A true 20th-century man such as myself is, after all, refined and sensitive."

Harrington ignored him and was back in the cab. "Highball, Mr. Clary!"

Clary gave the whistle cord two tugs, answered in the same way by Meath, and then by Ford, back in the 1154. Harrington was leaning out the left door, moving his lantern up and down movement, signaling "Highball" as well. It was a signal as old as railroading itself, and it left no doubt in anyone's mind, the X-800 was ready to clear the way east. Meath continued opening his throttle, sending steam into the cylinders that powered the big wheel. Clary was hanging out the door on the right staring into the night; Kelly's lamp from above sent a faint beam of light ahead into the falling snow. Smart was on the clutch lever, waiting for Harrington's signal to engage. The plow gave a slight lurch forward and began to move.

"Wind her up, gentlemen!" Harrington hollered, his head still outside.

Smart pulled the clutch lever back. The blades of the fan began a rhythmic clank as each one rounded the apex of the arc and flipped position. Meath opened his throttle, feeding more steam into the reciprocating engines. The wheel increased speed. The noise made by each blade slowly blended together to produce a steady whine. Snow began to exit the chute. Smoke erupting from the stack of the plow directly behind the cab and that of the pusher engine added to the symphony, creating their own syncopated beat to the chorus of sound.

Harrington wiped at his nose and the snow that had already lodged on his moustache. He watched the lights of Skykomish slowly disappear into the night.

The headlight of the 1154 shown bright over the tender of the snow plow, but its beam was shredded apart by the boiler head and roof of the X-800. Robbed of its strength, the light did its best to filter forward along the side of the plow, weakly illuminating the stream of snow being tossed from the fan. On the opposite side of the machine the other branch of light gave form to the trees and rocks on the uphill side, but was barely able to illuminate fifty feet because the shadow of the plow's fan kept everything directly ahead in the dark. Only the narrow beam from Kelly's lantern, his sharp eyes, and hard raps of his fist on the roof gave the men hanging from the doors of the plow an idea of what lay ahead.

Harrington squinted into the night, the snow causing his eyes to water. He ducked his head back inside every few minutes to quickly wipe the tears. His vision cleared, he again leaned from the door and studied the forms ahead.

Much to Harrington's relief, the "meets" with the opposing trains at Nippon and Scenic went without a hitch. By the stroke of midnight, the X-800 and the parade it was leading was making track time approaching Corea. The accumulated snow posed no problem for the power of the fan and made for easy plowing.

"Okay, boys, we're coming up on the trestle," Harrington called out. He held his lantern straight out, signaling the pusher to slow down. Clary sent two long whistle blasts, followed by a short and another long into the night. The plow slowed with the whistle from the pusher responding in kind, the thick clouds gobbling up the muted echoes like helpless prey.

Pulling his head back in, Harrington barked at Meath. "Back out of her, Bobby." "When we get to the other side we'd better wind her back up and plow through the tunnel cut."

Harrington passed to the opposite side of the plow and leaned from the door. He was now on the inside radius of the curved trestle, looking down into the dark abyss below. It was a scary feeling, crossing the trestle in the dead of night. He often thought that was what it was like to fly.

Across the long Martin Creek Bridge, and back on firm ground,

Harrington held out his lantern and moved it up and down. "Okay boys, wind her back up!"

The response was immediate. The fan was at full speed when the plow slammed into the snow drifting in the rock cut leading into the Horseshoe Tunnel. The crisp eruptions of exhaust exploding from the stack of the plow were music to Harrington's ears.

She's biting into it good.

The procedure was repeated as the plow approached the portal of the Horseshoe Tunnel. With the plow stopped, Harrington popped his head out the door and inspected the snow now barely clearing the chute. "You clear?" he called up to Kelly on the roof.

Kelly slid down the side of the fan and climbed into the cab.

"Ge-ge-getting c-c-cold out th-th-there," he shivered as he made his way back to the boiler to warm up.

"Let's button her up and head on through," Harrington ordered.

Clary gave the pusher engine the highball. With the doors and windows closed to keep the smoke from the plow and pusher out of the cab, they entered the tunnel. Rounding the Martin Creek Loop, the plow was now traveling in the opposite direction. Harrington spun the large wheel mounted at the very front center of the cab, changing the direction of the deflector on the chute. Meath had closed off his throttle and pulled the reverser lever all the way back. The fan would now spin clockwise, throwing the snow to the right side of the machine. Clear of the tunnel, Charlie Smart took his turn guiding the plow from the roof. Whistle signals were exchanged, and within minutes they were back up to speed, sending snow off the flanks of Windy Mountain and into the night.

Within half-an-hour they were rounding the narrow precipice of Windy Point, high above Scenic. The wind that had been meandering up the Tye River Valley regrouped in the Scenic Basin far below, and was making a final, violent thrust up the canyon, hoping to escape through the narrow summit gap above Wellington. Harrington was ready for it, and pulled his hat down hard on his head. Halfway around the loop the gusts hit, rising up from the black void directly below the right-of-way. A tailwind, it sent the flakes of snow on ahead of the plow, driven at a 45-degree angle and at a speed that matched the intensity of the driven air. Snow splattered on Harrington's back with such a force he could feel the flakes hit. He watched the snow exiting the plow's chute. Even that stream was being bent forward by the wind.

Christ, turning into a bad one. Hope it blows itself out in a few hours. He looked across the cab. Clary was shining his lantern on the slope above the plow.

"How's she look, Ira?"

"Hard to tell, Bill. The bank seems to be holding."

They ducked into Snow Shed 3.3. Exiting, Smart began to pound hard on the roof. "Slide ahead!" he called out.

"We've got a small slide!" Clary repeated in a yell.

"Small slide!" Harrington repeated back to Meath. Both men glanced at the steam pressure gauges positioned in the cab and alongside Meath on the boiler. Meath notched his throttle wide open, and without slowing, the plow gathered up the blockage and tossed it aside like a scrap piece of paper.

Pulling into Wellington, the outfit stopped abreast of the depot platform. Will Avery, the third trick operator, appeared with the signal staff, giving half to Harrington.

"Mr. O'Neill in there?" Harrington asked.

"He just left to get some sleep. I think a shift with Sherlock was about all each of 'em could take."

"You'll get your orders at Cascade, but looks like you'll be meeting 25 at Chiwaukum. 27 is later than shit comin' off the Rockies, so you won't see them 'til you get to Leavenworth."

"What's the snow like eastside?" Harrington inquired.

"From what I hear, not bad. This goddamned wind isn't hitting too hard over there yet. Should have an easy trip."

A set of electric motors moved off the siding and coupled to the tender of the 1154. Avery handed the other half of the staff to Ed Campbell, the motor's conductor. With a clear signal board ahead, the "white coal" of electricity shoved Harrington's steam-powered outfit through the 2.5 mile tunnel under the summit spine of the Cascades.

Conductor Ed Lindsay, with his brakemen Will Duncan and Johnny Gilmore, were standing under the eves of the depot at Cascade Tunnel Station when the X-800 was spotted at the water tank to the west. Harrington dropped down off the plow, and along with Clary, Smart, and Kelly, hiked to the stationhouse.

"Good run tonight, boys. I thank ya for your help."

"Our pleasure, Bill," Ira answered, heading into the depot to sign off duty. "You got it easy, Ed. It's all down hill from here."

"Hell, Ed, your toughest job will be keeping the Snow King here awake," chimed in Kelly.

"Snow King, hell, I'd worry more about keeping that 20th-century wheelman from dozing off." Smart laughed at his own joke and followed the crew inside.

"I got our orders," Lindsay said, giving Harrington his copies. "A clear run to Chiwaukum. We'll meet the 801 and 25 there, then a clear run to Leavenworth."

A warm blast from the coal stove greeted Harrington when he passed through the station door. Conductor Homer Purcell was leaning against the coal bunker, reading through a set of orders.

"Here Bill, you might want to read this," Purcell said, handing Harrington an order sheet. "It's from O'Neill. He's worried about the progress of 27. Says we need to make an all-out effort to expedite its passage across the mountain."

Harrington yawned as he glanced at its contents, then let the message fall to the desk. *Got nothing to do with me. That train will be on the mountain when my head's on a soft pillow.*

"Hell, Homer, 27 will be in Seattle before I roll my ass outta bed tomorrow. Anyway, it's blowing pretty good from Windy Point to Wellington. We hit a small slide east of Shed 3.3. Nothing to worry about yet, we went right through it, but the snow in that damned draw is must still be pretty unstable."

"I'm going west once 26 clears to bring 28 up. I'll look the situation over when we pass through. If I see your buddy Blackburn, I'll give him your regards."

"Ah give it a rest, Homer," groaned Harrington. "Leave the troublemaking to Meath and Dougherty. They're the experts."

With his plow serviced and on the move, Harrington climbed aboard as it drifted past the depot.

He glanced up on the roof. *Can't tell who's up there. Wearing everything he owns.*

"Well, Mr. Lindsay, why don't you give a few tugs on that

whistle cord. Wake up ol' Meath back there. Let's get on down to Leavenworth."

Harrington's face was nearly frozen by the time they reached the small station of Chiwaukum, located at the entrance to the Tumwater Canyon. Easing down the siding, he pulled his head in when, in a flurry of light and motion, they met the X- 802 and Train 25 running close behind, hustling past in the opposite direction.

With the line having just been cleared by the 802, Harrington and the parade of trains he was leading made quick time to Leavenworth. Emerging from the confines of the canyon, they entered the yard. On the west end of the siding Train 27 waited. Engineer Ed Sweeney hung from the cab and hollered "Outta my way!" as Harrington's outfit crept by. In a hurry to keep the mail moving, Sweeney had 27's rear markers disappearing into the canyon the instant number 26 had rolled clear of the switch.

"A good run, boys," Harrington told his crew as they signed off duty at the Leavenworth depot. "I'd say Mr. O'Neill should be right happy with things. 27's got a clear track all the way to Seattle."

Wednesday, February 23, 1910, 2:30 a.m.
Anthony John Dougherty, Brakeman

A heavy hand shaking his shoulder brought Dougherty out of a sound sleep. He cracked open an eye and muttered, "Not already."

"If you want some breakfast you best get your ass outta bed, Al," came a voice in a hoarse whisper.

Vision blurred and not yet awake, still Dougherty recognized the figure of Johnny Bjerenson standing over him in the subdued light.

"Huh? Oh, Johnny, it's you. I'll be along." Dougherty threw the blanket back over his head.

Could skip breakfast. Sleep another half hour. Grab a bite when we turn down at Sky.

The smell of Harry Elerker's buckwheat cakes filtered through the blanket.

Well damn. Awake now, might as well get up.

Dougherty tossed back the blanket and swung his legs over the cot. He pulled on his trousers and work boots. Still untangling the suspenders, he stumbled from the back of the Cascade Tunnel Station cookhouse and out into the dining room. Not totally awake, he sat down hard on the first available chair and began to lace-up his boots.

"You're looking bright and cheery this morning, Al," said engineer Ben Jarnigan as he poured a healthy amount of syrup over a stack of buckwheat cakes.

"You got a strange idea of what's morning and what's night, Ben, that's all I can say." Dougherty pulled himself up from the chair, yawned, stretched, and rubbed his hand through his shaggy hair. "I'd sure like to have a talk with the bloke that figured you can railroad at night."

Dougherty wandered into the kitchen where cook Elerker and his helper, Bjerenson, were busy flipping flapjacks poured out on the large, cast-iron surface of the wood-fired cook stove. Bjerenson handed Elerker a plate and, with flair unmatched by the best chefs in Seattle, Elerker started flipping pancakes in the air, catching each on the plate, four to a stack. With a grin that filled his entire face, Elerker passed the hot plate to Dougherty. Bjerenson stood alongside with a cup of steaming coffee.

"Now where else are you going to get service like this and not pay for it, eh Al?"

"You're the best, Harry."

Dougherty sat down at the table with Jarnigan, his fireman, Lou Ross, and fellow brakeman Sam Duncan. Seated at the table next to him was rotary fireman Will Courtney and wheelman Fred Stafford. No sooner had he settled in when the door flew open and a gust of cold, snow-filled air swirled through the building. On the tails of the draft, conductor Homer Purcell blew into the room. He shook the snow off his coat and joined the men eating breakfast.

"Jesus, Joseph, and Mary, it's getting downright nasty out there."

Purcell pulled the running orders from his vest pocket, and gave a set to Jarnigan. Grabbing a chair from another table, he wedged his way between Dougherty and Ross.

"Best eat quick, boys, they want us on the move by 3."

"So what's going on out there, Homer?" Dougherty asked.

"Blowing harder than a twenty-buck whore on the west side. Goddamned trains and plows spread out over the whole mountain. That's what. Let's see, well, we're headed for Sky to bring up 28, that's what I know for sure. Probably meet Blackburn coming west with 44 at Alvin."

"Where's Harrington? I see Clary's crew is back there asleep." Dougherty washed down another bite of pancake with Eliker's strong coffee.

"Lindsay relieved Clary around one or so. Your buddy Meath is with Harrington still, going all the way to Leavenworth before signing off. That reminds me—" Purcell paused and shuffled through his orders. "Got a directive from O'Neill himself. Yes sir, says right here, all conductors and trainmasters are instructed not to allow brakeman Anthony John Dougherty and engineer John Robert Meath to serve on the same plow crew." Purcell dropped his glasses to his nose and peered at Dougherty.

"Let me see that!"

Dougherty grabbed at the paper in Purcell's hand but missed. He heard laughter coming from back in the kitchen where Bjerenson and Elerker were busy washing the dishes created by the early breakfast shift.

"As I was saying, Harrington's gonna turn and come back later this morning. White and Mackey are on their way up now on the 802. 25 and 27 are behind them. They might hold 25 here until 27 catches up and take them down together. Probably run the mail train around 25 and take it down first." Purcell leaned back on his chair and cocked his head towards the kitchen.

"You hear that, Harry?"

"Hear what, Homer?" Elerker called out from the kitchen.

"I said they might hold 25 here until 27 catches up. Looks like you'll be having guests for breakfast."

The rattling of pots suddenly stopped.

"Son of a bitch! And I just sent the lace table cloths out to be washed," Elerker hollered back.

The cookhouse door opened a crack. Motor conductor Jack Scott popped his head inside and was greeted by a choir of voices in unison: "Close the damned door!"

"Hey, don't get mad at me. We're coupled and ready to go." He tossed half of the signal staff over to Purcell. "Here you go Homer, we're official."

Purcell grabbed the staff out of the air, just shy of Dougherty's head.

"Shoulda let it hit'em, Homer. Look's to me like Al still ain't awake," grinned Duncan, as he rose from his chair.

Purcell folded his orders and put them in his vest pocket. Getting up from his chair, he lightly hit the top of Dougherty's head with the staff rod. He grabbed the brakeman's heavy work coat and scarf, draping them over Dougherty's shoulders.

"Wake-up Al. It's time to get moving."

Dougherty began to eat his breakfast in earnest while Purcell went over their running orders. With wind-driven snow drifting at Wellington, Purcell wanted the crew to be ready for tough plowing as soon as they exited the tunnel. His mouth stuffed with the last two bites of breakfast Dougherty, slurped a final swig of coffee. His lecture complete, Purcell headed for the door.

"Let's get to it, boys."

Out of the warmth of the cookhouse and into the raging storm, Dougherty began experiencing a familiar excitement welling up in his stomach and throat. As often as he had been assigned to snow plow runs, it was always the same for him, a nearly childlike anxious anticipation of the job ahead.

He stumbled, half running through the accumulated snow, holding onto his hat, which the wind was doing its best to claim. Already breathless, both from effort and excitement, he came abreast of Duncan.

"If you want to run the clutch, I'll start out on watch, Sam."

"Suit yourself, Al. If you want get your face froze staring out into this goddamned storm, that's fine by me."

Crew on board and whistle signals exchanged, the electric motors began shoving on the tender of Jarnigan's steam engine. The Cascade Tunnel Station operator reported to the dispatcher: the X-807 was on the move at 3:05 a.m. Dougherty took-up his position on top of the cab. Gusts of wind, one branch coming down through the summit gap above the plow, another being forced through the tunnel just ahead, combined efforts as they crossed the Nason Creek bridge, just west of the yard. The cold blasts drove the snow into Dougherty's face. He flinched. Each flake felt like a pin being driven into his exposed skin.

Damn, this is bad. Never seen it quite like this.

The yellow light from his lantern cut a thin shaft through the snow. Through its narrow alley, the portal of the Cascade Tunnel loomed ahead. Dougherty gave four sharp raps on the cab roof with his fist, warning the crew inside they were approaching the tunnel entrance.

Stafford backed off on the plow's throttle. Duncan let the fan slow before pulling back on the clutch lever. Dougherty stepped down on the ledge of the side cab window and swung through the door.

Though protected from the snow once inside the tunnel, a howling gale rushed up through the bore. Despite the boiler of steam to their backs, the temperature in the cab of the plow plummeted. A chill ran up Dougherty's spine, and found its way to his lips.

"Must be really blowing over at Wellington," Purcell hollered across the cab.

"M-m-must be," was all Dougherty could muster from his quivering lips and chattering teeth. He pulled off his gloves, already soaking wet. *Better get these dry.*

Passing through the narrow doorway directly behind him, Dougherty stuffed his gloves under a steam pipe running on the outside of the boiler's smoke box. Stafford, sitting mid-way back, cracked a grin.

"Need to dry your gloves already, Al?"

"Yeah, gonna have cold fingers today."

Stafford came forward, pulling his set of gloves from his hip pocket. "Here, take these, I got another pair. You're gonna need to wear one set and keep the other pair drying anyway. Now get your ass ready to go back up there, we need your eyes."

"My fingers thank ya, Fred."

Dougherty made his way back to the firing deck, where Courtney was tending the fire.

"Want me to stuff a few coals down your britches, Al?" he asked. "Keep you warm up there."

Dougherty just smiled. He carefully pulled back the canvas curtain and shone his lamp into the dark. Although they were still shy of the west portal, he could see that snow was being driven into the tunnel. *Can't tell for sure if we're outta the tunnel. Better be careful climbing out.*

Gingerly, Dougherty leaned from the gangway. Through the snow he could see the concrete wall passing a mere foot from his head. He looked ahead and saw what he thought was the portal. He turned up the flame on his lantern. Stafford began notching out plow's throttle, and on command by Purcell, Duncan pulled back on the clutch lever, engaging the fan. Still inside the tunnel, the exhaust from the plow struggled to escape. The sharp reverberations bounced from the arched walls. Dougherty thought of covering his ears but in an instant the sound dissipated.

Outta the tunnel. Jesus, look at it snow. Can't see a damned thing.

As he swung out onto the side ladder, Dougherty let his lantern slide down to his elbow. Taking a tight hold on the rungs, he climbed up to the plow's roof. The combination of the wind and the curved roof caused Dougherty to teeter as he carefully made his way forward. He hunched against the gale and side-stepped around the stack, where hot exhaust erupted into the night in an ear-splitting cadence. On top of the cab, he brushed away a small accumulation of snow and settled in, sitting on the roof directly behind the fan housing.

The plow began digging into the snow that had drifted into the cut leading to the tunnel entrance. Dougherty peered ahead, squinting. The blowing snow devoured the light from his lantern, and the headlight of Jarnigan's engine, like a famished beast.

Must still be in the tunnel cut. Exhaust echoing a little.

Being careful not to give a confusing signal with his lamp, Dougherty began inspecting the bank directly abreast of the plow, trying to pick up an indicator of where they were. The swirling mass made such observations nearly impossible.

Christ, where the hell are we? Worried, anxious to try and get his bearings, Dougherty kept shining his lantern side to side. *Lights ahead. Bailets? Motormens' bunkhouse. Comin' around the curve above the upper spurs.*

"Bunkhouse, five car lengths!" Dougherty bellowed down to Purcell, who was hanging from the door.

Haskell Creek bridge next.

"On the bridge! Depot, five car lengths!" Dougherty shouted.

Dougherty's nose and ears had grown numb, but he scarcely noticed. He sat on the roof peering through the blizzard. The excitement he felt just prior to leaving Cascade Tunnel Station now consumed his mind and body. Lantern in hand, he knew it, he felt it, he truly believed it—all of the Great Northern Railway was depending on him at that moment.

Approaching the station, Dougherty signaled to Duncan, who grabbed the whistle cord and gave it two long tugs followed by a short. They slowly drifted by the depot.

Where's the operator? On the platform. Waving us through. Train order board at 19.

"Highball Wellington!" Dougherty called out to the crew below him.

Duncan collected the staff and folded orders as they passed the depot, and handed them to Purcell. Proceeding west, the outfit was spotted by the water tank. Dougherty climbed down from the plow and made his way back to help uncouple the electric motors. Courtney came out from behind the curtain on the fire deck and was on top of the plow's tender, pulling down the spout.

"Hey, Al!" he called. "Don't be in a hurry to cut out the motors. The way the snow is blowing, we might get froze in here. Might need the bastards to buck us out."

From a position alongside motor 5002, Dougherty relayed signals from the men servicing the plow and steam locomotive ahead. The wind-driven snow swirled around him as if the flakes had gone mad. Some came to rest at his feet and quickly piled up on his legs. Shining his lantern towards the heavy frame of the electric, he could see snow lodging around the locomotive's wheels as well.

"Jesus Christ, Al, we're gonna have to dig you out if you stand still too long." Scott was leaning from the window of the electric engine, his hands cupped over his mouth. "If you weren't just a dumb brakeman, I'd feel sorry for you standing there."

"Thanks, Jack, you're all heart, you asshole," Dougherty said, not even looking up.

A weak, diffused light from downgrade slowly materialized into Purcell, wading through the snow. Pulling his half of the signal staff from his coat, he tossed it up to Scott, who was still hanging from his window.

"Here you go, Jack. Thanks for the push."

"Always a pleasure, Homer."

"Okay, Al, let's bust him loose and get rolling."

Like the filling in a steel sandwich, Dougherty wedged himself between the pilot of the electric and the rear of the tender of Jarnigan's engine. He brushed packed snow off the two angle cock valves on the air hoses connecting the two locomotives. Frozen open, Dougherty gave each a couple of hard raps with this gloved fist before the levers worked free, cutting off the compressed air passing through the hose. Jumping clear and standing to the side of the tender, he grunted when he pulled up on the coupler's release linkage.

"Need a hand, Homer. Damned pin is froze up."

Working together, the two men were able to force the coupler pin free. While Dougherty held the lever, Purcell waved the motors back. The iron grip of the couplers released, the air hose stretched, and with a loud and sudden "pop," the connection broke. The motors slowly accelerated, backing upgrade and disappearing into the fog created by the snow.

Dougherty and Purcell remained quiet as they walked back to the plow, their heads down as a weak defense against the wind. Snow had already filled in the footprints left earlier. They broke a new trail through the accumulation.

This keeps up we're in trouble. Better stay cold. Let this stuff set so it don't slide.

West of Wellington, the plow crew made quick work of the first mile. Chunks of snow had broken from the banks lining each side of the right-of-way. Landing on the track, they acted as a barrier to the blowing flakes, quickly being covered, allowing the snow to build up. Barely two feet deep, none posed a problem for the fan and its insatiable appetite for snow.

Just clear of Snow Shed 2, his eyes squinting against the attacking snow flakes, Dougherty picked up the shadow of something large on the tracks. His heart leaped to his throat.

"Slide! Half a car length!" he hollered to the crew below. He madly pounded on the roof and swung his lantern in a large arc.

Duncan gave a long blast on the whistle. He reached for the plow's brake lever and pivoted it into "Emergency."

"Keep the fan turning! We're gonna hit it!" Purcell had leaped across the cab and was now hanging out the door behind Duncan.

Dougherty dropped to the roof, laying flat on his stomach. He grabbed the front edge of the cab with one hand, while with the other he continued to shine his lantern ahead. He hunched his shoulders and lowered his head, his nose pressing against the snow built up on the top of the plow. He took one last look at the fast approaching white wall. His body tensed in anticipation of the impact.

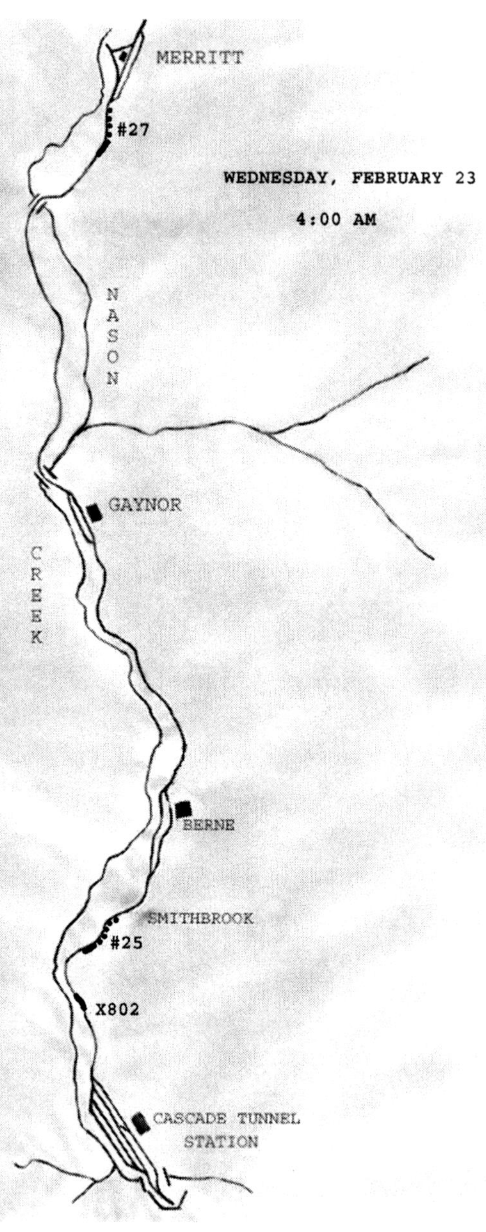
MERRITT
#27
WEDNESDAY, FEBRUARY 23
4:00 AM
NASON
CREEK
GAYNOR
BERNE
SMITHBROOK
#25
X802
CASCADE TUNNEL
STATION

In pusher engine 700, Jarnigan was lightning quick with his reflexes. Even before hearing the whistle blast, he felt the brakes take hold. Hands and arms, well trained by experience, acted without thought or contemplation. In an instant, the engine's throttle was closed off, the reverser lever brought back to the neutral position, the sanding valve was opened and the whistle response given.

"Hang on, Lou!" Jarnigan roared to his fireman.

Wheels locked, the plow slid through the first large chunks of snow that had rolled off the slide and onto the right-of-way. More like rocks, the fan chopped through them and hurled the pieces through the chute, making the sound of a Gattling gun as the hard bits of ice were flung to the side.

"Come on, stop, stop you son of a bitch," Dougherty mumbled under his breath.

Purcell was spinning his lantern in a full circle. Duncan gave the whistle chord three short tugs. The hood of the fan disappeared into the wall of snow towering above the plow.

Jarnigan heard the call for reverse, but hesitated. He knew he had to slow down more. Jerk the plow back now and he risked breaking a coupler or drawbar.

The force of the snow exiting the chute had cut a small trough in the slide, but was now barely clearing the fan. Purcell glanced up at the steam gauge.

"We're dying! Down to 60 pounds!" Purcell was hoping against hope that Jarnigan could pull them free before the fan plugged.

Jarnigan had to decide between the lesser of the evils: jerk the plow back and risk breaking a drawbar, or ease it back with a plugged fan. He pulled his reverser lever back and slowly began notching out his throttle. Ignoring the wind and snow, he leaned far out his cab window and watched his drive wheels, locked up and sliding on the slick rail. This time it was his turn to lay on the whistle chord, telling the plow crew to release the brakes.

Dougherty prepared himself for another backwards jolt, but it did not come. Jarnigan felt his engine shudder. Its drive wheels spun wildly in reverse. The engine and plow eased to a stop. He closed off his throttle.

Jarnigan wiped his brow and looked over to his fireman.

"Hot damn, didn't break a drawbar," he sighed.

The plow gave a slight lurch. Jarnigan was trying to get his engine on firm footing and pull them out of the slide. After three attempts without luck, he whistled "all stop." It was as if the slide had gathered the plow in its clutches and refused to let go.

Lanterns in hand, Purcell and Duncan jumped to the ground. Dougherty was picking his way across the hood, inspecting the chute and fan with his lantern.

Goddamn it. Middle of the blizzard of the century and we plug the damned fan. Can't even get the plow broke loose. Starting out to be one hell of a day, Dougherty thought as he climbed down from the plow.

"I'm going to check out the slide. See what we're up against. You boys break out the tools and see if we can shovel our way clear," Purcell ordered.

Stafford made his way back to the firing deck and gathered the hand tools from the box on the tender, handing them down to Courtney.

"How bad is it, Al?" Courtney asked.

"We buried the fan up past the chute before stalling out," Dougherty answered as he approached the two men.

A shovel over one shoulder and a bar over the other, Dougherty trudged downgrade, the other men falling in behind. His lantern handle was resting in the crook of his arm. Swinging side to side with each step, its beam of light cast an odd, oscillating pattern across the swirling snow.

Purcell stumbled over the large chunks of snow sent down the mountain by the slide. Even in the dim light of his lantern, the disgust on his face could be plainly seen.

"Slide's a small one," Purcell informed his crew. "I'm headed back to Shed 2. I'll call Wellington and see if we can get an engine and shovelers."

Duncan climbed on top of the fan. Holding onto the roof of the cab, he was facing backwards, kicking downward at the snow lodged in the chute, trying to push it back into the fan chamber.

"Here, I got a bar for you, Sam!" Dougherty, with a strength developed from years on the family farm, tossed the heavy tool up to Duncan as if it was a stick.

Their lanterns sitting in the snow alongside the front of the machine, each man began digging at the snow piled against the plow's fan. They had to stand back and thrust their shovels and bars at the hard-as-concrete snow, chipping away only a small portion of the icy mass with each try.

Suddenly, blocks of snow tumbled down from above, hitting Dougherty on the head and shoulders.

"I got the chute clean," Duncan called out.

Backing away and brushing the snow off of himself, Dougherty looked up at Duncan. "Ya don't say, Sam!"

Sliding down the side of the fan, Duncan came alongside of Dougherty. He grabbed an extra steel bar and also began attacking the entombed machine.

Between the men shoveling and Jarnigan's skill as an engineer, they broke the plow free from the slide before Purcell hiked back. Returning to the outfit, he found the men busy cleaning snow from the plugged fan.

"Well shit!" Purcell hollered. "I just told O'Neill we need an engine and some shovelers."

Purcell turned on his heels and headed back upgrade to the telephone for a second time to call off the requested help.

All fell silent. There was only the wind, the grunts from the men and the occasional loud clang of a tool being forced into the snow, its edge striking a blade of the fan. Their faces grew red. Steam began to rise from their cheeks and from under their hats. It was tiring, miserable work.

An hour passed. Purcell, having returned from phoning Wellington, dropped his bar. He reached into his back pocket and produced a flask. Unscrewing the cap, he took a swig.

"Pass it around, boys, something to warm your gut and brighten your spirits."

Dougherty put the cold flask to his lips. The cheap whiskey burned its way down his throat. He winced, shivered slightly and handed it to Jarnigan.

"So bad it's good, Benny."

Grabbing his shovel out of the snow, he went back to work.

Time to bid outta here. Ain't getting younger. No sleep. Arms hurt. Back aches.

A sense of rage began building inside of Dougherty. He started to attack the snow with quicker, harder strokes. Throwing his shovel into the blade, he swore aloud with each toss.

"You … god … damned … son … of … a … bitch!"

No one commented, no one teased. They were all feeling what Dougherty felt.

Colorless light began to creep into the mountains. It was a black and white scene: the bending trees black, the never-ending white snow blowing from the gray clouds and fog. It took hours of exhausting work before the fan was ready to tackle the slide that lay in their path. Weary, the men resumed their positions. Purcell whistled a "Highball," and Jarnigan eased the spinning fan into the white barrier. With the arrival of dawn, visibility had improved slightly, giving the men a better view of their progress and allowing Dougherty to remain in the cab as a lookout. It took three attempts, hitting the slide, backing out and letting the snow tumble forward, and then hitting it again. On the fourth charge the plow broke through.

"Halleluiah!" shouted Dougherty, when they passed through a final time to clean up the remains.

Get past Shed 3.3. Be home free. Just give us another mile of clean track, that's all I ask. Just one more mile.

Then Dougherty saw it. His heart sank.

"Slide! Five car lengths!" he shouted.

With time to react, Jarnigan eased the plow to a stop just as it butted up against the main body of the slide. Dougherty stared up alongside of the mountain, trying to see if additional snow was about to come down.

"Snowing too hard, can't tell if any more's ready to fall," he reported to Purcell.

It was a huge slide. As the plow retreated to a safe distance, Purcell and Dougherty waded through the snow inspecting the obstruction, sometimes sinking to their waists. Nearly thirty feet deep and two hundred feet wide, it was more than their plow could handle.

"Shit, shouldn't have called off the shovelers back at Shed 2," was all Purcell said. He disappeared into the dark confines of Shed 3.3, but quickly returned.

"Damned phone's dead," Purcell muttered. He began picking his way back towards the plow. Dougherty followed in a dejected silence.

"Snow's too deep to get back up to Wellington. I'm going to have to send you on foot for help," Purcell told Dougherty.

"I'll hit her hard and try and get back as soon as I can," Dougherty replied.

As they reached the plow, Courtney came down off the fire deck. By the look on his face Dougherty, knew things were not right.

"Jesus Christ, don't tell me the plow's low on water," Purcell asked, exasperated.

"'Fraid so, Homer," Courtney answered.

"Damn it, damn it, damn it!" Purcell exclaimed, slapping his hat against his thigh. "Al, you better get going. Tell O'Neill he'd better start doubling the rotaries. We'll stay here and start shoveling snow into the tender."

Even with the wind to his back, Dougherty's hopes for an easy two-mile hike back to Wellington were soon dashed. Less than a mile from the plow, he began to encounter small slides caused by the snow banks sloughing onto the tracks. Drifts had formed, two and three feet deep. It was like wading against a rushing current in knee-deep water.

Need a rest. Twenty steps, then rest. Go forty. There's Shed 2. Stop when I get inside. Catch my breath.

An interminable number of 20 steps later, the station door burst open and Dougherty, soaking wet, panting, stumbled in. He closed the door and immediately doubled over, hands on his knees, his lungs heaving. O'Neill, Flannery, and Longcoy stood in startled silence, staring at the snow covered, exhausted man.

"Hit a big slide." He gathered another breath. "Shed 3.3" He coughed up some phlegm. "Need a crew to shovel."

O'Neill crushed a half-spent cigar and walked to his side. "What's that you say? Take your time man. Catch your breath."

"Dougherty. Purcell's crew. Just east of Shed 3.3. We've hit a big slide," Dougherty repeated. He took another deep breath, slowly exhaling. "We figure it to be about thirty feet deep and two hundred or so wide. Need a crew of shovelers. Our plow is low on water but the track's filled with too much snow. Can't get back up here. They're shoveling snow into the tank. Mr. Purcell told me to suggest that you start doubling up the plows. Phones are dead too."

"Very well," O'Neill answered, seeming to take the news in stride. "Get some coffee and warm up, Mr. Dougherty. You look about spent."

Longcoy grabbed a chair and set it by the stove. Dougherty collapsed into its seat, slumping down slightly and stretching out his legs. He closed his eyes for a moment. Watering and stinging, he could only imagine how bloodshot they were.

"Here's some coffee for you, sir."

Sir? Calling me sir?

He opened his eyes and gladly accepted the steaming cup from Longcoy, his hands still inside his wet gloves.

"Mr. Longcoy, go over to the tool house. I believe Section Foreman Harley is there. He is to round up at least fifty men and tools and start west immediately."

"Yes sir." Longcoy buttoned his coat and headed outside.

"Mr. Flannery, ring up Cascade Tunnel Station. Trains 25 and 27 will have to continue to hold there until further notice. Also, tell the operator there to have the X-802 turn to an eastward-facing position. They need to make ready to double with Harrington. Get an order down to Leavenworth—I want Harrington to begin west right away. Also, tell Leavenworth to hold Train 3 until a rotary escort arrives."

Flannery was busy scribbling down O'Neill's orders on a note pad.

"Damn it, wish to hell I sent that engine after Purcell when he first called," O'Neill said, half under his breath. "Can't get down there with just an engine, can we, Mr. Dougherty?"

"Afraid not, sir. She's drifting in real bad. Wouldn't be wise to send a plow down less it was doubled, if you want to know the truth, sir," Dougherty added.

O'Neill paused for a moment. Staring out the window, Dougherty watched him light another cigar and shift it from side to side in his mouth.

"Don't know where Blackburn is. No communications west." O'Neill muttered as he resumed smoking and staring outside at the blowing snow. "Write out an order to Mr. Purcell. He is to proceed to Alvin and double with Mr. Blackburn at all possible haste. If you would issue that right away, Mr. Dougherty here can be back on his way as soon as he warms up and catches his breath."

O'Neill turned and walked over to Dougherty.

"Tell Purcell we haven't heard from Blackburn. He should be near Alvin. I'd send him east to help, but right now, I don't know where the hell he's at to tell him."

"Yes sir, I'll tell him."

"Now then, how long do you think it will take to buck through that slide?"

"Well, unless this storm breaks, I'm afraid it could take most of the day, sir."

O'Neill took a long puff from his cigar. Sighing, he scribbled a note on a telegraph form. Dougherty saw O'Neill's brow furrow with a look of concern not present a few moments earlier.

"Well, boys, I guess that settles it. Send this wire to St. Paul, Mr. Flannery. Include Mr. Brown. I'm shutting down the mountain."

Wednesday, February 23, 1910, 3:15 a.m.
Arthur Reed Blackburn, Trainmaster

"What the hell was that?" came the panicked shout of Trainmaster Art Blackburn.

A violent forward lurch of the X-801 rocked Blackburn off his feet, and caused him to nearly fall from the door of the plow. For a moment, he hung precariously outside, his arm wrapped tightly around the grab iron, his feet scrambling to find the rungs of the ladder. Inside the cab, brakeman Milt Hicks was equally surprised by the jolt, and was sent sprawling onto the floor. He used the clutch lever to raise himself back up. Across the cab, conductor John Parzybok was clinging awkwardly to the door jam. On the roof, Archie Dupy struggled to keep from rolling off the machine.

Irving Tegtmeier rushed from the passage alongside the boiler. Blackburn felt a powerful grip on his free arm, and the next thing he knew, he was back inside the plow.

"You alright, Mr. Blackburn?" quizzed Tegtmeier, a smoking pipe clenched in his teeth.

"Yes, no thanks to that fool Osborne. What the hell is he doing back there?"

"Lookin' like the fan's a doin' just fine, Mr. Blackburn." Hicks had regained his balance and was now hanging from the opposite door, shining his lantern forward.

Through the thick snow falling from night sky, a lone, long whistle call worked its way forward.

"Stop signal from the pusher!" Parzybok called out, returning the signal with the plow's whistle.

Blackburn was now looking back towards the 1118. He spotted a lantern signaling "stop" being waved by the fireman.

What the hell's going on back there? Damned black night, can't see a thing. Get a flagman out there. 44's gonna nail our ass if we don't.

"Did they signal for a flagman?" Blackburn asked.

"Haven't heard anything but the stop call, Mr. Blackburn," came the calm reply of Tegtmeier amid puffs from his pipe. "Something must have happened behind us."

Dupy climbed down from the roof and came up alongside the plow.

"Dupy, get out there and flag our rear. Quick! 44 has to be right behind us!"

"Yes sir." Dupy disappeared into the storm, lantern in hand.

"Mr. Tegtmeier, come with me. Need to get to the bottom of this damned fast."

Swinging down off the plow, Blackburn was taken aback by the amount of snow that had accumulated along the right-of-way. They just traveled that portion of track not three hours earlier, yet there was already nearly half a foot of fresh snow. The large, fat flakes continued to fall, so thick Blackburn felt he would have to part them like a curtain to pass through.

Good God it's snowing hard. Damned well better be the last of it.

Walking ahead, Tegtmeier held his lantern nearly at eye level and as far ahead as his arm would reach. He was leaning forward as well, as if such a position might cast just enough light ahead that he would be able to see a little better.

"What the hell?" Tegtmeier's voice tailed off into the wind.

Blackburn was also confused by the glow of lights now becoming apparent as they approached their pusher engine. Men with lanterns could be seen walking about.

"Looks like another engine is coupled to us. How in the hell …," Blackburn's pace quickened.

Thomas Osborne, the engineer of Blackburn's pusher, came forward. The lanterns dimly lit his weathered face and darting, eyes.

"It's the damnedest thing I ever seen, Mr. Blackburn. 44 hit us!"

"What do you mean … I don't see 44."

"No sir, 44 is back behind. That's his light you can see down yonder."

"You're making no sense. What the hell happened, man?"

"Well, just as we got underway, you know, pulling from the water plug, they came around the corner, 44 that is, sir. They musta been slowing down but they hit us. We didn't see'em come up. I was watching your signals ahead. Felt a jolt, but we kept going and pulled their helper right off them."

"What? I'll have that engineer's job! Where is he? Who's on that engine?" Blackburn asked in a rage.

"It was me, sir. Conrad." A short man in greasy overalls stepped into the circle of light.

"We came around the corner this side of the switch. Knew you were ahead, but didn't see a flag man or stop lantern so we just kept coming. You know, at a restricted speed. This damned wind and snow—hard to judge distance. Your tender came up on me, we were all but stopped, you know, pulling up to the water spout, I saw you were moving, looked back for just a second, just a second. When I looked ahead we were right on you. Thought we just kissed you. Went to grab the brake, but somehow you jerked me right off Day's engine. I'm telling you, Mr. Blackburn, I didn't see a flag."

"Mr. Blackburn, we best get this outfit rolling. Stand around here too long and we'll all need to get bucked out." Tegtmeier was kicking at the snow, shining his light toward the still wheels of the 1118.

"This goddamned sloppy railroading has to stop! No time now, but there will be disciplinary action, Mr. Conrad. Now help Mr. Tegtmeier check over your engine and our tender. Let's get that engine uncoupled and back on 44. Mr. Osborne, whistle in Dupy."

"No need, sir, I'm right here," said Dupy, stumbling through the snow. "Just got done talkin' to Otis Day on 44. Says his pilot coupler's busted all to hell, but he's on the rail. Thinks he might have problems behind someplace, was headed back to check."

"I'm going to check with Day. Stay here and help Tegtmeier get this engine uncoupled," ordered Blackburn. "I'll be right back. We need to keep going east."

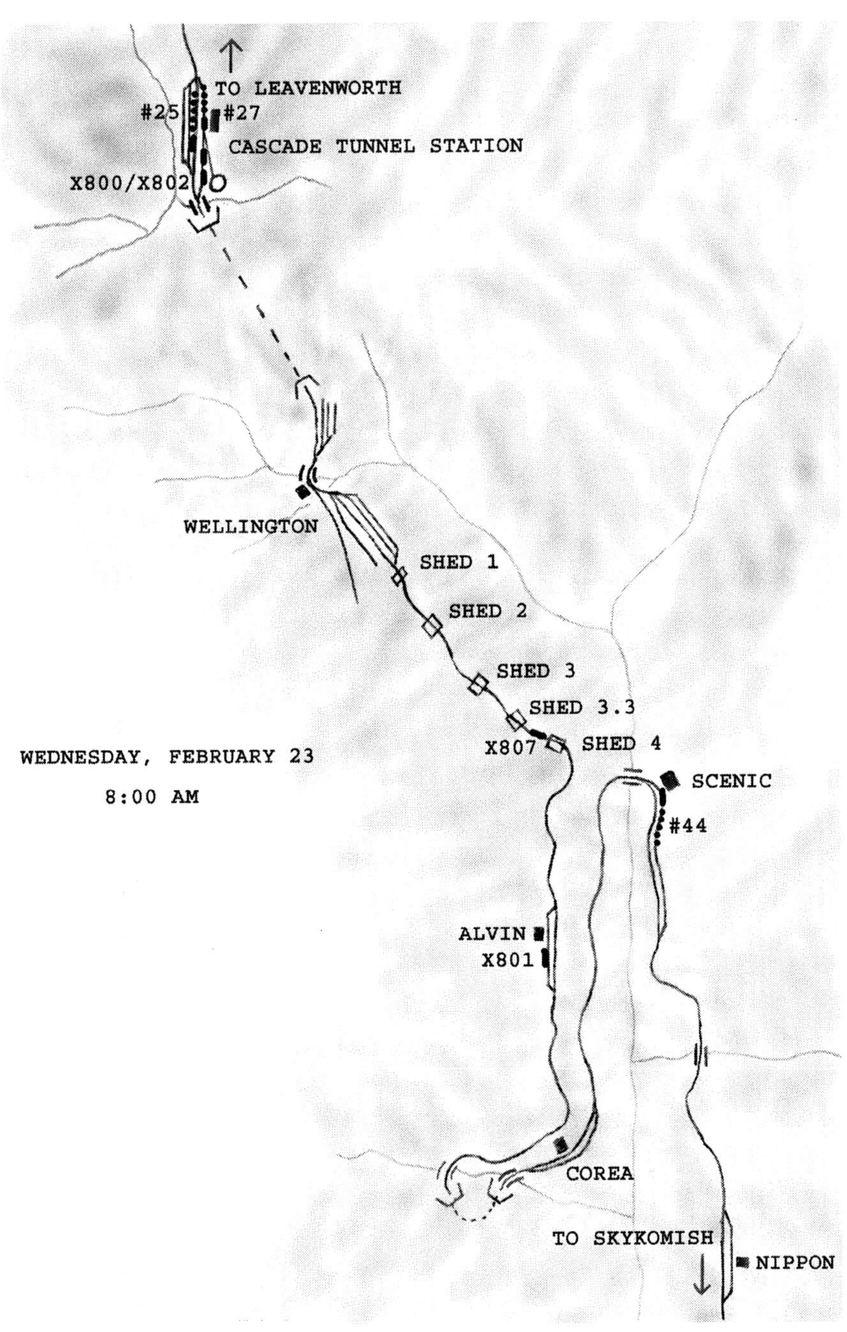
TO LEAVENWORTH
#25
#27
CASCADE TUNNEL STATION
X800/X802
WELLINGTON
SHED 1
SHED 2
SHED 3
SHED 3.3
X807
SHED 4
WEDNESDAY, FEBRUARY 23
8:00 AM
SCENIC
#44
ALVIN
X801
COREA
TO SKYKOMISH
NIPPON

Swear to God Scenic's jinxed. Tied up 27 last night. Now this. Gotta keep things moving. Stick the mail train again, O'Neill will have my ass.

Blackburn walked past the pilot of engine 1069, its coupler bent downward at an odd angle. While shining his lantern to inspect the damage, he fished out his watch from under his wet work coat. He knew Purcell was now west of Wellington and needed to get to Skykomish to escort the eastbound mail train.

Christ, half past three. Can't hold up Purcell. Gotta get going, Blackburn decided.

Blackburn was alongside the locomotive's tender when he caught up with Otis Day, making his way back up grade.

"Mr. Day, is there damage to your train?"

"Oh, it's you, Mr. Blackburn. Just coming to fetch ya. I've got a broken drawbar on my baggage car. Didn't pull her completely out. Be a bastard to fix in this, though."

Blackburn's stomach turned. *Damn it. Bad as yesterday.*

"What the hell happened to Conrad?" Day asked. "I had my light out, running behind him. Didn't see a thing. Got off my engine and he was gone."

"He ended up coupled to our engine," Blackburn snapped.

Day cracked a grin. "Now if that don't beat all."

"More important, is the rear of your train clear of the west switch?"

"Aye, sir, that it is."

"We need to keep plowing east. I'll inform the operator at Scenic of your condition and have him send some section men down to help you. There should be extra knuckles at Scenic. Get your train back together. If you have to use Mr. Conrad's engine as a rear helper, so be it. Whatever you do, the main line must be kept clear. Is that understood?"

"Yes sir. Am I to understand you are moving on east without us?"

"You get your train back together and hold here for new orders. Probably have you come up behind 28. Don't try coming up without a rotary escort! Now, I need to get my outfit moving."

It felt good to be back underway. Blackburn watched the snow stream from the chute, arcing high and into the night. It was hypnotizing, like staring at a waterfall. Being on the move, getting something accomplished, calmed him. His mind wandered, justifying to himself the decision he just made.

Not good leaving 44 behind. Had to keep moving, reasoned Blackburn. *Get things clear for the mail trains. Hope O'Neill understands.*

He continued to watch the snow, his eyes nearly glazing over. The whine of the fan and the steady, easy progress of the plow put him in a reflective mood.

This the best Mother Nature can do? Handling it, Blackburn allowed himself to believe. *Throwing snow aside like it ain't even here. Like to see those UP boys doing what we're doing.*

Conductor John Parzybok's voice broke into Blackburn's quiet contemplation.

"We're coming up on Alvin. Arch, soon as we slow down, run ahead and see if you can open the siding switch."

There was the normal barrage of whistle blasts accompanied by the swinging of lanterns. As the plow slowed to a crawl, Dupy dropped to the ground. Parzybok, on his knees, reached down and handed the brakeman his lantern.

Blackburn passed over to the opposite side of the plow where Tegtmeier was watching the track ahead.

"Any sign of Homer, Tig?" inquired Blackburn.

"Tough to tell yet, Mr. Blackburn. If they're here, they haven't plowed down the main to this end of the siding," observed Tegtmeier, relighting his pipe.

The wheels of the plow thumped across the points of the switch. The machine swayed slightly as it left the main line and entered the siding and slowed nearly to a stop. In a moment Dupy scurried up the ladder, slightly out of breath.

"Got lucky. Damned switch wasn't froze up a bit."

As they rolled up the siding, the fan continued to gather the accumulated snow and toss it over the bank. Blackburn watched the track ahead, relieved that in spite of the hold-up at Scenic, it appeared they had not impeded of the progress of the opposing plow. Still, he was a little uneasy, calculating running times in his head.

Should be here. Out of Cascade at three. Even if they took water at Wellington, that's 45 minutes max. Another 45 to here, that's an hour and a half. Put them here by 4:30 at the latest. He took another look at his watch. *4:45. Guess no sense getting worried yet.*

"Station ahead, Mr. Blackburn."

"Very well, Mr. Parzybok. We'll stop here for a bit. I'll see if the operator has heard from the 807," replied Blackburn.

The small depot at Alvin was more like a large tool shed than a station. Blackburn burst through the door, startling the telegrapher on duty.

"Have you heard from the 807 yet?" Blackburn asked, handing the man the signal staff he was given at Scenic.

"Sorry, sir. Not a thing. All our lines went dead about a half hour ago. We rang them through Wellington a little before 4. Haven't heard a word since," the operator reported.

"So your staff machine is down?" Blackburn was hoping he could at least ring Wellington, letting them know he had arrived at Alvin.

"Sorry sir, right now I don't have any communication to the east. I've got telegraph west, but all the phones were out last I checked."

Blackburn motioned the operator out of his chair. Grabbing the headset and putting it to his ear, he pulled the speaker to his mouth and pressed the foot pedal.

"Dispatcher. Alvin." Hearing nothing, Blackburn wiggled the cord jacks in the vain hope the problem was merely a poor connection.

"Dispatcher! Alvin!" he repeated, his voice rising in anger.

Dead as hell. Christ Almighty, what else can go wrong today?

Getting up from the chair, Blackburn removed his wet bowler and shook the melting snow from its brim. He ran his hand through his dark, wavy hair. "Well, now it seems things are just as dead to the west."

One hell of a fix. Can't go east, no staff. Don't know where Purcell is. Can't back to Scenic and get 44. Could get stuck. Gonna have to wait it out here.

"Been able to raise anybody?"

Even without turning, Blackburn knew Tegtmeier had entered the room. The spiced smell of his pipe tobacco permeated the dank air that had been long trapped in the building.

"Everything's dead, Tig. Best we can do is wait for daylight and see if any wires are down close by. No sign of Purcell?"

Tegtmeier let a couple of puffs of smoke escape the side of his mouth.

"All's quiet out there. Hard to tell with this damnable wind, but my guess is they're still the other side of Windy."

"Looks like we ain't got a choice but wait it out." Blackburn rubbed his hand over his face, forcing back a yawn. He rubbed his eyes hard with his thumb and index finger.

Damn the luck.

Wednesday, February 23, 1910, 8:00 a.m.
John Robert Meath, Engineer

With a scant four hours of sleep behind him, Meath was in the yard at Leavenworth working on the fan of his plow. The machine had been turned and serviced while he slept, but Meath, a man who took snow duty seriously, preferred to inspect the rig personally. He rounded up a ladder. Leaning it against the fan, be began to meticulously check each stay bolt and keeper pin on the thick metal blades.

"You're up and about early, Bobby. Hard at it, eh?" Harrington, having just come from the depot, steadied Meath's ladder.

"Like they say, a maiden's work is never done."

"Christ, Meath. The sooner you give up this high brow act of yours, the sooner I'll go back to trying to learn to like you."

"Why William, such remarks not only hurt, but make it very clear the need for me to bring civilization into this snowy hell." Meath continued working on the fan, placing the closed end of a heavy wrench on the heads of the stay bolts and giving a hard tug. A slight grunt escaped his lips, his frosty breath mixed with the light snow falling.

"Well you better let the shop boys finish this and get a quick bite. O'Neill wants us outta here right away."

"Never send a shop boy to do a wheelman's work, you know that, Bill. I'm about done here. I'll down a stack of Harry's buckwheats when we make Cascade."

Meath grabbed a hammer from his back pocket and beat on a keeper pin that did not quite suit his eye.

"So what's going on up there, Bill?" Meath asked. "A little surprised they're sending us back up so quick. Things getting tough?"

"From what they tell me, it's blowing like a bastard up there. I guess Homer's up to his ass in it. Hit a pretty good-sized slide …"

"Let me guess," interrupted Meath, "just east of Shed 3.3. We hit a little bump there when we went through last night, as I recall."

"You guessed it. Had to send back to Wellington for shovelers. They're holding 25 and 27 at Cascade right now. Gonna turn 3 when it gets here, send it back. They want us up there to double with Whitey."

Meath climbed down from his ladder. He pulled it away from the fan and laid it alongside the plow. "27's held up at Cascade. O'Neill must have his long johns worked up past his jewels over that," Meath quipped.

"My guess is we'll take 25 and 27 on down. We're gonna stay in the westward-facing position, so we'll be doing all the work. Homer is supposed to double with Blackburn over at Alvin sometime this morning. They'll work back to Wellington. Things should be pretty clear for us until we get past Alvin."

"Oh yes, and where is our favorite Trainmaster?"

"Don't know. Guess the lines west are down. Tell you the truth, Bobby, I got a bad feeling about all this." Harrington had turned and was now looking west, where the mountains rose like an impenetrable wall above the town.

Meath paused a moment and scanned the mountains as well. Thick clouds unfurled a white blanket that hovered below the jagged summits. "Al's with Homer, ain't he?"

"Think so. If he is, he's getting a snoot full of it about now, I'd guess." Harrington turned to face Meath, grinning.

"What's so damned funny all of a sudden?" Meath demanded.

"Oh, just struck me funny. Best part of this storm is we finally got you two separated," Harrington admitted. "I could just see you and Al hatching some goddamned scheme in the middle of all this just to get O'Neill and Blackburn. You two bastards would probably get all of us sacked."

Meath shrugged. "Might be the best thing we ever did."

"She's drifting in the cut ahead, Bobby, lean into her!" Ed Lindsay bellowed over his shoulder to Meath.

Left foot propped against the frame of the big reverser lever, Meath's gloved left hand had already released the catch on the throttle. He gave it two hard tugs, bringing the cast iron arm against the stop at the final notch.

"You got her all," he hollered back. His voice cracked slightly, already hoarse from the constant yelling of instructions back and forth between himself and the crew in the cab ahead.

Hate these kinds of runs. No snow for a half-mile, then a six-foot drift. Freewheeling one minute, stalling out the next. Throttle arm's falling off.

Vibrations rattled the plow, causing the wood cabin to creak when the X-800 slammed into the drift. Meath hardly noticed. Just by the sound of the plow and the position of the needle on the steam gauge, he knew exactly what was happening up front. The steam pistons powering the fan kept a steady cadence, the whine of the fan was a tone only slightly lower than normal, the steam gauge was holding rock steady, and the exhaust sharp.

Chewing right through. Bat's got a damned nice fire going. Bastard's steaming better than it has all winter.

"She's taking her all, Bobby," Lindsay turned back and gave Meath a grin.

When it came to being a wheelman, Meath developed a sixth sense. Anticipation, being one move ahead of the snow, that was how to run a snow plow. The challenge, the battle of wits, his mind versus nature, is what Meath relished. It was what made him one of the best plow engineers on the hill.

First cut west of Berne. Short one. Fan's picking up speed, hear it, feel it. His arm instinctively reached slightly above him, his hand once again squeezing the release. He closed the throttle off two notches.

"You can slow her down, Bobby," Lindsay shouted over his shoulder.

Should keep score how many times I beat them at their own orders.

Meath was operating blind. East of Merritt he closed the door next to him. Passing through a narrow gap in the Nason Creek Canyon, they encountered a cold wind that drove the snow into the cabin. It was times like this he was glad to be the wheelman, tucked back in the plow alongside the boiler. The crew up front in the cab was taking the brunt of the blizzard as they hung from the open doors and windows, watching ahead. Still, he had to concentrate, picturing in his mind where they were and what might lie just ahead.

Smithbrook's next. Deep cut on a bend. The way the wind's blowing, be the worst one. Need to get a running start.

He gave the throttle another notch.

"Smithbrook! The cut's plugged!" Lindsay shouted.

Give her the last notch. Don't let them see me grinning. Done all I can do. Let the fan eat away at it. Reminds me, getting damned hungry.

Again, the plow rammed into the snow forced by the wind between the steep rock walls of the cut. Again, the machine shuddered. Again, Meath took it in stride, calmly watching the brass needle of the steam gauge.

Quarter of the way through, holding steady. Coming up on the deepest part I'd guess. Pressure dropping. Down to 90. Fan still sounds okay. Keep her coming, boys. Don't get stuck here. Too hungry. Pressure holding. Into the worst. Fan sounds good. Exhaust about right. She's got her.

"She's taking her all, Bobby!" came the call from the cab.

Meath bit his tongue. He came dangerously close to yelling back, "No shit!"

Free of the cut, Meath hesitated. Steam pressure rose to normal running level, but it sounded to him like the fan was lagging, the exhaust slightly slow and labored.

Upper canyon. Snow's heavy. Wet. Like the slush on the west side. Might as well settle in. Keep her wide open until we hit Cascade.

Cramps began pinching their way up Meath's legs. Getting up out of his little seat, he kicked each leg out and shook each in turn. He yawned and stretched. Cracking open the door to his right, he peered out. Rocky Ridge had disappeared behind a wall of white. Snow blew by the plow in giant white waves, propelled through the trees by a menacing wind. It was an awe-inspiring sight. Meath watched, allowing himself to be mesmerized by the patterns generated by the windswept scene.

The shrill blasts of the plow's whistle brought him out of his trance.

"Coming up on the yard limit, Bobby. Passenger trains on the passing track. Watch my signal for shut down," Harrington ordered.

Meath climbed back into his chair. As he felt the plow's speed decrease, he answered in kind by squeezing off his throttle, ever so slowly reducing the speed of the fan. It was another game he played, having the throttle completely shut off the instant the brakeman was given the command to disengage the clutch. It was as much his ability to feel his plow as it was his ability to observe and interpret the movements of the conductor just beyond the narrow doorway in front of him.

Okay, last notch … one, two, three … shut her off.

"Disengage, Mr. Gilmore! Shut her off, Bobby!" ordered Harrington.

Walking forward, he joined the rest of the crew in the cab. The mail cars of 27 were passing within an arm's reach of the plow. As they eased by the two locomotives powering the train, Meath shouted to the crews, "Outta the way!"

Passenger coaches were next. Meath hung slightly out the door, making faces at himself in the reflection of the windows, getting scowls back from the few passengers inside staring out at the storm.

"Christ, Meath, we're trying to get people to ride our trains, not scare the hell outta them," scolded Harrington. "I swear to God, I'm gonna get a lock and chain and keep you back by your throttle outta sight."

"Tell ya what, Bill. Let me off of this thing for some grub and I promise to behave."

"That'll be the day, but yeah, you best get something in your belly. We'll take on water and double with the 802. Kerlee, Gilmore, you boys might as well go too. Me, Ed and Bat ate down at Leavenworth, so we can handle things."

The three men stumbled across the tracks behind the plow's pusher engines. Head down against the wind, Meath glanced sideways and stopped.

Snow's really piling up against the wheels of the passenger train. Gonna take an act of God to get them moving again. Better start rocking her.

"How much you bet Frank and Sweeney are in here stuffing their faces instead of keeping their train loose?" Meath called out to Kerlee and Gilmore as they were about to duck into the cookhouse.

"Ain't taking that bet Bobby," Gilmore called back, "I see'em both in here."

Meath strode into the porch just outside the dining room. Head still down, kicking the snow off his work boots, he yelled into the room.

"Martin! Sweeney! You lazy bastards! If you want me to plow your sorry asses to Seattle ..." His voice trailed off as he walked into the dining room. Inside there was dead silence. He looked up. Every table was taken with passengers. Everyone seemed frozen, not able to move. Women in dresses with heavy coats over their shoulders, their faces red, held forks laden with bites of flapjacks in midair. Men in suits glared at him, loudly clearing their throats, finding their napkins and nervously wiping their mouths.

"Sorry, folks. Used to this being a railroad cookhouse. We can get a little crude when we're with our own." Meath, his face suddenly red, took off his cap, and made his way across the room toward the kitchen. As he passed a table of businessmen he heard one mutter, "These men are the scum of the earth."

He came so close to stopping and challenging the man. For one of the few times in his life, embarrassment overrode his natural instinct to use his wit and counter what seemed to him a personal attack. Instead, he ignored the remark, pretending he did not hear.

Scum of the earth. Arrogant bastard. Meath silently worked to control the rage that was overriding his embarrassment.

Meath stomped into the kitchen fuming. Head down, he nearly bumped into Kerlee and Gilmore, who were walking out.

"Harry says he can't feed us," Kerlee confessed. "This is only the first shift. Another bunch of passengers are coming in. Says we'll have to eat at the cookhouse over at Wellington."

Saying nothing, Meath turned for the door.

Going back into this goddamned blizzard hungry. Work all night getting you off this mountain. Scum of the earth. Plow this railroad for the women folk and children. Our duty. Be damned if I'll do it for asses like you.

Meath put his cap back on and strode across the room. He made a point of returning the glares of those still staring at him. Nearly to the door, the smell of Harry Elerker's buckwheat cakes finally registered. He paused for a second, turned and faced the room.

"Hope you folks enjoy *my* breakfast," Meath announced.

Robert Meath walked from the cookhouse, back into the blizzard.

Wednesday, February 23, 1910, 3:30 p.m.
William Harrington, Assistant Trainmaster

Next to the tender of his snow plow, Harrington looked down the long line of three steaming locomotives and plow X-802, which was now coupled facing east. Above, Bat Nelson was on top of the tender. His foot was planted on the water spout, his head buried against his chest to break the wind and blowing snow. He swung the water spout clear, climbed down the icy ladder, and joined Harrington.

"What's eating on Meath?" Nelson asked. "Came back from the cookhouse and hasn't said shit to me since."

"Hear tell me he made an ass outta himself over there," Harrington answered. "Started cussing out Sweeney and Martin, you know, just joking around like he always does, before he saw all the passengers in there. Guess some passenger called him a name, and then they didn't feed him. Harry has to feed all those bastards on the trains. Reckon he's worried he hasn't got enough stores to do the job."

Harrington chuckled. *Poor Bobby. Can understand him getting bent outta whack. Frustrating. Feeling it myself. Can't get a warm meal in your own cookhouse. Woulda been fun to see his face go red. Get a taste of his own medicine.*

Martin "Whitey" White, conductor of the X-802, dropped down from his plow and waded through the snow toward Harrington.

"They want us over at Wellington, Bill. 27 needs to pull up and get water. Guess they're gonna pull 25 into the tunnel for a bit to clear."

"Oh, that'll be nice. They gonna use a motor set? I can just hear those good citizens griping about the smoke if they don't."

"Can't. Motors are stuck over at Wellington. We gotta plow 'em out after we take coal. Sounds like they got ten foot drifts between the station and the tunnel." White yawned. "Gonna be one hell of a night, Bill. Here's the staff. I'll see ya over there."

"Have our boys take a nap, Whitey. Looks like we'll be handling things for awhile." Harrington watched him trudge back to his plow, kicking the snow with each step. *Whitey looks beat already.*

"Back on duty, Bat." Harrington turned and walked forward to the cab of the X-800. He reached up and pounded on the side of the cabin, opposite where Meath was stationed. He yelled at the closed door.

"Hey, you fouled-mouthed 20th-century asshole! Wake up in there, we're heading out!"

Emerging from the west portal of the Cascade Tunnel, Harrington's outfit immediately slammed into the drifts choking the tunnel cut. Unlike what they had encountered climbing the east slope of the pass earlier in the day, what they were bucking now was wet and heavy. The snow clung to the blades of the fan, threatening to stall it at any moment. It exited the chute not in a long graceful plume, but in fits of thick wads, like giant, poorly-formed snowballs. Whistle orders blended into each other. Engineers became confused, and their whistling for a repeat of the original order only added to the problem.

Progress slowed to a crawl as the snowdrifts became deeper than the diameter of the fan. Twice the plow had to be backed from the white wall they were attacking, the fan dangerously close to plugging. To knock the accumulated snow off the blades, the rotation of the fan was reversed, which required Meath to constantly push and pull both his large reverser lever and the throttle.

Concerned about the physical strain being placed on his engineer, Harrington glanced back along the boiler where he was stationed.

Meath had stripped off his coat, and sweat was carving white streaks in his grease-smudged face.

"How you holding up, Bobby?" Harrington asked.

"Please, sir. A bite of stale bread, a cup of dirty water, anything, anything, kind sir," Meath whined, doing his best to mimic a London street urchin.

"Damn it, Meath, do you need a relief? I can have Mackey spell you off."

"The X-800 is my baby, Bill. I'm fine."

Hanging from the door, Harrington became tired of standing. He dropped to one knee, his left leg stretched out the door on the second rung of the ladder. His right arm was across his forehead. Leaning forward on the doorframe, he watched the snow struggle from the chute when the flanger below caught the corner of his eye.

Damn! Snow's piling up! Gonna derail!

"All stop! Raise the flanger!" Harrington yelled.

Whistles filled the air as Gilmore applied the brakes. The sound of escaping compressed air could be heard as the brakes took hold and the pneumatic winch lifted the heavy flanger.

"Hold her right here. Kerlee, Gilmore, check each side, make damned sure the forward truck isn't starting to ride up on the snow. I'll go back and round up some tools. Gonna have to dig the bastard out."

Harrington walked down the dark gangway leading to the fire deck at the rear where the shovels were stored. Meath rose from his chair and was stretching his back, rotating his head to relieve the pain in his neck.

The bloodshot eyes and the red, running nose of Bat Nelson greeted Harrington when he emerged from the plow's cabin out onto the fire deck. The wind was whipping at the heavy canvas curtain designed to protect the area from the elements. About the time a little heat from the firebox and boiler head would make the area comfortable, a gust of wind would lift up the curtain, allowing the warmth to escape, only to be replaced by blowing snow and artic air.

"Flanger's plugged, Bat. Need you to go back and get Whitey's boys up here to help."

Nelson was holding his gloved hands up to the boiler head. Once they began to steam, he pressed them against his face.

"Okay, Bill … I'm going through the water pretty quick. We'd better make the water tank in a couple of more hours or else we're gonna be in a world of shit."

"If we can't go a mile and a half in a couple of hours, this whole goddamned railroad will be in a world of shit!" exclaimed Harrington.

Harrington threw two shovels and an iron bar over his shoulders and struggled forward. Driven snow was already lodging between the plow and the steep banks of the cut.

Gotta get outta here. Get snowed in damned quick if we don't.

Kerlee and Gilmore were under the plow. On their bellies, they were digging at the snow piled up against the front truck with their hands.

"Look out boys," warned Harrington. "Let me knock it loose with my bar."

On his knees in the loose snow alongside the plow, Harrington began jabbing his iron crowbar into the packed snow, prying apart chunks with each thrust. As the snow loosened, Kerlee and Gilmore pitched it out from under the machine with the shovels Harrington had tossed to them. They worked like men possessed, knowing snow was gathering in the cut almost as fast they were casting it aside. After minutes of concerted effort, their chests were heaving. White's crew arrived from the trailing plow with additional tools, and lent a hand. They too found themselves gasping from the quick exertion needed to clean out the jammed snow.

"That'll … have to … do it, boys," Harrington panted. "Better get … the hell moving … while we can."

With everyone crowded into the cab, Harrington whistled "Highball." Meath cracked his throttle, supplying steam to the pistons turning the ring and pinion gear. Three engineers put steam to the cylinders of their locomotives. The plow once again began its advance, attacking the growing wall blocking their way.

Making steady progress, the X-800 churned its way clear of the tunnel cut. Night had set in when they bucked the last of the big drifts near the new bunkhouse east of the depot. Harrington, hanging from the left door with a lantern in his hand, allowed himself to heave a slight sigh of relief. White, leaning on Harrington's back, felt him relax.

"Know how you feel, Bill," he hollered into Harrington's ear. "Can't say as I've ever seen the tunnel cut that plugged up."

Harrington nodded an agreement, but said nothing.

In the last light of day, he examined the yard. It was completely plugged with snow. Deep inside Harrington there was a growing anxiety that conditions were fast getting out of hand.

Better check with O'Neill. Blackburn and Homer must still be west.

"Let's hold up at the depot," Harrington ordered his crew. He poked his head through the back doorway. "Bobby, I'll get Jim Mackey to take over for you. Get your ass up to Bailets with the rest of the crew and grab a bite of supper."

Wednesday, February 23, 1910, 6:00 p.m.
Arthur Reed Blackburn, Trainmaster

It was as if a jury had just acquitted him of a crime for which he was falsely accused. A giant sense of relief passed through Blackburn's entire body when Irving Tegtmeier came running from the station at Alvin a few hours earlier.

"Phone's working. Just talked to Purcell. They've been hung up all day the other side of 3.3. There's another slide this side of the shed. Got a conditional staff. They need us to come up."

The day-long wait at Alvin had been agonizing for Blackburn. By late morning they had cleared the main line and siding, and filled their tenders with water. He considered going further east, but quickly dismissed the idea. He feared a slide might come down behind the outfit, cutting him off from his only hope of communication and leaving him stranded out on the main line with no staff. Needing to conserve coal, there was no choice but to park his plow and wait it out. He sent Dupy ahead on foot to try and locate Purcell, but after an hour, the brakeman returned, nearly collapsing as he entered the depot at Alvin.

"Sorry, sir. Didn't even make Windy. Couple a times almost walked off the cliff. Can't see a damned thang. No sign of Purcell."

Blackburn fumed over the loss of time.

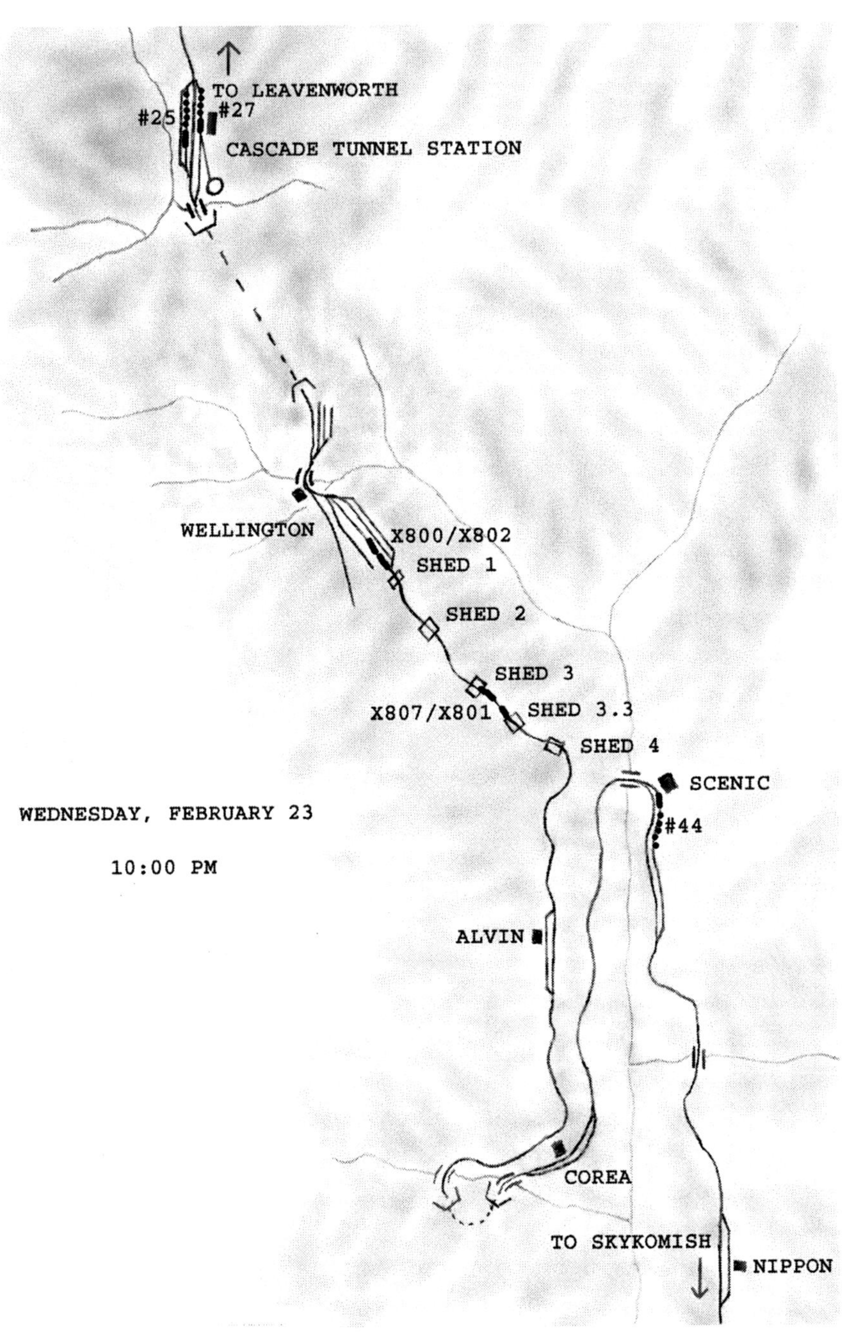

TO LEAVENWORTH
#25
#27
CASCADE TUNNEL STATION
WELLINGTON
X800/X802
SHED 1
SHED 2
SHED 3
X807/X801
SHED 3.3
SHED 4
SCENIC
#44
WEDNESDAY, FEBRUARY 23
10:00 PM
ALVIN
COREA
TO SKYKOMISH
NIPPON

Whole damned day shot. Nothing's moved since 26 last night. Got to get things coordinated better. No goddamned clue what anyone's doing.

Plowing the three miles from Alvin to Shed 3.3 was far from easy. Heavy drifts slowed their progress. It was a vicious circle. Deep, wet snow forced them to slow down, yet the slow speed allowed the wind to drift even more snow between the wheels of the equipment, slowing them even further. Twice snow had packed so hard between the drive wheels of the 1118 that they spun out, forcing the men to stop and break the hard chunks loose. The dark blanket of another stormy night covered the mountains when Blackburn's crew began digging into the slide, opposite Purcell and the X-807.

Blackburn grabbed a lantern and headed down the ladder.

"Take charge, Mr. Parzybok. I'm going to find Purcell."

He stumbled over the small mountain of snow separating the whirling fans of the two plows. About twenty-five of Harley's section crew were still spread about the mound. Looking like ghosts in the dim light of the lanterns, they shoveled snow either forward into the fan, or over the hillside. Despite the long, hard day, Harley's voice had yet to his lose its strength. What his crew now lacked in energy was more than compensated by the loud cussing and constant pacing of their foreman.

"Jesus God, we've been out here all damned day! The way you sissy boys are shoveling, gonna be here all damned night! Come on, boys! Shovel hard! Ten minutes, be done. Be done! Ten minutes hard work!" Harley was holding his gloved fingers up, pushing them in the faces of the men as he stormed by each. Exasperated, tired of the stares of the Italians, he grabbed the first available shovel. Head down, he began pitching snow so hard and fast he did not even notice that one shovel full nearly hit Blackburn. Only the sudden chuckles from the foreigners caused him to look up.

"Jesus, sorry, Mr. Blackburn. Didn't see ya there. About at my wits end getting these dagos and drunks to put in a day's work."

"Keep your men shoveling. Have you seen Mr. Purcell?" Blackburn asked.

"Back checking on his water and coal, last I heard, Mr. Blackburn." Harley looked back at his crew. "Goddamn it, work! I talk! You work!"

Blackburn crossed over to the uphill side of the 807 to avoid the plume of snow exiting its chute. He took a careful look back, sizing up how much of the slide was left to be plowed.

Fifty feet or so left. Half hour, we should have her.

Holding up his lantern, he caught the attention of one of the men in the cab of the 807.

"You there, where is Mr. Purcell?"

"Mr. Blackburn! Purcell here. Good to see you. Be right there!"

Making a clumsy leap from the cab of his plow, Purcell landed nearly face down in the snow at Blackburn's feet. Unabashed by his lack of grace, he promptly picked himself up and brushed away the snow still clinging to his day's growth of beard.

"I'm telling you, Mr. Blackburn, I've had my hands full since leaving Cascade last night. This damned wind's the problem. Blowing snow in quicker than we can throw it out."

"Yes, yes, we've hit the same, Mr. Purcell. What's the status of your plow?"

"About spent, sir. Been shoveling snow all day for water. Getting down to our last ton of coal, maybe less. Gonna have to shut her off if we want to keep a fire going for the trip back to Wellington."

"Our plow has plenty. I want you to back out and let us finish up here. I take it the line to Wellington is plugged?"

"Snowed in real bad, sir. Real bad. Sent Dougherty to Wellington this morning. He barely made it back. He brought back an order from Mr. O'Neill. Got it here." Purcell rummaged in his coat. The order, written on flimsy paper, had all but melted away in Purcell's wet pocket. "O'Neill wants us to double at Alvin as soon as we can get there, and plow back to Wellington. Got the order this morning. Haven't heard anything since."

"Has O'Neill moved 25 and 27 over to Wellington?"

"Don't know. We left Cascade Tunnel long before they showed up. When Dougherty was at the depot this morning, O'Neill said he was gonna hold them over the other side. Dougherty said O'Neill's shut down the line until we get a handle on things. That's all I know."

"Shut down the line. Brass must be happy about that," Blackburn said, wiping melted snow from his face. "Guess it's up to us to get it opened back up."

"Seems like a tall order right about now, Mr. Blackburn," Purcell allowed.

Not happy with the information he garnered from Purcell, Blackburn kicked at the snow as he stomped back towards his plow, now nearly halfway through the remainder of the slide. He told Harley to split his crew, with 15 men riding on the tender of the 1118 and the remainder stationed on Purcell's outfit. He stood on the hillside watching the progress.

Harrington must be doubled with White by now. Trains should be in Wellington. Fast sweep back upgrade can take 25 and 27 right on down. Puts 27 a full day late. Jesus, late with the mail two days running. Be lucky to get 28 over the hill tonight. Meet with Harrington and O'Neill. Start working together. Don't know what's happening any farther ahead than I can see with this damned lantern. No way to run a railroad.

Blackburn pulled his head back inside the plow.

"Looks like everyone's onboard. Highball, Mr. Parzybok."

Two whistle blasts were answered by two more, then two more, and finally two more. With a jolt, the X-801 and the 1118, now doubled with the X-807 and the 700, moved east from Alvin. Blackburn pulled his watch from his vest and noted the time, 10:35. He let a large yawn escape as he rubbed his face with his wet gloves.

Jesus, on duty over 24 hours. Not going to be quick trip to Wellington, either.

"Mr. Blackburn!" Parzybok called across the cab. "You able to raise Wellington before we left?"

"Barely," Blackburn answered. "Those blasted phones. Too much static to talk long. Told them we were leaving Alvin. I guess they understood me."

Not having the energy to carry on a shouting conversation with his conductor, Blackburn resumed staring ahead into the dark. Retracing their steps, it was easy plowing around Windy Point and east towards Shed 3.3. Blackburn relaxed, and his mind wandered. His thoughts turned to his wife.

Gone too much. No kinda life to bring up a family. Too late now. She's in Everett I'm up here. Doesn't seem to bother O'Neill, away all the time. Takes a different kind a man to railroad. Takes a different kinda woman to live with a railroad man. Can't wait to see Rosie again. Hold her. Little Grace. Miss them both. Wonder if they miss me. Best keep my mind on my work.

"Coming up on Shed 3.3," Blackburn called out. "Need you over here with your lantern, Mr. Tegtmeier."

As they passed through the slide area, both men did their best to study the hillside above them. The track remained open, the plow easily casting aside what snow had fallen since the slides were cleared.

"Looks to me like we got her, Mr. Blackburn. Can start running trains again."

"We'll see, Mr. Tegtmeier. I'd feel a lot better if I could see what's up that hillside. Nothing up there to hold the snow back. Longer it takes us to get back to Wellington the better the chance another slide will come down here," Blackburn fretted.

"Heavy drifts, wind her up!" Parzybok pulled in from the opposite side of the plow.

Blackburn knew it would be difficult plowing east of the slide area. Still, in the back of his mind he was hoping by some miracle they would simply march up the line and be in the warmth of the Wellington depot within the hour.

"Snow's building up around the flanger, Mr. Blackburn." Tegtmeier was completely outside, hanging from the ladder. It was a precarious position, but it was the only way he could get a clear view of the machinery under the plow.

"Raise the flanger!" ordered Blackburn.

Going too slow to flange. Better get shovelers ready to go.

Turning back into the cab, Blackburn motioned to crew foreman Harley.

"Work your way back and get your boys ready to shovel. Can't flange, going too slow. Damned wind. Snow's gonna bind the wheels."

Again Blackburn turned his attention to the murky shadows ahead. Snow nearly as deep as the fan was piled in the narrow trough that had formed from the numerous plow runs throughout the winter. With each encounter, the plow shook, exhaust exploding from the stack. The whirl of the side rods on the pistons, the grinding of the pinions doing their best to keep the giant ring gear spinning, emphasized to Blackburn the strain being placed on the machine, the strain being placed on the men.

It hit home.

This is a goddamned war.

Wednesday, February 23, 1910, 2nd Trick Wellington
Basil Sherlock, Telegrapher

Sherlock stood nearly at attention alongside the switch stand leading to the runaway track. Two Italians were with him, periodically digging into the snow accumulating around the switch points and tossing it over their shoulders. The strong smell of wine on the breath of the laborers repulsed Sherlock, but with the deep snow banks surrounding the switch, he had no choice but to stand next to the men. Sherlock kept a close watch on the double rotary set now parked at the depot, a mere 50 feet east of his position. In the dark he saw a number of forms swing off the lead plow. One walked into the depot, while the others made their way toward the Ballets Hotel.

Wretched night. Good to get out of that stuffy depot. O'Neill, that constant smoking. Pressure worse than the steam in the boilers of those engines. Lines down off and on. One minute messages going out in code, the next over own lines. Never been through such an ordeal in all my life.

Even without the usual movement of trains, O'Neill flooded Sherlock with work. The telegraph key, when working was constantly clicking as messages for the superintendent came in from throughout the division. The heavy snow in the mountains meant torrential rains in the lowlands. Rivers were on the rise, lapping at the railroad north of Everett. Trackwalkers across the mountain had completed their inspections and were reporting the status of their territories.

It seemed there was trouble everywhere. Flooding up at Ferndale was threatening a bridge. Slides down in the Tumwater Canyon were disrupting communications to the east. It occurred to Sherlock that O'Neill's railroad was a mess.

A highball whistle cut through the wall of falling snow. The outfit began to move, slowly bearing down on Sherlock and his two companions. Still intimidated by the size and menacing appearance of the spinning fan of a rotary, Sherlock was quick to wave the plow on through the switch and backpedal as far from the track as the snow drifts would allow. The two men shoveling grinned at his retreat, muttering something in Italian amongst themselves.

"Hey, Sherlock!" came a voice from behind. "Take over the wheel while me and the boys grab a bite to eat!"

Even under the cloak of the snow filled-night, Sherlock immediately knew the source of the jab.

Will Meath ever take a situation seriously?

Inside the station, Sherlock recognized the powerful frame of Harrington by the stove. He was pouring himself a cup of coffee, his back to the room. O'Neill stood next to him in silence, a cigar dangling from his mouth, himself holding a cup of the black brew. For the moment he seemed content to allow his assistant trainmaster to warm up.

Back at his desk, Sherlock busied himself. He rang the dispatcher, informing him of the passage of the X-800. Dots and dashes filled his earpiece as yet another coded report came in from the east side of the pass. Grabbing a note pad and his copy of "The 1910 Great Northern Railway Telegraph Code Book," he deciphered the message.

He spun around and faced O'Neill and Harrington.

"That was Chiwaukum. Track walker there reports two minor slides to the east. One's a quarter-mile east of the east switch, the other about a mile and a half beyond. They are preparing a slide report and will send it along."

"Well, so much for sending 25 and 27 back down the mountain." O'Neill let out a sigh.

"Were you thinking along those lines, Mr. O'Neill?"

To Sherlock, Harrington seemed surprised by O'Neill's comment.

Always interested in what was happening, Sherlock kept a close ear on the conversation.

"It crossed my mind earlier today. Double you up and send you right back down, but then we started getting reports that the Tumwater is sliding; plus you need coal. Easier to clear a couple miles west of here than try and open up twenty-five miles east. Weather's still not as bad over at Cascade."

"That's changing quick, Mr. O'Neill. Believe me, it's getting goddamned bad over there too." Harrington countered.

"Be just our luck we try to send them back down the hill just in time to hit a slide down in the Tumwater," O'Neill said. "If they get into trouble down there, no way to find out. Nothing between Cascade and Leavenworth except canyons and rocks. No, best to hold 'em over at Cascade until I know the line west is clear. Won't know that until I hear from goddamned Blackburn."

There was silence. O'Neill took the last puff off his cigar. Displaying his frustration, he threw the smoldering butt as hard as he could into the coal box next to the stove.

The ringing of the telephone helped break the tension that was building in the room. Sherlock was acutely aware of both O'Neill and Harrington staring at him as he plugged in the receptacle.

"Wellington."

Through the crackling of static he could barely discern the voice on the other end. Weak as the tone was, he recognized the voice of Trainmaster Blackburn.

"This … Blackburn. We're at Alvin …"

There was a disruption in the line. Sherlock looked up at O'Neill and mouthed the words, "It's Blackburn."

"Repeat please, Mr. Blackburn."

" …lea … Alvin. Dou … with Purcell … sli … cleaned up … heavy work."

The line went dead.

"Can you repeat, Mr. Blackburn? Sherlock paused.

"I say, can you repeat, Mr. Blackburn?" The line was dead.

Sherlock spun around in his chair and faced O'Neill.

"That was Blackburn, sir. He's at Alvin," Sherlock told his boss. "Near as I can tell he has doubled with Purcell and I believe they're just now leaving, coming east. Said something about a slide being cleaned up and heavy work. Very hard to hear, sir. Phone line west went dead again."

O'Neill removed another cigar from his pocket and put it to his mouth. Striking a match on the side of the stove, he lit the wrapped tobacco and slowly put it to his mouth. He left it there, precariously hanging from his lips. He finally gave it three quick puffs, pulled it from his mouth and inspected the ashes hanging from the end. The smoke lingered in the thick air of the depot. All the while Harrington slurped at his coffee, drops falling from his moustache adding to the water dripping off of his coat.

Just going to stand here with blank looks on their faces? Tension's giving me a helluva headache.

"Just now leaving Alvin. Christ, nothing is going to move all night." O'Neill resumed smoking.

Again the phone rang, and again Sherlock felt relieved at the prospect of having something of importance to do.

"Wellington." He placed his hand over the receiver and looked up at O'Neill. "It's Cascade Tunnel Station."

"Go ahead, Cascade Tunnel," Sherlock answered, leaning slightly into the mouthpiece.

"I've got Mr. Pettit here, conductor off train 25. He wants to know the status of getting his train underway," came the voice of the operator.

Again covering the mouthpiece, Sherlock turned to O'Neill.

"The conductor from train 25 wants to know when he can expect to get his train underway."

"Tell him I'm conferring now and will issue orders within the hour."

Sherlock repeated the message. Behind him, O'Neill and Harrington found two chairs and sat across from each other. Sherlock pulled his headset slightly off his ear so that he could eavesdrop on their conversation.

"With Blackburn coming this way, the sooner we get the trains over here the better, if you ask me," O'Neill was saying. "Need to have them here, ready to roll, when his outfit makes it back."

"Easier said than done, Mr. O'Neill. They've been rocking the trains trying to keep the bastards broke loose, but it's a losing battle. We're gonna have to go over there and bust them out as soon as we get serviced."

"All the more reason to get your outfit serviced and back over there."

"44's still on the siding at Scenic, right?" Harrington asked.

"They broke a drawbar. Was thinking you could plow them out when you take 25 and 27 down sometime early tomorrow morning."

"Christ, Mr. O'Neill," Harrington raised his voice. Glancing over at Sherlock, he controlled himself and once again spoke in a low mumble. "It's going to take us the better part of the night and on into the morning just to get serviced and get those trains here. That's if we're lucky. Let's face it, right now it's snowing harder and faster than we can clean the shit off the line, and that's not even taking into account hitting slides."

Sherlock watched as Harrington, fearful that he might have overstepped his bounds, bowed his head and stared at the floor. His large hands encompassed his mug, gently swirling the coffee.

So this is how decisions are made? One man smoking cigar after cigar and the other staring at the floor. Be getting things done if it were up to me.

Sherlock shuffled a few papers on his desk, acting as if he was completely engrossed in his work.

"Well, Mr. Harrington, it doesn't sound like the back edge of the storm is passing through yet. We're getting snow all the way to Index. Seattle papers are even talking they might get more snow before all of this is over. Makes no difference whether or not we're keeping up, we must keep plowing."

"And what about the crews? Have you thought about them?"

Sherlock nearly gasped.

Would never dream of challenging the superintendent like he is. Harrington's not long for this division.

O'Neill cast a quick glance at Sherlock who immediately lowered his eyes.

"We're short-handed as hell. None of the plows are double-crewed. You can't keep these men on duty for days at a time, no food, no sleep."

"Nonsense, Bill. We've got them doubled up, one crew in the forward position working, the crew in the trailing plow can rest."

"It don't work that way and we both know it. A fella can't sleep good in a goddamned plow." Harrington's voice trailed off. "Sorry sir, just speaking my mind, that's all."

Give him his due. You're the boss. Discipline must be maintained. Sherlock leaned back in his chair. Still intimidated by the presence and manner of Harrington, he was eager to see the Snow King put in his place by O'Neill.

"I know I'm pushing the boys hard, Bill. I'll bring relief up on the next train. Unfortunately, for now, I'm going to have to hold everything at Sky and Leavenworth. The boys are just gonna have to hang tough until we can clean the line."

"Well, at least keep 'em fed. My boys couldn't even get fed over at the cookhouse at Cascade on account of those goddamned passengers. They can work tired and cold, but you can't work 'em hungry."

"I'll leave word at Bailets he is to feed the crews and bill the railroad. That way the crews can eat there or at the company beanery. Mr. Longcoy, make those arrangements now."

"Yes sir." Longcoy emerged from the back of the room. On the run, he slipped into his coat and was out the door.

One way of maintaining discipline. O'Neill's right. Keep the wild beasts fed and they'll do tricks for you. Sherlock allowed himself an indiscernible smug grin.

"Now then, here's what I want done." O'Neill pulled his chair closer to Harrington and looked him in the eye. "As soon as your outfit is serviced, buck out the motors and take them over to Cascade to bring 25 and 27 through. After Blackburn gets back and serviced, I'll send him west. He can plow out 44 on his way down and bring up 2 and 28 with relief crews. Once you get 25 and 27 over here, you can get serviced and take them on down."

"Alright, sir." Harrington rose from his chair. "I'd better get back to my outfit. Just hope things go as smooth as all that sounded."

O'Neill opened the front of the potbelly stove and flicked off the ashes clinging to the end of his cigar. He slammed the door shut. "Wake up, Sherlock!"

Striding across the room, Harrington paused at the door.

"You get all of that, Sherlock?" A weak grin came out from under his moustache as he headed out.

Sherlock glared back at Harrington but kept silent.

If they wanted privacy should have left the room. Embarrass me in front of Mr. O'Neill.

"Break time's over, Mr. Sherlock. Back to work." Once again O'Neill was at Sherlock's side, towering over the slightly built man in the operator's chair. "First things first. Ring up Cascade and copy four to C&E trains 25 and 27. Plow returning from the west. Hold at Cascade Tunnel Station until can verify conditions west of Wellington. You can initial that JHO. Now take a second message, send this to Skykomish, copy four to C&E trains 2 and 28. Hold at Skykomish. Skykomish to Leavenworth still closed. JHO."

"Finally, ring up Delta and find out the status of the X-808. I have a feeling we're gonna need every plow we can lay our hands on."

Just like O'Neill. All of a sudden he's operating under full steam. Can't keep up with his head when he gets going.

"Now then, Mr. Sherlock, read those back so you can get them sent. I need to get a status report put together, coded, and sent to Brown and Gruber before your shift is out."

"One moment, sir," Sherlock said, still scribbling.

Good God, my head's killing me.

Thursday, February 24, 1910, 3:30 a.m.
James Henry O'Neill, Superintendent

The last thing O'Neill felt like doing was going back outside. He and Longcoy retreated to his private car shortly after Avery came on duty at midnight. Lewis Walker was waiting with steaming bowls of beef stew and hot biscuits set on the table. A meal under their belts, O'Neill gave Longcoy instructions for the upcoming day and sent the young man to bed. Not bothering to take off his clothes, O'Neill set his alarm clock for 3 a.m. and lay down for a nap.

Sleep away this snowstorm, was his last waking thought.

If anything, it was snowing and blowing even harder when he stepped from his car. Lantern in hand, O'Neill turned up the collar on his coat and worked his way down the track towards the coal chute. Two days pacing the floor at Wellington station was enough. For O'Neill, it was time to get out and deal with this storm head on.

Three, four foot build up on the sidings, gotta be a foot or more here on the main line. Harrington must be still servicing his outfit. Blackburn's still gone. Starting right where we left off.

He passed a group of men cleaning the switch leading from the main line to the siding. Another, larger group was struggling to keep the track clear ahead of the set of four motors parked on the passing track. The square, dark hulks of the electrics looked more like a group of derelict boxcars than the most powerful locomotives on the railroad.

Through the dark fog of the falling snow, O'Neill began to make out the diffused lights of Harrington's plow set. It appeared to O'Neill the crews were having difficulty spotting the locomotive behind the westward facing plow at the coal chute. He quickened his pace, eager to become an active part of the scene before him.

"You there!" O'Neill hollered, hailing the first man he encountered. "Where's Mr. Harrington?"

He was met by the blank stare of an Italian shoveler. The man smiled and politely shook his head side to side. He went back to work scraping snow from the wheels of the X-802.

"Is that you, Mr. O'Neill?" A tall figure emerged from between the plow and pusher engine. "Clafflin, sir, I'm firing the 802. Didn't expect to see you out here this time of night. Can I help you?"

"Clafflin, yes, well. Seems you've been here all night. What's been the hold up?"

"Sir, let me tell you, it's been just awful. The second we stop to fill a tender with coal or top off a water tank, why this damned wind and snow locks us in right tight."

"Locks you in?"

"Yes sir, that it does. Snow blows in right under the wheels. When we go to move, nothing will budge. Have to keep digging the whole time. Even then, we have to buck back and forth a half dozen times to get the outfit moving. Then we end up over shooting the whole show and have to do it all over again. Been like this all night, sir."

"I see. Any sign of Mr. Blackburn?"

"Can't say as I know. Mr. Harrington is down yonder by the coal chute. Lindsay is with him. Whitey is around here somewhere, shoveling."

"I see. And how are you holding up, Mr. Clafflin?"

"Well sir, it's like this. I'd like to be in bed with a belly full of food, but I'd like better to get this damned railroad back running again."

"What if I were to grab your shovel and order you back onto the fire deck of your plow? You think that would set right with you?"

"This bastard is yours, Mr. O'Neill!" Clafflin handed his shovel over. He tipped his hat and climbed back onboard his plow and called out, "I need to get my fire up anyway. We'll be doing all the work when we finally get outta here."

Shovel in one hand and lantern in the other, O'Neill continued down the line of steam locomotives coupled between the plows. He paused by each group of shovelers, lending a hand at digging out the snow from between the drivers and pilot wheels. While working, he asked them the status of their equipment, the status of each man. He made a mental note of the names of the men on the plow and engine crews, and the hours they had been on duty. Harrington's challenge earlier that night still stung.

Brown, Clafflin, Francisco, Baker, Imberg, Pettit, Allen, Ford, all over twenty-four hours straight. Nothing but a ham sandwich for any of them. Harrington's right, have to do better if they're going to keep going. Harley's dagos working twelve-hour shifts. Bastards are better off than my engine crews.

Whistles sounded up the line and lanterns waved. Orders were shouted man to man, "All clear! Moving east! All clear! Moving east!" Men emerged from between the three locomotives and two plows. "All clear" was repeated down the line.

O'Neill gave his shovel and lantern to the nearest worker and leaped aboard the 1154. Entering the cab, he stood alongside engineer Pete Imberg and watched him try to get his engine moving in the snow.

"Three engines and you can't move a damned inch?" O'Neill shouted.

"This goddamned snow and wind. Freeze right to the rail just like we're welded." Imberg replied, his head out the window, his eyes on his drivers. "We keep notching 'em out. Hold on. When she finally breaks loose we'll spin out and buck like a bastard!"

Francisco's big mallet engine was the first to break loose. Its two sets of drive wheels spun wildly on the rail, generating a shower of sparks, and sending a shaft of smoke from the stack up through the falling snow. The jolt broke the other two engines free. Imberg was quick to react, easing off his throttle but keeping some movement on his spinning wheels.

"We don't dare shut'em clean off. One of us shuts off while the others are spinning and they take hold, we'll start snapping drawbars."

Sanding valve open, more whistle and lantern signals exchanged, Imberg began to work at putting his engine on firm footing. His movements were duplicated by Ford, in the engine in front of him, and by Francisco, in the engine ahead of Ford. There was a slight rumble, and then a jolt. Legs braced, O'Neill was ready for it. He stood on the gangway between Imberg and the tender and looked to the rear. Slowly, they moved upgrade. An engine ahead spun out. They stopped, lurched, and again moved ahead. Suddenly Imberg's engine spun out, then Ford's. Stopped, they could not get started. Back-up signals were sent through the night along with a stream of profanity from a number of voices. Again a jolt, movement backwards. All stop. Two whistle blasts, answered three times and another attempt to move ahead. O'Neill looked at his watch. It was 4:25 when the tender of the X-800 was finally spotted at the coal chute.

"Been like this all night?" O'Neill inquired.

"That it has, sir. Getting enough shoveled now, this one went easy. Earlier on we were an hour just getting one of us spotted for coal."

O'Neill gave Imberg a slap on the back. "You're doing fine, Mr. Imberg. You'll hear no complaints from me."

Back on the ground, O'Neill plodded alongside Imberg's engine. A group of men were gathered near the tender. Another man was sitting on the ground gasping for air, his face bloodied.

"What happened here?" O'Neill demanded.

Two of the sectionmen helped the injured railroader to his feet. Catching his breath, he slowly stood straight.

"Mackey, sir. James ... Mackey, traveling ... engineer," the man said, still puffing. "Might need ... to lay down in the station ... for a bit. Sorry, sir."

"Yes, by all means go, Mr. Mackey," O'Neill said.

"Damned fool thing for me to do," Mackey confessed. His nose and forehead was scratched from hitting face first on the packed snow. He wiped the blood with the sleeve of his coat. "Yes sir, damned stupid of me. Heard the whistles, tried to level out one last pile of coal before the outfit started to buck its way out."

"Fine, Mr. Mackey," O'Neill interrupted. "Get patched up and get a little rest."

Mackey limped towards the depot, still chattering at one of the sectionmen helping him along.

The excitement over, the men poked their shovels in and about the drive wheels, pitching away the snow deposited by the ever-present wind. O'Neill recovered his shovel and took his place with the group, working in-between the front of the 1154 and the tender of the X-800. Within minutes, snow was lodging against the engine's pilot wheels. O'Neill was forced to drop on his knees to reach underneath and remove it.

Never seen it like this. Not this long. Not blowing this hard. Storm's gotta be close to passing. Tough work. Need to stand up. Stretch my back. Better not, snow's getting ahead of me.

"Need another man in here! Anyone around?" O'Neill yelled to no one in particular.

Above O'Neill, three men were on the tender of the X-800, manning the coal chute. While one operated the gate at the bottom of the bin, the other two, armed with scoop shovels, spread the coal across the tender's bunker, making sure it was filled to capacity. One of the men, hearing O'Neill's shout, jumped from the coal pile and peered over the edge of the tender.

"Be right down. I'll grab my shovel."

The man dropped off the tender and came alongside O'Neill. His face, sporting two day's growth of beard, was black from the coal dust sticking to the snow melting on his skin. No orders were required. The man immediately began pitching snow.

"Why, Mr. O'Neill, out for an early morning stroll?" he asked, without pausing.

It took a moment for O'Neill to take note of the man.

"Mr. Meath, apologies for not recognizing you. The way your face is blacked up I thought you were a stage performer."

Meath produced a greasy rag from his rear pocket and made a halfhearted attempt to wipe himself clean. If anything, he spread the black paste even further across his face.

"Three engines and two plows—got a snoot full of coal tonight, Mr. O'Neill."

"Then this is the last of it?"

"Last of the coaling, thank God. Still have to water Imberg's engine and my plow here."

"So, what's this I hear ... about Bailets getting a turkey lifted?" O'Neill asked carefully, watching Meath's reaction

"I've heard some talk," Meath said, without breaking stride with his shovel.

"Saw … that reward poster … at the depot," O'Neill panted. "Must be … more than talk."

"Wouldn't put much stock in that," Meath replied, still showing no emotion.

O'Neill momentarily stopped pitching snow to catch his breath.

"Funny thing is, Everett yardmaster ... told me a couple of his car knockers ... found a dead turkey in a cage inside an empty a while back. Wonder how that happened?"

"Well, you know as well as I do, Mr. O'Neill, the damnedest things can happen on the railroad."

Both men continued shoveling, the fog from their breath mingling to form a small cloud above them.

"Play chess, Mr. Meath?" O'Neill finally asked.

"Never took up the game," Meath replied.

"Learn it. We'll play. You'll like it. I see Mr. Harrington and Mr. Blackburn ... coming this way. If you'll excuse me, Mr. Meath, I need to talk things over with them." O'Neill crawled out from between the engine and plow.

"I think I know just the person to teach you the game," he said as he parted.

"I'm looking forward to it, Mr. O'Neill. But who's the guy you think will be a good teacher?"

O'Neill, walking away, hollered over his shoulder. "Basil Sherlock, of course."

Battle of wits with Meath. Just what the doctor ordered. Got the cobwebs cleared out. Thinking clear now. Need to figure our next moves.

Blackburn, Harrington and Lindsay did not notice O'Neill approach. Cold, they climbed into the cab of the X-800 to get out of the storm and warm up. O'Neill secretly laughed at the surprised looks on their faces when he, too, scampered up the ladder and entered the cab.

"Good morning gentlemen." O'Neill's booming voice seemed to fill the small cab beyond capacity. "Mr. Lindsay, I know you must be tired, but I need to ask a favor of you."

Ed Lindsay, who had long been intimidated by the superintendent, quietly mumbled, "What can I do, sir?"

"I need you to go forward and locate Mr. White. Tell him I want this outfit moved to the depot as soon as the watering is done. Mr. Blackburn and Mr. Harrington and I need to stay here and lay out today's work. And by the way, slide the door shut as you leave."

"Yes sir," came the suddenly meek voice of Lindsay. He left them alone.

The three men ultimately responsible for the operation of the railroad stood in the light of two lanterns. There was an awkward silence. Harrington and Blackburn eyed the wood box covering the giant ring gear, a flat surface large enough for only two men to sit. They waited for O'Neill to take the seat.

"Bill, Art, sit down. You boys need it worse than I do." O'Neill purposely lowered his voice.

Time for my "I'm just one of you" routine. Both about at the end of their ropes. Brow beat them now, won't get a thing out of 'em or their crews.

Seated, Blackburn was quick to speak. "Harrington tells me the trains are still over at Cascade. Need to have them here, Mr. O'Neill. With this outfit serviced, if we had the trains here, Harrington could take them right on down."

Trying my patience right off are you, Art? Bite your tongue. One problem at a time.

"First things first, Art. I need to know exactly what you encountered to the west."

"Well sir, as you know, Purcell hit that slide at Shed 3.3. We could have come up and helped if we knew, but the damned lines were down. Sent some men out to try and find Purcell, but it was just storming too bad. Was afraid to go out on my own, no staff, didn't want to get my rear blocked by the banks sloughing, you know. I'm telling you, Mr. O'Neill, we need to get some reliable phones up here. We wasted the whole damned day down there for no good reason."

"Art! I understand that! Right now I need to know the condition of the line to the west. These other problems we can take care of later."

"Sorry sir, just mad about how things are going, that's all."

"None of us are happy about any of this. Now listen, both of you. We're fast entering unmapped country. Before we can make any decisions we need to be clear about the conditions. Understood, gentlemen?"

Both nodded and mumbled agreement.

O'Neill reached into his coat and produced a cigar. Pulling up the lens of one of the lamps, he lit it and began to smoke. Wisps of spent tobacco mixed with the thick odor of hot grease and coal smoke.

"We hit heavy work all the way up from Alvin, Mr. O'Neill," Blackburn continued. "The plow chewed through the drifts all right, that wasn't what slowed us down. The problem was the banks. Big chunks would break off and fall under us. We'd have to stop, back up, sometimes dig ourselves out. There were times we were afraid we'd rise up on the snow and derail. It's the banks sloughing, that's the problem."

"What about the area at 3.3?"

"It was clean when we came back through, other than the snow that drifted in. The only thing is, none of us have gotten a good look up the mountain. I ain't got a ghost of an idea how much snow is still hung up on the ridge."

"So as of right now, you feel the line is open."

"I'm telling you Mr. O'Neill, if we had those trains here right now, we could take them right on down."

"Moving the trains just wasn't in the cards, Art," Harrington said. "Best to have them over at Cascade. Weather still ain't as bad over there. Closer to the cookhouse and out of our way."

"Gentlemen, let's get one thing straight. The movement of those trains will be my decision and my responsibility." O'Neill removed his cigar and pointed at the men. "I want you two to concentrate on your plows and your crews, pure and simple. Right now I'm inclined to believe we can send the trains west, but I want to do it in the daylight. I'm worried about the banks too. If they caused so much trouble with the plows, the same goddamned thing is going to happen when we run those trains through there."

"We can send shovelers with the trains," Blackburn countered.

"True enough," O'Neill allowed. "What I don't want to do is hold those trains here for any length of time. Bill's right, too unhandy for the passengers and for us. Don't want a bunch of people walking around."

There was a flurry of whistle calls. Bracing himself against the clutch lever, O'Neill swayed slightly as the plow began to move.

Getting ready to water this rig, O'Neill realized. "Now then, Bill chewed my ass a bit earlier about working the crews. We need to get the men organized so all of us can grab some rest. Art, how are your boys faring?"

"We need to eat, but we're pretty well rested from the layover at Alvin. Purcell's crew is about dead. They took the brunt of it. Even coming back, they had to help shovel."

"In that case, Art, have your outfit follow us on up." O'Neill was now in his element, zeroing in on problems, solving them one at a time. "Get everybody either up to Bailets or in the sectionmens' kitchen for a meal before you start servicing your plows. Release Purcell's crew for a rest break, and as many of your boys as you can and still get the plows and engines serviced."

"Yes sir," Blackburn answered.

"When you get serviced, I want you to head right back out and make another flip to Alvin. I don't want this drifting snow to get ahead of us," O'Neill decided.

"Understood." Blackburn sounded less than enthused. "Be better to send this outfit west, wouldn't it? It's ready. Besides, you got the 800 here on the point. Has a bigger tender."

O'Neill pulled a few long puffs off of his cigar.

Gotta point. Be good to have the 800 working west. Big tender. Good machine. Harrington's boys need some rest. Best get those trains busted loose first. Better stick with the plan.

"No, Art," O'Neill decided. "We'll take this set on over to Cascade. I want to drop off one engine. Don't need all three of these bastards eating coal. I can get Clary's crew to relieve Bill's boys."

"Suit yourself," shrugged Blackburn.

"So, what about your boys, Bill?" From his earlier conversations with the crewmen, O'Neill had a fairly clear idea, but he wanted to hear Harrington's view of the issue.

"Kind of a toss up. Both my boys and White's have grabbed rest along the way. Clary's bunch has been off since midnight last, so they're in good shape to relieve either Lindsay or White."

"Still leaves us a full crew short." O'Neill's voice trailed off as the plow began to move.

Sliding the door open a crack, O'Neill looked out as the outfit moved upgrade. He gazed at the electric motors sitting silent on the siding as they glided past.

Use men off the motors.

"Art, Bill, who can we take off the motor crews to help us on the plows?"

Both Blackburn and Harrington stared at O'Neill for a moment.

"Well, let me think," Harrington began. "Chambers for sure, and Ed Campbell, he's been conductor for plow trains."

"Bloemeke has worked snow plows too. Purcell has a couple of extra brakemen with his outfit, they came down with Harley's boys. Jenks and some other kid, don't know his name," Blackburn added.

"That'll help," O'Neill said. "Bill, you and I will head straight over to Cascade. I plan to take three of the motors with us. We'll use them to pull out the trains. I can pull Campbell off the motors. He can take charge of this plow and come back and plow out the yard ahead of 25 and 27."

Harrington yawned and stretched. He got up from his seat and joined O'Neill at the door.

"Boys are getting a little owly. Goddamned snow just won't let up. Art tells me things are balled up on down the hill. What about 44? God only knows when we're going to make it back down there."

The plow came to a stop. O'Neill moved to the opposite side of the cab and slid open that door as well. Through the dark frame shone the lights of the depot. "I'm going to wire Delta immediately. The 808 should be repaired and ready for service. I'll start it east. I'll have Dowling take charge. They can bring up 2 and 28 from Sky and relieve 44 at Scenic."

"What about coal?" Blackburn asked. "Pulling pretty heavy out of here."

"I'll have Dowling bring some with him. Bastards missed our switch this week. Left our coal in Everett. I gave them hell about it." O'Neill took a draw from his cigar and shrugged. "Little good that does us now."

O'Neill swung out on the ladder. "Any questions gentlemen?"

"Guess that about covers it," Harrington allowed.

"No sir. I best get back down to my outfit and bring that tired bunch on up for some grub," Blackburn replied.

"Very well, men," O'Neill said as he dropped off the plow. "Let's hope by this time tomorrow we'll be sound asleep and all of this will be behind us."

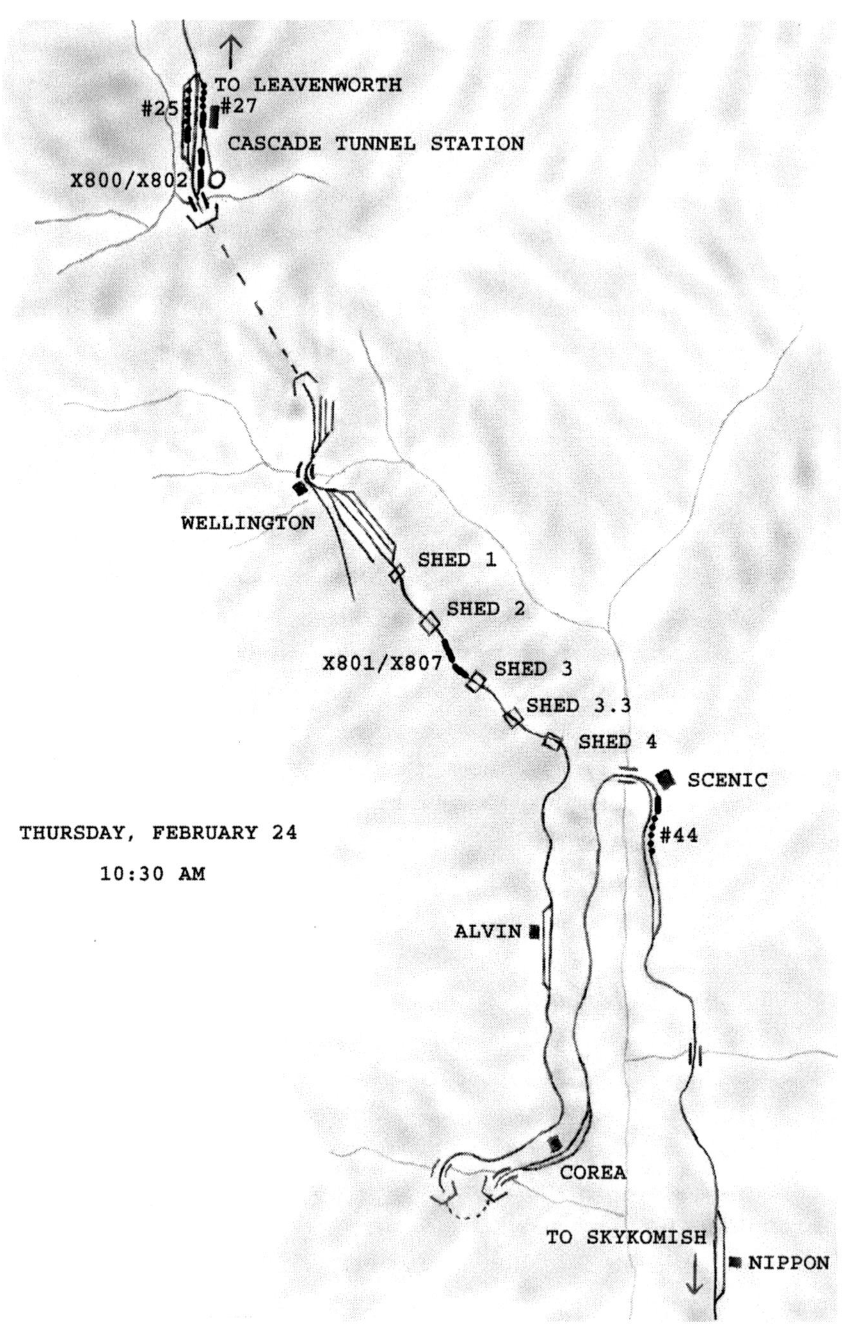
TO LEAVENWORTH
#25
#27
CASCADE TUNNEL STATION
X800/X802
WELLINGTON
SHED 1
SHED 2
X801/X807
SHED 3
SHED 3.3
SHED 4
SCENIC
#44
THURSDAY, FEBRUARY 24
10:30 AM
ALVIN
COREA
TO SKYKOMISH
NIPPON

Thursday, February 24, 1910, 10:30 a.m.
Arthur Reed Blackburn, Trainmaster

"I tell you this, Mr. Blackburn, they should've had them trains waiting for us when we got back to Wellington." Irving Tegtmeier was leaning over Blackburn's shoulder, hollering into his ear. "The line was clean when we come up last night. Harrington's boys could've taken 'em right on down and this damnable business would be done."

Blackburn continued to hang from the door of the X-807. Dawn had long since broken, but the heavy snowfall was keeping him from getting a clear view of the tracks ahead. Like sheets of rain, the snow seemed to come at him in waves. In one moment he could catch a glimpse of what lay ahead; in the next, it was gone behind a white curtain.

"What's done is done, Mr. Tegtmeier," Blackburn snapped back over his shoulder. He pulled his head back in and glared across the cab. Harley's section crew was traveling with the outfit. Men were crowded along the enclosed boiler catwalk and spilled out into the cab.

Damned Tig. Shouldn't be talking down O'Neill in front of these dagos. Blank stares. Damned well understand every word.

"They'll play hell getting them trains dug out today," Tegtmeier continued, ignoring Blackburn's reply. "Snow's really piling up. Looks like ten, maybe twelve feet on the level."

Blackburn simply nodded in agreement. The day did not begin

well. As with Harrington's plows, the blowing snow slowed the process of servicing Blackburn's plows and engines. Hours later than he had hoped, they were finally headed back west. The delay allowed the storm to pile even deeper drifts along the right-of-way, further slowing their progress. Although now a double set, the engineers of the two pushers were having a difficult time keeping a steady push on the plow. Snow continued to slough off the banks and blow in and around the drive wheels, robbing the engines of both power and traction.

"Well, all I can say is, I hope Harrington and O'Neill have them trains waiting for us when we get back," Tegtmeier continued. "Missed a good chance this morning, that's for damned sure."

"We've got our hands full right now. I'm not going to worry about what O'Neill and Harrington are doing." The impatience in Blackburn's voice finally silenced Tegtmeier. Instead, he leaned even harder on the trainmaster's back and shoulder.

Soaked. Getting hell of a chill. Wonder if Tig can feel me shivering? Give anything to be home with Rosie. Kitchen warm. Probably finished her second cup of coffee. Fussing around with Grace. Shaking his head, Blackburn cleared his mind. He wiped the melting snow from his face. *Concentrate. Keep a sharp eye.*

Through the blowing snow and the rotary's plume, something dark caught Blackburn's attention. Instinctively he bent forward, trying to force his vision to pierce through the veil of white. Another gust of wind sent a sheet of snow into Blackburn's face blinding him. Even Tegtmeier was forced to turn away.

"We're blind here!" Blackburn hollered across the cab. "Watch ahead! I saw something!"

"The bank's got our view cut off, sir!" Brakeman Al Dougherty's voice was hoarse and anxious.

Christ. Whole mountain might have slid up ahead. Won't know until we hit it.

Both Tegtmeier and Blackburn saw it at the same time. Each could feel the other tense for a split second before they both yelled, "Slide ahead! All stop!"

For a moment, whistle blasts rose over the howl of the wind. The sound of escaping air filled the cab as conductor Homer Purcell grabbed the brake handle and slammed it into "Emergency." Not braced for such a quick stop, a number of the Italian shovelers lurched forward with the sudden decrease in forward momentum.

As the fan cleared and the plume from the chute dissipated, Blackburn and Tegtmeier finally got a better view. Another slide, much larger than any previous, had come down just ahead of the entrance to Snow Shed 3.3. The dark object that had caught Blackburn's eye was the trunk of a burned tree, packed in the snow as it was carried down off the mountain by the force of the avalanche.

"Christ help us, that's a big one," Tegtmeier said in nearly a whisper.

Blackburn saw all he needed. He pulled his head back into the cab and began barking orders.

"Mr. Harley, get your boys out there. Better take axes, looks like we're gonna hit some timber. Mr. Tegtmeier, I want you to give the fan a close look. We're going to be chewing some logs, maybe some rocks. Mr. Dougherty, get back there and tell the engineers we're gonna be bucking a tough one. Climb back to the 801 and tell Parzybok to get his boys up here. We're gonna need them. Mr. Purcell, follow me. I want to see what we're up against."

Just getting to the base of the slide took a considerable amount of effort. The snow berms lining the right-of-way had gotten so tall Blackburn felt like he was walking through a dark, narrow canyon. The wind was cascading snow over the sides and onto the track like waterfalls, piling up at an alarming rate. He and Purcell were soon up past the tops of their heavy mountaineer's boots, wading through the white mass.

Leading the way, Blackburn began to climb the front face of the slide. He was a strong man, and with each stride he distanced himself from the shorter, struggling Purcell. The snow was dirty. It was streaked with mud and speckled with bits and pieces of branches and small rocks. Parts of the slide were still moving, tumbling down over the steep bank to Blackburn's left. He squinted and looked up towards the top of Windy Mountain. *A dirty bastard. Snow's scraping the ground. Can't be much more up there to come down.*

"How big you make it to be, Mr. Purcell?"

Out of breath, Purcell came up alongside the trainmaster. He took a long look around.

"She's gotta be 30, maybe 35 feet deep right here. What, maybe 1000 feet wide? A big son of a bitch, sir. Gonna have to ram our way through, can't just chew it."

Section Foreman Bob Harley joined the two men, already bellowing orders.

"Peter! Fan the boys out just below us! Get your boys shoveling! Our boys will handle the axes!" He turned to Blackburn. "Damned dagos. They can shovel, but they can't handle an ax worth a damn."

"So how long is it going to take to clear this bastard, Bob?"

Harley took his first close look at the slide. He pulled the wool stocking cap off his head and used it to wipe snow off his weathered face. At first he said nothing, seemingly more interested in making sure his hat was back on his head and covering his ears.

"All goddamned day and well into the night, if it's the truth you want. If we get this thing cleared in under 12 hours it'll be a damned miracle, and that's only if this goddamned wind dies down and the other half of the mountain don't come sliding down on top of us. Peter! Goddamn it! Get those boys over there working! I gotta tend to things, Mr. Blackburn."

Voice shouting, hands waving directions, Harley stumbled down the front face of the slide towards the shovelers. Blackburn took another hard look up into the clouds draped over the side of the mountain.

"Sure wished to hell I knew what's still up there," he wondered half aloud.

Hard labor yielded minor results. Within hours, the wet snow set up, becoming as hard as concrete. Working together, Ben Jarnigan and Tom Osborne would back their engines to a point about five feet from the base of the slide, and then speed forward, ramming the spinning blade against the wall of snow. Even with such a force behind it, often the wheel would bite only a few inches before the drive wheels of the locomotives would lose their grip on the rail and the entire outfit would stall. While the plow was pulled back for another charge, shovelers and ax men would work down the face, removing large bits of timber and rocks. Driving their tools into the pack, they tried to loosen the snow enough for the plow to cast it aside. It was slow, frustrating work.

Needing to warm up, Blackburn replaced Parzybok in the cab of the X-807. Dougherty came in out of the storm as well. He was manning the clutch and sending signals back to Tegtmeier, who was engineering the plow. Dougherty stood in the cab with Blackburn, nearly at attention, both hands on the large clutch lever protruding from the center of the floor. Blackburn was at his usual post, gazing ahead from the left cab door, impatiently waiting for Harley's men to get in the clear so they could make the next charge. Neither man spoke.

Dougherty. Him and Meath—good railroaders. Tough men to handle. Meath, too smart for his own good. Dougherty too dumb not to fall into Meath's schemes. Got the signal.

"Okay, Mr. Dougherty, wind her up, here we go." Blackburn gave the whistle cord two short tugs and braced himself against the door.

The plow jolted forward and quickly picked up speed. Instinctively, Blackburn clinched his teeth. He jammed his heavy boot against the doorframe and braced himself. Behind him, 200 tons of iron and steel were propelling him toward what amounted to a brick wall. The thought of the plow derailing with the impact and the heavy locomotives crashing through on top of him, never crossed his mind. It was a procedure he endured a thousand times before. He had the utmost confidence in the machinery and its ability to withstand the strain.

To Blackburn, the impact seemed like the very moment separating life from a sudden, violent death. The instant the giant fan encountered the face of the slide, exhaust erupted from the stacks of the plow and two pusher engines. Even the wind and falling snow did not mute the roar. The plow vibrated, and the forces sent both Blackburn and Dougherty forward despite of their braced stances. The torque of the wheel grinding against the resistance of the snow caused the machine to shudder even harder, leaning slightly to the left. More like glacial ice, large chunks of snow slammed against the spout of the chute as the fan tried to cut through the mass and cast it aside. A tree limb, nearly 6 inches in diameter was thrown aside like a javelin tossed by an athlete.

Just as the plow was about to stall, the blades cut into a soft pocket of snow. Regaining their footing, the pusher engines jolted forward, thrusting the plow into the pack until the fan and hood were completely immersed. Just then their forward progress began to falter.

Blackburn was back in the cab in an instant.

"Keep her turning!" he yelled at Dougherty and Tegtmeier. Grabbing the whistle chord, he gave the reverse signal.

The plow slowly began to retreat. The fan, still spinning, cleaned itself of the last of the snow and debris as it emerged from the bank.

"Stop! Stop!" It was Purcell, waving his arms and yelling from the bank alongside the plow.

Knowing not to question his men, Blackburn immediately applied the brakes just as Dougherty whistled "Stop." The machine came to a rest at the leading edge of the cut they were making through the slide.

"Now what the hell's wrong?" Blackburn shouted back, clearly irritated.

"Something's caught up underneath, sir. Between the fan and the front truck. Whatever it is, you were dragging it and pushing snow. Was afraid you'd lift up off the rail."

"Tig!" Blackburn was staring down the side of the plow's boiler. "Need you out here. Got problems under the plow."

The banks of snow were closed in around the plow making it difficult for Blackburn and Tegtmeier to work their way underneath the machine. Snow was packed solid between the back of the fan housing and the facing of the front wheels. With little room to work, both men dug as best they could by hand, trying to see what had caused the snow to become so impacted.

After a few minutes of futile effort, both men stopped.

"Better raise her up, Mr. Blackburn. Whatever's under here, we ain't gonna dig it out from here."

Climbing out from under the machine, Tegtmeier disappeared into the cab. Blackburn stayed outside, on the snow bank, even with the door. He could hear Tegtmeier order Dougherty to raise the plow. The big brakeman eased the clutch lever forward until it clicked into the hoist position. Under the plow, the drive chain powering the jackscrews snapped to life.

The cab and fan began to lift. Suddenly, it faltered. A loud, sharp, "b*ang*!" came from under the plow and the left side of the machine came crashing back down onto the frame of the truck. The machine sat stationary, listing to the left like a ship taking on water.

Blackburn was enraged. "What the bloody hell did you do?" he yelled at Dougherty. "Try again. Get this damned plow lifted and level!"

He glanced at the men shoveling. All had stopped and were staring back at him and the plow. "Mr. Harley! The rest of you! Get back to work, goddamn it!"

Tegtmeier came out from his position along the boiler and took the clutch lever from Dougherty. He carefully feathered it into position, but the plow did nothing. He and Dougherty pulled up the floor covers to inspect the clutches.

Blackburn leaped from the bank and into the cab. "What the hell's wrong? We gonna get this plow lifted or stay here all goddamned day?"

Down in the hole, Tegtmeier inspected the grease-filled recesses of the clutches and main shaft. He pulled free the broken remains of a drive chain.

"She ain't gonna raise up, Mr. Blackburn. Snapped the drive chain. The way she's leaning, things must be bent to hell under there. Can't tell for sure until we get her shoveled out."

"Can we keep plowing anyway? We need to keep at this slide." Blackburn knew full well the answer, but was hoping his Master Mechanic would live up to his title.

"We gotta get her cleaned out so I can see what happened. Maybe then we can figure out how to level her out and keep plowing. One thing's for damned sure, we can't be ramming her into this bank off-center like she is. Could tear the truck right out from under us."

Blackburn placed his thumb and forefinger over the bridge of his nose and rubbed his eyes. Hunger and fatigue was ganging up on him. A headache sprang to life.

Having little choice, Blackburn relented. "Damn it. I hate to take men off the slide. Round up some shovels, Mr. Dougherty. I'll get a couple of Harley's boys to help us out."

Piece of shit, Blackburn fumed. *Should've sent the 800 down here like I wanted. Tearing this goddamned relic apart.*

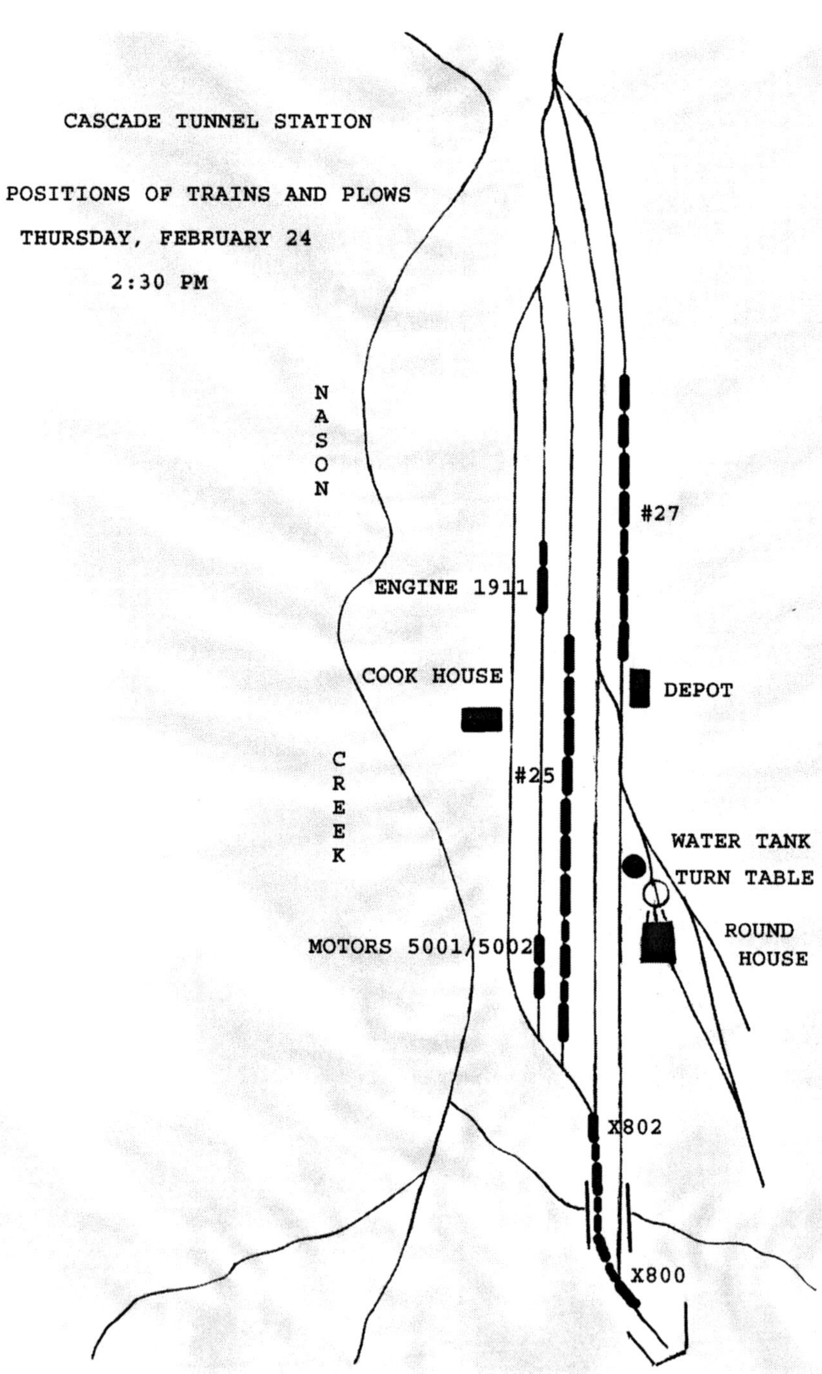
CASCADE TUNNEL STATION
POSITIONS OF TRAINS AND PLOWS
THURSDAY, FEBRUARY 24
2:30 PM
NASON
CREEK
#27
ENGINE 1911
COOK HOUSE
DEPOT
#25
WATER TANK
TURN TABLE
ROUND HOUSE
MOTORS 5001/5002
X802
X800

Thursday, February 24, 1910, 2:00 p.m.
James Henry O'Neill, Superintendent

O'Neill, head down, thumbing through a group of telegrams, burst from inside the depot at Cascade Tunnel Station and nearly ran into the conductor of Train 25, Joseph Pettit.

"Sorry sir, didn't mean to block your way," Pettit stood aside and politely tipped his cap, which proudly bore the shiny brass "Conductor" emblem.

"Ah yes, Mr. Pettit. Here for a report, I assume? Keeping your charges calm, are you?" O'Neill stuffed the messages into an inside pocket. He buried his hands into the pockets of his soaked overcoat and gave the conductor his complete attention.

"Well, yes sir, to both questions. The women and children are comfortable enough. There are a handful of business types onboard that are somewhat demanding. I try to keep them penned up in the observation car. Keeps them from stirring up the rest of the passengers, don't you see."

"I see, very good. Well, I suppose they want to know when we'll get you back on your way." O'Neill fixed his look on Pettit.

"Yes sir. I told the passengers I'd get the straight story from you." Pettit, not the least bit intimidated by O'Neill, held his ground and looked O'Neill straight in the eye.

Like this man, O'Neill thought. *Better he's on that passenger train than me. Have the lot of them out here shoveling. Cussing them the whole time.*

"I'll give it to you right, Mr. Pettit. We are having a devil of a time moving in this storm. The plows are handling the snow, but it's slow going. Mr. Blackburn hit a slide west of Wellington, but they're clearing it right now. We're here to break your train out. You can tell your passengers we plan to take you through to Wellington. As soon as Blackburn returns from the west, just as soon as we know that line is clear, you can proceed. I'm not prepared to say exactly when. It all depends on what Blackburn's crew is facing to the west."

Pettit took in what O'Neill told him. "What about backtracking east? Back down to Leavenworth at least until the storm breaks?" Pettit knew such a move was out of the question, but also knew that very thought was going through the minds of some onboard his train.

"Too risky, Mr. Pettit. I'd much rather concentrate our efforts on a few miles of track to the west, than 25 miles of track to the east. Besides—and this is just between you and me—our telegraph lines to the east keep going down, have been since last night. The Tumwater is sliding. For now, we're cut off to the east. If they ask, just tell them all our plows are working west and will continue to do so."

"Very well sir, I understand." Eyeing his train, Pettit pointed towards the cars. "Can you pull our train straight out?"

O'Neill looked past Pettit and carefully studied the passenger train as well. Other than the windows, snow had completely engulfed the cars. The heavy drifts covering the roofs did not concern him, but he knew the snow packed under and in-between the cars would play havoc when it came to getting them to move.

"I doubt it, Mr. Pettit. Pass the word to your passengers we're going to pull each car out separately. They'll need to either stay onboard in their assigned car, or in the cookhouse, until we're done. Make sure people don't try to pass from car to car while we're pulling your train out. They'll be times the engines will not be coupled to the train, so tell your passengers to dress warm if they stay onboard. Understood?"

"Indeed, sir," Pettit once again tipped his cap. "I'll let you get back to your duties. I'll spread the word that you have things well in hand. I appreciate your time."

Pettit turned and began to walk back towards his train.

"Mr. Pettit!" O'Neill stopped walking toward the plow and turned back. "The job you're doing onboard that train will not go unnoticed. I'm personally grateful."

Pettit said nothing. Smiling, he again put his finger to the bill of his cap, and resumed walking back to his train. O'Neill continued towards the plow, his hand in his pocket still clutching the messages he just received.

Damn the luck. Get two freight trains over the hill with hardly a delay. 27 stuck. Under a hundred miles from home. Two days late. Damned messages from Brown and Gruber burning a hole in my coat pocket. Get that mail train to Seattle with all due speed. Christ-a-mighty, they should be here.

The news from across the division added to O'Neill's worries. Snow was due in Seattle, which meant at least another day of the same in the mountains. Of additional concern was the possibility of a quick melt causing the rivers to flood and mud to start to slide along the Sound.

Whole damned division falling apart. Just keep working. Keep the boys working. Hard work. Break in the weather. Our only way clear.

Suppressing a yawn, O'Neill trudged past the cookhouse. The smell of coffee mingled with fried bacon. He considered going in for a quick bite but dismissed the idea when a group of passengers emerged. Politely nodding to the men and women, he quickly walked away.

Last thing I need right now is explaining myself to a bunch of nervous passengers. Let Pettit handle them.

Clary and Harrington, shovels in hand, were pitching snow away from the front truck of the plow. Section Foreman Charlie Bergstrom was helping as well. He had his crew spread out along both sides of the plows and engines, keeping their wheels free of the blowing snow.

"Mr. Bergstrom," O'Neill called, making his presence known.

Bergstrom, a tall, rugged, squared-jawed man, looking every bit his Viking heritage, paused from his shoveling.

"Yes sir."

"I'll make you a deal. Fetch me a sandwich and a cup of coffee and I'll make myself useful on the business end of one of your shovels." O'Neill continued to size up the plow and work crews. "Looks to me like we've got an all-hands-on-deck situation if we're going to get a damned thing done this afternoon."

"Yes sir," Bergstrom snapped, motioning to one of his men. "I'll see to your food."

"We're going to need every shovel you can muster. Can you find us a few more?" O'Neill wanted to make sure every man not directly operating a rotary was employed in breaking out the two stalled trains.

"I'll get right to it, sir. I know where there are at least a dozen more." Hollering at a group of men, they left in a fast walk to dig out one of the tool houses now covered with snow.

"Mr. Clary, let's get these plows underway. Here's a written order giving you permission to make a reverse move to the tunnel portal. I want the yard plowed out so the motors can start pulling out the passenger train."

"Harrington's boys are still taking their rest and eating, sir—no one's manning the trailing plow or engines," Clary countered.

"Christ, Ira, get that burr outta your ass. Get your boys out of the 802 and have them man the 800," Harrington snarled. "My boys need as much rest as they can get right now."

"Mr. Clary," O'Neill quickly interrupted. "I agree with Mr. Harrington. Now get that trailing plow manned and let's get going. Have the operator get the engine crews called and back on duty. If we have extra board men, call them to crew. We need to double-crew anyway. I want that plow moving, now!" O'Neill felt his temper slipping away.

It was the second time he had to deal with Clary and Harrington arguing. Earlier in the morning, while trying to reach the water tank, the lead plow had derailed. Tempers flared when Clary and Harrington locked horns over how best to rerail the machine. Harrington even went so far as to take O'Neill to task over the refusal of the cookhouse to serve his men the day before. O'Neill took a deep breath.

Calm down. Tired's no excuse. They're all getting tired. At each other's throats. Have to stay calm to keep them calm.

O'Neill turned his attention to Harrington. The big man was now stooped, leaning hard on his shovel. He ordered his crew to rest, but taken none himself, opting to stay with the outfit while it was being serviced.

"All last night getting coal and water, half the day today doing the same. We're getting nowhere fast, eh Bill?" O'Neill began to shovel snow from around the plow.

"Damned snow builds up so quick, can't keep these goddamned plows on the rail. So how we doing to the west, any news from Blackburn? He got the line clear?" Harrington resumed his digging as well.

"He phoned Wellington. Guess they hit another slide at Shed 3.3," O'Neill reported.

"Goddamned hill just won't hold," Harrington commented in a dejected tone.

"Still blowing hard over there from the sounds of things." O'Neill paused from his work. "As soon as we get these trains moving again, I'm going to call out 26."

Harrington stopped mid-scoop and stared at O'Neill. "What the hell for? We can't even get a damned plow across the hill."

"You forget, Bill, I've got bosses too. There's times when I have to say 'yes sir' just like the rest of you. Brown wants to get trains moving. I told him we expect to have the line open sometime within the next 24 hours. Besides, I've got the 808 coming out of Delta. They'll open to Scenic and get 44 back to Sky for car repairs."

Doubting O'Neill's plan, Harrington shook his head.

"How far is the 808 gonna get before it goes to hell on us again? That goddamned bucket of bolts is a piece of shit and we all know it," Harrington muttered.

"Dowling is coming out with her. He'll keep her going," O'Neill countered.

The men fell silent.

Harrington's right. Making assumptions on information I don't have. Hoping Blackburn isn't locked up too bad. Hoping Dowling can keep the 808 running. Hoping this damnable storm gives us a break. Hope's about all I got. O'Neill leaned into his shovel, matching Harrington scoop for scoop.

Clary and his crew walked by in silence, climbing aboard the X-800. The shrill "highball" whistle sent Bergstrom's section men scurrying clear as the engineers of the pushers answered in kind and the outfit began to move.

"Bill, you'd better get our boys out here too. The only way we can get these trains busted outta here is to get everyone digging."

Harrington, resigned to the fact rest would come only after the two stalled trains were well on their way to Seattle, offered no argument. As he started walking, he motioned to O'Neill's back. "I think that guy wants to talk to you."

Spinning around, O'Neill found himself towering over a short man standing an arm's length away, food and coffee in hand, his head slightly bowed.

"Excuse me, sir. Your food."

Back aching, nose running, O'Neill kept digging away at the snow packed underneath a sleeper, fifth of the seven cars that comprised train 25. He had set the pace all afternoon, driving the men hard, leading by example. By now digging out a car had become routine. With a tenacity and agility that impressed O'Neill, Bergstrom's sectionmen would literally surround the car and begin pitching away the snow lodged around the wheels and underframe. Harrington, O'Neill, and a number of the available trainmen lent a hand, breaking the snow loose with heavy steel bars and clearing the ice between the rails so the wheels of the car would not ride up on the pack and derail. Once the outer portion of the car's under frame was clear, the section hands would crouch down and burrow into the snow packed under the coach. Tossing the snow outward, the larger trainmen ringed the perimeter of the car shoveled it clear. Like all other jobs undertaken in the storm, it was slow, agonizing work.

"She's cleaned out good enough. Get your boys clear, Mr. Bergstrom." O'Neill stepped back and motioned to John Scott to bring the electric motors forward. The slow, even pulling power of the electrics worked well providing the force necessary to release the ice-age grip the storm had on each passenger car.

Two square box-cab electrics coupled together hummed down the siding toward the car. Blue bolts of electricity shot from the trolley poles as they bounced across ice on the overhead wires. Harrington and Charlie Smart broke chunks of snow from the car's coupler, freeing the locking pin. About 50 feet from the car, the motors slowed to a stop.

"Bring 'em on in! Bring 'em on in!" O'Neill yelled, motioning with his arm.

John Scott, the conductor onboard the motors, appeared in the front doorway.

"They just went dead on us! Don't know what the hell happened! Rich is checking the back motor! Might have popped a relay."

O'Neill threw his shovel to the ground.

"Goddamn it!" He stomped to the dead locomotives, his face red, kicking at the snow with each step.

"Mr. Bloemeke, snap the trolley poles on and off the overhead—see if you can get them to spark," O'Neill ordered.

Anthony Bloemeke stepped out onto the narrow porch on the front of the engine. He released the ropes and the two forward trolley poles swung into position. He pulled at the ropes allowing the contactors on the tip of each pole to slap harmlessly against the overhead wire.

"Deader than a doornail, Mr. O'Neill," Bloemeke remarked.

"What the hell's stopping us now?" Harrington, weary of fighting what seemed to him a losing battle, joined O'Neill.

"Overhead's dead. Transmission lines must be down," O'Neill snapped. He wiped his face and yawned. The men stood silent for a moment, staring at the dead electric motors.

"We'd, better get those useless bastards outta here. Anything not moving is gonna get snowed in damned quick." Harrington's sarcastic tone did not set well with O'Neill, and he knew it.

What was a valuable asset a moment ago was now a useless liability. With no means to propel themselves out of the way, there was no time for O'Neill to dwell on this most recent bout of bad luck. He had to act before the motors became snowed in as well.

"Mr. Scott, I'll issue orders for Frank on the 1418 to tow you back to Wellington. You will secure your locomotives and your crew will come back with him. Is that understood? We need every available man back here."

"Yes sir, understood."

O'Neill caught Clary's attention as the plow set eased past, clearing an adjacent track. Jumping from the plow, the short Irishman joined Harrington.

"The motors are down, Ira. We're dragging them back to Wellington.

Break the double set," O'Neill ordered. "I want you to take the 800 and clear the way. Stay over at Wellington and get the yard clean. Looks like we're gonna have to hold these trains over there. Can't move past Wellington until I hear from Blackburn. Time's a wasting so let's get to it!"

The impromptu meeting broke up. Harrington and O'Neill walked away together in silence. Out of earshot from the rest, O'Neill finally spoke.

"I need you to stay here and help me, Bill. I'm counting on you and Bergstrom to keep the boys working. They're tired. Harder to keep 'em going. The only way we're going to beat this storm is to keep fighting. You understand? We can't slow down now."

For a moment Harrington said nothing. He let out a long sigh and glanced at the snow tumbling from the sky.

"We ain't gonna get these goddamned trains down the hill today, are we." Harrington said, still not looking directly at O'Neill.

"The day ain't over yet, Bill. Let's hope Blackburn is making progress on that slide."

Thursday, February 24, 1910, 4:30 p.m.
Anthony John Dougherty, Brakeman

Dead tired, Dougherty sat on the brake wheel in the left front corner of the 807's cab. The machine was still tipped to that side, so it was easy for him to rest against the window. Half of Harley's section gang was with him, returning to Wellington for food and rest. Harley managed to convince the other half of his crew to keep working the slide, with the promise they would be relieved as soon as the plows returned. Steam rose from their wet wool coats. Some of the men even took off their shoes and placed their wet socks back on the plow's boiler to dry.

God, it stinks in here, Dougherty thought. *Should go back on the fire deck with Will. Be warm, smell hell of a lot better. Too damned tired to push my way through all these drunks.*

The shovelers kept a steady chatter, their mumbles largely inaudible. Dougherty caught the eye of Archie Dupy and motioned his head towards the workers. Dupy, sitting on the edge of the box covering the ring gear, merely shrugged and went back to dozing.

At least Blackburn's gone up front. Son of a bitch's been on my ass all afternoon.

Dougherty rubbed his hands against his face. His cheeks felt like they were being stuck with a thousand sharp needles. He wiped his nose with the wet sleeve of his coat, but felt nothing. His swollen fingers ached to the point he could hardly bend them. Even back on the farm in Minnesota, he could not remember being this wet, cold and miserable.

As Dougherty watched, the workers continued their hushed chatter. They were not smiling or joking. Whatever it was they were talking about, they were taking it seriously. Dougherty was curious, but too tired to care.

It was the worst afternoon Dougherty ever spent on the railroad. Working underneath the plow, he and others dug out the snow and chopped out a stump jammed between the plow's fan and leading truck. The entire time, Blackburn paced between them and the men shoveling at the slide, urging them on in one moment, cursing at them the next. It seemed to Dougherty that the pressure of the railroad being blocked and his plow out of commission was wearing on the trainmaster.

The snow bank was only two feet from the sides of the plow allowing little room for Dougherty to maneuver. At first he was on his stomach, using a short iron bar to loosen the packed snow. Dougherty would knock a block of snow out from the plow; a shoveler would pick it up and pass it back to others, as the banks were too steep to toss it aside. Eventually he was able to clear a hole large enough for him to sit upright under the machine, and then finally make room for Irving Tegtmeier to join him. As Dougherty jabbed snow from the twisted roots of the stump, "Tig" pulled it out and handed it to the shovelers standing alongside the plow. Dupy and his helpers were enduring the same torture on the other side. All the while, the engine crews and the men off the trailing plow were shoveling, trying to keep the storm from entombing the outfit where it stood.

"Get me an ax," Dougherty finally called out. "You boys get out from under here. Best let me chop this bastard out myself."

With no room to get the weight of his body into each swing, Dougherty had to concentrate all of his strength in his shoulders and forearms. With each swing the blade bit into the gnarled fir roots and Dougherty let out a loud grunt.

"Get me another ax!" he called out. "A sharp one, goddamn it!"

He tossed splinters of wood out from under the plow. Once, recognizing Blackburn's boots, he made sure a particularly large chunk of wood came spinning out from under the plow, slapping hard against the trainmaster's legs. To his satisfaction he saw the boots stomp off to the ladder and disappear up into the plow's cab.

When the last of the stump rolled out from under the plow, Tegtmeier crawled in and joined Dougherty to survey the damage.

"So … whatta ya think, Tig? Can we … get her leveled up?" Dougherty asked, still winded.

Tegtmeier studied the drive shaft extending from a broken bearing bolted to the plow's under frame. He scrambled further under the plow to get a closer look at the jackscrews and the worm gears that the bent shaft powered. When he slid next to Dougherty, his hat, and coat sleeves were smeared with grease from the mechanisms.

In an instant, Blackburn was crouching down, staring at the two men.

"Well, what the hell went wrong, Tegtmeier? Can we get her leveled up and keep bucking this slide?"

Sighing, Tegtmeier rose up to his knees.

"We're gonna have to go back to Wellington, Mr. Blackburn. I think we can block her up level, but we'll need the bridge jacks to do it. If we can get the pressure off the down side, we can get a pipe wrench on the drive shaft and work the jack screws level, then block her into place." Tegtmeier paused and studied the look on Blackburn's face. "You have to understand, Mr. Blackburn, with this broken bearing, she'll never hold the drive chain if we try to put power to the hoist. If we get her set, we still won't be able to raise or lower her, but she'll plow."

To Dougherty's surprise, Blackburn offered no argument. He seemed resigned to their retreat from battling the slide.

"Very well," Blackburn relented, "let's get the boys gathered up and get going. I need to get word to O'Neill that we're broke down."

A shake of his shoulder brought Dougherty out of a restless sleep.

"We're here, Al. Y'all might want to grab a bite to eat with me before Tig catches up to us." Dupy peered into Dougherty's still-blurry eyes. Once frozen tobacco juice was now dripping from the stubble on his chin.

"Damn, Arch, how long was I out?" Dougherty said, yawning.

"Dunno, I was sawin' 'em off myself. Maybe an hour. Harley's dagos piling off woke me up."

Still a little disoriented, Dougherty looked around the empty cab of the X-807. He glanced outside. It was still light, but snow continued to blow by the window. He pulled off his hat and rubbed his hand through his hair. He stretched, then slowly rose from the brake wheel.

"Damn, my ass hurts. What the hell time is it?"

"Your ass is gonna hurt one hell of a lot more, Al," Tegtmeier climbed into the cab. "It's half past four, if you must know. Harley and his boys are getting the jacks. Now set the brake and let's see if we can get this goddamned plow fixed. You can eat after we get her patched up."

"Christ, Tig, you're getting to be another Blackburn," Dougherty mumbled. "Let me find my gloves and I'll be out."

Blackburn spotted the outfit at the Wellington depot, near the section house that contained the tools needed to fix the plow. Climbing down from the cab, Dougherty stumbled upgrade alongside the pusher engines, toward the station platform where Harley's section crew was piling heavy wood blocks, chains, and dragging out the bridge jacks. Ben Jarnigan and Tom Osborne had climbed down from their engines. Hands inside their overalls, they paused their conversation as Dougherty approached.

"Hey Al," Jarnigan called, "We're gonna grab a bite. Wanna come along?"

"Love to, Ben, but Tig grabbed me. I guess he figures it's gonna take a couple of old farm boys like us to monkey rig the plow back together."

"We'll save some crumbs for you," Jarnigan teased.

Dougherty walked on past, hardly giving the men a glance. He looked up at the lights shining inside Bailets and the depot.

Nice and warm in there. Getting so hungry, don't feel hungry. Homer's bottle is still up in the plow. Pull a drag off it to stay warm. Best quit thinking of that. Blackburn's around somewhere.

It took both Dupy and Dougherty to pack one of the jacks from the station platform down to the 807. Dupy, his burly arm wrapped around the top, led the way as Dougherty manhandled the thick cast iron base. Tegtmeier and Homer Purcell followed with the second jack. Others trailed behind carrying armloads of wood blocking.

Dropping the heavy jack in the snow near the front of the plow, Dougherty rotated and rubbed at his right shoulder.

"Damn, don't remember those bastards being that heavy."

"Hell, Al, y'all's just getting fat and lazy with this easy-time railroadin' job," Dupy drawled, stuffing his cheek with another plug of tobacco.

Blocking and jacking was nothing new to the men. Dougherty grabbed a shovel and began to dig down through the snow, eventually hitting the ballast and the edge of the wooden ties. He and the others spread the gravel level, creating a base for the blocking. On their knees, the sharp edges of the exposed, frozen ballast dug into their pants. Dougherty and Tegtmeier grabbed thick hardwood blocks handed to them, jamming the bottom pieces against the rail. Once happy with the stability of the foundation, they stacked additional blocking in an alternate, cribwork formation to create a wide, level base for the jacks.

"Reminds me of the time me and the old man had to level up the barn after a tornado came through," Dougherty quipped as he laid one of the last blocks into place.

"Guess we've all done that a time or two," Tegtmeier answered. "Leveling up a barn. Sure seems like an easy job all of a sudden, don't it, Al?"

Crawling out, they brushed off the snow packed on the knees of their pants. Dougherty straightened up and then arched himself backwards, trying to ease the pain stabbing at his lower back. Tegtmeier was doing the same.

"This damned railroad is making old men out of us, Tig," Dougherty commented.

"Yeah, well, you think this is bad, just wait til you get married. Now grab that jack."

Made of heavy cast iron, each jack stood about three feet tall and weighed nearly 100 pounds. Dougherty and Gerry Jenks each took a grip on the iron ring handles at the top and, with a coordinated heave, swung the jack up onto the just-completed platform. Tegtmeier crawled back under the plow and carefully positioned the head of the jack to lift against the junction of a heavy steel cross member and the plow's outer frame.

"Okay boys, swing that other son of a bitch in here," Tegtmeier called out.

"I want her right here," he said, pointing.

Jenks and Dougherty slung the second jack into position.

Tegtmeier was precise in his final placement of the second jack, as well. "Now get that tie over there and lay it across the heads. You boys will jack against that tie, it'll push against the plow frame. Should be able to keep the jacks level that way."

Now the real fun, Dougherty thought. *Lifting this bastard up ain't gonna be easy. Need to get all of us on the jacks.*

Grabbing a long iron cheater bar, Dougherty inserted it into the jack. Dupy did likewise with the second jack. Protruding at a slightly upward angle, the end of the bar was nearly level with the big brakeman's shoulders. Dougherty and Jenks, being the tallest of the crew, worked the end of each bar. Jenks and Wells lent their strength to the jack manned by Dupy, Purcell and Parzybok gave aid to Dougherty.

"Now, when I say 'Give,' you boys raise your jacks one notch. The closer you do it together, the better off we'll be," Tegtmeier instructed.

The first four notches came easily as the heads of the jacks lifted the tie up against the frame of the plow. With each succeeding "Give!" the men pulled down hard on the cheater bars, lifting the jacks up one more notch. As the weight of the plow came to bear, the blocking began to snap and crackle due to the bases of the jacks pressing down into the wood rather than raising the front of the plow.

"The blocking holding up?" Dougherty called out.

"Doing fine, now give!" Tegtmeier hollered from under the machine.

The jacks ratcheted up another notch. The front of the plow began to rise. Suddenly there was a loud "crack!" as Dougherty's jack slipped and began to lean.

"Goddamn it!" Tegtmeier came bolting out from under the plow.

The men on the jacks knew the crib work would have to be shored up, and were already dropping the jack heads back down.

Dougherty joined Tigtmeier on the ground, inspecting the blocks.

Grabbing a splinted piece of wood from under the jack, Dougherty tossed it aside.

"Damned piece of fir. No wonder," Dougherty observed. "Arch, grab that chunk behind you. Make sure it's oak."

The cribbing rebuilt, the men again worked the cheater bars, slowly lifting the plow. Although each jack began to lean slightly as the front frame of the plow began to rise, the blocking held.

"One more time, boys," Tigtmeier called out. "Now, give!"

Grunting, their heavy breathing turning to steam in the cold air, the men on the jack handles pulled down with all their strength. For a moment, Dougherty's jack hung between notches. With a final burst of effort he reefed on the iron bar, putting all of his weight into the downward motion. The lock clicked into position.

Instinctively, Dougherty scrambled under the plow, and the remainder of the crew began to pitch blocking in after him. It was imperative to get the plow stabilized, in case the jacks slipped. Tegtmeier had crawled up against the frame of the front wheel set. Quickly, Dougherty began handing him wood to jam between the top of the wheel assembly and the bottom of the plow.

"Throw me a sledge!" Dougherty called out. Grabbing the heavy maul, he held it shoulder high and pounded the last of the blocks into position.

"That … should hold her … for now." Dougherty sat back in the snow to catch his breath.

"You boys have any idea what you're doing under there?" James Mackey was crouched down, looking under the plow.

"Jimbo! You're just the man I want to see. Crawl under here and take look," Tegtmeier exclaimed.

"Get us a couple of lanterns, will you, boys? Tig and Al are gonna need all the light you can muster," Mackey ordered, as he crawled in to join the two men.

"Jesus, what happened to you?" Dougherty asked as Mackey sat alongside. "Your face is cut all to hell."

"Let's just say Pete Imberg ain't quite ready to take a passenger train out of a station without spilling any water," Mackey commented. Seeing the confused look on both men's faces, he explained. "I got bucked off Pete's engine last night while we were servicing the outfit. Damn ice gets sharp when you hit it face first."

"How's Harrington's boys doing?" Dougherty asked.

"Not worth a damn," Mackey answered, joining Tegtmeier to inspect the damaged jackscrew drives. "Got 25 about half dug out and the overhead went dead. Got word you boys were down, so O'Neill split the outfit and sent me over to help. I come over with Lindsay on the 800. Frank's right behind us. Gonna shove the motors up on the coal track if you boys ever get outta our way. Jesus, Tig, things are busted all to hell under here."

"Bobby running the 800?" Dougherty asked.

"Sure is, but don't you get any ideas, Al. Got too damned much work to do," Mackey warned.

The men fell silent. Dupy handed Dougherty two lanterns. He held one up so that Mackey and Tegtmeier could get a better look at the broken mechanisms deep within the frame of the truck.

"Just what I figured, Jimbo," Tegtmeier interjected, "sheared a pin on the left side worm gear. Gonna be a bastard to fix. Got any ideas?"

Mackey was shaking his head. Grabbing the main drive shaft, he shook it.

"Here, Al, wrap this pipe wrench around the drive shaft and let's see if we can turn it. About the only way out of this is get the right side lowered, then drop the left side down onto a couple blocks to keep her level."

Dougherty slapped a large pipe wrench onto the drive shaft. He gave the handle a couple of hard tugs, barely turning the shaft.

"Get me a cheater pipe," he called out.

Damn. Must be getting tired. Weak as a kitten.

A three-foot section of pipe slipped over the handle of the pipe wrench gave Dougherty the leverage he needed. Pulling down hard on the very end of the pipe, the shaft spun, dropping the right jackscrew. Mackey and Tegtmeier helped Dougherty reposition the wrench for another bite. Again Dougherty jerked down hard on the cheater. Slowly the right side of the plow began to lower.

Two hours after arriving in Wellington, Dougherty, Mackey and Tegtmeier rolled out from under the plow. They slowly dropped the bridge jacks, and, the left side of the plow settled on the blocks that the men chained to the frame of the truck.

"Think she'll hold?" Dougherty asked.

"Doubt it," Tegtmeier admitted. "Not the way we're ramming her into that slide. Won't know until we try."

"Damn, here comes Blackburn," Mackey said. "If you boys want to get some supper, you'd better head for the hotel. I'll get Harley to send his boys down here to pick things up."

Dougherty, Dupy and the others walked around to the opposite side of the plow, avoiding the approaching trainmaster. Stooped against the wind and driving snow, they said nothing as they passed the shovelers working to keep the outfit clear.

In the last light of day, Dougherty could make out the X-800 halted east of the depot.

"Hey, Homer," Dougherty called out, "think I'll grab a couple of sandwiches and head over and see how Bobby's faring. I'll catch up with you boys down at the coal chute."

Thursday, February 24, 1910, 6:30 p.m.
John Robert Meath, Engineer

Hands numbed by the cold, senses and reflexes deadened by hunger and fatigue, Meath struggled with the master link on the hoist chain. He was crouched down in the small compartment below the floor of the cab of the X-800, straddling the clutch housing surrounding the machine's main drive shaft. "Bat" Nelson squatted beside him, his hands cupped to catch the link in case Meath dropped it. Above them, Ed Lindsay and Dan Gilmore, held lanterns. They had succeeded in repairing the broken drive chain that powered the hoist. All that remained was to slip the keeper into place to hold the master link.

Hundred million dollar railroad. Lose a two-cent keeper and we'll be shut down. Move slow. Concentrate.

"Keep your hands under that link, Bat," Meath cautioned. "We loose this keeper we're in a fix. Probably the only one between here and Everett."

Simple job's a major pain in the ass.

Pocketknife in hand, Meath carefully looped the closed end of the keeper over one of the exposed pegs of the master link. With the tip of his knife, he pressed on the thin metal until it snapped into the tiny machined groove. Keeping it in place with his thumb, he spread the keeper's open end. He held his breath as he used his knife to keep the end open and to pry it over the opposite master link peg. Slowly, carefully, he pulled his knife blade out. Meath let out a long sigh of relief when the sprung metal snapped into position.

"That should do it, boys." Meath said. "She's all yours, Ed. Hey, by the way, I have it on good authority that Mr. O'Neill wants you to try and keep it running."

"Ahhh, up yours, Bobby," Lindsay answered, with a smile.

Nelson made a half-hearted attempt to wipe the chain grease off his hands before putting his gloves back on. He handed the grimy rag to Meath.

"No thanks, Bat, I got enough grease on my hands already." Meath gave Lindsay a slight wink and then grabbed the rag.

Back alongside the boiler, Meath settled into a chair he had taken from the station the night before. Tired of the simple seat box, he had "removed" the piece of office furniture when Sherlock wasn't looking. He closed his eyes.

807's down. Poor Al. Must be catching hell. Damned trains are gonna get snowed in here just like over at Cascade. Food, sleep, a break in the storm. Take any one of the three.

Meath felt his strength ebb from his body. The nagging headache he was enduring for the better part of the day lessened. The loud, painful ringing in his ears brought on by the din of the plow eased as consciousness slowly slipped away. In his semi-lucid state, the heat radiating from the boiler conjured up an image of home in Meath's mind.

Hot summers. Milking those damned cows. In-between those damned churn heads. Heat coming off their coats. Flies everywhere. Not sure this is much better. The old man. Done milking by now. In the house with Mother. Nice and warm, stomach full.

The plow's shrill whistle caused Meath to snap his head forward.

"Wind her up, Bobby," Lindsay called out.

With a long sigh, Meath grabbed his whistle cord and gave it two short tugs, which Pete Imberg, pushing in the 1154, answered in kind. Meath slammed the reverse lever forward and pulled the throttle out. He felt the plow lower into position. He widened out the throttle and pushed the reverser into the furthest notch. A gentle jolt shook the machine as Imberg's engine began to bite the rail and the outfit moved forward. Meath's eyes were barely half open during the entire process.

"Hey, you lazy ass, wake up! I brought you something to eat!"

Eyes fully open, Meath focused on the form of Al Dougherty standing in the gangway door. For a brief moment the two friends stared at each other.

"Al, how come you're on our outfit?"

"Aw, just hitching a ride down to the coal chute. We got the 807 monkey-rigged back together. While they coaled her up I went and grabbed a bite. Here, Bailets fixed ya a couple of ham sandwiches. On the house, he said." Dougherty handed Meath two thick sandwiches wrapped in a napkin. "He wants the napkin back, though."

Meath took the parcel and set it up on the boiler, near the steam dome.

"No sense in eating cold food."

"Coming up on the runaway track switch, Bobby, slow her down," Lindsay called out.

Still standing, Meath pulled back on the throttle and reverser lever. He looked closely at Dougherty. Deeply sunken, bloodshot eyes, peeling, red skin, the growth of beard—his friend had aged ten years. Meath figured Dougherty was looking at the same sight.

"Wind her up, Bobby, plowing a full hood," Lindsay ordered.

"I tell ya, Al, they're never happy up there," Meath complained, as he pushed the Johnson bar forward and jerked on the throttle. He settled back in his chair, propping his right foot against the big lever.

"So how ya making out, Bobby?"

"About like you, from the looks of things." Meath glanced up at the steam gauge. "Bat's having one hell of a time with his fire. We stand too long in one place, snow melts down through the coal. Stoker pulls that wet shit through into the firebox. Can't keep this bastard steamed up. You boys having that problem, Al?"

"Can't say as I know. Been doing nothing but shoveling all day. Haven't even been in the plow."

"Coming up to O'Neill's car—slow her down, Bobby!" Lindsay hollered.

Meath pushed the throttle back by half and pulled back on the reverser. Lindsay was on the whistle cord signaling "all stop" and then "back up" to Imberg. Hearing the fan begin to race, Meath closed off the throttle and pulled the reverser lever into the straight up "neutral" position. He reached up and grabbed his now warm sandwiches, falling hard into his chair as the plow lurched backwards.

"So, got any plans when we finally get outta here, Bobby? Overdue for a stay in Everett, wouldn't you say?" Dougherty asked.

With a mouthful of ham sandwich, Meath held up his hand. He chewed quick and swallowed hard.

"Now you wouldn't be talking about a certain birthday coming up in a few weeks, would ya, Al? Hear you're about to turn 29. Be your last good year."

"How'd you know my birthday's coming up?" Dougherty was leaning against the plow's wall, his arms crossed.

Meath continued to devour the first sandwich. He gave Dougherty his best "innocent" look.

"Oh, word gets around, Al, word gets around."

"That's for damned sure. So you want to see if some of the boys want to meet up down at Everett when we get done up here?" pressed Dougherty.

"Bat" Nelson burst through the gangway door behind the two men.

"Bat, just the man I wanna see," Meath called out.

"Hey, Al, whatta you doing here?" Nelson inquired.

"He's looking to take a group of willing gentlemen down for a night on the town on Market Street," Meath offered, getting ready to bite into the second sandwich.

"Well, if you're buying, count me in. Tell Lindsay we've got less than an hour's worth of water." Bat turned and headed back out to the fire deck. Pausing in the doorway, he turned. "Hey Al, keep Blackburn busy and off our asses, will ya?"

"I'll do my best, Bat."

Nelson took a long look at the brakeman. "Take care of yourself, Al. When this is all over, I'm buying the first round. Hear tell you're turning 29. Another year and you'll look as old and wrinkled as Meath here." Nelson gave the two men a slight salute and headed back out onto the fire deck.

"I'd better get back to my outfit, Bobby. You ain't gonna get a drop of water until we get outta your way. I'll tell Lindsay about the water."

Meath rose from his seat and finished his sandwich. He carefully wiped his mouth with the napkin and gave it back to Dougherty.

"Make sure Bailets gets his napkin back, Al. He'll skin both of us if it comes up missing."

Meath followed Dougherty forward into the plow's cab. They were stopped next to the depot. Kerlee and Gilmore were on the ground, struggling to align the snow-clogged switches so the plow could continue cleaning the yard tracks. Lindsay stood alone, peering out the side door.

"Bat's got some bad news, Ed," Meath said. "Got about an hour's worth of water."

Lindsay pulled his head back in and merely shrugged.

"I figured we were getting low. You going back to your outfit, Al?"

"Yeah, best get going before Blackburn comes looking for me," Dougherty replied.

"Al's gonna be 29 in a few weeks, Ed. He wants us to join him for a drunken orgy down on Market Street soon as this is all over. You in?" Meath offered.

"You buying, Al?" Lindsay asked.

"Me buying? It's *my* damned birthday. You should be buying the women for me!" Dougherty protested.

"Well, if you boys get there before I do, save a nice plump one for me," Lindsay requested. "You know the old saying—the more there is of 'em, the more there is of 'em to love!" Lindsay cracked a big grin and slapped Dougherty on the back. "Be careful out there, Al. We're all getting a little rummy."

"You got it, Ed. See ya in Everett or see ya in hell."

Dougherty jumped down from the plow into knee-deep snow, Meath right behind him.

"How bad is it down there, Al?" Meath asked, with a look of seriousness Dougherty seldom saw on his friend.

Dougherty paused. Staring down, he kicked at the snow with his wet work boots.

"Real bad, Bobby. Real bad," he finally admitted . "The slide down at 3.3 is a big one. Solid. The fix we put on the 807, it ain't gonna hold. God's truth, Bobby, them trains ain't going anywhere until we get a break in this storm. Every hour we spend plowing out the slide, it takes us two hours to get back here for water and coal. We're losing ground, Bobby. God knows what it's like west of Windy Point."

"So what's Blackburn think?"

Dougherty frowned.

"He's just like us. Just trying to deal with shit as it comes up."

"About like Bill. He's working all of us hard too, but you can tell, he's scared as hell. We're all scared we ain't gonna get those trains off the mountain until this goddamned storm decides to blow itself out," Meath added.

Again there was silence.

"I gotta go, Bobby. We'll get that slide bucked so you can be the hero and lead those damned trains down the hill to glory. We'll have a time of it down in Everett when this is all over."

Meath was a man who seldom displayed emotion, and yet, even to his surprise, his arm went across the shoulders of his friend Dougherty.

"You look about as beat as a man can be, Al. Make Harley's boys do the hard work. Blackburn needs you on that plow, not on a goddamned shovel. You got that?"

"Wish it was that easy, Bobby, but we all gotta do our share and then some. You know that," Dougherty countered, stopping shy of scolding.

He threw his arm over Meath's shoulders.

"If you get to Market Street before I do, save a sweet little miss and warm bed for me, will ya, Al?" Meath joked.

"Only if you'll do the same for me, Bobby. I'll see ya down the line."

The two men separated. Dougherty turned and began to walk toward his plow set.

"Hey Al," Meath called out. "Thanks for the lunch. I know it wasn't on the house. I owe ya."

Not even turning, Dougherty waved and slowly disappeared into the storm.

Kerlee and Gilmore came up alongside of Meath.

"Al sure looks tough, don't he," Gilmore said.

"We all do, Dan." Meath climbed back into the plow.

Thursday, February 24, 1910, 2nd Trick Wellington
Basil Sherlock, Telegrapher

Sherlock's lunch sat tantalizingly close on his desk, but every time he reached for a sandwich, the telegraph key came to life. Each telegram had to be transcribed, with copies kept for O'Neill's secretary, Earl Longcoy. Across the mountain, the operator at Cascade Tunnel Station was also making copies to give directly to the superintendent, who had been there all day.

Finally a lull. Sherlock glanced to the rear of the room where Longcoy was sorting through the pile of messages. *Hate having him in here. Buzzing around like a fly. Watching every move I make. Probably keeping a list so he can tattle to O'Neill.*

Sherlock opened his lunch pail and pulled out a corned beef sandwich. He spread a napkin out on the desk, rested his elbows to each side, and took a big bite out of the middle of the thick slices of homemade bread. Althea bought the meat on her last trip to Skykomish, a few days before the storm had started. She cooked it yesterday, and they had a rather grand feast before he went to work. He awakened this morning to the smell of frying corned beef hash, his favorite.

The ring of the phone ended Sherlock's enjoyment. The sound immediately brought Longcoy from the back of the room to his side.

"O'Neill here. Do they have the lower yard cleared yet?"

"The plow is still down there, sir. I can't really see, the wind's blowing snow too hard," Sherlock answered, peering outside.

"Find out where they are and get back to me immediately. We're ready to send 25 over. Send Longcoy. Give word to the operator here as soon as you find out what that plow is doing. Is that clear?" O'Neill's voice snapped.

"Yes sir, Mr. O'Neill."

"Blackburn still to the west?"

"He left a little over an hour ago, sir. Had full tenders. I'm not expecting him anytime soon," replied Sherlock.

"Find out about the lower yard, and if Blackburn returns, I'm to be notified immediately." O'Neill abruptly hung up.

"Yes sir, Wellington out," answered Sherlock into a dead phone.

Sherlock hung up the receiver and looked at Longcoy. "When you came back from supper, did you notice where that plow was?"

"They had finished cleaning the yard and were headed back down to the coal chute," Longcoy answered with a tentative voice.

"Are you positive both sidings are clean?"

"Yes sir, I believe they are."

"Mr. O'Neill wants to bring 25 over. We need to know for certain if the sidings are clean and the plow is in the clear. The plow still has the staff, so I can't clear the block."

Longcoy, realizing Sherlock was not about to move from the warmth of the station, put on his coat.

"I'll be right back," he said.

"And get the staff," Sherlock ordered, as Longcoy slammed the station door.

No sooner had Longcoy walked out than he came right back in. On his heels was Ed Lindsay. Through the bay window in front of him, Sherlock could see Imberg in the 1154, pulling the snow plow to a stop alongside the station platform.

"Here's the staff, Sherlock, we're done. Ring up Cascade Tunnel, I need to get word to O'Neill," Lindsay ordered, handing both halves of the signal wand to Sherlock.

"Mr. O'Neill was just on the phone," Longcoy interjected. "We need to report to him the status of the passing tracks. He is about ready to move ..."

"I've got Cascade, Mr. Lindsay." Sherlock interrupted. He rose from his chair, allowing Lindsay to sit. Melting snow dripped from Lindsay's hat and coat. It formed a small puddle on the floor. Sitting at his desk with the receiver to his hear, Sherlock could tell the man was trying his best to control the waves of shivers engulfing him as the warmth of the station began to replace the cold that had permeated his body.

"Lindsay here, is Mr. O'Neill there?" He paused and listened. "Yes sir, the yard is clear, but you need to get those trains over here if you're going to. She's blowing hard. Snow will drift in the sidings. Yes, he's right here."

Sherlock reached for the phone.

"Not you, Sherlock. Mr. O'Neill wants to talk to you, Longcoy."

Irritated, Sherlock stepped away, allowing Longcoy to assume the operator's chair.

"Training a new operator, are you, Sherlock?" whispered a voice from behind. "Or is Longcoy teaching you the ropes of being O'Neill's right-hand man?"

Lindsay chuckled as he walked by. "Sorry, Sherlock, thought we had Meath under lock and key back in that plow. Didn't mean to turn him loose on you."

Furious at Meath, and wanting to listen in on the conversation Longcoy was having with O'Neill, Sherlock did not know which way to turn or how to respond. He glared at Meath.

"Will you please be quiet," he scolded in a loud whisper. "We are having an important meeting with Mr. O'Neill!"

"We?" Meath questioned. "Looks more like *them* to me."

"Come on, Bobby. Grab your coffee. Don't wanna get too warmed up. Get too comfortable we'll never wanna get back to work," Lindsay said.

"And I want my chair back, Mr. Meath!" Sherlock snapped. "I know you took it!"

Meath wandered over and poured himself a cup of coffee. He walked toward the door in silence. Just before stepping out, he looked beyond Sherlock and pointed.

"I believe Mr. Longcoy wants you to speak to Mr. O'Neill." Meath tipped his hat and left.

Face red, Sherlock wheeled around, nearly colliding with Longcoy.

Without saying a word to the young secretary, Sherlock sat down hard in the operator's chair. He took a deep breath to compose himself before he spoke.

"Sherlock here."

Instead of O'Neill, he heard the voice of the telegrapher at Cascade Tunnel Station.

"Sherlock, get things set up for 25. I'll ring you on the staff machine so you can clear Lindsay."

"I copy that, but where is Mr. O'Neill? Doesn't he need to talk to me?" Sherlock asked.

"He's headed back out. Guess they derailed the observation car pulling it out. He just told me to tell you to get the staff machine clear for 25. We'll let you know when 27 is ready. Longcoy can fill you in on the details."

"Very well," was all Sherlock said, but by then the operator at the other end of the line had hung up.

"Well, Longcoy, what are my orders, since it seems you have the details?"

"Train 25 is to go on the westward passing track, 27 will follow to be placed on the eastward passing track."

"That's it?" Sherlock asked, a little surprised at the lack of specifics.

"He had some personal things he wished me to handle. He'll follow 27 through and be here himself in a few hours," Longcoy allowed. "I'm sure he will have more specific orders for you once he arrives."

At 7:25 p.m. Sherlock cleared the staff machine for the movement of Train 25; at 7:35 p.m. the train slipped by the Wellington depot. Sherlock, stomping on one foot and then the other, stood out on the station platform. Hand extended, he caught half of the staff from Lou Holmes as he eased his lead helper engine past. Sherlock watched the coaches slip by. Inside, the passengers stared back through little holes they had wiped in the fogged windows. Leaning from the platform of the observation car, Conductor Pettit tossed off his half of the staff baton with an OS Form wrapped and tied to the shaft.

"Get ready. Passengers are gonna want to send telegrams!" he called out, as the train continued west into the siding.

"He must be joking," Sherlock muttered, hustling back into the warmth of the depot. Ignoring Longcoy, he rang Cascade Tunnel Station on the staff machine. The machine answered back with a loud "clang!" at which time it unlocked, allowing Sherlock to place the wand back into its slot. He released his palm from the button, ending the process that cleared the signals through the tunnel for the next train.

Sherlock took off his coat and settled back into his chair, pulling the scissored mouthpiece towards him. He pressed the foot treadle.

"Dispatcher. OS Wellington."

In a stuffy office in a nondescript building in Everett, Carl Johnson pressed his foot treadle. "Dispatcher."

"West, w-e-s-t First Class train 25, two five, by at seven thirty seven p.m. seven three seven p.m. seven, s-e-v-e-n cars, held on westward, w-e-s-t-w-a-r-d passing track 2, t-w-o, until further orders."

Johnson repeated back the information as he wrote it down on his nearly empty train sheet.

"That is correct," Sherlock intoned in an unemotional monotone.

"Any idea how long they're going to hold them up there, Sherlock?" Johnson asked.

"Haven't heard anything from Mr. Blackburn plowing to the west. Mr. O'Neill is coming through with Train 27 at any moment. Both trains will be held here until Blackburn returns and reports the line clear. Have no idea when that will be."

"A real mess up there, is it Sherlock?"

"I've never seen snow like this, I can tell you that, Mr. Johnson. Seven, maybe eight feet on the level. Getting drifts ten to twelve feet, maybe deeper."

"Copy that. Stay warm, Sherlock. Dispatcher out."

"Copy that. Wellington, out."

Nearly two hours passed before Train 27 was ready to come west. Sherlock whiled away the time with busy work around the depot.

Hate lulls. Glad Longcoy isn't here. Have a tough time looking busy.

He glanced at the clock. *Two more hours. Althea's got the stove stoked with more coal than one of these plows. Buried underneath a stack of quilts, no doubt. How do O'Neill and Harrington take it? Away from their wives all the time. Not my idea of being married.*

The ringing of the phone forced Sherlock to refocus his thoughts.

"Wellington. Sherlock."

"Cascade Tunnel Station, here. Sherlock, we're ready to send 27. They've got his helper pulled off and are gonna use it to give him a shove. Mr. O'Neill says that he'll just have his road engine, so keep him moving. He wants you to make sure everything but the runaway is lined, then call us back"

"The snow's blowing too hard, I can't see the yard from here," Sherlock countered.

"Well, you need to find out for sure, those are Mr. O'Neill's orders."

"You mean he wants me to walk down to the lower yard and check? No one will be here manning the station," Sherlock protested. "Even Mr. Longcoy has left for the time being."

"Don't know what to tell you, Sherlock. Those were Mr. O'Neill's orders. Best get a move on. You waste too much time and this train will get snowed in again. That happens you may as well head out into the storm and never come back."

"Very well. I'll ring you on the staff machine when things are ready."

"Break a leg, Sherlock." The line went dead.

Sherlock fumed as he donned his heavy coat.

No heavy boots for walking. Feet going to get soaked. Probably freeze off.

Sherlock made a point of staying out of the storm since it had started. Except for his brief walks from his house to the depot and the occasional mad dash for coal, he managed to stay indoors. Now faced with a quarter-mile hike down to the lower yard, he became engulfed with self-pity.

Easy for that operator at Cascade to tell me what to do. Stays in his warm little cozy office. Why does second trick get stuck with all the work? Clean the station, haul the coal, I handle more trains than anyone else. Sherlock do this, Sherlock do that. All in this God-forsaken hellhole.

Leaning against the wind, his nose was numb and running within minutes. He passed two Italian section men making a halfhearted attempt at keeping the runaway switch clean.

"Make sure that switch is not frozen!" he barked at the men.

They stared back at Sherlock in silence with their usual expression of non-comprehension.

"You know, back and forth!" Sherlock grabbed the switch lever and tugged at it. The mechanism refused to budge.

"Make it work! Make it work!" he hollered.

Again the men did nothing. Exasperated, he continued to walk down the tracks. In the distance he could make out the rear marker lights of Train 25, parked on the Number 2 track. Groups of men were huddled around small fires they built alongside the switches. Taking turns, one group of men would work at keeping the switch tracks clear of snow, while the others tried to keep warm in the gale.

"You there!" Sherlock called out, stumbling into the light of the first fire. "Train 27 coming. Number 3 track ready?"

To emphasize his point, Sherlock swung his arm in the direction of the station and then pointed down the route the train would take into the eastward passing track.

"Understand? Train coming. Go there!" Sherlock again pointed, hoping for a glimmer of understanding.

"I understand you, sir," one man said, his accent thick. "The yard tracks are ready. She can come right on in. We keep the switches clean, you tell them that."

Relieved, Sherlock turned and hustled back towards the station.

Running a railroad with ignorant foreigners. Come cheap. By the time you get through to them, normal person would have gotten the job done.

With his head down, Sherlock barely noticed the two men manning the runaway track switch. It was aligned for the steep ascending grade of the runaway route as per instructions and that was all that concerned Sherlock at the moment.

Once back inside the station, he headed straight for the staff machine, knowing that O'Neill was eager to get 27 moving. Not until the machine was cleared and confirmation received from Cascade Tunnel that a staff wand had been removed, did he finally take off his coat. Dripping wet, he hung the heavy garment near the coal stove to dry. He looked down at his shoes. They, too, were soaked, and his socks and feet felt nearly frozen. Sherlock was contemplating taking them off as well, and drying his socks, when the phone rang.

"Wellington, Sherlock."

"Just OS'ed 27. As soon as it's by, clear the machine. Mr. O'Neill wants to follow behind on the plow."

"I copy that."

"Remember, keep 27 moving. Sweeny said he's gonna start whistling for the runaway switch soon as he clears the tunnel."

"Don't worry," Sherlock said, getting a little irritated with the continual warnings. "I made it clear to the men keeping the switch clean they need to keep it from freezing up."

"Good."

In the usual abrupt manner, the line went dead. Concerned about the runaway switch, Sherlock put on his coat again. He grabbed a lantern off the wall and headed out the door.

To Sherlock's horror, no one was manning the runaway switch. Two shovels were leaning against the stand, but the men were nowhere to be found. Sherlock set down his lantern and pulled hard on the lever, but the switch points would not budge. Try as he might, he could not realign the track for the main line. In a near panic, he grabbed a shovel and began wildly tossing snow from between the rails and the mechanism operating the switch. He jerked hard on the lever yet again, but to no avail.

"Goddamned dagos!" he shouted as he continued to pitch snow. From the east he could hear the clear notes of a steam engine whistle. His heart was racing. He drove the shovel in-between the switch points and the main rail, prying so hard he broke the handle. In a rage he threw both pieces into the night.

By now, the diffused beam of the train's headlight cast a yellow glow in the thickly falling snow. The whistle blasts—four in rapid succession came clear and loud, and still Sherlock could not get the iced-over switch to move. Fearful that in the storm the engineer would not see the "Stop" signal outside the station, Sherlock grabbed his lantern, and with clumsy lunges tried his best to run upgrade, madly waving his arm in a wide semi-circle. Seeing the signal, engineer Ed Sweeny eased his train alongside the station platform and applied the brakes.

"Damned dagos," Sherlock puffed as he came up next to the engine cab. "Took off on me," he wheezed now nearly bent over. "Switch still froze. Need some help." Sherlock straightened up and for the first time looked at Sweeny.

"Jesus Christ, Sherlock, can't stay here long. I'll never get her going." Sweeney pulled his head back in and hollered across the cab to his fireman. "Hey, Harry! Sherlock's got his tits in a wringer. Give him a hand with the runaway switch."

Weary from the hard work of breaking loose the trains, Harry Partridge dropped down from the engine onto the platform.

"Never thawed out a switch before, Sherlock? What kinda railroader are you anyway? Shovel out some hot coals from your stove into a bucket and get 'em down to that switch damned fast!" Rolling his eyes at Sweeny, Partridge was still shaking his head as he stepped down from the platform and made his way to the switch.

Hands smudged with coal soot, Sherlock was still breathless when he arrived with the coals.

"Dump this load right here at the base of the switch stand. We'll get the pivot gears thawed first. Now run back and get another bucket."

"That will just about put out the fire in the station stove," Sherlock argued.

"I don't give a damn about your stove. Get me another bucket of goddamned coals and make it quick!"

Sweeney, not about to let the storm's grasp overpower his train, whistled for a reverse move. Pushing upgrade against the cars on a slick, icy rail, he barely moved ten feet before his engine lost its footing. He tried easing ahead, but without being able to gain any speed and momentum, found himself becoming quickly hemmed in by the blowing snow.

"The snow's binding me in!" he hollered at Sherlock, who was sprinting from the station with another bucket of coals. "Get your ass moving!"

"Sprinkle 'em next to the hinges on the switch points, there!" Partridge ordered. "Take your foot and work 'em in close."

Ruined my shoes, Sherlock thought, nudging the red-hot cinders of coal against the rails of the switch. *Those goddamned dagos. Harley and O'Neill are going to get a full report. Railroad owes me a pair of shoes.*

"Get over here on the lever with me, Sherlock!"

Partridge, having fun being a taskmaster at my expense.

"Okay, grab a hold with me. When I count to three, pull for all you're worth. One! Two! Three!"

Both men gave the switch lever a quick, hard jerk.

"She gave a little, Sherlock, but I was doing all the pulling. One more time and this time put your balls in it. One! Two! Three!"

Sherlock planted his feet and with his teeth clinched, pulled on the lever as hard as he could. To his surprise, Partridge suddenly let go and stood aside. The switch was already broken free. Caught off balance, Sherlock was still straining against the lever when it slammed against the stop, sending him wheeling into the snow.

"No time for playing in the snow, Sherlock. Best get back up to the depot and get Ed moving," Partridge teased. He grabbed Sherlock with his grease-stained, gloved hand and pulled him up. "And don't forget your coal bucket. Might have to use it to rebuild your fire."

Given the "all clear," Sweeny began rocking his train back and forth. It took three attempts to gain enough momentum to break loose from the snow that was already piling against the wheels of the engine and cars.

As the cab moved past the end of the platform, he handed off his half of the signal staff to Sherlock. "That was a close one," is all Sweeny said as he moved on by.

Walter Vogel, the conductor, tossed his half of the baton off as well. "Had to show the delay on the OS. Sorry!" he called out.

Sherlock went back into the station. His hands were raw and numb, his fingers refusing to move. The sleeves of his coat were filthy, covered with a mixture of coal soot and melting snow. Taking it off, he saw that even the cuffs of his white shirt were black. He looked at himself in the reflection of the window. He had black smudges along his red cheeks and forehead.

What a night, he thought as he cleared the staff machine.

He sat at his desk and OS'ed Train 27 to Dispatcher Johnson.

"Why the delay, Sherlock?" he asked.

"Runaway switch froze up," Sherlock replied.

"That's your responsibility to keep it open, you know that, don't you?" Johnson reprimanded.

"I had two section men stationed there, but they took off. Not my fault!" Sherlock's temper was about to snap.

"Alright, alright, calm down. Dispatcher out."

The telephone was ringing.

"Wellington, out." Sherlock picked up the receiver. "Wellington. Sherlock."

It was O'Neill. "What's going on over there? Clear the damned staff machine so we can come west!"

"Sherlock! Ring up Cascade Tunnel Station!" Blackburn boomed, bursting through the door and slamming it shut.

"Dear God, man, you scared the hell out of me!" Sherlock stammered.

"What's that you say?" O'Neill asked.

"Mr. Blackburn just arrived, sir," Sherlock said into the phone.

He looked up from the desk at the towering frame of Blackburn. "I'm talking to Mr. O'Neill right now," Sherlock told him.

"What's that you say, Sherlock?" O'Neill asked. "What the hell's going on over there?"

"Give me that phone, I need to talk to Mr. O'Neill." Blackburn all but pushed Sherlock aside, chair and all, in an effort to grab the telephone.

"Mr. Blackburn is here. I'll give him the phone and clear the staff, sir."

Sherlock gladly gave his headset to the agitated Blackburn and busied himself clearing the staff machine. He kept a close ear to the conversation the trainmaster was having with O'Neill.

"Blackburn here. The 807's down for good. Afraid we didn't make much progress down at 3.3. As soon as we bucked into the hard snow, the blocks slipped out and she went back down." Falling silent, Blackburn listened.

"Very good sir, we'll hang tough right here. I'm going to need the 800 as soon as we can get her coupled in. I want to get back west right away."

Again Blackburn listened.

"Yes sir, if that's what you think is best, I'll wait. I guess we might just as well drop off the 807. We'll spot it behind 25 on the number two track and drop the fire. Blackburn out."

Ignoring Sherlock, Blackburn bolted up out of the chair, slapping his hat hard against his thigh.

"Goddamn it anyway! No damned reason to wait around for him to get here. Grab the damned 800 and get back to that goddamned slide!" Blackburn opened the door. "When O'Neill gets here, tell him I'll be back as soon as I get the 807 out of the goddamned way."

Storming out of the station, he slammed the door.

Sherlock pushed on the release button on the staff machine.

God help me. Blackburn's on a tear. O'Neill and Harrington on their way over and I look like hell.

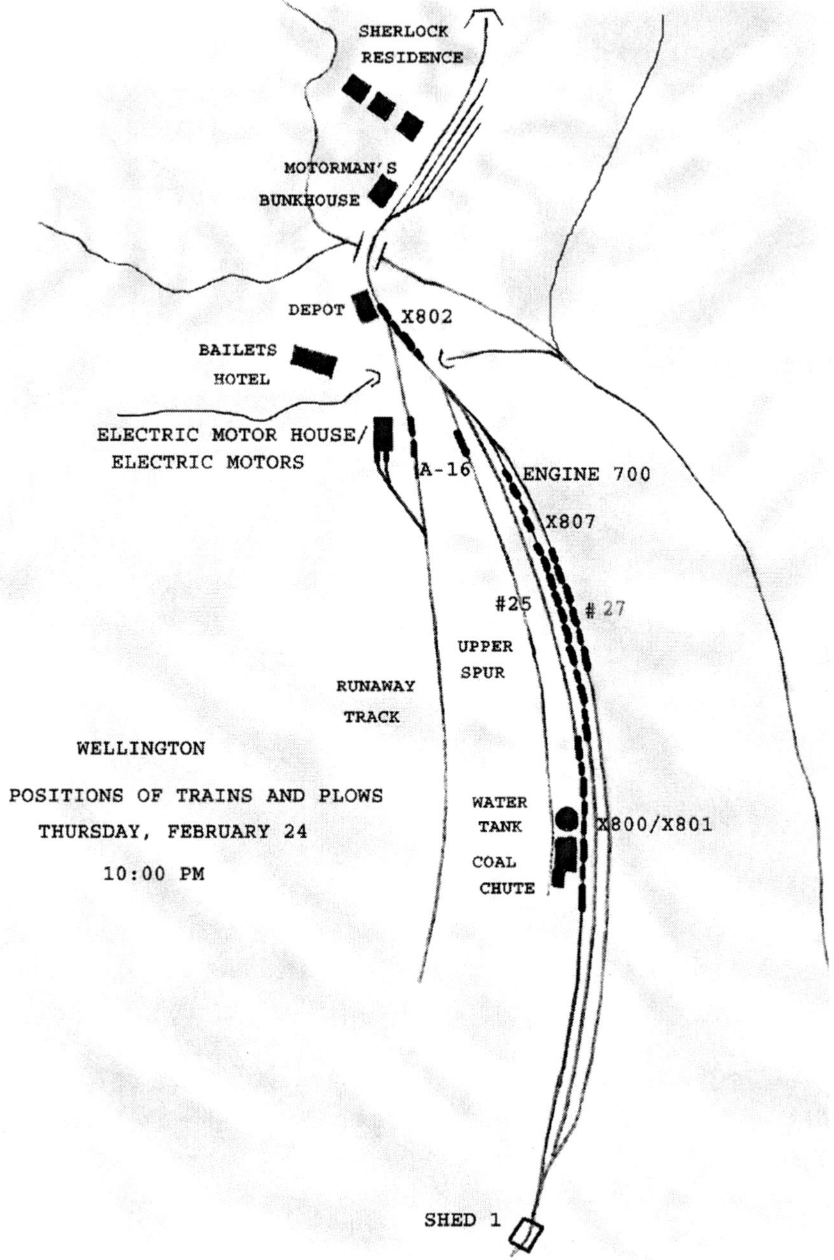
SHERLOCK
RESIDENCE
MOTORMAN'S
BUNKHOUSE
DEPOT
X802
BAILETS
HOTEL
ELECTRIC MOTOR HOUSE/
ELECTRIC MOTORS
A-16
ENGINE 700
X807
#25
#27
UPPER
SPUR
RUNAWAY
TRACK
WELLINGTON
POSITIONS OF TRAINS AND PLOWS
THURSDAY, FEBRUARY 24
10:00 PM
WATER
TANK
COAL
CHUTE
X800/X801
SHED 1

Thursday, February 24, 1910, 10:30 p.m.
James Henry O'Neill, Superintendent

Jumping from the moving snow plow, O'Neill paused for a moment on the platform outside Wellington station. He hadn't changed clothes since arriving Tuesday morning. Beyond just being cold, he felt dirty. He rubbed his face, the palm of his hand scratching against the stubble of his beard. A hot bath, dry socks and a fresh shirt would be a luxury, but he knew now was not the time for such indulgences.

O'Neill reached for a cigar, staring at the lights of his private car. He inspected the wet tobacco and threw it to the ground. *Can't have dry clothes. By damned I'm going to have dry smokes.*

Harrington swung down off the plow, hollering over his shoulder at Clary, his voice noticeably hoarse. "Tie her down on the runaway clear of the main, Ira! Better tell the boys to get some grub and a little sleep while Blackburn's outfit takes coal!" Harrington opened the station door and paused, "Coming in, Mr. O'Neill?"

A tattletale fog escaped O'Neill's lips as a sigh combined with a yawn. He rubbed his eyes and shook his head, trying to overcome the weariness that was fast overtaking his body and mind.

"Was thinking about getting clean clothes," he allowed, " but I see Mr. Blackburn is in there, best not keep him waiting."

O'Neill followed Harrington into the depot. He ignored Blackburn and Sherlock. Instead he fixed his eyes on Earl Longcoy.

"Mr. Longcoy. Hate to send you out in this, but I need some dry cigars. Run over to my car and have Lewis hunt some up. Wouldn't mind a bite to eat too. Have Lewis send something back with you."

"I'll be right back, sir," Longcoy said with his usual enthusiasm. He grabbed his coat and hustled out the door.

"Sherlock, what is the latest from Dowling?"

"Haven't heard a word from Skykomish, sir."

"Probably broke down," Harrington mumbled.

"Get them on the phone, telegraph if you have to, I want to know where he is and the status of his plow."

"Yes sir."

"Mr. Blackburn, Mr. Harrington, get your coffee and let's go to the back room. We need to get things hashed out. Sherlock, when Longcoy gets back, tell him we're in the back. If you hear from Dowling, relate the message to Longcoy."

"Might it be better if I give you the message directly when received, sir?" Sherlock argued.

"It might be better, but I want you by this key at all times. Now do what I tell you!" O'Neill snarled, raising his voice.

Sherlock's face became red. Without saying another word, he turned back to his desk.

"Gentlemen, after you," O'Neill motioned towards the back room. He grabbed a dirty cup from a hook on the wall and filled it with the last of the pot of coffee. "Just my damned luck, the dregs."

The smell of kerosene was thick in the small room located off the main office. With the electricity out, Sherlock lit all the old lamps that were still affixed to the walls. Grabbing a chair, O'Neill half-carried, half-dragged it across the floor. Blackburn and Harrington settled in on either side of the door. O'Neill slammed his chair against the wall opposite the men and motioned to Harrington to close the door.

"Forgot just how smelly these old oil lamps were," O'Neill observed. "Never noticed it back before we had juice."

"So the 807 is busted all to hell?" Harrington asked Blackburn as he unlaced his boots.

"Fraid so. Hoist is broke," Blackburn replied staring at the floor, hat in hand.

"Christ, picked a fine time to tear up a plow." One of Harrington's boots hit the floor.

"We probably shouldn't have brought the trains over so soon. Gonna be awhile before we can get that slide bucked out," Blackburn told O'Neill, ignoring Harrington. "Damned passengers are going to be underfoot and right in the way."

"Your busted up plow's a bigger problem then the damned passengers." Harrington kicked off his other boot in a fit of temper.

"Forget about the damned plow! It's down and that's that!" Blackburn shouted back.

Need a smoke. Don't need those two fighting. Harrington's beat. Not his usual easy-going self. Been working like a slave all damned day. Blackburn's been ordering the boys all day. Not really working. He can go a little longer, looks to me.

"Well, at least we got the trains busted loose and moving. All we need now is get that slide bucked out," Harrington said with a hint of sarcasm.

"What do you mean by that? What the hell you think we've been trying to do for two goddamned days straight? Picking our goddamned asses?" Blackburn threw his hat to the floor.

O'Neill heard enough.

"What's done is done, gentlemen. The decision to move those trains was mine and that's final. And yes, that plow going down is a problem, but nothing we can't figure out." O'Neill's voice was measured, steady, and firm, leaving no doubt in the minds of his trainmasters this was not the time for bickering.

"Now then, Art, I need to know exactly the status of things down at Shed 3.3."

"We're about half through the slide. Maybe another 500 feet to buck. We're through the deepest part, don't really need shovelers, just need a plow that we can buck with. The 807 just can't handle being rammed into the cut. Not with that busted jackscrew. If we keep bucking with her tilting the way she is we'll tear the forward truck right out from under her."

"So you tried blocking it up level?" O'Neill asked.

"We did, but they won't hold when we buck," Blackburn conceded.

"The blocks just pop right out. Tig and Jimbo are re-blocking it right now."

"What the hell for?" Harrington asked. "If the son of bitch won't hold together, why bother?"

"You can clear loose snow with it, just can't buck a slide." Blackburn was obviously becoming defensive. "I've got to have the 800 straight away. I need another engine too."

"Another engine? Jesus! Next you'll want my whole damned crew!" Harrington snapped, dropping his hat to the floor.

"The pilot of the 700 is cracking, all that ramming into the slide. We're sidetracking it along with the 807," Blackburn admitted.

"So now you're gonna rob me of my lead plow and engine?" Harrington asked, trying to control his growing rage. "Christ, just redouble me with the 800 and I'll work west."

"Seems to me your boys are about done in," Blackburn insisted. "Best send my crew back, we know what we're up against."

"So now I don't know how to buck a slide?" Harrington countered.

Blackburn opened his mouth to respond but was cut short by a gentle knock at the door.

"Yes, come in," O'Neill said.

Harrington reached behind himself and flung open the door. Longcoy walked in, a covered tray in hand.

"Excuse me, gentlemen. Lewis sent along your cigars and this platter of hot beef sandwiches. He says there should be enough here for the three of you."

"Thanks, Earl. Put the platter over on that shelf. Sherlock heard from Dowling yet?" O'Neill asked, already lighting up a cigar.

"Yes sir, just arrived at Skykomish. They're going to take a meal while they get serviced then head straight out for Scenic. They hit heavy snow from Index on up, but report the line from Everett to Sky clear. The spreaders seem to be keeping up."

O'Neill blew a puff of smoke out of the side of this mouth. He rose from his chair and walked to the door.

"Don't be shy. Eat up, boys. I'll be right back."

With Longcoy at his heels, O'Neill left the room.

Gotta get out of there. Let those two get a little grub in their stomachs.

Maybe they'll quit yelling at each other. Good men separate - a couple of hissing wildcats when they're together.

"Sherlock! Ring up the dispatcher! I need to talk to him," O'Neill bellowed. *Something about Sherlock … fun hollering at him.*

"Right away, sir!" Sherlock locked in his phone wires and pressed the foot treadle.

"Dispatcher. Wellington. Mr. O'Neill is here, hold on."

Getting damned tired of trying to run a railroad from the middle of nowhere.

Sherlock moved from his chair and handed the headset over to O'Neill. Cigar dangling from his lips, O'Neill sat down.

"Mr. Johnson, copy … let's see, two, four, six, make it copy seven To C&E First Class trains 2, 26, 28. T-w-o, two, six, and two, eight." With that, O'Neill dictated orders that would send the three trains waiting in Skykomish back west to Everett, to wait for the line to reopen.

As he rose from the chair, O'Neill took another quick puff off his half-burned smoke; a long ash was about to drop off.

"Keep in close touch with Skykomish, Sherlock. I want to know when Dowling clears town. Any news from Devery in Leavenworth?"

"None of late, sir."

"Damn it. Need to know the status of the Tumwater," O'Neill mumbled.

O'Neill turned and walked back into the small room, now smelling of warm beef.

"What'd Lewis send up boys?" O'Neill snubbed out his cigar and grabbed a thick sandwich from the plate.

Mouths full, neither Blackburn nor Harrington could answer.

Biting into the warm bread and meat, for the first time in days, O'Neill allowed himself to relax. He devoured the sandwich, wiping his mouth on his coat sleeve. "Okay, boys, let's get down to business."

Unsuccessfully suppressing a yawn, O'Neill rubbed his eyes and face. He pulled out another cigar. Striking a match against the seat of his chair, he lit up.

"Bill, I'm going to give Art the 800. She's ready to go, and you have to service the 802. We can get back down there quicker this way."

"Understood," Harrington said, "but we need to start getting these outfits double-crewed. With the electrics down, we've got extra men. Meath and Nelson haven't left that plow since yesterday morning. All of the boys are about dead on their feet."

"My crews have been pressed just as hard, maybe harder, Bill," Blackburn countered. "Need to keep our crews together. They're used to working with each other. Makes it a damned sight easier to oversee what's being done."

"Oh bullshit, Art! You can't run a man like a goddamned machine. They need regular food and rest. None of us are getting either. No reason to push us until we drop dead from exhaustion."

"Nonsense, Bill!" Blackburn argued, his voice matching the strength of Harrington's. "Give me a good plow and my boys will buck that slide in a matter of a few hours."

"You're full of shit, Art, and all three of us know it," Harrington continued to press his point. "Your boys are just as beat as mine. You need a good plow alright, I'll give you that, but if you're gonna buck that slide, you need fresh men under you."

Goddamn, listen to those two. Like kids fighting over a piece of penny candy. O'Neill puffed hard on his cigar, working to control his temper.

"Alright, both of you! We're not getting a damned thing decided." O'Neill got up and walked over to the food tray. He grabbed an apple. Giving it a quick polish, he sunk his teeth into its crispy, juicy flesh. Cigar in one hand, apple in the other, the big bite in the side of his mouth, he stared down his trainmasters.

"Imberg and the 1154 are behind the 800, right Bill?"

"Yes sir."

"We don't have a choice here. They'll have to be doubled with the 801 and go west to buck that slide." O'Neill took another big bite, the crackle of the apple echoing in the bare room. He flicked the ashes off his cigar. "Any idea how we're doing for coal? Wish to hell we got that delivery. Been going through it pretty good the last couple of days."

"Plenty still coming out of the chute. I think there's still another partial car on one of the upper spurs," Blackburn said.

"We should be good for a day or so yet, then," O'Neill surmised. Finishing his apple, he resumed smoking. "I'm going west with Art on the double set. Bill, once your boys are fed and rested, I want you to team up with Mr. Harley and try and keep those goddamned trains from getting snowed in like what happened over at Cascade Tunnel."

"Be nice to have the 801. Gonna be running her the whole time, that 15 ton tender would make life easier," Harrington suggested.

"I need both 15 ton tenders," Blackburn interrupted. "We've been bucking hard each time we come back from 3.3. If we run out of coal trying to get back here, that's it, we're done for."

"Art's right, Bill. Besides, we've been having one hell of a time switching in this storm. I don't want to start busting these plows apart if I don't have to."

"You can double with the 807 if you need to, Bill. She'll plow, just have to go easy," Blackburn suggested.

"So you're telling me you don't want to take the time to switch out and give me a decent lead plow, but it's fine if I spend the rest of the night switching in a piece of junk you've busted all to hell."

The sarcasm in Harrington's voice hung as thick in the air as the smoke from O'Neill's cigar. He re-laced his boots in silence, finally looking straight at O'Neill.

"I'll do what I can with the 802. What about double crewing?"

"Use Jarnigan and Ross off the 700 along with the crew off the 807 for relief," Blackburn snapped.

"You've got Lindsay, Purcell and White already. If you're going to take the 800, then leave me Parzybok to relieve Clary," Harrington bartered.

Blackburn was about to offer a complaint, but O'Neill stopped him short.

"That should work. Lord knows with me and Art and three conductors, we'll have more chiefs than warriors."

O'Neill rose from his chair, yawned and stretched. He felt he should say something, some words of wisdom or encouragement, but fatigue dulled his mind.

Just want to get this line open. Get these goddamned trains outta these mountains, he thought. *Need to set the example. If I don't look confident, never keep the men working.*

"We're gaining on it, boys," O'Neill said. "The trains are busted loose, we get another 500 feet of track clear and we can send those snooty businessmen on their way to Seattle and be rid of them." He walked by Harrington and gave him a good pat on the shoulder. "Get your plow down to the coal chute after we leave. While they're coaling her up, get a few winks, Bill. You need it."

"Art, I'm going to grab a few more smokes from my car. I'll meet you at the coal chute. Don't you leave without me. I wanna be there when we finally clear that goddamned mess at Shed 3.3"

Striding out the door, O'Neill boomed across the room, "Sherlock! Look sharp, man!"

Damn, I like yelling at that poor kid.

Friday, February 25, 1910, 3:30 a.m.
William Harrington, Assistant Trainmaster

Wrapped in a blanket on the cold floor of the motormens' bunkhouse, Harrington struggled to get comfortable. In one position, pain shot through his lower back. If he rolled over and tried sleeping another way, the dull ache around his neck and shoulders prevented him from relaxing. All around him, men were fast asleep. Their heavy breathing and snoring alone were enough to keep a person awake. Even when Harrington felt himself drift into unconsciousness, he snapped awake, his mind involuntarily racing with thoughts of the coming day or regrets for being there at all.

Getting too old for this. Should've listened to Lil. Never should've taken this goddamned job. God, I miss Lil.

"Bill, it's half past three," came a voice. "You said you wanted me to roust you out."

"Oh God," Harrington mumbled, slowly sitting up. He rubbed his face and yawned, trying to focus on something in the dark room. "That you, Harley?"

"It's me alright, Bill. Jarnigan and Ross, you know where they're bedded down? I'll get them up too."

Harrington leaned to his right and shook the prone body next to his.

"Wake up Benny, Mr. Hill needs you," he whispered. "Thanks, Harley, I'll get the boys going. Still snowing?"

"Hell yes, and just listen to that goddamned wind," Harley said as he left.

Jarnigan sat up. "Jesus, Joseph, and Mary, would you listen to that wind. You sure you want to go out in this, Bill?" Jarnigan asked.

"Best get your buddy Ross woke up. I'll grab Ira and have him get his boys going. Parzy and his crew will need to take a break," Harrington said, throwing off the brown-checked blanket he had taken from Train 25's baggage car earlier.

God, feel worse now than before I laid down, Harrington thought, rotating his stiff shoulders. *Shoulda just kept working instead of taking a nap. Another tough day, can just feel it.*

His coat buttoned to his chin, Harrington stepped out into the storm. A fierce wind was blowing down from the east out of the summit gap in the mountains. Grabbing his hat, he turned his back to the gale and walked towards the depot. Snow drifted heavily across the main line. The outfit cars spotted on the three short spurs directly across from the bunkhouse were nearly covered. Even the section house was buried. The only visible parts were the stovepipe protruding from the top, and the door on the side.

With a firm grasp on the handle, Harrington opened the door to the station. The door gave a quick lurch as the wind pushed it open, nearly pulling the wrought iron latch out of his hand. Quickly entering the room, he leaned his shoulder against the door in order to shut out the storm.

"When did this wind start kicking up, Mississippi?" Harrington asked.

"Not long after I relieved Sherlock, I reckon, Bill. Long about half past one or so," Avery told Harrington in his thick southern accent.

"So what's the latest?"

"Well, can't say as I can tell ya much, Bill. Phone's dead between here and Cascade, so is the staff machine. O'Neill and Blackburn just got back. They're down at the coal chute. Still ain't through that slide down at Shed 3.3. Needed to get more shovelers. I sent Harley over to wake you up since he was out scramblin' for shovelers anyways."

"Any good news? Where's my plow set?"

"Ain't seen them all night. Reckon they's down yonder gettin' coal, too. Be good if you could make a pass up this way. Sure would help out the boys trying to get over to the cookhouse car," Avery suggested.

"I'll see what I can do, making no promises, mind you. Staff machine down, you say?"

"Yep, happened couple of hours ago, near as I can tell. Went to call Cascade on the phone and it was dead, so tried ringing them up on the machine. Never got a response. No sense in worrying about it till it gets light. Ain't no trains moving anyways."

"Telegraph still working?" Harrington asked.

"To the west. Everything east is still dead. Hell, can't even key Cascade right now."

The station door flew open. Clary and his crew hustled inside. Cold wind rushed in with them like a demon, swirling about the office. It sent a stack of telegrams into the air, driving them to one side of the room, just as it was doing with the snowflakes outside. Al Dougherty and Archie Dupy were the last to walk in, both men fumbling at the door handle.

"Hurry up and close the goddamned door!" Avery scowled, flopping his arms and body over his desk in an attempt to keep the remaining papers in place.

"So where the hell is Parzybok? We gonna have to go on a forced march to relieve him?" Clary asked.

"Down in the lower yard somewhere. We'd better get on down there, boys," Harrington sighed.

Again the door flew open. Charlie Baker, who had been tending the engines at Cascade Tunnel Station, stumbled in.

"Slide hit! Cookhouse...gone!" he gasped.

His clothes soaked, his face beet red, he immediately doubled over, dropping his lantern on the floor. As he wrapped his arms around his chest, his entire body shook. Clary and Harrington grabbed him by an arm to hold him steady.

Coughing, Baker leaned hard on Harrington and allowed himself to be led across the room. He fought to catch his breath and regain his composure as he sat down next to the stove.

"You say a slide? How bad, whereabouts?" Harrington knelt, eye level with Baker.

"Hit the cookhouse. Bjerenson, Elerker gone."

"Whadda mean gone?" Clary interrupted.

"Too dark, can't find them. Probably dead."

Harrington's head jerked upward at the news. "Mississippi, you say O'Neill and Blackburn are down at the coal chute?"

"Jesus, God." Avery looked to be in shock as well.

"Are O'Neill and Blackburn still coaling?" Harrington repeated, loader.

"Reckon they still are," Avery finally answered.

"Al, Archie, get down there now! Find O'Neill and tell him Cascade's been hit by a slide." Harrington barked. The two men grabbed their lanterns, and, holding their hats, were out the door in an instant.

"What about the station?" Harrington asked.

"Yeah, anyone else get killed?" Jarnigan interjected.

"What about Bergstrom's boys? Any of them in the cookhouse when she hit?" Clary added.

"Shut up! All of you!" Harrington roared. "One question at a time and I'm doing the asking."

"What about the station?" Harrington asked once again, his voice turning patient.

"Just missed it. Miracle it's not gone. Bergstrom was trying to get a head count when I left. Not sure if any of his boys got killed. Couple got a little banged up, but were walking around. Francisco, all of us trainmen are fine." Baker finally sat upright, taking a deep breath. "Feeling a little better. The snow between here and the tunnel is deep, Bill, real deep. Damned near has the portal of the tunnel plugged."

"What about over at Cascade? How big is the slide?" Harrington continued to draw from Baker as much information as he could.

"Hard to tell. Still dark when I left. Wind's been drifting snow all night just like here. I'd guess the slide is only ten, maybe twelve feet deep, not sure how wide, maybe five hundred feet, could be more."

Harrington got to his feet and found himself surrounded by the rest of the crew.

"We'd better get a move on, boys. Charlie, you work with Mississippi. Get a telegram out to Brown and Gruber straight way. Send it line and coded. Might as well start filling out a slide report. I'll pass the details to Mr. O'Neill." Harrington paused and patted Baker on the shoulder. "Get some coffee, Charlie."

Head down, one hand stuffed in a coat pocket, the other holding a lantern, Harrington followed behind Clary and the rest of the crew. Wind-blown snow covered the tracks to the point the men took turns breaking a trail through the drifts. The stand marking the runaway switch loomed out of the predawn darkness and the blinding white torrent. Harrington glanced back towards the station, but its muted lights had already disappeared. Squinting, he looked toward the hill to his right for the hotel, but it too was lost in the blizzard.

Two dead. God be with 'em. Gotta break soon. Gotta. Can't see ten yards.

"Keep your lanterns swinging boys, and listen for that goddamned plow. They'll never see us in this," Harrington warned.

"I see her up ahead. They're stopped!" Clary called out.

Once alongside the idling plow, Harrington shouted up into the cab. "What goes here, John? You broke down?"

Clary had already climbed inside when Parzybok stuck his head out. Jarnigan and Ross continued down the line to the pusher engine.

"We're stuck, Bill. Snow sloughed in behind us, can't go forward or back. The boys are behind the engine shoveling. Sent Charlie Smart down to get Blackburn to plow up behind us," the young Parzybok told Harrington. "Making things worse, damned wind's been blowing the snow right back into the fan. Bastard just doesn't want to blow."

Following Clary into the cab, Harrington knocked the snow off his broad-brimmed hat.

"Got bad news, John. A slide hit the cookhouse over at Cascade last night. Not sure yet, but they think Harry and Johnny are dead," Harrington said in a somber tone.

"Oh God." Parzybok was noticeably shaken.

"Are you certain O'Neill and Blackburn are coming this way? I need to get word to them."

"They were coaling up. Been a couple of hours, I'd guess. Sent Smart back a good hour ago," Parzybok related. "They must be close."

"Okay. Hang tough, John," Harrington said. "I'm going to walk back and meet up with them."

Lantern in hand, Harrington climbed off the plow and made his way back. Passing behind the tender of the 1128, he met up with the men shoveling at the mound of snow that had fallen across the tracks. A few of them paused from their work. Harrington heard a few voices mumble "too bad about Harry and Johnny" before they went back to their labor.

Jesus Christ. Never seen anything like this.

As he passed the cars of Train 25, he saw its coaches were already becoming snowed in. Harley and his Italian section men had been working around the cars throughout the night, but were losing ground to the storm.

Even if they get the line open, gonna take all day just to bust these trains loose. Just like yesterday. Harrington stopped and listened for a moment. The unmistakable sound of the spinning fan of a rotary and its hurried exhaust could be heard. Stepping to his left, he skirted alongside the passenger coaches, weaving his way between the shovelers working around the wheel sets.

No goddamned way these trains are moving until it quits snowing. O'Neill and Blackburn best come to their senses. Take a couple days after the storm passes just to dig out.

The diffused light from Harrington's lantern revealed the churning blade of the X-801. Gusts of wind bent the plume of snow exiting the chute back against the car body, covering the machine to the smoke stack. As the plow inched by, Harrington hooked his arm around the grab iron and scurried up into the cab.

"Dupy and Dougherty tell me a slide has come down over at Cascade Tunnel. Two men missing and the cookhouse gone," O'Neill said in a matter-of-fact voice.

The son of a bitch. Not a bit upset. Harrington glanced at Blackburn, who pulled his head in from the door briefly, but already resumed watching the progress of the plow. *Figures he don't give a shit.*

"Yes sir. Baker came through the tunnel and told us."

"Goddamn it," O'Neill muttered. "God help them." Sitting on the ring gear cover, O'Neill pulled out a cigar and lit it.

"Mr. Blackburn," O'Neill called out. "A moment, if you please."

"We've been making good progress down at 3.3, Bill. I don't want to stop work there to go back over to Cascade. A couple more good attacks and we should have it bucked clean at least to Alvin I should think. Can you buck over there with a single?"

"I told you last night, if I'm going to get anything done east, I need this plow. The 802 is just too light to handle this stuff. Drifts are so heavy in the tunnel cut, the portal is damned near plugged from what we're told. I need this plow. If I'm going to make Cascade there's no argument anyway, I got to have this 15 ton tender."

"You're gonna have to make good with the 802, Bill," Blackburn insisted. "The longer we stay bucking the slide west, the tougher it is for us to get back for water and coal. We gotta have this plow trailing in order for us to get back."

"Goddamn it! Parzybok's been trying all night to get from the coal chute to the depot and hasn't got there yet!" Harrington protested. "There's two dead over at Cascade and we're fighting over a goddamned snow plow?"

"Lanterns ahead, all stop!" Conductor Ed Lindsay called out.

"Mr. Lindsay, the rest of you men, see what needs to be done to get the 802 underway," O'Neill ordered. "Mr. Blackburn and Mr. Harrington and I need to discuss a few things."

When the cab was empty, O'Neill rose and paced across the floor, drawing smoke from his cigar. He leaned against the clutch lever. Their eyes fixed on the superintendent, Harrington and Blackburn remained silent.

"Gentlemen, you know as well as I we're a long ways from being out of the woods. I'd feel a lot better if I knew just how much coal is up in the bunker. Been going over our usage in my head … the bunker has to be half empty, maybe more."

"There's that car on one of the spurs," Blackburn interjected.

"Buried in snow. It's too far from the main line to hand shovel into the tenders. You ain't gonna get it outta there until the spring thaw," Harrington argued.

"How much coal is stored at Merritt? You know, Bill?" O'Neill asked.

"Three or four cars. Three for sure," Harrington answered.

"Can you make Merritt?" O'Neill asked.

"Not with the 802," Harrington responded.

"Jesus Christ, Bill! When are you going to get it through your head, we have to have these 15 tonners," Blackburn insisted.

Tired of arguing, Harrington said nothing.

Blackburn can yell all he wants. My argument's with O'Neil, Harrington silently reasoned. *Choose your words careful. Don't give O'Neill any options.*

"I'll leave the 807 here along with the 700," Harrington began. "If I run into trouble and you need extra coal for your set, you can rob off of them. 807 would just be a pain the ass for me anyway. Can't lead with it. Give me this plow. I can top off our coal over at Cascade, that way I'll have a full 15 tons before heading for Merritt. I can turn on the "Y" at Merritt, bore out one leg with the plow, take along some of Bergstrom's boys to shovel out the other leg. Give me this plow, Mr. O'Neill, and I'll bring back those cars for you."

O'Neill glanced at Blackburn.

Keep your damned mouth shut, Art.

"What about the crews?" Blackburn challenged.

"Ira's boys are rested and can take over this plow, the engine crews can stay as is. Jarnigan and Ross are rested, they can stay with you. I can pick up fresh engine crews over at Cascade. Duncan and Francisco are still over there," Harrington offered. "Let me take Mackey along in case we break down, since Tig is with you guys."

For a moment there was silence. O'Neill finished his smoke and dropped the butt to the floor.

He's seeing it my way.

"Okay, Bill, you can have this machine," O'Neill decided. "Let's just swap 'em out, engine and all. You take the 801 along with the 1118, and we'll take the 802 and the 1128. Clear the slide at Cascade, then plow to Merritt. I'd feel better knowing I had a little extra coal on hand. Goddamned storm just ain't easing up. Mr. Blackburn, are you in agreement here?"

"No sir, I'm not," Blackburn groused. "Wasting more goddamned time switching. Seems that's your final decision. No reason to keep arguing. If we're gonna make a swap, we'd better get to it."

"As long as we're switching, bore up the siding," Harrington added. "I need the helper off 25. Just can't move in this with one engine."

Exiting the plow, Harrington dug underneath his coat and removed his pocket watch. He let it dangle on its chain while he pulled off a wet, greasy work glove. Even at that, his numb fingers fumbled at the latch, finally releasing the protective gold cover.

Quarter after seven. Christ, time's ticking away.

O'Neill and Blackburn disappeared into the fog produced by the blowing snow. Backing their outfit down to the west end of the yard, they began cleaning the side track leading to the 1413 coupled to Train 25.

Harrington waited ten minutes, giving O'Neill's outfit time to clear, before calling for his plow to follow. He was to back his plow down to the siding switch as well, where the plows would be exchanged.

The sudden hissing of escaping air filled the cab of the plow. Instinctively Harrington braced himself for the quick stop that immediately followed. He looked back at Tom Osborne, who was leaning from the cab of the pusher, madly waving at Harrington to come back, and then pointing back toward his tender.

Goddamn it, now what? Hope to Christ he's not off the rail.

Harrington dropped out of the cab and picked his way back to the locomotive.

"It's them goddamned passengers, Bill!" Osborne shouted, clearly agitated. "They walked right out behind us! I damned near ran over 'em backing up. Too goddamned stupid to know we can't see the sons of bitches."

Saying nothing, Harrington stomped past to the rear of the outfit, fueled by accumulated rage. His gait quickened. By the time he came around the corner of the tender, he was kicking at the snow. Huddled between the rails was a group of four men. They stood a few feet from the back of the engine's tender, using it for a windbreak. Harrington pounced on them like a hungry cat on a wounded sparrow.

"What the hell do you think you're doing back here? You wanna get killed? Get back on your train and stay the hell outta our way!" he roared.

The shocked look on the faces of the men was exactly the reaction Harrington had hoped he would receive.

"I don't know who you are, sir, but none of us will addressed in that tone or with such profanity," one man said.

"We are going to get breakfast at the hotel is all. Thought we'd use the train here for a windbreak. I hardly think that is being in your way," another countered.

"Yes, and now that we have you here—I am assuming you have some authority—when are we moving west?" the third man asked.

"Yes, indeed," agreed the other, "when are we moving? These constant delays are ridiculous. You can be assured all of this, including your behavior Mr ..."

"Harrington. H-a-r-r-i-n-g-t-o-n," Harrington said.

"Well, ah, Mr. Harrington, as I was saying, myself and those of us businessmen on this train intend to make a full disclosure of what is going on up here as soon as we reach Seattle," threatened the man.

"Get off this goddamned track now! Get back in that train! You understand? All of you, get the hell outta the way of my plow!" Harrington bellowed, not the least bit intimidated by the threats being made.

Harrington purposely stepped between the coupler of the tender and the most vocal of the men, making sure he pushed against the man. He planted his legs in the snow and folded his arms, brushing against the man. There was an awkward silence.

"Come on, gentlemen, let's get back to the train and report this Mr. Harrington's behavior to Conductor Pettit. I'll have your job, sir."

The men turned and stumbled back across the tracks towards the nearest open passenger car vestibule. Harrington was right behind them, stride for stride.

Having seen the confrontation from inside the coach, Pettit was on the porch when the group arrived. Before the passengers could say a word, Harrington was on the offensive.

"Joe, you gotta keep your people onboard until we're clear of the depot. We can't see a damned thing backing up. You understand. I chewed these gentlemen out good. They should know better. I'll let you handle things from here."

"Very good, Mr. Harrington, I understand," Pettit said in his usual calm, agreeable tone. "Climb back aboard, if you please, gentlemen. We need to let the "Snow King" here get back to work. He has enough on his mind without worrying about running us over."

Harrington tipped his hat at Pettit.

As he turned away, Harrington considered saying something a little more pleasant, but quickly dismissed the idea.

Put the fear of God in 'em. Leave it at that.

Friday, February 25, 1910,11:30 a.m.
Anthony John Dougherty

Feeling like the eyes of the world were on him, Dougherty tried to keep his back to the passenger train as much as possible. Although those who ventured off the train stayed clear of the workers, he could not help but feel their curious looks. Most walked in groups towards the hotel and a warm meal, helping each other wade through the snow. More than once, Dougherty glanced up from his shoveling to meet the stares of men and women as they returned from eating and climbed back aboard their coaches. The activity of the plows being exchanged had given some of the passengers hope that the train was about to be moved west.

Dougherty worked alongside Harley's Italian section men and the crew off the X-801, clearing away snow from Train 25's helper. The plow had cleared the side track, but the arduous task of cleaning the snow from the engine's wheels and tender was left to men with shovels. Knowing a slide had hit over at Cascade Tunnel Station added to their frustration and anxiety. Knowing they could do nothing without the additional power of the 1413 kept them working at a brisk pace despite of their fatigue.

Between a rock and a hard place, Dougherty thought. *Need the 1413's power to run the plow. Gotta get her dug out. Harry and Johnny dead. Can't believe it. Wanna help but can't even get over there.*

Like ants on a large crumb of bread, the men swarmed about the engine. They chiseled and dug at the snow packed around the giant drive wheels and under the coal tender.

Doing more digging than railroading, Dougherty mused. *Just want things back to normal. A week from today, all this will be behind us. I hope.*

The job nearly done, Dougherty began digging with the enthusiasm of a kid, madly throwing snow aside. Amused by his show of strength, even the Italians picked up their pace, quickly clearing the last of the snow from the locomotive. Within minutes Holmes had his engine out on the main line.

"Finally get to do some railroading!" Dougherty shouted at no one in particular, tossing his shovel aside. He took up a station near the rear coupler of the 1118's tender and guided Holmes into a gentle union of the two locomotives. He ducked under the heavy iron knuckles of the couplers. Grabbing the air hoses to each side, he quickly snapped them together, and gave them three hard jerks to make certain they were locked securely. Crawling out from under, he opened the petcock valves to each side. There was a gentle hiss, and the hoses snapped taught with the pressure of the air. Happy with what he saw, he headed upgrade towards the plow.

As Dougherty walked under the cab of the 1118, engineer Tom Osborne leaned from the window and gave a quick look up and down the tracks.

"Climb on up, Al, got something for you," he beckoned, giving Dougherty sly wink.

Dougherty scampered up the ladder and met Osborne on the deck of the tender. Reaching into the toolbox, Osborne produced a bottle of whiskey. Popping the cork, he handed it to Dougherty.

"Take a good hard belt, Al. Get your belly warmed up. A little shot of bottled encouragement will do you good. Hell of mess we're in. Hell of a mess."

Dougherty titled his head back and closed his eyes. The smell of the whiskey quickly permeated his nose, bringing at least some relief to his plugged sinuses. The liquid burned its way down his throat, its alcohol-induced heat settling into his stomach. He wiped his mouth clean, then handed the bottle back.

"Thanks, Tommy, that hit the spot," Dougherty said. "Tough morning, what with hearing about Harry and Johnny and all."

"Terrible way to go. Getting buried under a wall of snow," Osborne added, taking a quick gulp from the bottle.

"Better take a hit for the road, Al," Osborne suggested. "A toast to Harry and Johnny. God let their souls rest in peace. At least they're clear of this damned business. Lord knows when we'll get off this goddamned outfit. One hell of a mess, that's for damned sure."

"You drunks better hurry, some passengers are coming this way," fireman Stan Meredith called out from the cab. "Harrington's coming too. Probably looking for you, Al."

Another shot of whiskey quickly found its way down Dougherty's throat. Choking on it slightly, he winced, coughed, and wiped a few tears from his eyes. Quickly, he put the bottle back in the toolbox and closed the lid.

"That'll hold me, Tommy. Just what I needed. Put it on my tab, my good man." Dougherty gave Osborne a pat on the shoulder and dropped off the engine.

Climbing into the X-801, Dougherty made his way across the cab, careful not to exhale as he passed Ira Clary. He poked his head out the left door as if he had taken his station. Clary, not fooled, was by his side in an instant.

"Stop off at the Osborne Saloon, did you, Al?" he asked.

"I gave my greetings to Tommy, if that's what you mean," Dougherty answered, still not facing Clary.

"Yes sir-eee," drawled Archie Dupy, leaning against the clutch lever. "Ol Tommy. He's got the best damned hooch on the mountain, that's for damned certain."

"Goddamned Osborne serves up almost as much whiskey from his engine as Bailets does in his damned saloon," Clary countered.

"Yeah, well, you better hope Blackburn and O'Neill don't come across the jug you got stashed down on the 800," Dougherty said, pulling his head back in and facing his adversary.

"Al, my boy, I'm pleased to report the X-800 is operating under all the proper rules concerning strong drink onboard railroad equipment," Clary replied with a smile. He carefully patted his side coat pocket.

"Yes sir, the X-800 is a dry machine. All onboard her are on the wagon, except for a hit or two I stashed for Bat."

"You're forgetting, Ira, Meath's still on her," Harrington scowled, climbing aboard. "That bastard will take it as a personal challenge to get boozed up right under O'Neill's nose. Now let's get some snow plowed."

The extra power supplied by the 1413 kept the plow moving through the deep drifts formed by the wind. In under an hour they had plowed the main line alongside Train 25. Hanging out of the right side door, Harrington and Dougherty kept a close eye on the train's coaches, fearful that curious passengers might step out for a close look of the machine at work. A few small children wiped circles in the fogged windows and pressed their noses to the glass as the plow inched by. Harrington never failed to wave at each of them.

Bill's sure missing Lillian and the kids, Dougherty thought. *Can see why. Remember the time I met them. Bill's one lucky son of a bitch.*

Just east of the station, Harrington halted the outfit. On the platform he saw John Parzybok and his crew, along with Jim Mackey. They were fresh from their rest and ready to rejoin the effort.

"We need to make room for Paryz's boys," Harrington ordered, as he headed for the depot. "We're double-crewing from here on out."

Extending a hand, Dougherty pulled Parzybok, brakemen Julian Wells, Charlie Smart, and John "Pattie" Kelly into the cab. Jim Mackey made his way back to check on the flywheels and help engineer Joe Stafford "oil around" before resuming east.

"Gonna get crowded in here, that's for sure," Dougherty said, rubbing shoulders with Charlie Smart.

"Jesus, Al, you musta stopped off down at Osborne's engine. You smell like a cross between a pig sty and my old man's still," teased Smart.

"Overdue for a hot bath and change of clothes, that's for damned sure," Dougherty admitted. "So what's the latest from Cascade, any of you boys know?"

"Guess they found Harry," Parzybok said. "Last we heard they still hadn't found poor Johnny. He's the only one missing. A few of the agency boys got a little banged up, but nothing serious."

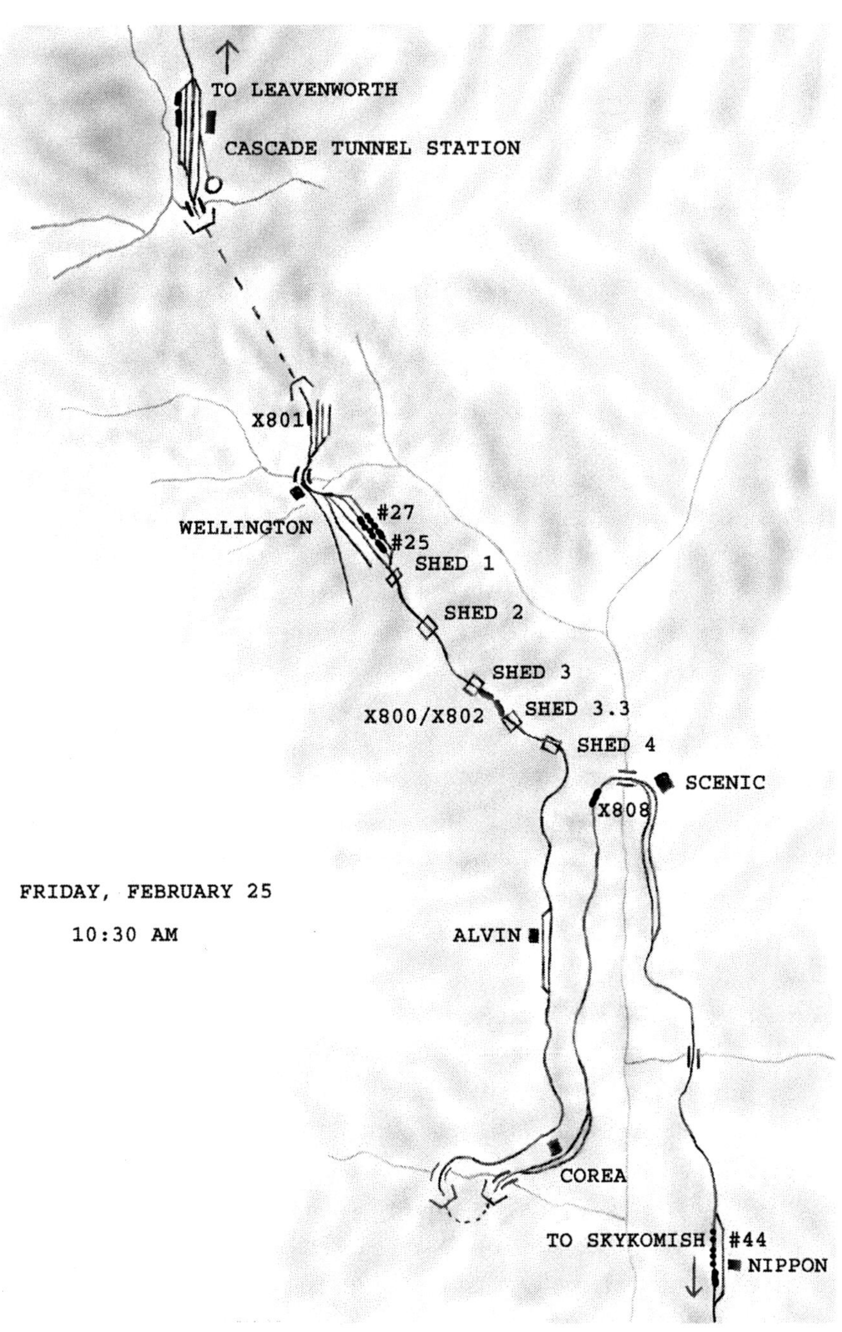

TO LEAVENWORTH
CASCADE TUNNEL STATION
X801
WELLINGTON
#27
#25
SHED 1
SHED 2
SHED 3
X800/X802
SHED 3.3
SHED 4
SCENIC
X808
FRIDAY, FEBRUARY 25
10:30 AM
ALVIN
COREA
TO SKYKOMISH
#44
NIPPON

Half of the staff in hand, Harrington elbowed his way into the cab.

"Jesus, got a bigger crowd in here than they'll draw for the Jeffries fight," Harrington grumbled. "Parzy, break up your boys. Have each one help out one of the firemen. Arch, you're on the clutch. Al, you and I will take the right side; Ira, you and John watch the left. Now, let's get rolling."

Dupy pulled two long tugs on the whistle cord. Poking his head out into the wind driven snow, Dougherty braced himself and squinted.

Wonder how bad it is over at Cascade.

Taking forever to get through this damned tunnel, Dougherty thought.

From the time they bucked the last drift at the west portal of the Cascade tunnel, Dougherty began to feel a growing sense of sober anticipation well up deep within. He wanted to see the damage done by the slide, but could not deny the unsettling thoughts caused by the deaths of Bjerenson and Elerker.

Poor Harry and Johnny. Wonder if they heard it coming? Wonder if they lived awhile under the snow? God, don't want to go that way. Hope they never woke up. Jesus, quit thinking about it.

With the electricity still out, the motors normally used to pull trains through the tunnel were useless. The exhaust of the two steam pusher engines, amplified by the narrow confines of the tunnel, reverberated in Dougherty's ears. The noise only added to the constant ringing in his head, spawning a throbbing headache. Even though the locomotives were not working hard, the natural draft in the bore whisked their smoke forward, making breathing difficult.

"Seeing daylight!" Clary called out.

Dougherty welcomed the sight of light streaming into the east portal.

Get back to plowing, get my mind off Harry and Johnny.

Dougherty turned and motioned to Mackey that they were about to hit the drifts of snow piled just outside the tunnel. The pusher engines eased the plow from the tunnel. The big wheel engaged. They immediately hit a snow bank ten feet deep.

It was difficult for Dougherty to concentrate on the operation of the fan. His eyes wanted to look beyond the plow, hoping to catch a glimpse of where the slide had swept away the cookhouse and the lives of two of his friends. Although the fierce east wind that was buffeting Wellington was not as intense at Cascade Tunnel Station, it still whipped the falling snow into an opaque, white cloud. Slowly working east, the minutes seemed to stretch into agonizing hours.

"Work crew ahead!" Dougherty finally called out. "Five car lengths!"

Standing right behind him, Harrington dropped one foot down on the ladder and swung out from the plow to get a better look. Dougherty extended his hand, placing a firm grasp on Harrington's free arm.

"Haul me in, Al," Harrington finally said. "Can't tell where the drifts stop and the slide starts. She must be pretty clean. Let's bring her to a stop and see what we've got."

Off the plow, Dougherty and the rest of the crew waded through the snow to where a large group of men were working around the site where the cookhouse once stood. Splinters of wood littered the scene. Parts of chairs and tables jutted out from the snow, themselves being slowly covered with the flakes still falling from the sky. The force of the avalanche sweeping down off the mountain and across the canyon had even overturned the big cook stove. Its hot coals had scattered, melting small holes in the snow. A small ring of melted water circled its black cast iron form.

Groups of sectionmen were cleaning snow from the collapsed roof, while others chopped away at the jumble of shingles and broken rafters. Grabbing an ax from one of the workers, Dougherty began to take clean swings, cutting through two-by-fours with easy strokes. Once a chunk of roof was loosened, the sectionmen would lift it and toss it to the side.

"Go easy with those axes and shovels, boys," section foreman Charlie Bergstrom warned. "There's a man under there somewhere."

Long dead, Dougherty thought. *Be one hell of a miracle if he was still alive.*

Dougherty on one side and Duncan Tegtmeier on the other, the two men hacked through another section of roof.

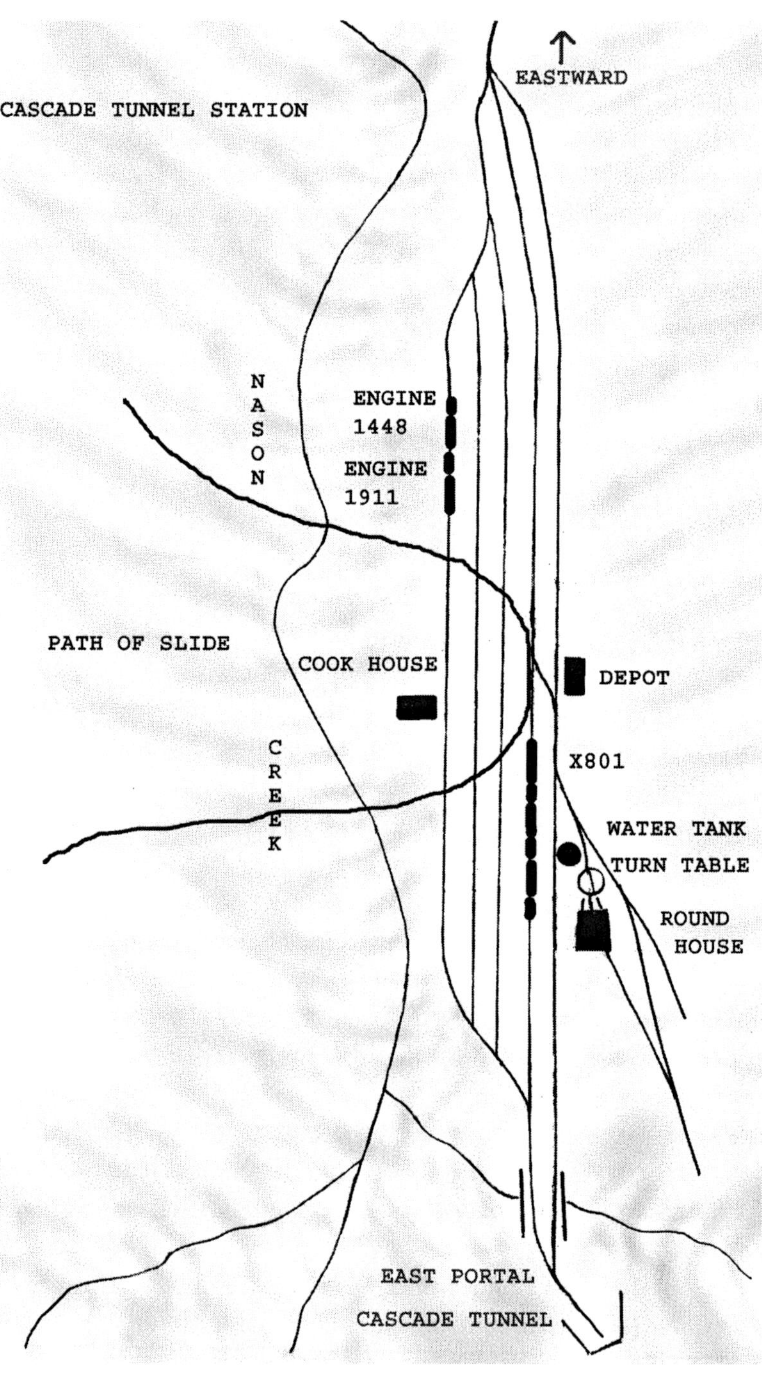

EASTWARD
CASCADE TUNNEL STATION
NASON
ENGINE 1448
ENGINE 1911
PATH OF SLIDE
COOK HOUSE
DEPOT
CREEK
X801
WATER TANK
TURN TABLE
ROUND HOUSE
EAST PORTAL
CASCADE TUNNEL

"Where'd they find Harry?" Dougherty asked Tegtmeier between swings.

"Out by the rear door there," Tegtmeier answered, pointing out the spot with his ax. "He must have been awake and heard it coming. Probably went out to the back porch to take a look when it hit. He was pretty beat up. The body's wrapped in a blanket out behind the depot. Not sure right now what to do with him."

"God, you think he saw it?" Dougherty tried to block the horror of such a moment from his mind.

"Guess only the Good Lord knows," Tegtmeier said.

The two men continued to work in silence. The laborers cleared off another large section of the roof. Tegtmeier and Dougherty quickly hacked it into chunks that could be removed. Placing his ax aside, Dougherty grabbed part of a rafter and heaved, closing his eyes and grunting with effort. He rolled the timber and the roofing it supported over his head and threw it to one side. He opened his eyes and then quickly shut them again.

"We found him!" Tegtmeier called out.

Dougherty looked again. Bjerenson's hands were exposed, stiff and blue. The snow covering his torso was red with blood. A section of rafter lay across the top of his head, but Dougherty could clearly see the blank stare of death in Bjerenson's wide-open eyes.

Dear God. Dear Jesus. Look after Johnny's soul. Dougherty crossed himself. He turned away for a moment and looked up into the snow-filled sky. *Terrible way to go.*

Taking a deep breath, Dougherty turned back. He grabbed the two-by-four that was lying across the dead man's face, and with Tegtmeier's help carefully pulled it away. Other men gingerly swept the snow from the lower body.

"He never knew what hit him, Al," Tegtmeier said. "Probably never woke up. Still lying in his bed, see there? Happened fast. Snow hit, the roof came down, this two-by-four did him in, God save him."

Dougherty said nothing. He helped remove the stiff, frozen body from its icy tomb. Bjerenson's lower body had been badly mangled by large slivers of wood propelled by the snow. Once pulled clear of the debris, some of the workers covered their mouths and ran out of the sight of the others, vomiting.

Holding on to Bjerenson's shoulders, Dougherty handled the corpse of the dead man like he would a newborn baby, carefully, reverently laying it down. Tegtmeier knelt down and tried shut Bjerenson's eyes, but they were forever frozen in a terrified stare. The body was wrapped and the blanket bound with twine.

"We'll lay him next to Harry for now, I guess," Tegtmeier solemnly decided. "A terrible thing, Al. Appreciate your help."

Dougherty still could not say a word. He gave Tegtmeier a quick nod and walked away.

His eyes were open. He saw it. He felt it. Dear God, he saw it and felt it.

Dougherty wiped away tears and headed for the toolbox on Osborne's engine.

Friday, February 25, 1910, 1:30 p.m.
Arthur Reed Blackburn, Trainmaster

Watching O'Neill, Blackburn could not help but be impressed. He seemed tireless. While plowing west from Wellington, they decided O'Neill would concentrate on keeping the Italian and temporary shovelers working, with Blackburn supervising the operation of the plow. O'Neill had a way with the foreign workers that Blackburn had yet to master, and both men knew it.

Hard to handle the crews with him here, Blackburn thought. *Men wait for him to say something. Don't listen to me.*

Despite the harsh wind and blowing snow, Blackburn opted to stand outside on the bank ahead of the plow, relaying signals back to the plowmen and the engine crews pushing. The men on the plow were running blind, not only by the strong winds and blowing snow, but also because the slide was located on a curve in the tracks. Whistle signals alone were not enough to coordinate the movements of the two engines, nor sufficient warning for the men digging on the slide to keep clear of the spinning blades of the plow each time they attacked the solid white mass.

Any man not actively operating the plow was out on the slide, alongside the sectionmen, pitching snow. Even O'Neill grabbed a shovel, and was setting a pace few of the men could match.

Blackburn stomped on the snow, packing down a larger area on which to stand. His continuous pacing along the narrow ledge between the trough created by the plow and the sheer drop-off down the flank of Windy Mountain had left an icy trail between the rotary and the front face of the slide. The product of nervous energy and impatience, Blackburn's constant motion had also helped keep him warm.

"Too tired to be tired," Blackburn said half aloud peering through the blowing snow at O'Neill still directing the laborers. "Wish I could lick this goddamned headache. Betcha Clary hid a bottle on that plow somewhere. Could use a good swig about now."

Blackburn realized he had been talking aloud and looked around sheepishly. His worry that someone had noticed were quickly eased. Even the men close enough to hear seemed to be in no condition to notice or care. *No sleep. Getting to us. Taking three men to do the work could get out of one. Damned dagos. Doing more standing than shoveling. I'd be on their asses. Good thing O'Neill's there, I'm here.*

"Blackburn! Mr. Blackburn!" Shouts from O'Neill and members of the plow crew on the slide brought Blackburn out of his trance. *Goddamn, getting as rummy as everyone else.*

"Bring her on in!" O'Neill bellowed, waving the 'all clear.'

Rotating his arm, Blackburn relayed the "highball" to Tegtmeier on the plow, and fireman John Pettit, leaning from the cab of the 1154. The plow rolled past Blackburn. He kept pace with its progress, slipping on the ice formed in the trail he had worn in the snow bank. The fan hit the slide with a violent collision. Blackburn's eyes darted from the fan, to the plume exiting the chute, to White, hanging from the door of the plow. For an instant, a sudden rush of energy replaced his fatigue. He loved watching the blades of the big machine chew away at the ice and snow.

"Keep her coming, boys! Keep her coming!" Blackburn hollered, his arm rotations matching his excitement.

He knew few could hear his shouts, yet he could not contain himself. He felt like a general, leading his troops into a desperate battle against overwhelming odds.

Gotta buck this slide today. We gotta. Be home free.

The plume of snow cascading over the bank began to falter. The exhaust of the plow became labored and sluggish.

"We're losing her!" White called out.

Blackburn spotted O'Neill. He was signaling them forward.

War, he thought. *Goddamned war.*

"She ain't down yet!" Blackburn shouted, waving harder than ever. "Keep at her!"

Another foot. Another five feet. Hand to hand fighting. No retreat. We'll beat this goddamned storm.

With an explosion of exhaust, Imberg's engine spun out, and the 1128 quickly followed. The sudden loss of tractive effort caused the plow to momentarily slow and the fan to clear itself of snow, temporarily racing. Not wanting the charge to stall, Blackburn continued to yell encouragement, unheard as it was. The skill of the engineers put their locomotives back on firm footing, and forced the fan further into the slide.

"That's it, boys! Give her all your snoose!" Blackburn shouted.

Begrudgingly, another five feet of the slide yielded to the power of two locomotives driving rotating steel into the snow. A second time the engines slipped out. Momentum lost, they had no choice but to back up and make another attempt. Undaunted, Blackburn called for yet another charge, not stopping the process until the hood of the fan became engulfed in snow and O'Neill signaled a halt. The plow backed away, its boiler building up steam for the next encounter with the enemy.

No longer content to stand, Blackburn made his way over to the slide and found a shovel stuck in the snow. He took a place between two of the Italians and began pitching snow down onto the partially cleared track below.

"What's the matter, Mr. Blackburn? We not getting the slide shoveled fast enough for you?" O'Neill called out.

"Not at all, sir," Blackburn answered. He paused to catch his breath. "Need every shovel working, that's all."

He had not realized how weak the long hours on duty had made him until he started digging into the packed snow. A man proud of his strength, Blackburn's forearms were soon burning, the muscles tightening. His back became stiff, pain shot down his left leg. To maintain an even pace with the men on each side of him became a battle between his desire to stop and his pride in working harder than the next man.

Fortunately, digging the hard snow required no thought. Head down against the wind, Blackburn closed his eyes as he worked.

Twenty good shovel fulls, then I'll blow, he thought. Counting in his head, once he reached nineteen he dared himself to do another twenty.

Yesterday I couldn't keep my eyes open, Blackburn thought. Opening his eyes into a narrow squint, he took a look around before driving his shovel into the snow with the power of his boot. *Now I can't keep them closed.*

Blackburn finally paused. He straightened up, hoping to ease the pain and catch a second wind. The men on either side said nothing. Their eyes, the looks on their faces, gave Blackburn no clue as to what they were thinking, if they were thinking of anything at all. It occurred to him that, like him, they were operating more on instinct than any logical progression of thought. In them he saw his own fatigue.

Blackburn put his head down and resumed his work.

Easy, he cautioned himself. *Don't break the goddamned shovel handle. If I were running the show, have Bergstrom at Wellington right now keeping the trains clean. All the dagos down here. Half the dagos here, half the dagos shoveling at Wellington just ain't getting it done. O'Neill must know what he's doing.*

O'Neill was slowly walking his way, stopping periodically to redirect some of the men. As he approached a group of workers they increased their pace, then immediately stopped and watched as he passed by. To Blackburn's eye, at least half were leaning on their shovels doing nothing once O'Neill's back was to them. He nearly hollered, "Get back to work!" but bit his tongue.

The closer O'Neill got to Blackburn, the harder he worked. Blackburn could not help but chuckle at himself. *Not that much different than the dagos after all.*

O'Neill came up alongside of Blackburn and sank his shovel into the slide.

"This crew is about done in, Mr. Blackburn," he said, not the least bit winded. He had a cigar hanging from his mouth, but as near as Blackburn could tell it was no longer lit. "We'll need to head back for water in a few hours. If we can get another 100 feet or so bucked between now and then we'll be lucky, wouldn't you say?"

Blackburn seized the opportunity to take a short break. He straightened up and at least appeared as if he was looking over the slide.

"Maybe. Just can't seem to keep this bunch shoveling. Need some fresh men."

"That's what I'm thinking," O'Neill concurred, still not breaking stride. "We'll haul this sorry bunch back with us. Let 'em eat, get warmed up, and have them work on the trains. Take the crew that's up at Wellington now, back down here. Keep trading them off like that. This bunch has been grumbling about quitting."

"Let the bastards quit. We can grab Bergstrom's crew." Blackburn offered. "Have them keep the trains clean, bring all of Harley's crew down here."

"Bergstrom's got his hands full over at Cascade with that slide," O'Neill countered. "Have to wait and hear what happened over there before we can bring him this way. Damned shame about the two cooks."

The two men fell silent. O'Neill paused and scanned the workers. All that could be heard was the howl of the wind, the crunch of shovels being driven into the snow by the heavy boots of the men, and the faint panting of the plow and pusher engines.

"This is the toughest part of running a division, Mr. Blackburn. Making the men work like dogs when you know they're damned near dead on their feet and wanting to quit," O'Neill admitted. "Now's when you have to be your sharpest, because the boys aren't. You have to put how you feel behind you and go on like it's just another day's work."

Blackburn did not answer. His nose and cheeks were numb, and his ears felt like they were being poked with sharp needles. He was one of the men about whom O'Neill spoke. He was dead on his feet.

Picked a fine time to give me advice on how to be a super, Blackburn thought.

"I suppose you're right, Mr. O'Neill," Blackburn finally said. He turned his head and put his thumb to each nostril. Blowing hard, he cleared his nose. "Still, sometimes I think we need to ride these men harder. Not our crews, Harley's section boys. Look at 'em. Especially those agency men we brought up here. Only about half are really working. None are earning their keep."

"They're close to breaking, Art. A fine line. You have to be able to judge it. Ride them hard now and they'll be gone tonight. Trouble is, we need them more than they need us right now. Don't fool yourself—if we know it, they know it."

O'Neill finally stopped digging and took another long look around.

"So, you ready to bring your plow on in for another round, Art?" he asked. "Besides, looks to me like you're damned close to breaking yourself."

"I'll round up the plow crew and we'll hit her, Mr. O'Neill," Blackburn answered. He headed across the face of the slide to where Tegtmeier and the rest of the plow crew were working. He turned and looked at O'Neill.

"I might be a little tired, sir, but I'm a long ways from broke."

Friday, February 25, 1910, 4:30 p.m.
John Robert Meath, Engineer

Meath sat quietly on his seat next to the boiler of the X-800. He was bone tired, both from running the plow and joining the crew out on the slide, manning a shovel. Thankfully, O'Neill and Blackburn had ordered them back to Wellington for coal and water. Both of Meath's superiors had opted to ride back on the eastward-facing X-802, which was doing the work.

Lonesome, Meath decided to join Bat Nelson on the fired deck. Having just finished shaking the grates, Nelson was busy spreading out the hot coals in the firebox. He adjusted the stoker and water, then closely examined his fire one last time before slamming shut the firebox door.

"Pull up a chair, Bobby," Nelson said, motioning to one of the small fold-down seats built into the tender. Dropping down the seat on his side of the deck, Nelson settled in, his back against the tender, his feet propped up on the feeder valves, his arms folded. Meath did likewise.

"One tough day, eh Bobby?"

"Don't know about you, Bat, but I'm about done in," Meath admitted. "You ever get a relief?"

"Had Earl Bennington back here awhile. Tried to grab a nap. Pretty hard to do, what with all the back and forth bucking this damned slide. Want a drink, Bobby? Ira left us half a bottle."

Meath shook his head. He pulled back the curtain and for a moment watched the snow blow past the plow. The cold wind rushed through the opening, and Meath quickly repositioned the heavy canvas in order to keep in what little warmth was radiating from the boiler head.

"What about you, Bobby? You've been at the throttle the whole time. Blackburn gonna get you a relief?"

Meath just shrugged and stared ahead. He searched the pocket of his overalls for a cigar, but soon realized his supply had run out.

Maybe I could bum one off O'Neill.

"So how's Blackburn been? He never comes back here. He been giving everybody hell all day?" Nelson asked.

"Aah, he's been pretty good. Having O'Neill around helps. The bastard's so scared of him he stays pretty quiet. Besides, Blackburn's as wore out as the rest of us. Takes energy to be an asshole," Meath responded.

Never seen snow like this. Never quits. Meath thought. *Buck this slide, line between here and Scenic's gotta be plugged. Take the rest of tonight, all of tomorrow just to make Scenic. Don't know what they're telling the passengers. Trains ain't going anywhere anytime soon.*

"Wonder if they found Harry and Johnny?" Nelson asked. "Been thinking about them. They have family?"

"Don't know, Bat," Meath sighed. "Bill's crew must be over there by now. Guess it depends on how big the slide was. Don't know about kin. Probably like us, Bat—out here by ourselves, a long goddamned ways from home."

"Father and Mother talk about moving back to Denmark," Bat admitted. "I don't remember much about the place, came over here when I was four or five. They still talk Dane around the house. What about you, Bobby? You never talk much about home."

"I go back every now and again," Meath confessed.

"To visit your family, or a certain lady I've heard about?" Nelson teased.

"I stay at the farm. My little brother's running it these days. Never was much on farming, so best he's there and I'm here," Meath confessed.

"Been thinkin' some of Lizzie lately. I guess that's no secret. Her and her sister are running the family store since her old man died."

"We ain't getting younger, Bobby," Nelson said. "Fact is, this storm's turning all us old quick. I'm sure thinking its time to start settling down."

"And get ourselves married, eh Bat?" Meath added. "You might be right. Maybe it's time. If Lizzie will have me."

The two men fell silent. The fire deck grew dark as night descended into the mountains. Light from the fire occasionally flashed though the seams of the firebox doors and cast its red glow on the weary, hardened faces of Meath and Nelson.

"Ever tell you about the time me and my brothers stole a body?" Meath asked, breaking the silence.

"You did what?"

"Yeah, we were having a wake for some old uncle or somebody at our house. My brothers and me figured it'd be funny to boost the coffin out the window so when folks came in, the old boy would be gone," Meath explained.

"So where'd you hide it?" Nelson asked, clearly amused by the tale.

"We stuffed it under some hay out in the barn. Funny thing is, folks were too busy drinking and eating to really miss him, so we brought him back in the next morning. No one really liked the old bastard anyway."

"Now Bobby, are you going to sit here and tell me it was all your brothers' doing?"

With his normal dead pan look, Meath shrugged.

"Oh, I might have put the notion in their heads to begin with."

"Now I see why you had such an easy time of it boosting ol' Bailets' turkey out from under his nose," Nelson chuckled.

Meath said nothing while Nelson rummaged through the toolbox and produced the bottle of whiskey left behind by Clary. He pulled out the cork, taking a long smell before downing a gulp.

"You'd better take a hit, Bobby. We're slowing down, must be about at the coal chute. Blackburn will on our asses before we know it."

Meath put the bottle to his lips. He filled his mouth with the liquid, and held it there, letting the strong fumes permeate his stuffed head. He slowly let it trickle down his throat.

"Tell ya what, Bat, I'll help you coal and water up and you can buy me supper up at Bailets," Meath offered, handing back the bottle.

"That's a deal, Bobby."

As Meath walked into the dining room of Bailets Hotel, he was uncomfortably reminded of his confrontation with the passengers two days earlier, at Cascade Tunnel Station. The room was nearly full of well-dressed men and women from the stranded passenger train. They stared at the railroad men as they filed in and split up, trying to find places to sit. Grabbing extra chairs from along the wall, Meath and Nelson retreated to the back of the room, each using one chair for a seat and another for a table. The sound of knives and forks on the plates and the smell of ham and bacon being fried filled the stuffy room.

God, same people who were in the cookhouse over at Cascade, Meath thought, looking across the room. *It's all gone now. Didn't even see Harry or Johnny that morning. Gonna miss 'em both.*

A waiter brought them a plate of bread, boiled potatoes, and strips of bacon.

"This is the best ol' Bailets can do for us? I see a lot of ham out there under the noses of all that high society," Meath challenged.

"Sorry, we're running low," the waiter said with a shrug. He motioned his head towards the passengers. "They're gonna be down to two meals come tomorrow and eating the same stuff you are."

He poured the two railroaders cups of coffee and hurried off to seat the passengers still entering the dining hall.

"I see Blackburn and O'Neill are nowhere to be found," Meath observed, laying two strips of bacon on a thick slice of bread.

"Guess I can't blame them," Nelson answered. "These folks would be all over them."

"Been trying to pick up what they're saying," Meath admitted, "but my hearing's shot. Ears ringing to beat hell."

"Mine too, Bobby," Nelson admitted.

"Boiled spuds on an empty stomach. You're gonna be glad you're by yourself out on that fire deck in a couple of hours there, Bat," Meath teased. "If I knew I was gonna be up in the cab with Blackburn, I'd order me another plate just to make his life miserable."

Meath cleaned his plate with the last slice of bread. Pushing away the chair he was using for a table, he leaned back on the rear two legs of his own seat, his back against the wall. He cradled his cup of coffee and studied the faces of the people in the dining room.

Look scared, some of them, he noticed. *Lady over there with the three kids, just picking at her food. She's scared. Funny, them being scared. Got a warm place to stay, safe from the storm. No reason to be scared.*

Meath sipped from his coffee cup.

"Must be running low on coffee too," Meath told Nelson. "Weak, even for Bailets."

Nelson finished his meal as well. The hot meal and the warmth of the room overcame the fireman; chin touching his chest, he was fast asleep.

Gonna be heading back out, better find a privy. Get a head start on Bailets' spuds and bacon fat, Meath decided.

A number of the passengers fell silent as Meath passed. As he weaved between the tables, he heard bits and pieces of remarks, but tried to ignore them. One man, whom Meath recalled from the cookhouse at Cascade Tunnel Station, asked his companions in a voice loud enough for Meath to hear, why these men were wasting time here eating when the line was still blocked.

Good thing about being dead tired, Meath thought, *got no energy left to start a fight with bastards like him.*

He openned the door to leave and nearly bumped into a man and his small daughter coming in. Standing aside, Meath held the door open. He smiled at the child in the gentleman's arms.

"Thank you," the man said, hustling in out of the storm. "Davis is my name, George Davis. This is my daughter Thelma. I'd shake your hand, but, well, got my hands full."

"Bob Meath, nice to meet you, Thelma."

The girl said nothing. She burrowed her head into her father's neck. Meath closed the door behind them and stood surveying the room.

"Most the tables are taken, Mr ..."

"Davis," the man repeated. "Just call me George."

"Well George, see that man back there asleep in the chair? You can kick him out and grab his chair and the one next to it. We're heading back out in a few minutes anyway," Meath said.

"Oh no, wouldn't think of it. Let him sleep. You men must be exhausted. I'm a motorman. A rail of sorts too. I work the Seattle-Renton interurban," Davis explained.

"Oh really? Well, come on up here. You can take over running our juice boxes once we get 'em back on line. Good Lord knows our boys ain't got the foggiest notion how to run 'em." Meath said, his usual light nature returning. "Your little girl here can lend a hand."

Meath extended a grimy finger and tickled the child. She had been sneaking peaks at him but again hid her face, this time with a slight giggle.

"Better yet, you got a job for me down there?" Meath continued, still smiling and tickling the now-laughing girl.

"Well, you never know, Mr. Meath." Davis said, boosting his squirming daughter up further on his chest.

"I'm Thelma," the girl finally said, now looking straight at Meath.

"I'm Thelma," Meath repeated.

Again the girl giggled. "No, I'm Thelma!" she said, pointing at herself.

Again Meath mimicked the antics of the child.

"I hate to ask, I'm sure everyone else has, but how bad is it to the west?" Davis questioned looking embarrassed.

"We're bucking a big slide, that's for sure. But we're making progress. The plows are working fine. It's just gonna take time, that's all. We'll get you out, don't worry."

There was a moment of awkward silence. Meath wondered if the man actually believed his shallow optimism.

"Well, good. I know you men are doing your best. Tough to railroad in this storm and with all of us people around," Davis admitted. "I get it some just running the trolley. Can't imagine what it's like for you boys."

"Hey, a rail's a rail. We gotta stick together," Meath told the man slapping him on the shoulder. "Nice to meet you, Thelma. Take good care of your Daddy."

He gave Thelma a smile, a wink, and a wave before walking out the door.

Friday, February 25, 1910, 2nd Trick Wellington
Basil Sherlock, Telegrapher

It was the predictability of the railroad that appealed to Sherlock. Once he had learned the intricacies of the operations at Wellington, he quickly settled into the routine of his shift. For Sherlock there was comfort in the regular arrivals and departures of the passenger trains, the scheduled time freights and the movement of the electric motor helpers through Wellington. There were the occasional variations, minor derailments, mechanical problems, or landslides that disrupted the schedule, but even at that, more often than not Sherlock could fall back into his routine before turning the chair over to "Mississippi" Avery every midnight.

A methodical young man who relished normality, the disruption of the snow storm was trying his nerves. Taking over earlier from first trick operator Will Flannery, Sherlock was warned that the first few hours of his shift would be busy.

"You won't see a single damned train, but the passengers will start showing up around dinner time to send telegrams," Flannery told him.

Well into his shift, Sherlock had yet to see a single person enter the station, but the telegraph key seemed to click nonstop. Messages for O'Neill were coming in from throughout the division; none carried good news.

Line to Seattle blocked. Line south of Bellingham blocked. Lowland snow melting. Rivers rising. Bridge at Ferndale threatened. Two derailments in Seattle. Dowling fighting heavy drifts east of Scenic, not sure when he'll make Alvin. All in just two hours.

He stared out the window, watching the snow blow past the narrow cocoon of light produced by the lanterns out on the platform. The pit of his stomach felt unsettled. It seemed he was in the midst of an ever-increasing crisis, yet he was powerless to do anything to ease the situation.

O'Neill acts like there's nothing wrong. Eight feet of new snow. Two stalled trains. Doesn't dare show how he really feels. Maybe it's not beyond what he's handled before. Be my only winter in this hellhole.

The clearing of a man's throat and a loud "Excuse me, young man," startled Sherlock. A middle-aged man had come in the passenger's entrance to the depot and was standing at the counter, peering through the open window.

"Yes sir, may I help you," Sherlock stammered, rising from his chair and pulling off his headset.

"When the telegraph operator returns, I need to send a wire to Seattle. How soon will that be?"

Sherlock's back stiffened as he pulled out a Western Union note pad and produced a pencil. "I *am* the telegraph operator," he said, slightly indignant.

"Are you capable of wiring Western Union?" the man asked, obviously not convinced of Sherlock's competence.

"I can assure you, sir, that I am a fully qualified telegraph operator for both the railroad and Western Union. Now if you will clearly print your message and its destination on this pad, I will gladly send it for you."

Still skeptical, the man took the pad and wrote a short note. He tore off the top sheet and handed it to Sherlock.

"Am all right. Plenty to eat. Good bed. How are you? Albert Mahler" Sherlock read. "Is that all?"

"No reason to send the newspaper," Mahler replied sarcastically. "Your people are telling us we'll be out of here by tomorrow morning. Correct?"

"Very good, sir." Sherlock purposely avoided the man's question and constant staring. Returning to his desk, he plugged into the Western Union connection and tapped out the message. While waiting for the confirmation, he filled out a receipt and filed it.

"There won't be any charge, Mr. Mahler. The railroad is paying for all messages sent by the passengers," Sherlock announced.

"Well, I should hope it would!" Mahler exclaimed. "What have you heard about the slide on the east side of the mountain? Terrible thing about those two cooks."

"One of our plow crews is there now, sir." Sherlock paused as the key rattled to life. "I have confirmation, Mr. Mahler. Western Union will have your message to your family this evening. We are putting a priority delivery on all telegrams being sent."

"Very good. Now tell me, where they have the trains parked. Is it safe there? The mountain on one side, the canyon on the other. I must say, I'm not one bit happy with the situation. Some of the women... well, you know how they can get."

"The officers in charge have been here longer than I have, Mr. Mahler. I can assure you they have a firm grasp of the situation and under no circumstances would they place those trains in harm's way," Sherlock stated, wondering if the man believed a word of it.

"I certainly hope you're correct, young man." Mahler tipped his hat, buttoned up his coat and walked out.

Looking out his bay window, Sherlock could see Mahler standing under the eaves, talking with another gentleman. Even in the dark he saw the men pointing toward the hillside above the siding where the trains were parked.

O'Neill or Blackburn need to talk to these people. Calm them down.

Anticipating being asked to send another telegram, Sherlock stood at the counter, Western Union pad ready. Presently, the man strode into the station. Without saying a word, he took the notepaper, scribbled a message to his wife, and pushed the pad through the window.

"Get this sent right away. You are capable, I presume?" the man snapped.

He glanced at the message for the sender's name. Sherlock again swallowed his pride and kept his temper in check.

"I am fully capable, Mr. Bethel. If you will wait for a moment I will send it priority delivery and get a confirmation for you."

Sherlock tapped out the message, taking out his anger on the key.

Who are these people? Questioning my abilities, Sherlock fumed.

"And I'll want a copy of the receipt stating this is being paid for by the Great Northern, young man," Bethel interjected when Sherlock had finished.

Receipt and confirmation in hand, Bethel turned to leave.

"If your boss…what's his name?"

"O'Neill, Mr. Bethel, Superintendent O'Neill," Sherlock answered.

"If your Mr. O'Neill shows up, you tell him some of the men on the train want to meet with him. We want to be kept informed on how soon we will be leaving. I for one am not convinced conductor Pettit knows if he's been punched or bored. We expect to be kept informed. You tell him that."

"I will tell him if I see him, sir. He could very well return west with the plows and not even check in tonight, but I will leave word with my relief," Sherlock offered.

"See to it, young man." Bethel stormed from the hallway, slamming the door behind him.

Hope that's the last of them, Sherlock thought. *Can't get those trains out of here soon enough. Get things back to normal.*

Sherlock busied himself around the station. He turned down the lamp in the hall outside the office, hoping to discourage any more passengers from coming in to send telegrams. He stoked the coal stove and put on a fresh pot of coffee, using snow for water. In the absence of Longcoy, he went through the stack of messages addressed to O'Neill that had arrived throughout the day, arranging them in the order they were received.

Wouldn't mind Longcoy's job. Be a real help. Be gone too much. Althea would never allow it, Sherlock concluded.

He stood up, stretching his back and arms, sore from shoveling the accumulation of snow off the roof of his house earlier that day. Fearful of the weight, Althea had told him when he woke up that if he did not take on the task, she would don a pair of his pants and do it herself. He tried to argue that the pitch of the roof was such that excess snow would naturally slide off, but his wife was hearing none of it. She took a pair of trousers from the dresser drawer and began to put them on under her dress. Reluctantly Sherlock gave in and ventured out into the storm, shovel in hand, for no other reason than to avoid the embarrassment of having his wife doing a man's work.

"You're a strong-willed woman, Althea," he complained as he headed out the door. "I swear I'll never win with you."

"Oh pooh, Basil. Think of those poor men out there working day and night in this," she countered. "A few minutes up on the roof will do you good."

Cup of coffee in hand, Sherlock slumped in his chair. The station was silent and deserted. The ticking of the clock echoed in the empty room. He glanced at the face, 7:15 p.m.

Shift's going to last forever. Althea's right, can't fathom what it must be like for those men out there. Dago shovelers have it the worst. Out in this hour after hour. Getting paid pennies. 'Bout all they're worth, though.

The sound of heavy boots stomping outside caused Sherlock to sit upright in his chair. Grabbing a handful of already-sorted messages, he attempted to look busy. The door flew open and in walked O'Neill, mid-sentence.

"…can you get me a crew or not?" O'Neill asked, brushing the snow off his coat.

Behind him was section crew foreman Bob Harley.

"Well, my full-time boys ain't the problem. It's those part-timers we brought up from Seattle last month that's raising the hell," Harley explained. "My boys been carrying the weight. Need to trade them off for the part-timers tonight, but the bastards say they're too tired to go."

Workers. Ignorant lot, Sherlock judged. *Maybe ignorance is bliss. No cares.*

O'Neill grabbed the pile of telegrams Sherlock had laid out for him and leafed through them. It seemed to Sherlock he was so engrossed in the messages that he did not hear a word Harley had said.

"Can you muster 10 or 15 good men, Mr. Harley?" he asked.

"I can do that, sir," he answered.

"I fully intend to be bucked through that slide tonight. Once we're through we can send the lot of them packing. For now, tell them I'll meet with them and hear them out in the morning when we get back." O'Neill calmly replied.

"Very good, sir. I'll get some boys together and get them on the plow train." Harley turned, but before leaving, caught Sherlock's attention.

"Passengers have been coming in, ain't they?" he asked.

"A few have."

Taking Harley's lead, O'Neill stopped reading. "Yes, Sherlock, not a word about what you've just heard to a soul. Is that understood?"

O'Neill's cold stare sent a chill down Sherlock's spine. For a moment he could not say a word.

"Company matters are strictly confidential, sir, I understand that," Sherlock mumbled, secretly proud of his reply.

Harley nodded and strolled out of the station. Sherlock watched him become slowly engulfed by the storm. His lantern cast an eerie glow in the fog formed by the snow, and then disappeared altogether.

"I'm going back west in a few minutes with Mr. Blackburn. I'll dictate the necessary responses to these messages to Longcoy before I leave."

"Yes sir, there is one thing," Sherlock said.

"Just a minute, first I need to know the latest from Cascade, I don't see anything here." O'Neill was leafing through the papers yet another time.

"Here, sir, sorry, this came in about half an hour ago, I was sending Western Union for the passengers, got distracted …"

"Yes, yes," O'Neill interrupted, taking the paper.

"Not good, eh Sherlock. A real shame about Bjerenson and his helper. Next of kin will need to be notified. I'll have Longcoy work on it. Now then, you were saying?"

O'Neill put down the messages, dug out a cigar and lit it. He pulled two quick puffs and then pulled the cigar from his mouth, staring at the smoke drifting from the end.

"Well sir, one of the passengers, a Mr. Bethel I believe, wanted you to meet with some of the men onboard the train. He says they want to be kept informed of the progress, when they are going to be able to leave, things of that nature."

Sherlock paused to judge O'Neill's reaction. Again the icy stare caused Sherlock to cower.

"I made no promises on your behalf, mind you, sir. I just said I'd relay his concerns," Sherlock quickly interjected.

"I see. Well, no time now. Too damned busy. Even if I wasn't up to my ass in all of this, I'm too damned sleepy to meet with any of them. If anyone asks you about such things, you simply tell them all important information concerning the passengers will be given directly to conductor Pettit. My time is best spent getting this railroad open. You got that, Sherlock?"

"Understood, sir," Sherlock uttered, fearful he had over-stepped his bounds with the superintendent.

O'Neill snubbed out his cigar and threw it in the wastebasket. Clearly perturbed over what Sherlock had told him, he gathered his messages and left without saying another word.

Once again alone, Sherlock slumped down in his chair.

Just want things back to normal.

Friday, February 25, 1910, 7:30 p.m.
James Henry O'Neill, Superintendent

"Do I have any dry socks, Lewis?" O'Neill called out, as he unlaced his boots. Pressing the heel of his right boot against the toe of his left, he pried his wet foot from the cold confines of the heavy shoe. Wincing, he pressed the numb toes of his right foot against the hard heel of the left boot, and with a loud "clunk," that shoe also hit the floor of his private car. He pulled off his soaked wool socks and tossed them in a corner of the rear parlor.

"Damn, I smell," O'Neill announced to his secretary, Earl Longcoy. "Getting as ripe as those good-for-nothing shovelers, wouldn't you say, Earl?"

"We all could use a bath, I guess, Mr. O'Neill," Longcoy replied.

Always the diplomat, O'Neill thought.

O'Neill's steward, Lewis Walker, hustled into the room with a dry pair of socks and a plate of hot ham and boiled potatoes.

"Now Mr. O'Neill, you're gonna need to sit and eat this. That snow plow can wait another five minutes," Walker instructed his boss. "If you come back home to Mrs. O'Neill weak and sick, why, she'll make sure I'm fired for sure."

"Well, the last thing I need is a guilty conscience from you getting fired, Lewis," O'Neill relented, pulling on the fresh socks. He swung around to the table and began to eat.

"By the way, Lewis," O'Neill paused to swallow, "there's no need in us hoarding food. I understand Bailets is getting low on provisions. Dole out some of our stores and get them up to the hotel."

"We ain't got much left either, and that's the truth. But I'll give him what I can spare. Might as well help out with some of the cookin' up there too," Walker suggested.

"Just don't bake them anything as fancy as what you cook for me, Lewis. Don't want folks to know how easy I got it around here," O'Neill teased.

"I swear, Mr. O'Neill, I don't know how you do it. Dead tired and still giving me the dickens." Walker cracked a wide grin and disappeared to the front of the car.

Revitalized by a warm meal and dry feet, O'Neill turned his attention to the telegrams Longcoy had spread out on the table. Realizing O'Neill had little time to spend, Longcoy was anxious get his boss's mind on the business at hand.

"Now sir, about the Everett – Vancouver line," Longcoy began tentatively, and outlined conditions across the division. Rising waters were threatening a major bridge at Ferndale. Messages from Seattle indicated even the rival Northern Pacific and Milwaukee Road lines through the Cascades were closed. To the south, the railroads built along the north and south banks of the Columbia River were blocked with rock slides. From San Francisco north, there was no rail service to the west coast.

"Amazing," O'Neill muttered. "The whole region completely isolated. Amazing."

Stifling a yawn, O'Neill sat silent for a moment. The slow progress at Shed 3.3 and the constant snowfall was wearing on him. More than once during the day he had to fend off a secret fear that the tide of battle had turned against him.

Tired. Have to think. Harrington's east, Dowling east of Scenic. Heard his whistle today. Tumwater blocked. Have to reroute trains even if we get the west side open. Keep an eye on the other lines just in case.

Turning from the table, O'Neill grabbed his boots and began to pull them back on. He could hear the plow train working east up the main line toward the station and the crew Harley had assembled.

"Looks like it's time to get going, Earl," O'Neill said, lacing up his shoes. "There're three things I want accomplished tonight. First, get this wire off to Bellingham to ready the pile driver. I'm worried about that Nooksack trestle in Ferndale. Second, you'll need to get a wire to Everett. When the clerks come in tomorrow, we need to find the names and addresses of Bjerenson and Elerker's next of kin. Not a pleasant task, but must be done. Legal will need to be notified, and the State."

O'Neill paused to allow Longcoy to catch up with his note taking.

"Very well, sir."

"Finally, I want our dispatchers to keep in contact with the NP dispatchers. I need to be kept abreast of the conditions of their line over the Cascades. They can help us monitor the North Bank line along the Columbia River, too."

"Are you thinking of rerouting trains over the NP or up the Columbia Gorge, sir?" Longcoy asked, realizing the reason for O'Neill's directives.

"Not yet. I'm confident we'll break through the slide to the west by morning. Still, I need to have a plan to fall back on in case things really go to hell," O'Neill stated, half joking, half serious. He rose from his chair and lit a cigar.

"Come morning maybe we'll be clear of this. I don't know about you, Earl, but I'm ready for a night or two at home."

Longcoy paused from gathering up the paperwork spread out across the table.

"Indeed, sir. This has been a bit more of an adventure than I expected."

O'Neill bundled himself up in his wet coat and walked to the rear door of his car.

"Lewis!" he called out, "You stay out of my bed!"

"Now Mr. O'Neill, I wouldn't think of it!" Walker answered from the kitchen. His words fell on empty ears, for O'Neill had already left.

The unmerciful bite of the wind caused O'Neill to linger on the porch of his car. Four days of unrelenting snow had buried his division. In all his years of railroading out on the Northern Plains or even in the Rockies, he had never seen such a series of violent storms.

Stay confident, O'Neill thought, trying to fight off that ever-increasing uneasiness. *Four plows operational. Have the manpower. Storm's bound to break.*

O'Neill dropped off the bottom step into knee-deep snow and waded down the embankment where the plow train waited. The sight of the dull lights shining from the passenger coaches, now nearly buried in the snow again gave rise to a growing sense of anxiety. *Don't panic. No need,* he secretly implored as he struggled to the X-800. *Every hour it snows, another hour closer to when it quits. We'll lick this. Stay calm in front of the men.*

Out of the corner of his eye, O'Neill saw a form approaching from the passenger train. One hand in the pocket of his long rain slicker, the other holding down his short-billed cap, O'Neill quickly recognized the man.

Damn, here comes Pettit, he scowled. He took a last puff off his cigar and threw the smoldering butt to the ground, where it was instantly covered with snow. He thought back to Sherlock and the passenger that had confronted him. *Shouldn't think that way. Poor devil has his hands full. Needs to be kept informed.*

"Mr. O'Neill," Pettit called out. "A quick word if you have time?"

"Past time for me to report, is it, Mr. Pettit?" O'Neill asked. "Here, let's get alongside the plow and out of this wind."

Ushering the conductor around the front of the giant fan of the X-800, the two men huddled alongside the hood. Shoulders hunched, hands in their pockets, they instinctively tipped their heads towards each other like school boys whispering a secret.

"I'm going to give to you right, Mr. Pettit. You can decide how best to tell the passengers. The bad news is you're going to be here tonight, that's for certain. We're about half way through the slide at Shed 3.3. We're going back right now. I fully expect to buck through tonight. Once it's clear, I want to plow west to Alvin before coming back for you. It's quite possible we'll meet up with Mr. Dowling working east from Scenic there."

O'Neill stopped and turned his head to sneeze. He cleared his throat and spat.

"Better off staying out in the cold, Mr. Pettit. Every time I go inside and come back out, my sinuses start raising holy hell."

"I can only imagine, sir. So, you're confident about getting through that slide by morning?" Pettit reiterated.

"Yes, no reason to believe otherwise. Now then, Bailets has told us his stores are running low. He's going to limit us to two meals a day. Shouldn't be a problem, since in all likelihood you'll be safely in Seattle by this time tomorrow. Still, keep that in mind."

"I might hold off saying anything about that. No sense in getting the folks riled up over nothing," Pettit decided aloud.

"That's probably best. Finally, just a matter for your information. My plan is to combine trains when we leave. If we can seat your passengers in the smoker and day coach that would help. We can go over the details when the time comes."

Pettit remained silent, staring at the ground, kicking at the snow. He took a deep breath and let it slowly escape, producing a fog that was quickly whipped away by the wind.

"I need the truth, Mr. O'Neill," he said, now looking straight at O'Neill. "I'm of the opinion we're not going anywhere until it quits snowing. Even if we combine trains, we're locked in worse now than we were over at Cascade. I've kept my feelings to myself, but am I correct?"

"We've got enough men and engines to get you moving, you can be sure of that, Mr. Pettit," O'Neill said, picking his words carefully and in a confident tone of voice. "We're having fits at Shed 3.3, but you can assure your charges, we will get through this slide and there will be no delay in getting your train loose and moving west."

Pettit extended his gloved right hand. Taking it, O'Neill felt the man's firm grasp. Matching Pettit's grip, O'Neill placed his left hand on the conductor's shoulder while they shook.

"You can tell the folks getting these trains down the mountain is foremost on my mind. All our efforts are centered on just that. I'm relying on you to handle things inside those coaches. A hell of a job, I know. I'm not the man for it. You are."

"Very well, Mr. O'Neill. Appreciate you taking the time to talk to me." Pettit pulled his hand away, walked back to his train.

O'Neill climbed into the X-800. He glanced at the men gathered inside. Blackburn was in his usual position at the left door; conductor Martin White on the right, near the brake stand. At the clutch was Dan Gilmore. Stationed on the roof, serving as the look-out, was Jim Kerlee. Across the back wall stood section-crew boss Bob Harley, along with extra crewmen. Over the last three days the men he worked with, the cabs of the snow plows he occupied, all had become more familiar to him than his own family, or the over-stuffed chair in the front room of his own home.

"Waiting for me, eh boys?" O'Neill asked, making his way across the cab. "Well, Mr. White, if all are aboard, let's get going."

Then began sounds and sensations so familiar, O'Neill would only register their absence. The two long blasts from the plow's whistle, answered by the two pusher engines, the grinding of the gears, the whine of the spinning shaft, the vibrations pulsing from the floor up through the body—all went unnoticed as the plow began moving back west.

"How many men could you muster, Mr. Harley?" O'Neill asked.

"Got twenty rounded up. Not sure how much work we'll get out of them, though," Harley admitted.

"Bodies are what we need right now," O'Neill dryly replied.

As the plow worked past the snow-covered cars of Train 25, O'Neill studied each one closely, estimating how long it would take to break the train free in the morning. Ahead, he saw engineer Frank Martin leaning from the cab of the train's locomotive.

"Give her hell!" Martin hollered as the plow passed by.

O'Neill returned his greeting with a formal salute.

Clear of the trains and the yard, Blackburn signaled for full power to the fan. Conductor White spun the large wheel mounted on the center-front wall of the cab, positioning the chute, while back alongside the boiler Bob Meath once again pulled the throttle out to the last notch. Within seconds, a heavy stream of snow was arcing to the left, disappearing into the dark, mixing and blending with the snow falling from the sky.

"What about the coal, Mr. Blackburn? You have enough for full loads?" O'Neill hollered into the trainmaster's ear.

"Full tanks all around, sir," he shouted back. "Started getting a few fines when we topped off the 802. Chute's getting low."

Worst comes to worst, can shovel off the 807 and 700 like Harrington said, O'Neill silently considered. *Need to keep some coal in the chute for the engine on the passenger train, come to think of it. If we buck through without coming back won't have to worry about it. If this, if that. Down to running this railroad on a handful of ifs.*

"Coming up on Shed 2, back out of her!" Blackburn called out.

Signals passed along, the fan slowed. O'Neill took the opportunity to walk back along the boiler. A handful of shovelers stood near the front of the warm smoke box. Walking sideways, O'Neill brushed by the men and approached Meath, the plow's engineer.

Hunched over on his square seat box, Meath's left arm was drooped over the throttle. His jacket and overalls were pure black from grease, oil and soot. The clean, boyish face had disappeared, replaced with grease smudges, a dirty growth of beard, and furrows etched into his brow. The darting eyes, the only means by which you could read the feelings of the man, were now dull and blood-shot, surrounded with dark circles and sunk deep into his head.

"Want me to chase these men out of here, Mr. Meath?" O'Neill offered. "Must be hard to see your signals with them standing there."

"Well, truth be known, harder to see through you right now than see through them," Meath quipped, leaning hard to his right.

"Point taken, Mr. Meath." O'Neill sidestepped past the reverser lever and settled in alongside the seated engineer. Leaning against the sidewall, he put a cigar to his lips, striking a match on the sill of one of the plow's grimy windows.

"You smoke, Mr. Meath?" O'Neill asked.

"You know, a good strong stogie right now might just be what the doctor ordered," Meath replied, straight-faced as always.

"Clear of the shed, wind her up!" came the call from the cab.

Meath loudly exhaled. In an action smoothed by the plane of experience, he notched open the throttle while pulling back on the reverser lever. No hard jolts, no excessive vibrations; his efforts produced a smooth transition of pressurized steam into the raw power necessary to hurl hundreds of tons of snow off the side of the mountain.

Meath rolled the cigar handed to him to the corner of his mouth. As O'Neill knelt down to light its end, he yelled in Meath's ear.

"What happened to your chair?" O'Neill asked.

"With all these shovelers onboard, I figured it was just in the way," Meath replied, again showing no sign of emotion.

Still thinking quick, O'Neill surmised, holding back a chuckle; knowing that Blackburn had ordered it removed while Meath was eating.

"So when was your last relief, Bobby?"

O'Neill's sudden use of his given name obviously took Meath by surprise.

Ah, finally a hint of emotion in that poker face of ours, John Robert Meath. O'Neill put on his own deadpan expression, calmly examining the wisps of smoke coming from the end of his cigar.

"Getting a few winks each time we come back for coal, Ji … er, ah, sir. The 800's my plow, I'll run her." Meath was looking O'Neill straight in the eye, their cigars so close the smoke from the two mingled into one cloud.

"Slide ahead! Ten car lengths!" White called out. Whistle signals were exchanged and the plow began to slow.

"I guess it's time for me to get wet with the rest of the boys. You're good on this machine, Bobby, but there's a couple of other good engineers with us. Not telling you, just letting you know."

"Pride, Mr. O'Neill. I'm gonna be at the throttle when my plow bucks this damned slide." Meath pulled the cigar from his mouth and put a grease-soaked glove to his hat. Giving it a slight tip he winked at the superintendent.

"This is a damned good smoke, Mr. O'Neill."

Saying nothing, O'Neill tipped his hat and winked in return.

Saturday, February 26, 1910, 3:00 a.m.
Arthur Reed Blackburn, Trainmaster

"Nelson says he's got less than an hour's worth of water. You want us to get the steam hose back in the tender and start shoveling snow?" Conductor Ed Lindsay had just come from the X-800 and joined Blackburn alongside the plow. Halted by the depth of the snow bank ahead, Lindsay had backed the plow away and was waiting for the "all clear" before making another charge into the blockage.

Blackburn stood erect as a snow-covered statue. He shone his lantern towards the entrance to snow Shed 3.3, a mere fifty feet away. Nearly covered by the slide, the portal to that shed had been their goal for the last two days.

Shovel snow for water. Use the few good men I've got working the slide. Take that much longer to bore out last bit, Blackburn thought, weighing his options.

"No, Mr. Lindsay, we're too close to breaking through to start changing things," Blackburn decided. "I'm going to keep those men on the slide."

Orders given, Blackburn turned and approached the section crew working to shave down the slide. The men shoveling this last portion had slowed considerably. Both Blackburn and O'Neill knew a protest was brewing among the shovelers. Nothing was said, but Blackburn could see it in their eyes and how they were working. It was more than fatigue; it was a growing air of defiance.

O'Neill and Harley picked one hell of a time to go exploring, Blackburn thought, as he walked among the shovelers. Lantern in hand, he said nothing as he passed each man. Some began to work in earnest as he approached, but others purposely stopped, preferring to stare at him in silence. *Bastards just want me to yell at them. Want an excuse to drop their shovels and quit. Well, I'm not falling for it. Lazy sons of bitches.*

An uneasiness was eating at Blackburn most of the night. O'Neill and Section Foreman Harley left nearly an hour earlier to inspect the line beyond the snow shed, leaving Blackburn supervising both the plow train and the shovelers. A part of him wanted to be the man in charge when they finally broke through the troublesome slide, yet he loathed the responsibility of both the plow crews and the workers.

Satisfied that the snow had been dug down to the point at which the plow could make another run, he began to direct the shovelers away from the path of the machine's spinning fan. He swung his lantern signaling the "all clear." Two whistle blasts from the plow, answered by the pushers, pierced the darkness. The majority of the sectionmen slowly walked out of the way, but three men lingered. In the light cast by the lanterns, their stiff silhouettes made them look more like department store mannequins than living humans. Blackburn could take it no longer.

"Move, goddamn it! Plow's coming! For Christ sakes, get the hell outta the way!" he hollered. Blackburn stormed towards the stationary men waving his hands and lantern. "Get outta the goddamned way!" he bellowed into the ear of the closest shoveler. "Plow's coming!"

Homer Purcell, standing outside the cab of the plow, saw the trouble.

"Hold her up!" he hollered into the cab. "Blackburn can't get the damned workers off the slide."

"Move, goddamn it! Move!" Blackburn shouted, his voice cracking.

The three men dropped their shovels and causally strolled out of the way. In the dull light of the lanterns, Blackburn could make out smiles on the faces of the others in the crew. Furious, he snatched up the shovels and again gave the plow the "all clear."

Making a good run, the whirling fan hit the wall of packed snow with a force Blackburn had not witnessed all night. The berm below his feet shook with the impact. Large chunks of snow that were not immediately chewed by the fan flew in all directions.

Purcell was at Blackburn's side. Both men kept their lanterns shining on the hood of the fan. Lindsay, hanging from the door, was within an arm's reach of both men.

"She's taking her, Ed!" Purcell called out.

"Keep at her! Don't back out!" Blackburn added.

Chewing right into her. Snow's getting softer the closer we get to the shed, Blackburn thought. His trained ear could hear the fan beginning to falter, its revolutions decreasing.

"Ease up!" he shouted to Lindsay.

"Pressure dropping!" Lindsay hollered at nearly the same time. He bolted for the whistle cord, producing a single long and single short blast. Both Lindsay and Blackburn held their lanterns straight out. The engineers in the pushers reacted immediately, easing up on their throttles.

There was a momentary lag between the slowing of the pushers and the fan reacting to the lesser load. It seemed an eternity to Blackburn.

"Come on, you bastard," he mumbled aloud. "You can take it. Goddamn it, don't plug on us now."

Even before Lindsay called out that the steam pressure was rising, Blackburn could hear it. The pitch of the fan's whine began to increase, and the snow again flowed from the chute in an arc that quickly disappeared over the steep bank and into the night.

Lanterns in hand, O'Neill and Harley emerged from the shed, climbing up the wall of snow that blocked the entrance. They scurried across the face being attacked by the plow and joined Blackburn and Purcell.

"You gonna break through this pass?" Harley asked Blackburn.

Blackburn was moving with the plow. Gently waving his lantern in a counter-clockwise circle, he kept motioning the machine forward.

"She's breaking apart. If we don't spin out, we'll take her out." Blackburn answered.

O'Neill was at Blackburn's side.

"One car length!" Blackburn called out to Lindsay.

Blackburn ducked under the plume of snow exiting the fan and took up position at the corner of the shed. Shining his lantern into its darkness, he closely watched the remaining snow pack. The forward force of the plow could very well shove the last of the slide into the shed, where it would have to be shoveled out by hand.

"Half a car! Ease her up!" Blackburn called. O'Neill and Purcell relayed the orders to the plow and engines.

Chunks of snow began to break free and roll down into the shed. Cracks started to form as the final feet of the blockade gave way to the constant churning of the plow's fan.

"Quarter car length!"

Wall's holding firm, he thought. *Keep bringing her in slow.*

The closer the fan came, the more snow was pitched from its blades at Blackburn, hitting him on his legs and chest. He took refuge near the corner post of the shed, still shining his lantern on the snow. Suddenly, a large section broke away from the middle of the pack. Part of it was instantly devoured by the fan and cast aside, while the remainder fell into the shed. The fan, now partially exposed, sent a blinding cloud of snow and ice into Blackburn's eyes. Instinctively he waved his lantern back and forth. His signal relayed down the line, and he heard the plow's whistle "stop."

"You okay, Art?" O'Neill called out.

"Yeah, fine!" he answered. He cleared his eyes, wiping the tears from his cheeks. He came out from behind the post and carefully inspected what was left to be plowed.

"Bring her in a couple more feet!" Blackburn shouted. "Come in easy, just use one engine to push, watch for my signal to stop. We about got her, by God!"

He continued to rotate his lantern in a slow counterclockwise circle. The fan was throwing so much snow in his direction, Blackburn could only sneak occasional looks at the progress.

Suddenly, the flying chunks of snow ceased. The leading edge of the fan ducked under the eve of the shed. Blackburn immediately waved his lantern back and forth. The plow stopped and then pulled away. Backed well clear of the snow shed, Imberg brought the plow train to a stop and whistled that the brakes were set. Blackburn slid down the steep snow bank onto the freshly cleared track. Inside the shed lay only a three-foot mound of snow.

"Get some shovelers down here!" Blackburn ordered. "Throw a shovel down for me!"

Two shovels clattered as they were thrown from on top of the berm. O'Neill came sliding down behind them, closely followed by Harley and five of the Italians. Together the men cleared away the snow pushed into the shed by the plow, tossing it out where the fan could pick it up and cast it aside.

"What did you find to the west?" Blackburn asked O'Neill as they worked.

"Line's plugged. Drifted in bad," O'Neill stopped speaking to catch his breath, but kept shoveling. "Figured that. But no slides between here and Windy."

"Can make a clean-up pass," Blackburn informed his boss, panting as well. "About out of water. Probably low on coal. Won't be able to plow west until we refill."

A few more men slid down the embankment. Working shoulder to shoulder, within ten minutes the remaining snow had been pitched clear of the shed.

"Hallelujah!" Blackburn cheered. "Didn't think we'd ever buck through that bastard."

Crowded into the cab of the eastward facing X-802, Blackburn motioned to conductor Martin White to take his place watching the fan. He elbowed his way between a track worker and O'Neill, who was sitting on the ring gearbox along with Harley. Blackburn dropped down on one knee in front of both men.

`"You got trouble brewing, you know that," Blackburn said to Harley, his right hand cupped to the side of his mouth. "As soon as you left, that crew of yours wouldn't do a damned thing. Just stared at me."

"We know, Art, but now's not the time," O'Neill stopped lighting a cigar and was glaring at Blackburn.

"I suppose when those bastards drop their shovels and walk outta here, then you'll figure it's time," Blackburn mumbled loud enough for O'Neill to hear.

"I said now is not the time!" O'Neill put his smoke to his lips. "When we get back to Wellington, I'll get things hashed out."

"What about the trains? You still going hold them until we buck to Alvin?"

O'Neill snubbed out his cigar and tossed it to the floor.

"Christ, Art, calm down. Man can't even have a smoke in peace?" O'Neill complained.

"Sorry sir, just don't want to miss another chance of getting those trains moving, that's all," Blackburn admitted.

"When we get back to Wellington, get your men fed, Mr. Harley. Tell them I'll be over there in half an hour to meet with them," O'Neill ordered. "Art, you and me need to talk things over."

About time he sat down with me, Blackburn thought. *Talks to Harrington like they're long-lost brothers, leaves me out in the cold. Out in the cold, now that's a good one.*

Back at Wellington, Blackburn walked into the depot behind O'Neill. He grabbed two chairs and pulled them over by the stove. O'Neill was at the desk talking to Avery, picking up the stack of messages that had arrived from other parts of the division. He quickly thumbed through the telegrams, taking note of a few, then placed them back on the desk.

"Now then Art, guess you and me need to get today figured out." O'Neill sat down and yawned. "I'll look after the trouble with the section crew. You keep to the train crews. They're about to break too, I can feel it. Be careful, Art. Don't drive 'em too hard."

"Understood, sir," Blackburn said. He stretched out his legs and stared at the floor.

"Now then, about the coal," O'Neill continued. "Think the chute's about empty?"

"What I don't want to do is take all the coal out of the chute. Have to leave some to top off 25's and 27's power when time comes to pull them out and take them on down." Blackburn said. "I'm thinking we can pull coal from the 700 and the 807 to top off the engines and the 802 while we're sitting here. We can pull coal for the 800 out of the chute. How far west we going to plow before we come back for the trains."

"I was hoping no further than Alvin," O'Neill said. "Not looking good though. Message from Scenic, Dowling is tangled in a good slide just east of Scenic."

"Shit," Blackburn sighed. "We gonna have to try and buck all the way to Dowling down at Scenic before getting the trains?"

"I don't want to leave those trains here, but I damned sure don't want to hold them at Alvin," O'Neill answered. "Get them stranded down there, we'll be in a hell of a fix. You got any ideas, Art? I've about run out."

Finally. Didn't think the day would come he'd ask my take on anything, Blackburn thought. *Glad Harrington ain't here.*

"Well sir, I have been thinking on it some," Blackburn said, carefully choosing his words. "What say we plow down to the west switch at Alvin, then come back for the trains. If Dowling is still hung up down below and we have to hold the trains at Alvin for a few hours, well, if worst comes to worst, there's the old work trail there. We've got enough men on the plows to break that trail out and get the passengers and mail sacks down to the lower line. Hell, we make Alvin, we can grab one hell of a crew from Scenic to help out."

O'Neill sat quiet.

Tell me a better idea, Blackburn thought. *You don't have a better plan. Can tell.*

"There's women and children on that train, Art. You think they'd be able to handle that trail? Snow's gonna be deep there too, you know," O'Neill challenged.

"You get enough men helping, maybe ropes around the trees to hold onto, sure, they'll make it. That old trail ain't that steep. If Dowling is having that much trouble, it could be a couple of days before we get the line open. You want to wait that long? That goddamned hill above 3.3 might give way again if we wait. We both know it!" Blackburn took a deep breath. He realized his temper was on edge. *Get a hold of yourself. Quiet reason works better on him than shouting,* Blackburn silently said in an effort to calm down.

"God, I don't know, Art. It's pretty risky trailing a bunch of passengers out in this storm." O'Neill paused then rose from his chair. "But I ain't got a better plan right now."

Nearly out the door, he stopped. "We'll plow to Alvin. You and I can scout out the old trail, maybe find out for sure where Dowling is. Your idea might be our best bet. Get something to eat, Art. Go up to my car and have Lewis fix you something."

"Thank you, sir. I think I'll take you up on the offer," Blackburn said.

Still at the door, O'Neill looked straight at Blackburn. An expression of caring and compassion came across his face.

"You've been working like a slave, Art," O'Neill said in a soft voice. "I appreciate the job you're doing. Not many trainmasters could shoulder all of this."

There was an awkward pause. Blackburn could not tell if the flush of heat he was suddenly feeling was embarrassment, or simply the skin on his face beginning to thaw.

"We're all just doing our duty, sir," Blackburn mumbled.

"Well anyway, get your boys transferring that coal as soon as they've eaten. I'm going to see what's going on with Harley and his damned crew." O'Neill headed out the door.

"We'll get on it, sir," Blackburn replied, himself walking outside.

The two men parted ways, O'Neill walking over to the section house, Blackburn towards the men gathered around the plow train.

Finally seeing a few things my way.

For the first time in days a grin appeared on Blackburn's face.

Saturday, February 26, 1910, 6:00 a.m.
James Henry O'Neill, Superintendent

The last thing O'Neill felt like doing was dealing with a group of insubordinate sectionmen. He walked across the station platform, now covered with nearly three feet of snow. Only a narrow path between the station and the adjoining section house was being maintained.

Slide cleaned. Don't need all those shovelers, O'Neill reasoned. *Need men to bust out the trains. Bergstrom's boys over at Cascade can help. No reason to knuckle under to this bunch.* He rolled his cigar across his mouth. His thoughts collected, he pushed his way through the door into the tool room.

Foreman Bob Harley and his lead man, Peter Buno, were standing in the far corner next to the stove. Hanging from the rafters were wet rain slickers, steaming wool coats, and socks. A handful of men were scattered about, lying on thin bed rolls. Some were fast asleep, others merely rolled onto their sides and eyed O'Neill in silence. The atmosphere was dank, heavy with the smell of wet clothes, stale whiskey, and men long overdue for a bath.

Harley poured himself a cup of coffee from a pot that had long ago turned coal black. His mug was a tin can that matched the color of the pot.

"Care for a cup, sir?" he offered.

O'Neill declined with casual shake of his head.

"Just want you to know, these here are my regular boys. They ain't the problem," Harley explained.

"That's right. We do the work. We'll stay," added lead man Peter Bruno in a thick Italian accent.

"It's those bastards from that employment agency. They're causing all the ruckus," Harley claimed. "Got 'em over in the cookhouse, eating."

"They have a ring leader I can talk to, or are they gonna gang up on me?" O'Neill questioned.

"There's a couple of hotheads," Harley replied, looking at Bruno. "There's that one Italian that was trying to rile up our boys, then that big mean-looking fella, right, Peter?"

"The big man, they call him Hank. The other is Tony," informed Bruno. "They say Hank, he kill a man back east."

"Never knew a section gang yet that didn't have at least one murderer. I wouldn't pay it any mind," scoffed O'Neill. "Started on the gang when I was fourteen, Mr. Harley. Worked the gangs for a year and a half. These men don't scare me."

Show of force be best, O'Neill reasoned. *If they think I'm going to deal with a couple of bullies, they've got another thing coming.*

"I can have Peter go in there and get those two sons of bitches if you want, Mr. O'Neill," Harley offered.

"No, I think I'll go in there and raise hell with the lot of them, Mr. Harley. Nip this thing in the bud," O'Neill opted. "Mr. Bruno, you tell your men, they keep working and I'll see they are taken care of. Gonna tell that bunch across the way the same thing."

"Not about being cared for, they want more money," Harley muttered.

"I realize that, Mr. Harley, but they are not getting a dime more from me. What about your men, they griping about wages too?" O'Neill challenged.

"No! No! We keep working," Bruno interrupted. "We want to work!"

O'Neill looked around the dimly lit room. The men on their bedrolls were watching and listening closely.

"That true?" O'Neill asked, now looking around the room at the rest of the men.

There was a nodding of agreement from those who understood—and from those who did not, but knew enough not to cross O'Neill.

"So be it. Mr. Harley, come with me. Let's settle this thing with those bastards once and for all."

O'Neill left the tool room with confident strides, Harley at his heels. His cigar pressed hard between his lips, he set his jaw and burst through the door into the mess hall. The clinking of forks on tin plates immediately halted, then just as quickly resumed.

A long plank table stretched down the middle of the room. On each side, men were crowded shoulder to shoulder on benches. They were a tough-looking crew, clothes tattered and dirty. They grasped their forks like small children, shoveling in mouthfuls of boiled potatoes. They viciously ripped hunks of bread, slopped them in the grease left from the thick slices of bacon hanging from their plates and inhaled that as well.

Going to have choice words with that employment agency, O'Neill thought, sizing up the crew. *Rounded up every drunk in Seattle and Everett. Crooked bastards.*

"I'm told you have grievances," O'Neill boomed. "So let's hear them."

There was silence in the room.

"Oh, I see, big talk behind my back, no guts to stand and speak," taunted O'Neill. "I'll listen to any man that's willing to talk to me face-to-face. I'll fire any man I catch raising hell with my workers behind my back. Now let's hear it!"

Typical hotheads, not an ounce of courage in any of them, thought O'Neill. He calmly pulled a long puff off his cigar and blew the smoke straight down the table.

"We want fifty cents an hour and no charge for board. Take it or leave it," came a voice from the middle of the men.

"That's the man they call Hank talking," Harley whispered to O'Neill. "The big guy with the red hair there in the middle on the left side."

With a nod of his head, O'Neill centered his glare on the big, bushy-haired man. He strolled down the opposite side of the table, not once taking his eyes off him. Standing directly across from the man,

O'Neill exhaled another puff of tobacco smoke, making sure the white cloud blew across the table.

"Excuse me, sir, but my ears aren't what they should be, what did you say?" O'Neill asked, casually inspecting the end of his cigar.

Hank looked up from his food. O'Neill saw the eyes of someone suddenly unsure of himself, even frightened, staring back at him from under the worker's thick eyebrows.

You've killed a man, all right. If you're a murderer, I'm Jack the Ripper. O'Neill let a slight grin cross his face.

"I said, we want fifty cents an hour and no charge for board." His voice tailed off.

"And if I say no?" O'Neill challenged.

"Then we ain't working and your trains ain't goin nowhere," Hank replied, slowly gaining some confidence. Around him, heads nodded in agreement.

"Blackmail what you have in mind?" O'Neill asked. "Well, gentlemen, you picked the wrong time and the wrong man to try and pull a stupid stunt like this. The Great Northern Railway is not about to bow to the demands of a bunch of worthless drunks."

"Seems to me you ain't the whole damned railroad," Hank snarled.

"And that, sir, is where your weak mind is dead wrong!" O'Neill shouted, "I *am* the whole goddamned Great Northern as far as bastards like you are concerned! Now then, why the hell would I even consider paying you five times what you agreed on?"

O'Neill's outburst produced the impact he expected. Worried eyes darted from man to man, many settling on the man they had hoped would bully O'Neill into a raise. Hank himself looked like was just sent to the floor of a bar with a roundhouse left hook out of nowhere.

"We ain't doin' the work we agreed. You're working us day and night, out in this goddamned storm. Dangerous too. Damned snow slides. Nobody told us we could get covered and killed in some goddamned snow slide," Hank countered.

"You have a simple choice, gentlemen," O'Neill continued speaking, once again in a completely calm voice. "Work for the wages you agreed on when you signed your contracts with the agency, or leave."

"Leave? Whatta ya mean, leave? We're snowed in here just like everyone else!" blurted out another worker.

"Now you're blackmailing us!" another hollered.

"No blackmail, gentlemen, just a simple decision. Work and get paid, get food, get a place to sleep, or get out. If you decide not to work, all you have to do is walk that way," O'Neill pointed to the west, "long enough, and far enough and you'll find Everett. I have nothing more to say to any of you. Finish eating. Those of you who still want to work, report to Mr. Harley in the tool room. The rest of you, clear out!"

O'Neill turned and began to make his way to the door.

"Hey, what about the money we're owed for the work we've done? We're supposed to be paid come the first, you got the money?" Hank protested.

"Too bad you can't read, sir. Your contract plainly states we can pay you cash on site once each month, or issue vouchers and send our payroll to the agency and they'll pay you. Obviously the payroll has not yet been delivered. I plan to have the pay clerk issue vouchers to all of you for the work done thus far. You can redeem them at our office in Everett when your work here is done." Once again O'Neill began to leave.

"Oh, and I almost forgot," O'Neill turned and faced the stunned men, "from now on, to eat in this cookhouse, you will have to show a voucher proving you did a day's work. No work, no voucher, no food. Good day, gentlemen."

"Hey, you can't do that!" a man yelled.

"You and your goddamned railroad can go to hell!" came another shout.

Harley slammed the door behind him as he and O'Neill departed, shutting out the noise of the angry workers.

"I don't expect any of them to grab a shovel, Mr. Harley," O'Neill admitted. "I'll contact Brown and see if I can get the men who stay a nickel an hour raise, but keep that to yourself for now."

Back in the tool house, Harley looked around at his full-time gang. Most were now asleep. "They've been working like dogs, Mr. O'Neill. Just don't lump these boys in with that riffraff."

"I understand, Mr. Harley. Let your boys get a few more hours sleep, then get as many as you can digging out those trains. I want the engines cleared out first. I plan to combine the trains. Don't worry about the trailing three passenger coaches—my guess is we'll leave them here for now. Understand?"

"Yes sir, I'll muster as many men as I can that'll work. What about those vouchers?" Harley asked.

"Longcoy will give you a hand with the paperwork. We brought a bunch up with us on my car. We had no intention of paying those men in cash until we were through with them. Give men like that a dollar and you'll never see them again, wouldn't you say, Mr. Harley?" O'Neill threw the butt of his cigar into the stove and walked for the door.

"Aye, that's about how it goes," agreed Harley. "Appreciate you giving those bastards hell, Mr. O'Neill."

"All in a day's work, Mr. Harley."

Saturday, February 26, 1910, 6:30 a.m.
John Robert Meath, Engineer

Meath rammed his scoop shovel into the mound of coal. The tip tried to skip across the top of the pile, but he put downward pressure on the handle and jiggled until he had a full load. Lifting the shovel, he swung his arms in a long arc behind his back and, with a swift forward motion, propelled the scoop forward. Its load of coal flew across the gap between his position, in the tender of the 700, to land neatly on the pile in the nearly-full tender of the X-802. At Meath's left worked Bat Nelson and Rich Chambers; to his right Thomas Brown, and Irving Tegtmeier. Further down, another crew of trainmen pitched coal from the tender of the dead X-807 to top off engine 1128.

"You must be getting plumb wore out, Bobby," Brown commented between scoops.

"Wore out, wore out," Meath pondered, pausing from the work. "Let me see, what day is it, Thomas?"

"Saturday," Brown answered, now eying Meath as if he was losing his mind.

"Ah yes, Saturday. Well, near as I can remember I was tired on Thursday afternoon. Wore out didn't show up until yesterday. Don't remember a thing since." Meath went back to shoveling while those around him chuckled, shaking their heads.

"The fire's never out in your boiler, is it, Bobby," Tegtmeier commented.

"If you had as much whiskey in your belly as ol' Bobby's got, you'd have a full head of steam too, Tig," Nelson said.

"Sober as a widow church lady," Meath replied, not breaking stride.

In spite of the cold, Meath was beginning to sweat. The coal dust mixed with the melting flakes of snow and sweat on his face. Black streams of the salty water flowed off his forehead and into his eyes. Attempts to wipe them clean with his glove only aggravated the stinging. Digging into his coat, he pulled out his grimy bandana. He wiped his brow clean but left his eyes alone, hoping his own tears would eventually ease the discomfort.

"Stings like hell, don't it, Bobby," commented Nelson. "Do ya good to remember what it's like to be a fireman. Can tell you've been on the right side of the cab."

Meath resumed shoveling.

"When's the last time you had a hand-stoker, Bat?" Meath casually asked.

"Alright, you got me," Nelson relented. "Thought you were tired."

"That was Thursday."

Beat to hell, Meath admitted to himself. *Glad we finally bucked that slide at 3.3. A good run to Alvin. Be able to finally sign off for a shift.*

He straightened up and looked down from the tender. At some point it had become light, he hadn't even noticed. Reaching down, he grabbed the closest lantern and closed off the flow of kerosene. He watched the flame slowly flicker out.

Feel like that flame, Meath thought.

Through the snow, he saw O'Neill and Blackburn walking toward them from the depot. The image of the approaching men blurred as Meath focused his eyes on the falling snow.

Flakes getting bigger, fatter, full of water. Starting to warm up a little. Maybe this is about the end of it.

"Better get to shoveling, Bobby, Mr. Blackburn and Mr. O'Neill will have your job if you don't," Nelson teased, as their two superiors came alongside the tender.

"Good reason to keep leaning on my shovel, Bat," Meath replied in a loud voice. "I can only hope Mr. O'Neill sacks me on the spot and puts me out of my misery."

"Sorry, Mr. Meath," O'Neill called up. "I'm afraid I intend to keep you right here 'til the snow's melted away."

"We've got all the coal we need," Tegtmeier hollered down. "If you two gentlemen are ready, we can head on out."

"Lead plow serviced?" Blackburn asked.

"Yes sir," Tegtmeier answered.

"Well, let's get to it, boys," O'Neill announced. "I'm anxious to make Alvin. With a little luck we'll have those piles of snow over there on the siding out of our hair by nightfall."

The surroundings were all too familiar to Meath. Shabby wood tongue-in-groove car decking sides hemmed him in to his right. The long, hot steaming boiler rubbed his shoulder to the left. The narrow passageway to the cab in front, and the dark gangway leading to the fire deck behind, created a cramped, environment that Meath secretly detested. The towering mountains, the crisp mountain air in his face—that was his favorite part of running an engine. As much as he liked the challenge of engineering a plow, the untold hours in its confined surroundings never failed to put him on edge.

Born and raised in Wisconsin, his mind and imagination were fed by the rolling fields and open air. Being locked inside the dark plow for days wore on Meath, creating an ever-increasing strain that added to his physical fatigue. All that remained between himself and collapse was the stubborn spirit to finish what he had started. It was a spirit literally beat into him by his father.

On the move, they were working through a light accumulation of snow. Meath had the plow working at half capacity, but it easily cleared the track.

Be at Alvin by noon, Meath thought. *Easy running to 3.3. After that slow going. If we don't have to buck, just wind her up and let her go. Engineers on the pushers can jockey their throttles for a change.*

Steam escaped the cylinders under Meath's feet and drifted up through the boards of the gangway. It mixed with the ever-present haze created by hot grease and the coal smoke being pushed through the stack at the head of the boiler. The air was stuffy, laden with moisture. Rising from his seat box, Meath cracked open one of the grime-covered windows. Taking off his coat, he draped it over his seat for a cushion, and settled back in.

Bat's back there freezing to death. I'm suffocating. Keep the windows open. Keep it cold in here or I'll nod off.

Demons were haunting all of the men, and Meath knew he was surrounded by his fair share. He looked up at the steam gauge, its glass dial smudged. The needle was nearly pegged. Staring at it for a long moment, his mind began to drift and his vision blurred.

Damn it, pay attention! Don't stare at anything too long, Meath lectured himself, shaking his head. He got up and opened the second window and the door to his back. *Get outta here Satan. Gentle voice. Telling me to sleep. Boys up front are lucky. People around, things to see, gives a man a fighting chance to stay awake. Hate it back here alone when I'm this tired.*

Again Meath shook his head. He had been staring at the shiny handle on the reverser lever in front of him and his eyes had started to glaze over.

Hope Bat's cooling out his fire—pop-off valve's about to blow. Wasting all that steam., using too much coal. Blackburn'll be on our asses for that. I'll see if can bail Bat outta trouble.

To break the boredom, Meath began to juggle the position of his throttle and reverser, in an attempt to push more steam through the pistons. He kept his eyes moving by counting the notches he was taking on his levers and watching for the needle's response on the steam gauge. He forced himself to listen carefully for the slightest difference in the sound of the exhaust and the whine generated by the main shaft spinning the fan. Still, it was the steady drone of the gears that pierced most easily through the intense ringing in Meath's ears. The effect was hypnotic.

"Shed 2, five car lengths, Bobby," Conductor Homer Purcell called back. "You can start backing out of her."

Meath sat prone, his eyes fixed on the steam gauge.

"Mr. Meath. Mr. Meath! Slow down the damned fan!"

Blackburn's shouting snapped Meath from his momentary trance.

"Damn it," Meath mumbled. He reached forward and pulled the reverse lever toward him, then shoved the throttle away, reducing the flow of steam to the two pistons.

"You need to stay alert, Mr. Meath," Blackburn lectured from the front doorway. "Mother Nature is giving us enough trouble—we don't need to add to it by not paying attention to what we're doing." Blackburn turned and left for the opposite side of the plow's cab.

Darkness engulfed the plow as it rolled through the short snow shed. Peering ahead into the cab, Meath could tell by the intensity of the light coming through the small front window when the plow was about to emerge from the other side and encounter snow again. He gave his eyes a quick rub and slowly began to work his levers, putting power to the fan the instant they burst into the daylight.

There, you asshole, how's that for paying attention? Meath gloated.

He heard talking, even a few bouts of laughter from up front. Men were moving back and forth in the cab. He could see the outstretched legs of Ed Lindsay, obviously sitting on the floor, his back against the ring gear cover, taking a nap.

Demons, floating all around, Meath thought. *In this goddamned snow that won't ever quit. Demons trying to get my eyes closed. Inside my goddamned head. Got hammers. Trying to pound their way out. Demons taking the fun outta railroading. Gotta stay alert. Can't let the demons get the better of me.*

One long blast erupted from the plow's whistle.

"Slide, ahead! Eight car lengths!" Purcell called out.

Eight car lengths, Meath calculated. *That's about at Shed 3.3. Oh God, you didn't …*

As the plow slowed, Meath closed off his throttle. He sat for a moment. A deep sense of depression welled up inside the man the crew depended on for his happy spirit.

Don't even want to go up there and look, Meath thought. *Another slide in the same spot. How much more, Lord?*

"Another slide, Bobby, same damned place." Lindsay called back. He, too, had the look and sound of a beaten man.

"I don't even want to look. How bad is it?" Meath asked.

"Dunno, Blackburn and O'Neill are looking it over right now. Maybe not as big as the one we cleaned yesterday, but I'd guess we'll be here the rest of the day trying to buck it out. I just can't believe it." Lindsay turned and walked away, his head bowed.

Ain't got shoveler one with us either. Almost rather shovel than be stuck in this bastard another day and night bucking. Maybe I'll ask O'Neill if I can shovel and...naah, quit thinking nonsense.

"All right, Mr. Meath, we're going to wind her up and move in," ordered Blackburn having returned to the cab.

"What are we up against?" Meath asked.

"About three hundred feet long, but not as deep. Maybe fifteen, twenty feet at the deepest. Not as hard packed—must've just come down. We might be able to buck through it without those damned shovelers slowing us down," Blackburn informed Meath. "Stay alert now, we're going to be moving in and backing out. Keep a sharp eye on your steam. I don't want the fan to plug."

"Yes sir," Meath replied. Under his breath he muttered, "Easier said then done."

Be into snow right away. Soon as the clutch catches gonna have to wind her fast, Meath reasoned.

There was a slight lurch. Meath glanced out his open window. Through the falling snow, he saw the snow bank begin to move. There was a slight mechanical grinding and then the all-too-familiar drone of the main shaft spinning.

"Wind her up! Now!" Blackburn shouted back. "You're half asleep back there!"

While Blackburn yelled, Meath released the catch on the throttle and, in one quick motion, pulled it to the last notch. The needle on the steam gauge took a sudden dip, but as Meath slowly pulled back on the reverser lever, it began to climb upward.

Blackburn's right. Was late getting going, Meath admitted to himself. *Didn't even hear them engage the clutch for some reason.*

"Plowing a full hood! She's taking her!" Lindsay called back.

Watch. Listen. Concentrate, Bobby boy, Meath coached himself.

The fan was beginning to lug under the load; he could tell by the sharp, labored exhaust and the pitch of the drone of the main shaft. He slammed the reverser all the way forward, giving each piston the longest possible stroke to take advantage of the most steam he could force into the cylinders. Steam pressure began to slide.

Watch the gauge. Keep your eyes sharp. Blink. Look away. Look back. Damn, can't focus! Seventy-five pounds, no, sixty-five. She's lugging hard, better whistle for some brakes.

Meath reached for the cord, but before he could even grasp it, a single long wail exploded into his ears. The plow began to slow.

Damn it, behind the eight ball again. Gotta concentrate.

Again Meath pulled back on the reverser lever, trying to stabilize the dropping steam pressure, yet maintain ample power for the fan to throw the snow clear.

"How's the chute?" Meath hollered forward, hoping to get a visual idea of the snow conditions and the fan.

"The arc's starting to shallow out! Snow's coming over the hood!" Lindsay answered.

Holding at seventy pounds. Need to get ten more out of her to be safe, Meath decided.

He leaned forward and grabbed the reverser. His back was stiff, his shoulders aching from exertion and tension. He pulled it back two more notches. Sweat dripped into his eyes. He wiped his forehead with his filthy shirtsleeve.

Up to eighty but the fan don't sound right. Need more stroke. Give her two notches back. Sounds like she's trying to pick up speed.

Meath closed his eyes and yawned. *Gotta stay alert. Check the steam gauge. Steam dropping. Damnit!*

"She's stalling!" Meath called out. He lunged for his whistle cord and sent three short blasts into the air.

"Back this bastard up quick, goddamn it," Meath said aloud. He kept a full throttle but continued to work the reverser level. In near desperation, he tried to walk that fine line between keeping maximum power to the main shaft and depleting what little steam pressure he had left.

"Why the hell did you let it drop this far? You waited too damned long to call for brakes, goddamn it!" Blackburn pulled Lindsay out of the way and stood in the doorway. "If you can't run this goddamned plow right, I'll get someone who can!"

Once backed clear of the slide, the fan quickly cleaned itself and the steam pressure rose to an acceptable level. Meath again whistled off to the engineers in the pushers. Easing the plow forward, they resumed the attack of the slide.

Had that ass-chewing coming. My fault. Not running her sharp. Don't just stare at that damned gauge, make sure you read it, Meath instructed himself.

A gentle tap on his shoulder caused Meath to nearly jump from his seat. Eyes wide with the sudden scare, he turned to face O'Neill, standing behind him.

"You scared the hell out of me, sir," Meath hollered above the din of the working plow. He turned back around, maintaining his vigilant watch on the steam gauge.

O'Neill came to Meath's side, bent over and cupped his hands between his mouth and Meath's right ear.

"I went back to the 802 and got Mr. Brown. He's taking over for you."

For the second time, Meath spun around on his seat box. Behind him stood Thomas Brown.

"You done more than your share, Bobby, get some rest for God's sake," Brown pleaded. "Let me take her awhile. You've thrown more snow off the side of this mountain than all of us put together."

"Full hood!" came a call from up front.

Meath turned his attention to the steam gauge. *Holding at eighty five.*

He grabbed the reverser and gently pulled it back one notch, then two. Sighing, his shoulders sagging, Meath pulled the gloves from his hands. As he rose from his seat, his knees buckled. His right leg had gone to sleep and he hadn't even noticed. O'Neill grabbed him under his right arm and steadied the exhausted engineer.

"Not very polite of me to hog all the fun, I guess. She's all yours, Tommy," Meath said, doing his best to cover his disappointment in himself. "I'm okay, Mr. O'Neill, just got up too fast after that scaring you gave me, that's all."

Meath stepped back. Brown took Meath's coat off the seat box and draped it over the weary engineer's shoulders. Pulling on his gloves, Brown looked over the positions of the levers and the steam gauge. He looked up at Meath and gave him a nod and a grin.

"You're leavin' her in good shape, Bobby."

"You need shovelers out front, Mr. O'Neill?' Meath asked.

"Even if I did, I wouldn't tell you," Mr. O'Neill replied. He placed a strong arm across Meath's hunched shoulders. "Make your way back to the 802 and get some rest. I'll need you to run that old teapot when we go back for water. Mr. Brown is right, you've done more than your share. Already sent Nelson back, probably sound asleep. Bennington firing this rig."

Meath said nothing. He walked through the door onto the fire deck. Earl Bennington paused from tending the fire.

"The shits we hit another slide here, eh Bobby?"

Meath pulled back the canvas to see the wall of snow they were trying to clear.

We're licked. Can feel it. Goddamned storm beat me, now it's gonna beat the rest of us. Demons everywhere.

"You okay, Bobby?" Bennington was at his side.

"I'm okay, Earl. Just hate to walk away, that's all. Job half done and all."

Bennington spat a wad of tobacco onto the wet deck.

"Shit Bobby, weren't for you and Bat we'd still be here bucking that last slide, and that's God's truth." Bennington paused and spat again. "I told O'Neill them very words. Bat was here, he'll tell ya."

"I'm headed back to the 802. Keep my girl hot and happy, Earl," Meath quipped.

With the last bit of energy he had left, Meath vaulted off the fire deck and onto the snow bank alongside of the plow. He landed face first, his legs dangling over the edge. Kicking and clawing, he scrambled his way to the top, struggling to stand in the deep snow. Covered with snow, hands in his coat pockets, he waded past the two pusher engines.

Lou Ross, leaning from the cab of the 1154, held out his arm. In his hand was a small flask.

"You look beat to hell, Bobby. Need some liquid encouragement?" he asked.

"No thanks, Lou," was all Meath could muster.

Bob Ford had relieved Ben Jarnigan in the 1128. With his engine running backwards, he too was leaning far out his window.

"They told me they were giving you the boot, Bobby. You done good for an old man." Ford said, as his engine inched past.

Compliments were something Meath seldom heard growing up. Ten years away from home, he still was never sure what to say when praise came his way. His solution was always to turn a compliment into a joke about himself.

"Yeah, O'Neill finally figured out I hired out from that same agency that sent Harley those lazy shovelers, so he sacked me," Meath said, pausing to catch his breath.

Meath left Ford laughing, relaying what he had just said to his fireman, Gerry Jenks.

Tired. Hitting like a ton of bricks. Too tired to walk. Just stand here, let the 802 catch up to me, Meath thought. Squinting through the falling snow, he watched "his" plow slowly chew into the slide. *Tommy's got her running good.*

"You coming aboard, or just stand there and turn into a snowman?" Bat Nelson was leaning against the door of the 802.

"Too beat to jump, Bat. I'll slide down when she passes and catch up with you."

Limp as a rag doll, Meath half slid, half tumbled down the snow bank onto the freshly cleared track. He eased his way around the side of the lifeless fan of the X-802, to the cab ladder and Nelson's outstretched hand. The fireman's firm grasp and strong arm lifted Meath into the cab, his feet barely touching the rungs, his free arm sliding up the grab iron. In a blur of motion, he was standing inside.

"Just us, Bobby. O'Neill sent all the relief boys forward to help with the slide."

"Feeling kinda poorly all of a sudden, Bat. Headache's been killing me for a day or more now," Meath revealed. "Think I'll just settle here in the corner for a bit. A quick nap and then go on ahead and help shovel."

The floor of the plow seemed to pull out from under Meath's feet. For a moment, he thought a slide had hit the plow and it was being hurled on its side. Once again the firm grasp of powerful hands and strong arms took hold of Meath's faltering body and gently lowered him to the floor.

"Demons, Bat. Watch out for the demons."

John Robert Meath gave up fighting off his demons and fell asleep.

Saturday, February 26, 1910, 2:30 p.m.
William Harrington, Assistant Trainmaster

As Harrington's plow train worked east for the coal at Merritt, a sense of doom wormed its way into his mind. Things had not gone well right from the start. It took longer than Harrington hoped to clear a path through the slide at Cascade Tunnel Station. When that task was complete, one of his locomotives was spent, requiring it to be switched with another. The coal tenders of his plow and two pusher engines had to be filled by hand from the tenders of the spare locomotives stored on a snow-clogged siding. A caboose to house extra men had to be shoveled out and coupled to the rear pusher engine. More than time, all of this cost effort, and with the ebbing of the men's energy came the more dangerous loss of spirit.

Finally underway from Cascade late Friday evening, Harrington tried to force into his thoughts glimmers of optimism. The snow was deep, but loose. His plow made quick work of casting the drifts aside. Then they reached a giant avalanche at Berne, and in an instant, his budding hope was buried deep under the tons of snow blocking his way.

As much as he hated to, Harrington rousted out the exhausted train crews resting in the trailing caboose. The only hope they had of making Merritt and its important supply of coal was to shovel by hand as much of the slide as possible.

"The more we shovel, the less coal we put through the plow, boys," Harrington lectured. "There's no going back; if we run out of coal before we make Merritt, we're really going to be up shit creek."

"This is nuts," grumbled Ira Clary, working alongside Harrington. "Goddamned plow just sitting there while we bust our backs shoveling."

"Ahh, quit your griping, Ira. Hell, you've been pretty good at keeping away from a shovel handle from what I've seen," accused Dougherty.

"The hell I have!" Clary snapped back. "Just because I didn't grow up shoveling out a damned cow barn don't mean I haven't pulled my weight around here."

"That's the trouble with you little sawed-off shits," chimed in Duncan Tegtmeier, "you ain't got enough weight to pull."

"Yeah, and where were you when we kept derailing the plow over at Cascade the other day, wise ass?" Clary shouted, his temper already getting the better of him. " I was underneath that plow working my ass off while you were sitting on your ass in your goddamned engine!"

"All right!" Harrington roared. "That's enough. My kids act better than you bastards!"

The crew fell quiet. The silent snow continued to fall. Sounds seemed muted to Harrington; the pant of the plow and pusher engines, the crunch of shovels against packed snow, the grunts of effort escaping the mouths of the men— all were distant, a world away.

Ears ringing so loud things sound funny, Harrington silently concluded. Pausing from his work, he surveyed what was left of the slide. *Tempting to try and buck the rest,* he thought. *Fifty feet or so left to dig down. Better not. Need to chew straight through.*

"If they get the trains out today, they won't really need the coal from Merritt, will they, Bill?" Dougherty asked.

"Those trains ain't going anywhere, Al," Harrington grumbled, "Snowing as hard as ever. Believe me, they'll need that coal before this is over."

"Well, I guess a guy can hope," shrugged Dougherty.

Hope. Glad Al's got some. I'm plum out, Harrington thought, continuing to dig. *Making Merritt. That's where I'll put my hope. Lil's right, gotta keep little Donnie away from railroading.*

"Got a good head of steam building, Bill, plow's greased and ready—I say let's hit her," informed plow engineer James Mackey, just joining the group.

"I don't want to waste an ounce of coal bucking this thing out, Jimbo," Harrington warned. "Think you can take her in a couple of passes?"

"Yeah, I'd say a couple of hard runs and a clean-up should do her," Mackey predicted.

"No clean-up pass, waste of time and coal. There's nothing behind us. All I want is to bust through and keep heading for Merritt," instructed Harrington.

"Soon as we're clear of slide and are back into clean snow, we're gonna have to start filling the tanks. Water's getting low on the plow and engines," Mackey reported. "We got the steam hoses set up already."

"Ain't that just about the way things have gone, Bill? Goddamned creek fifty feet away, and we have to shovel snow for water," Clary said in a dejected tone of voice.

"Hear that, boys?" called out Harrington, "Jimbo here figures since we already got the shovels good and scoured, might just as well keep digging. Plow and engines need water."

The expected groaning and swearing rose from the crew. Still, each man knew all the complaining in the world would change nothing. Personal comfort, fatigue, even hunger no longer mattered. Whether it was shoveling a hard-packed slide, or snow for an empty tender, Harrington knew the men would do what he asked.

"Let's call her good, boys. See if Mr. Mackey can bust through and send us on our way," Harrington decided.

There was a time when Harrington felt a sense of excitement prior to making a run at a slide. The anticipation, the need for judgment and decision-making, the wondering whether or not the machine would overcome what Mother Nature had thrown into his path—all provided a source of energy that kept Harrington going, his mind sharp. Dulled by the long hours on duty, he was now content to stand aside with a feeling of detachment and merely watch the plow eat away at the last of the slide.

When the big fan broke through the final remnants of the avalanche, a cheer went up from the men. Harrington felt no elation, no sense of accomplishment.

Bucked that one. Wonder what's around the next bend? Coal in the plow already over half gone, Harrington silently worried.

The men out on the slide quickly dispersed, some climbing aboard the still-moving plow, others onto the pusher engines, with a few stragglers waiting and swinging aboard the trailing caboose. Harrington remained outside, wading through the snow ahead of the whirling fan. Trees closely lined the right-of-way, disappearing into the fog produced by the falling snow.

Too many trees. Snow's full of needles. Plug up the injector screen, Harrington concluded.

As the plow crept by, Harrington leaped into the cab. Strong arms grabbed him when his feet slipped on the wet floor.

"Thanks, boys, just getting too damned old for this, I guess." Harrington said. "You can wind her up, Mr. Clary, gonna need to get clear of these trees before we can stop to shovel."

"Easy plowin'," Dupy called out, his head out the left door, watching the plume exit the fan. "Got a full hood and she's takin' her all and then some!"

"That's more like it, eh, Mr. Snow King?" Dougherty asked, leaning against the clutch lever. "Be down at Merritt drinking coffee before you know it."

"I wouldn't be too quick to be pouring coffee, Al. Got some nasty country to get through yet," Harrington warned.

"This damned storm has made you plum sour, Bill," observed Clary, pulling his head in from the plow's right door. "That slide back there was a fluke—never had one there before."

"We've never had a storm like this before either, Ira. That slide at Berne is what's got me worried. Where else are we gonna hit trouble where there ain't been trouble before?"

"Hell, Bill, don't be looking for trouble where there ain't none." Clary poked his head back out the door and resumed his vigil with the fan.

Don't need to look for trouble. Been real good at finding us, Harrington thought.

The east end of the siding at Berne provided a clean field of snow. Harrington halted the outfit. Shovels in hands, the men swarmed from the shelter of the train and out into the storm. The wind was picking up, and the large flakes of snow fell to earth at a 45° angle. Knowing the coal supply was dwindling, the crew needed no prodding from Harrington. To a man, they pitched snow onto the tender of the plow at a furious pace. When the two men on the tender were overwhelmed, transferring the snow down into the tender's hatch, the crew on the bank moved down and began throwing shovel fulls toward the water hatch on the 1118, as well as the 1448. Clouds of white vapor billowed from the openings above each tank, as deep inside the tenders, steam was forced through the snow and remaining water.

"What's your glass reading?" Harrington called out to Will Courtney, working the fire deck of the X-801.

"About half full, Bill," he called back. "Enough to make Merritt if we don't run outta coal."

Damn it to hell. Shoulda never left the 807 behind. Could use her coal. We hit rough going and we're done for, Harrington surmised.

With everyone back onboard, Harrington whistled off and the plow train resumed its lonely journey east. In the heart of the Nason Creek Canyon, no trailing rotary, no hope for retreat, they were on their own, like soldiers on a mission from which there was no coming back.

Two miles of easy plowing did little to ease Harrington's mind. He had already gone back to check the remaining coal in the plow's tender. Courtney was doing what he could to conserve fuel and still deliver the needed steam to the cylinders, but Harrington could sense he was losing the battle ever so slowly.

"West switch Gaynor!" Clary hollered. "Least I think that's where we're at."

"West switch," John Parzybok repeated. He worked the handle controlling the flanger suspended under the plow, raising it up so it would not snag on the buried switch points.

As they rounded a sweeping bend to the left, Harrington leaned on Dupy's shoulder watching the plow throw a graceful arc of snow over the bank down towards Nason Creek. The slower-moving water along its banks had long since frozen over, and only the swift-flowing center channel remained clear.

"Heavy going ahead," Clary hollered from the opposite side. Harrington rushed over and peered ahead, squinting his eyes against the blowing snow.

"Better slow her down, Al. Give us some brakes, then whistle off so Tom and Duncan know," Harrington ordered. "I'm going to try and hike on down and check in at the depot."

Jumping from the plow into the snow, Harrington was immediately swallowed nearly to his waist by the soft white mass. He kicked and stomped an area large enough to get firm footing before trying to work his way out of the hole and onto the top of the pack. Try as he might, he sunk in to his knees with every step he took.

Side track's right here. Must be a good ten feet of snow on top of the rail, Harrington thought. *Weak as a kitten. Dumb idea. Can hardly wade through this stuff.*

Winded, coughing, Harrington had to stop every dozen steps to get his bearings and muster strength to continue on. A small slide lay just ahead of the plow. It had come down off the mountains to Harrington's left, sweeping across the valley and up the opposite side, spilling out onto the tracks.

They'll hit this one. Take it out with the plow. Won't need to shovel. Only fifty feet wide.

Harrington worked his way across the face of the slide at a good pace. Packed chunks of ice produced by the avalanche produced good footing. He walked through a small cut near the depot. The rock berm had served as a windbreak. He stopped and carefully looked over the entire area.

We stall out, be a safe spot to tie down.

The station was covered in snow, with no sign of life. The smokeless stove pipe barely poking out from the drifts is all that marked the whereabouts of the building. It told Harrington all he needed to know.

Bastards. Long gone. Abandoned the place. Probably no food or coal.

Just beyond, Harrington could see the entrance to the narrowest stretch of the Nason Creek Canyon. The site of a solid wall of snow made him physically ill to his stomach.

Blocked tighter than shit. Never bust through. Goddamned done for. Christ, now what?

Having smashed through the small slide upgrade, the plow was boring out the rock cut just west of the depot when Harrington returned. Perched on the bank to the side, he let the machine pass, its exhaust still crisp, tons of snow still flying from its fan.

Running good, sounding good. Son of a bitch! Stuck in the middle of nowhere. A couple of tenders of coal and we would have made it. Jesus Christ.

"How much you got left?" Harrington called across to Courtney.

The plow's fireman took another look in his tender.

"Maybe an hour. Coal's getting wet, burning colder. Taking more to keep steam up," Courtney reported, still standing in the coal bin, his head barely showing over the top edge.

See how much we got in the pushers. Could bring some forward, Harrington considered. *Waste of damned time. Don't have enough to buck through that mess down there.*

"How much coal you got?" Harrington asked Osborne as his engine moved by.

"Stan says he's down to about a ton," came the reply.

If they've got a ton, I doubt Duncan's got much more. That's it. Bore out this cut and shut her down. Fight's over.

A wave of exhaustion rolled over Harrington like the slides that barred his way east. For a moment, all he wanted to do was lay down in the snow and sleep. He did not care if he ever woke up. Tired of the snow, tired of the wind, tired of trying to do the impossible, for a moment death did not seem that bad an option. It was a coward's way out and Harrington knew it. A vision of Lillian and his three children brought him back.

Retracing his steps in the deep snow, Harrington worked his way forward climbing back into the plow.

"So what are we up against down there, Bill?" Clary asked.

At first he said nothing. He looked at Al Dougherty manning the clutch. Harrington was shocked by what he saw. The happy-go-lucky Midwest farm boy had vanished. In his place stood an old man with a gaunt face covered with whiskers, eyes blood red, sunk into his head, and ringed with dark circles. The skin on his face was beet red and peeling.

"Al," Harrington sighed, "I need you to go back and spread the word. We're shutting her down. We'll bore ahead to the east switch, then back out. I want to leave the outfit here in this little cut. When you get back to Duncan's engine, have him whistle stop and then reverse. Tommy will follow. You got that?"

"Guess so," Dougherty replied with a confused look. "Seems funny giving her up. Still got some coal."

"The entrance to the canyon is plugged with slides. We're still five goddamned miles from Merritt. There's no goddamned way we're gonna make it. No goddamned way. Now all of you listen up, spread the word on down the line to the boys in the caboose, we're hiking outta here tonight. Nobody's around. The sons of bitches abandoned the station, so we can't stay there. We can't fit in the caboose. Dropping the fires in the boilers. We'll freeze if all of us stay."

"Hike back? Tonight?" Dougherty shook his head. He still had some fight left in him. "If we stay we can cut logs and keep the fires up until a relief train shows up."

"Goddamn it, Al! We *are* the goddamned relief train! Jesus goddamned…" Harrington stopped himself. He glanced around the cab. Even Ira Clary looked surprised at Harrington's sudden outburst.

Laying his arm across Dougherty's shoulder Harrington could feel the big brakeman shivering under his wet clothes. He took a moment to calm himself.

"Just tell the boys we're shutting her down, okay? We ain't got a choice. It's snowing too hard, the wood's gonna be too wet. We'd clog the grates with ash even if we could get the wood to burn. You know that. Our only hope is to get back to Cascade. The sooner we can get going, the better off we'll be. I'm depending on ya, Al, so let's get to it."

Darkness was settling into the canyon. Dougherty grabbed his lantern and headed back through the plow. He paused at the door.

"You know you can count on me, Mr. Snow King," he said with his familiar smile.

Harrington retreated to the rear of the cab. For the first time since the previous night he sat down. He took off his hat and slapped it hard on his thigh.

"Goddamn it!" he shouted. "Goddamn it to hell!"

Ira Clary was at Harrington's side.

"We're beat, Ira. Goddamn it to hell, this storm's beat us down good."

Saturday, February 26, 1910, 3:00 p.m.
Arthur Reed Blackburn, Trainmaster

"So has there been any word from Harrington?"

Art Blackburn stood next to Superintendent O'Neill in the cab of the X-800. They had just finished servicing both plows and the twin pusher engines at Wellington. Once again the weary crews were plowing west to resume the attack on the slide at Shed 3.3. While Blackburn oversaw the coaling and watering of the equipment, O'Neill went to the depot for the latest information on the conditions elsewhere on the mountain.

"Cascade said they left east around eight or so last night. Got a short message from Berne. Sounds like they hit a slide over there. Don't know how big," O'Neill admitted.

"We know for sure where Dowling is?" Blackburn asked, himself wanting to be clear on the situation.

"Hasn't made Corea yet. We won't meet up with him anytime soon, from the sounds of things," informed O'Neill.

"You still want to try and get the trains down to Alvin sometime tonight?" Blackburn inquired.

"No," came the superintendent's short reply.

"Pettit know they're stuck here another night?"

"I told him."

"Bet that won't sit well with those folks onboard," Blackburn commented. "Pettit's gonna have some damned mad people on his hands."

"Guess there's been some trouble already with a few of them," O'Neill said with his voice lowered. "Some want to wire the Seattle papers and complain for God knows why. Pettit even said some of those dumb bastards want to hike out to Scenic. Want us to supply men to break a trail. I told Pettit they're free to go but we'll have nothing to do with it. No liability, no nothing. Big shot businessmen. More like the village idiots. Don't know when they've got it good."

O'Neill fell silent.

Damned ungrateful people, Blackburn fumed. *Killing ourselves out here and they want to cry to the papers. Give me ten minutes with them. Find out quick who's in charge.*

Blackburn elbowed his way through the cab, which was crowded by a crew of shovelers gathered at Wellington. Charlie Bergstrom's section crew hiked through the tunnel earlier in the day. With their cookhouse at Cascade Tunnel Station destroyed, the men soon used up the limited provisions salvaged from the wreckage. They had come to Wellington hoping for food and sleeping quarters. Blackburn and O'Neill quickly to rounded up a crew of shovelers from their ranks to replace the men that were refusing to work.

Lucky Bergstrom's boys showed up, Blackburn thought. The increased manpower of Bergstrom's crew had given him some optimism. *Good two hours of daylight left. Get most of the slide bored out. Get to Alvin before we have to head back for water. Bound to meet up with Dowling sooner than later.*

"Heavy going ahead!" called out conductor Homer Purcell as the plow train struggled west. "Better slow her down!"

The plume of the snow flying from the fan blinded Blackburn's view of the conditions ahead. Purcell's cry cut though his thoughts like the icy wind that was ripping across his face. He felt the brakes take hold as he watched O'Neill grab the whistle cord and fire off a single long blast.

Nothing coming easy. Blackburn felt his fragile sense of optimism crumble. *Only place on earth where we have to fight our way to the battlefield.* He became increasingly upset with how the plow was being handled. Watching and listening, his patience quickly wore thin.

Too slow. Just lugging along. Plow can take it, fumed Blackburn. *Use half our water just getting to the slide.*

Blackburn pulled his head back into the cab. He glanced at O'Neill who seemed to be lost in thought. Intimidated by his presence, Blackburn was torn between doing what he felt was right and the fear of overstepping his bounds in the eyes of his boss and the rest of the men.

Blackburn swallowed hard. *Here goes.*

"Mr. Purcell!" barked Blackburn. "Let's get going here. We're running too slow!"

Purcell gave Blackburn a confused look, then quickly shifted his stare to O'Neill. Blackburn found himself looking in the same direction as well.

Won't obey a single order I give with O'Neill around, thought Blackburn.

"Well, Mr. Purcell?" Blackburn questioned. "Are we going to pick up the pace or spend the rest of the day just getting to the damned slide?"

O'Neill remained silent, obviously choosing to stay out of the exchange.

"Very good, sir," Purcell finally said.

Satisfied that his orders were finally obeyed, Blackburn glanced O'Neill's way one more time. Catching his eye, O'Neill gave Blackburn a slight nod. Relieved by O'Neill's approval, Blackburn turned his attention back to the fan.

Letting me run things, Blackburn gloated. *Knows not to undermine my authority.*

It was an all-too-familiar procedure when the plow train arrived at Shed 3.3. Bergstrom set about deploying his crew out on the slide. Fortunately, in their absence no additional snow had slid down the mountainside. The plow resumed work at the point they had left off prior to returning to Wellington for coal and water.

"Mr. Blackburn, I'd like you to head out onto the slide with me," O'Neill said, finally moving from his position along the cab's back wall. "I'd be good if the both of us assess the situation out there."

"Yes sir," Blackburn responded. He took another long look ahead at the men beginning to dig away at the slide. "Mr. Purcell, you're in charge. Bergstrom's got his boys back far enough you can start bucking right away."

Hands in their pockets and heads bent against the wind, Blackburn and O'Neill climbed over heavy chunks of packed snow brought down by the slide. The snow was turning to rain, only adding to the misery felt by the men.

Wonder what he's got on his mind? Blackburn asked himself. *Not like him to stay quiet so long. Usually spouting orders left and right.*

The two men picked their way across the slide, and ducked under the covered entrance of the shed. O'Neill tried to light a cigar, but the wind and driving mix of rain and snow quickly ended his attempts. He stared up the troublesome avalanche chute and panned his eye across the slide.

"You really hit the nail on the head, Art," O'Neill finally said.

"Excuse me, sir?" questioned Blackburn, not sure to what O'Neill was referring.

"This new avalanche chute. A few months back. We hiked up there and you warned me that this son of a bitch was going to give us problems. I tried to talk Brown and Gruber into extending this shed this summer. Haven't heard back." O'Neill paused. "Guess it's a little late now."

"Well, the way I see it, this has to be the last that's up there, Mr. O'Neill. My guess is what we see here is that dome from the very top. Snow's pretty dirty, slid down a long ways. We buck through this and we'll have her," Blackburn added.

"Hear that?" O'Neill suddenly asked, pointing behind them. "Listen."

The valley below was completely obscured by the thick clouds. The wind ripped off shreds of the gray gloom and sent them wheeling past where Blackburn and O'Neill stood. From above, sheets of rain fell out of the sky into the abyss below. Somehow finding its way through this solid wall of moisture was the unmistakable sound of a whistle and working steam.

"Dowling's still down there," O'Neill said.

"If we can still hear him, he's a lot closer to Scenic than he is to Corea," concluded Blackburn.

"That's the way I figure it. Art, we're in serious danger of running out of coal up here before we can meet up with Dowling," O'Neill finally confessed. "He's not making near as much headway as I'd hoped. Neither are we."

"Harrington getting back here anytime soon is a long shot too, isn't it?" Blackburn asked, already knowing the answer.

"I'm starting to think having him run east might have been a mistake," O'Neill admitted. "Should've kept his plow here as a back-up."

"We're still getting coal outta the chute, but it's acting like she's about empty. Sending him to Merritt for coal was about our only option," Blackburn added in an attempt to help his boss justify the decision.

O'Neill bent over. Packing a snowball he threw it as hard as he could against the snow shed. It splattered on one of the timbers, a small portion of the snow sticking to the rough wood.

"Even if we can get the line open to Alvin before we run out of coal, what the hell then, Art? Dowling hasn't got far enough east to have the lower line clean. No goddamned way we can move those passengers or the mail sacks down that old trail. Gotta know he's got the lower line open back to Scenic."

"So what the hell you telling me, Jim?" Blackburn challenged. "Just head back to Wellington with our tails between our legs and wait for the spring thaw? We gotta keep at it. We're not that far off from breaking through."

"What I'm telling you, Art is we'd better start thinking about what we're going to have to do in case we don't make Alvin, in case Dowling can't get up to Corea for a day or two. What if we run so low on coal we have to decide between plowing and keeping the passengers warm? We're in a tight fix here. Right now we don't have a good plan of action."

"Well, it's gotta quit storming anytime now. Storms just don't last this long. Already turned to rain. A break in the weather will give us the chance we need to fight our way outta this," Blackburn replied.

"We're way past hoping the storm quits and things will be better. The damage is done, Art. Another foot of snow ain't gonna make a tinker's damn worth of difference. Right now we're snowed in tighter than any railroad's ever been. We're fast running out of ways to deal with it." O'Neill formed another snowball and sent it smashing onto the snow shed timbers. "Just between you and me, that slide over at Cascade has got me a little spooked. Art, if those trains were still over there, it would have taken out the ass end of 25."

"We got them outta there. No point on worrying about something that didn't happen," Blackburn countered.

"I'm doing nothing *but* worrying about things that have never happened up here, Art," O'Neill confessed.

"If you really think this has gotten beyond what we can handle, then we damned well better look to get some more help," advised Blackburn.

"Getting more help is going to take time, Art. I'm afraid we're living on borrowed time right now. Pettit is going to have a regular revolt on his hands if we don't figure out a way to get those damned people out of here. On top of everything else, Brown and Gruber are already riding my ass about the mail. Thank God the UP is having problems of their own right now or else my neck would really be in the noose."

Blackburn was taken aback by O'Neill's confession. It was unsettling for him to see doubt in the man he looked to for calm reason and focused direction. It bothered him even more that he did not have any solutions for O'Neill's concerns.

O'Neill let out a long sigh.

"You're a good railroad man, Art. I wouldn't have you up here if you weren't. You see something that needs to be taken care of, get it done. You don't have to wait for my blessing. The more of us doing some thinking, the better our chances of working our way outta this jam. I'm telling you all of this so you know where we stand and can think on it some yourself."

"Understood," Blackburn mumbled.

Looks like I made the right call back there on the plow, Blackburn thought.

"I'll work with Bergstrom out on the slide, you can run the plow crews," Blackburn ordered.

O'Neill cracked a grin. "That's more like it, Art."

The slide at Shed 3.3 would not give way easily. Bergstrom's men proved to be little better than the mutinous crew of Harley's. As the afternoon wore into early evening, their pace slowed to the point that Blackburn had to bring out the extra train crews resting in the trailing X-802. Six hours of hard plowing, of hard words trying to keep the men shoveling, did not yield nearly the results he wanted. He was beginning to understand the seriousness of the situation. O'Neill's concerns and doubts were becoming Blackburn's as well.

Came through here on the twenty-third, haven't got past here since. Three goddamned days to plow three miles. Still haven't busted through. O'Neill's right. In a tight fix, Blackburn silently admitted.

Four long blasts from the plow's whistle broke through Blackburn's thoughts.

"That's it for this shift, boys," Bergstrom hollered. "Don't suppose none of you lazy bastards are willing to stay out here and keep shoveling?"

Their shovels flung over their shoulders, the men ignored Bergstrom's suggestion and, in single file, walked toward the plow train.

"Sons of bitches," Bergstrom said to Blackburn. "They heard about the blow-up with O'Neill this morning. Now they think they need more money."

"They got the same deal. Work, get paid, get fed, or get the hell out. If you want, I'll tell 'em just that," Blackburn told Bergstrom.

"We'll see what happens when we head back out tonight, Mr. Blackburn. I might just have to take you up on that," replied Bergstrom.

With the section crews on the now-trailing X-800, Blackburn and O'Neill walked to the eastward-facing X-802 for the run back to Wellington. Between avalanche debris falling in behind them and wind-blown drifts, they were faced with heavy work just to get back to Wellington for water and coal.

"Let's take her on back, Mr. White," Blackburn told conductor Martin White. Looking back along the boiler, he saw the familiar figure of Bob Meath at the throttle. "Rested, are you, Mr. Meath?'

Meath gave Blackburn a nod, and with the "highball" echoing through the thick evening sky, he pulled the reverser back and opened up his throttle.

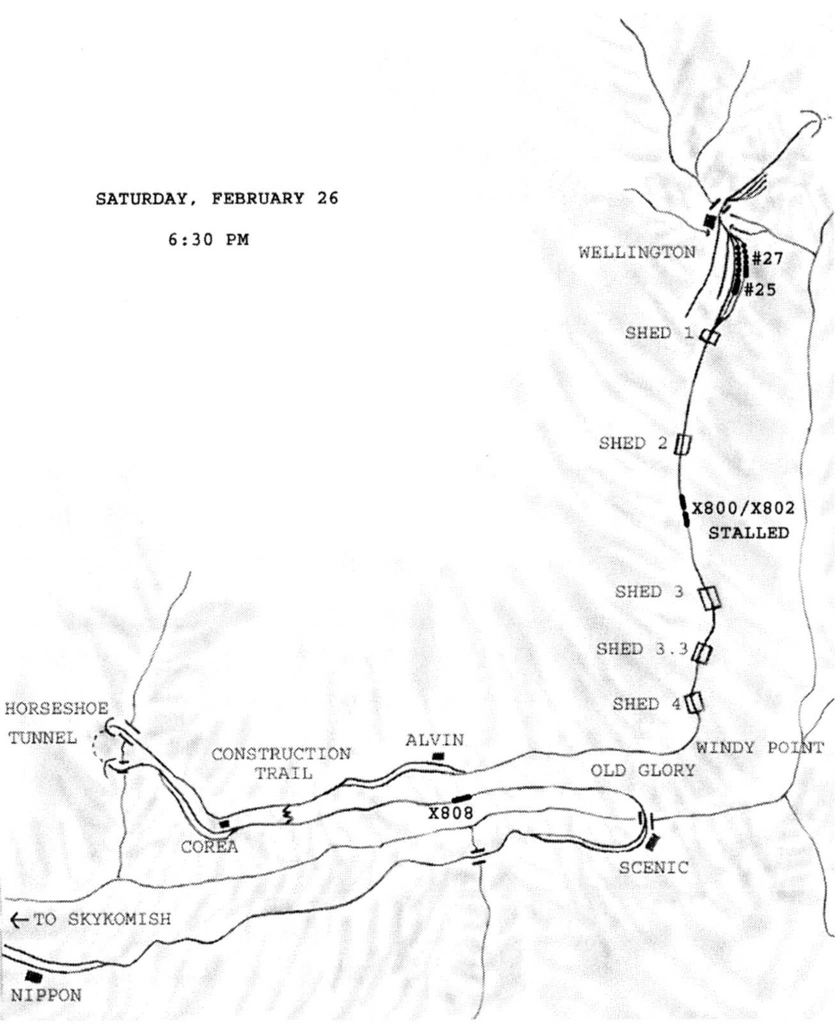
SATURDAY, FEBRUARY 26
6:30 PM
WELLINGTON
#27
#25
SHED 1
SHED 2
X800/X802
STALLED
SHED 3
SHED 3.3
SHED 4
WINDY POINT
OLD GLORY
SCENIC
ALVIN
X808
CONSTRUCTION
TRAIL
HORSESHOE
TUNNEL
COREA
← TO SKYKOMISH
NIPPON

Guess I got my answer, Blackburn thought.

Leaning out the left door, lantern in hand, Blackburn watched the plow chew through the drifts.

Steady progress. There's still coal to be had, just harder to get to that's all. Long as we keep at it, we'll eventually come out on top, Blackburn reasoned. *By next week all of this will be behind us.*

Lost in thought, something caught Blackburn's trained eye and suddenly dominated his attention. He squinted ahead, trying to focus, trying to understand what it was he was seeing. The lookout on top of the plow saw it, too; suddenly there was a loud thumping on the roof.

"Oh Jesus no," Blackburn groaned aloud. His stomach turned. "Snow and goddamned trees all over the tracks!"

"Slide! Five car lengths!" Blackburn shouted.

Saturday, February 26, 1910, 7:30 p.m.
James Henry O'Neill, Superintendent

The dim light of his lantern kept O'Neill from getting a clear grasp of the size of the slide, but 'how deep' and 'how wide' no longer mattered. All that mattered was the tons of snow and splintered trees that now separated his plows from the supply of fuel at Wellington.

Through the rain, he saw a lantern approaching. In its narrow sphere of light appeared charred logs and branches of fir trees strewn in a jumbled mass like a giant set of "pick-up sticks" thrown into the wind.

"She's a tough one, sir," Irving Tegtmeier admitted, coming from the dark into O'Neill's circle of light. "Don't need a plow, need a damned donkey engine to clear this one. More logs than snow."

"No way to buck it, Mr. Tegtmeier?" inquired O'Neill. "What about getting in there with axes and chopping out the biggest logs?"

"Near as I can tell, got big timber through the whole goddamned thing. You tie into one of them logs with the fan and she'll just tear herself apart before we can back her clear," Tegtmeier explained.

"Any chance of just easing into her?" O'Neill asked. "Just a slow steady forward push?"

"Snow's already set hard. We'd sit here the rest of tonight like a dog scratching his nuts. Wouldn't get a damned thing accomplished but burn up our coal. We have to buck her out, but if we do that and hit a big log ..." Tegtmeier paused, "Well, you understand what I mean."

O' Neill sighed. "What about the coal and water? Do we have enough to at least make a run at this slide?"

"Engines are good, they'll go on into the night. The 802 hasn't worked that much either—three quarters a tank of water, plenty of coal," Tegtmeier reported.

"And if we simply maintain enough fire and water to keep the boilers hot, how long will the coal and water supply last on each?" O'Neill asked.

"Well let's see." Tegtmeier rubbed the rough whiskers on his chin with his gloved hand. "The trailing plow, she's pretty low right now, probably make the night. The engines and the 802 here, they'd go into tomorrow easy before we'd have to start shoveling snow and somehow get fuel for their fires."

"Can we burn wood without plugging the grates with ash?"

"If all we're doing is heating the boilers, maybe. Doubt we could get enough heat out of this green stuff around here to work the plow or the engines. We start pulling a heavy draft through the firebox by working them, that's when all that ash would start raising holy hell," Tegtmeier explained.

Blackburn returned from the far end of the slide and joined O'Neill and Tegtmeier.

"It's a big one," Blackburn panted, out of breath. "All of 800-feet, maybe more. Good 30, 35-feet deep. Whole son of a bitch choked with big timber."

What the hell am I going to do now? Just want to walk away from all of this. The inner drive that had propelled O'Neill from a lowly track worker at age fourteen to the office of superintendent was finally beginning to falter.

"Too bad we're railroaders and not loggers," Ed Lindsay muttered to Marty White, the two having come forward from the plow.

"We're done for," White quietly replied out of the side of his mouth.

Shaking his head, Lindsay wandered off to explore the lower edge of the avalanche.

Waiting for orders. They'll wait a long time. Fresh out of ideas, O'Neill admitted to himself.

"Where's Bergstrom?" O'Neill asked. "Let's get as many axes and shovels out here as we can."

"Bergstrom asked me if you could come back to the 800, sir," spoke up Purcell. "Hate to add bad news on top of bad news, but the men, the shovelers, they say they ain't working unless you give them more money."

"Those dirty bastards," grumbled Blackburn. "Those dirty, goddamned bastards."

"Mr. O'Neill!" shouted Lindsay. "Slide took out at least two, maybe three poles. The wire's all down, ripped all to hell sir!"

Stay calm, O'Neill coached himself. *One problem at a time. Have to try and buck this thing out, start with that. If Harrington gets back he can start from the other side and work this way. Get his crew and our crews. To hell with those laborers.*

O'Neill yawned and rubbed his face. His stomach felt like a watch spring wound too tight. He tried to relax his muscles and clear his head, but to no avail. His teeth were clenched so hard, his jaw hurt.

Relax. Think. Make a decision, O'Neill told himself. *No right answer. Just get the boys doing something. Start giving orders. See what becomes of it.*

"Okay, gentlemen, I want to at least get started bucking this thing out. I want every man out here either shoveling or chopping out these trees. I want a couple of men to head for Wellington right away and gather up as many axes as they can muster, and any men willing to work. One hell of a job, gonna take us awhile, but I want to get started. Harrington should be back sometime tomorrow with coal and start working from the other side. Mr. Blackburn, you're in charge, the rest of you gather up your crews. Leave only a single fireman on each machine. Understood?"

Although there was vocal agreement amongst the men, O'Neill knew that, like him, they felt they had just played their last card in a losing hand. For the first time, O'Neill realized the challenge was not in getting the hired laborers to work, but to keep his own train crews from giving up hope.

"What are you going to do with those sons of bitches of Bergstrom's?" Blackburn asked as they picked their way off the slide.

Pausing next to the fan of the 802, O'Neill was finally successful at lighting a cigar.

"Same deal as Harley's crew. They stay, they get paid the going wage. They don't want to work, I'll clear them all out tonight," O'Neill finally answered between puffs. "They think they've got me over a barrel, I got news for the lot of them. It's a cold dark walk down off this mountain right now."

"Gonna have trouble getting our own boys to work." Blackburn looked back towards the slide. "Can chop all you want, still won't get fifty feet into this slide."

"Get some men out there digging and chopping. Let's see what we've got. When I get back from raising hell with the work crew, we'll figure out how hard to hit her, Art," O'Neill countered. "That sound fair?"

"Fair enough, sir."

By the time O'Neill made his way back to the trailing X-800, Bergstrom had gathered his workers behind the fan. Huddled together, they stomped their feet on the hard snow packed along the freshly cleaned right-of-way, their arms crossed, hands stuffed up their coat sleeves. A few lanterns gave the scene a ghost-like appearance. Their hardened faces glowed yellow in the subdued light.

Another crew of skid row drunks, O'Neill quickly surmised. *Make this short and sweet.* Taking the same tact that he had with Harley's men that morning, O'Neill gave them the same choice: work or get out. When they chose to leave, O'Neill showed no fear as he blocked their way to Wellington.

"The only way you're getting to Wellington is over that slide, and the only way we're gonna let you over that slide is with a shovel or ax in your hands, working." Turning, O'Neill and Bergstrom walked away from the stunned men.

Not knowing what to do or say, the crew slowly dispersed. A few came forward to help, but most disappeared into the night, hoping to find their way to Scenic.

"Funny they didn't just walk right over us and head for Wellington," Bergstrom commented.

"Drunks have no courage, Mr. Bergstrom. If they did, they wouldn't be drunks," O'Neill answered.

Spots of light from a dozen lanterns were scattered across the front face of the slide. Above the wind, the sharp ringing of axes mixed with the sound of shovel spades glancing off the limbs could be heard. Seeing O'Neill, Tegtmeier jumped down from atop a log he was bucking.

"We're beating a dead dog here, sir," he told O'Neill. "We're gonna chop all night before we can even hope to make our first run at this bastard."

"I see," O'Neill solemnly said. "Most of Bergstrom's crew just quit. As it stands, we're down to a handful of sectionmen and our boys."

"Guess that does it then. We're stuck." Ax in hand, Tegtmeier climbed back on top of the log he was chopping. Legs spread, he sent the bit of his ax into the charred bark, prying away large chips.

Find Blackburn. Get back to Wellington. Get word for more help, O'Neill decided.

Walking across the slide, O'Neill spotted the form of Blackburn, shoveling snow from around an uprooted stump.

"Stumps, rocks, logs, never quite seen a slide this big and dirty," Blackburn admitted as O'Neill came up. "Let's see if I got this stump dug out enough to move. Maybe if we put our shoulders into it, we can roll it to one side a bit."

Side-by-side, the two men leaned hard into the stump. As they pushed against it, the knurled roots began to rise out of the snow below their feet. Both O'Neill and Blackburn lost their footing, their boots suddenly breaking through the snow, causing them to sink to their knees.

"Goddamn it!" Blackburn cried out. "This is bullshit! Just goddamned bullshit!"

O'Neill helped Blackburn to his feet. "You're right, Art, we can't buck this slide with what we've got. Keep a few boys here to tend the boilers. Let the rest go to Wellington. They need some sleep."

"We're beat, aren't we," Blackburn said, throwing down his shovel.

"I don't know, Art. I just don't know."

Lantern in hand, O'Neill began the mile-and-a-half walk to Wellington. Buffeted by the wind funneling down the deep trough left by the numerous passes of the plow train, blinded by the darkness and the rain that was turning to snow, he struggled to keep moving.

Telegraph's probably out at Wellington, O'Neill surmised. *Head for Scenic. Never would've believed it. Biggest and best machines on the railroad. Can't move a goddamned wheel.*

For the first time in his career O'Neill was at a loss for what to do. He had no answers, no solutions. No amount of concentration was going to change the circumstances or ease the stress he was enduring. The problems he faced were beyond his ability to control.

A deep sense of anxiety dominated O'Neill's mind. He fought to keep it in check so that the men would not know. But shoots of doubts were growing, taking hold. O'Neill was scared.

Harrington's my only way out. If he's stuck—God, don't even think about that.

Saturday, February 26, 1910, 2nd Trick Wellington
Basil Sherlock, Telegrapher

"What do you mean you can't send any wires?" demanded passenger Edgar Lemman.

"The wires west are down. We've been without telegraph for a couple of hours now, sir," Sherlock informed the red-faced Lemman.

"And how do I know you're not just saying that to keep me from getting word out about how we're being held up here?" challenged the irate Lemman.

"The lines are down, sir. I can take your message, hold it and send it out as soon as service is restored. Beyond that I can do nothing," Sherlock answered, his voice starting to rise.

"And how hard are you trying to get the lines up and running? I don't see a damned thing getting done!" the lawyer snorted.

"I will have you know, sir, Mr. Flannery and I personally inspected all lines leading into and out of this building and as far west as we dare travel without leaving the station unattended. Linemen are out working. Again I say to you, sir, there is nothing we can do right now!" Sherlock's words were emphatic, his stance firm.

"I'll not be spoken to in that tone, young man. You tell your Mr. O'Neill we have formed a Citizen's Committee and demand he come meet with us as soon as he arrives back." Lemman grasped the message he had written and turned to leave. Pausing, he returned to the ticket window.

"And what about those men I saw walking by just now? Looks like your work crew's quitting. Do you have any men left working around here at all?" he demanded.

"I'm sure I don't know, sir," Sherlock snapped.

"Oh, I'm sure you do, young man," Lemman replied sarcastically. Still in a rage, he left.

The day had not gone well for Sherlock. He'd spent a restless night worrying about the increasing snow pack clinging to the mountains behind his house. Another foot and a half of snow had fallen since he cleaned his roof. The measuring pole he set up in front of his house earlier in the year showed over sixteen feet on the ground. He tossed and turned, trying to think of how to get out of this snowbound hell.

"As soon as they get the line open west, we're packing up and leaving," Sherlock had told Althea that morning. "I'm planning on telling O'Neill that very thing first chance I get. He can fire me on the spot, I don't care. I want out. I want to move back east. Back home."

"And use what for money?" Althea asked. "The railroad is not going to be interested in handing us free tickets and baggage car space for all our belongings, Basil. Not if you just up and quit."

"We've saved up enough to get out of here," Sherlock countered. "Might not get back to Iowa right away, but we'll get out of these god-forsaken mountains."

"And where will you work this time? Some other little out-of-the-way station where no one wants to live, just like here?" questioned Althea. "Face it, Basil, as long as you keep booming around we'll never be able to live in one place long enough to get our lives started."

"Well, we're not going to get our lives started here, and that's that!" asserted Sherlock. "And I'm not just a common boomer!"

Sherlock sat alone in the depot. Their earlier exchange kept spinning through his mind. He stared out the window. Through the light streaming from the window, he saw the rain had turned back to snow.

Boomer. Althea's right. That's all I am. Just another boomer, Sherlock thought.

Sherlock lifted his coat off the hook and went outside. He grabbed a shovel and began to clean the station platform. The snow had piled so high it began to cover the bottoms of the windows.

Not used to extended work, Sherlock was soon winded. He paused and leaned against the shovel to take a closer look at his surroundings.

Ghost town. No sounds, no people, nothing moving. Never know a railroad is within a hundred miles. No trains in days. All too strange.

Waste of time, he concluded. Sherlock propped the shovel against the door jam and walked back inside the depot. His coat still on, he sat at the desk, staring at the silent telegraph key.

Eight o'clock. Plow train should be back. O'Neill and Blackburn be here anytime. Last thing I want to do is tell them we have no communications, fretted Sherlock. *Be happy that Lemman character is gone. Him and Blackburn would really butt heads.*

Sherlock busied himself looking through the messages that arrived before the wire went dead. He knew they were for the most part private, and for O'Neill, but read them anyway.

Feeling guilty, he placed the telegrams back in the wire basket on the desk corner. There was an unwritten rule amongst the keymen; send, receive but do not read. It was a habit Sherlock had yet to develop. Knowing the details of the railroad, of people's lives as told through the messages he sent and received, was one of the aspects of the job he secretly enjoyed.

Don't read, he thought. *Wonder who the hell tries to follow that stupid rule?*

From the west, Sherlock could make out a light slowly approaching. His heart jumped.

Looks like O'Neill. Tell him the wire's down. See how he takes that. Then I'll tell him I want out, Sherlock coaxed himself. *Guess I should tell him about that passenger group too. Poor man, nothing but bad news.*

Watching out the bay window from his desk, Sherlock saw O'Neill stumble onto the platform. Puffs of vapor exploded from his mouth, not unlike the smoke from the stack of one of the engines. O'Neill paused at the door to douse the flame of his lantern. The powerful frame of the superintendent heaved as he tried to catch his breath. O'Neill's stature alone told Sherlock something was not right.

"Raise Everett, Sherlock," O'Neill ordered before he was even completely through the door. He set his lantern down and came over to the desk.

"Sir, the wire's down to the west. Been dead for the better part of my shift." Sherlock paused for a reaction from O'Neill. "Flannery has gone over to Cascade to round up a few more linemen."

O'Neill sighed and removed his soaking-wet hat. He found a chair near the wall and sat down.

"We were receiving messages all along, up until around five or so. They're here in the basket for you, sir."

"I see," O'Neill said in a tired, unemotional tone. "What about Harrington? Any news from him before the line went dead?"

"Couldn't say, sir," Sherlock lied. "Nothing on my shift. Flannery never said a thing about him. Most of these messages came in on his shift."

A weak smile crossed O'Neill's wind-burned face.

"I've worked the key, Mr. Sherlock. Is there any word from Mr. Harrington in those messages?"

"No, sir," Sherlock admitted. He could feel his face grow red with embarrassment. "Not since they ran into that slide at Berne."

"Very well, I'll look at those messages later." O'Neill spread his legs. He folded his hands across his knees, bent at the waist and dropped his head.

What the hell's the matter with him? Sherlock thought, alarmed at what he was seeing.

"Can I get you some coffee, sir?" Sherlock offered.

O'Neill simply shook his head, still staring at the floor.

Don't know what to do. Should I talk to him? Needs to know what's going on, Sherlock rationalized.

"Mr. O'Neill, there are a few developments that I need to tell you about if you're up to it," Sherlock began.

O'Neill violently shook his head. He rose from the chair and wandered back to the pot-bellied stove and stood over it for a moment. He returned to his chair and sat down. He began to unlace his shoes.

"Let's hear it, Sherlock," he said.

"Well, I suppose you saw the last of the hired laborers leaving on your way here. Guess they finally figured out they weren't getting fed, so they cleared out," Sherlock began.

"Passed that sorry bunch on my way up. None of the bastards would even look me in the eye." With a loud "clunk" O'Neill let one of his wet mountaineer's boots hit the floor of the station. "Don't know how far they're going to get in this storm, don't really care. Bergstrom's gang quit too. You might as well hear that bit of news from me."

"I see. Well, then a passenger was in, not but an hour or so ago. A Mr. Lemman, I believe he said his name was. Well sir, he was quite angry that the wires were down and all. He said he and some of the gentlemen on the train have formed some kind of a committee. Said—well, sir, to quote him, he 'demanded' that you go over to the train and meet with them."

"They're demanding, are they?" O'Neill repeated, pulling off his other shoe.

"His words, sir, not mine," Sherlock clarified, worried O'Neill might think he was putting words in Lemman's mouth.

"Well, it looks pretty quiet on 25 right now, no need in me going down there and stirring things up at this late hour, eh Sherlock?"

"Seems prudent, sir," answered Sherlock.

"I'll send Longcoy to tell them I'm just too tired to meet with them right now. By the way, you're going to have some company tonight, Mr. Sherlock. Expect them any moment now, as a matter of fact." O'Neill pulled his chair over to the stove. Sitting back down, he stretched out his legs, tucking his feet under the firebox. His chin fell to his chest. "We're stalled west of town. Can't get the plows back for coal. Slide came down blocking our way back. Probably took out your lines. Most of the boys are coming back for rest tonight. Hell of a mess, wouldn't you say?"

Sherlock had no answer.

"Well, Mr. Sherlock, there's not a damned thing more any of us can do tonight. Keep the station open and warm—a few of the boys might end up on your floor asleep. Get my feet warmed up, then I'm going to get a bite and grab a few hours of sleep. If I'm needed I'll be in my car." O'Neill fell silent, content to just sit and allow his frozen feet to thaw.

Can't tell him I'm leaving. Can't do it now. As trapped as everyone else. Sherlock actually felt a sense of relief that he had an acceptable excuse for not telling O'Neill what was truly on his mind.

Yawning and stretching, O'Neill finally arose from his chair and put his boots back on. On his way out the door, he gathered up the stack of messages from the basket.

"When the linemen show up, tell them the problem is about a mile and a half west of here. Gonna be awhile before we get you back on line. I'll be leaving for Scenic on foot the first thing in the morning. Going to wire for more help. If anyone comes in asking, tell them that. I'll catch up with Pettit before I leave in the morning. Good night, Sherlock."

O'Neill put on his hat and walked out the door.

"I'll tell them, good night, sir," Sherlock called back as the door slammed shut.

"This isn't good," Sherlock mumbled aloud. "Never have seen a man with authority act like him. If he's beat, we're all beat. Good God, he didn't even light a cigar."

Saturday, February 26, 1910, 9:00 p.m.
Anthony John Dougherty, Brakeman

Three quarters of an hour had passed since Harrington's crew began their trek back from the stalled plow at Gaynor to Cascade Tunnel Station. It was a strange sight: a group of fifteen men hiking through the mountains in the middle of the night, fighting off blizzard conditions. James Mackey and the five trainmen from the pushers and plow volunteered to stay and watch over the boilers. Under orders from Harrington, the remainder of the crew began the nine-mile hike back upgrade to Cascade Tunnel Station.

"Blacker than the ace of spades out here tonight," complained Ira Clary, walking beside Dougherty. "Can't see a foot in front of me and I'm carrying a goddamned lantern! None of us should be out here."

"You still griping, Ira?" Harrington, who was leading the pack, called back. "You'd better save your energy. We got tough going ahead."

The hike from Gaynor towards Cascade Tunnel Station began easily, even in the face of a fierce wind and increasing snowfall. Walking on hard-packed snow just cleared from the right-of-way, the men barely sank past the soles on their boots, maintaining a brisk pace.

Moving right along, Dougherty thought. *Be next to the stove in the depot in a couple of hours. Finally might be able to lay down somewhere. Get some sleep.*

"You men keep a move on," ordered Harrington. "Al, come up with me and let's scout ahead. Keep on our tracks men, and stay together. Get lost in this soup and we won't find you 'til the spring thaw."

Working his way forward at a slight jog, Dougherty was soon beside the "Snow King." In spite of his long hours of duty, the strong Minnesota farm boy was barely winded. Together they forged ahead of the group, breaking a trail in the ever-deepening snow. Approaching the spot where they had bucked out the slide at Berne, the two men stopped dead.

Dougherty let a slight whistle escape from his lips.

"Jesus, Bill, would you look at that."

Both he and Harrington held up their lanterns and gazed through the weak light. Just ahead of them was a wall of snow, the top of which was somewhere in the darkness above the small ring of light shed by their lamps. It was a frozen barrier, blocking the men from the warmth and safety at Cascade Tunnel Station.

"If I'd known we were going mountaineering, I'd have brought ropes," Harrington muttered.

"Guess that settles it, Bill. Even if we made Merritt, we'd have used up all the coal we were bringing back just bucking through this son of a bitch," observed Dougherty.

"Goddamn it," was the only thing the dejected Harrington could think to say.

"Now what the hell we gonna do?" came the voice of Ira Clary as the remainder of the crew caught up.

"How the hell should I know?" Harrington yelled back. "Do I look like a goddamned mountain climber?"

"Just gonna have to pair up. The big guys help the little guys over this thing," Dougherty suggested.

"And hope to Christ the rest of the mountain don't cut loose up thar somewhere while we're at it," drawled Archie Dupy.

"That's good thinking, Al. Pair up, boys and get moving," Harrington barked.

"Might just as well join the army, the way Harrington's shooting orders," Clary told Dougherty out of the side of his mouth.

"Come on Ira, jump on my back and I'll carry your sawed-off legs across," Dougherty joked, squatting down in front of the short, stocky conductor.

"Go to hell, Al," Clary hissed amidst the chuckles from the crewmen.

"Let me take the lead, Bill," Dougherty volunteered. You've been out front all night. Take a break. Come on, Ira."

Before either man could voice dissention, Dougherty, lantern in one hand, and Clary in the other, bolted past and began to work his way up the avalanche. It was slow, arduous going. Dougherty would set his lantern as far as he could reach, then scramble to its position. Stopping, he would extend his arm back and pull the struggling Clary up to his side. Digging out steps with his boots and packing down the loose snow, Dougherty slowly built a path for the rest of the crew to follow up the steep face of the slide.

For nearly a half hour, Dougherty and Clary labored in silence. Below them, men snaked upward along a weak line of light cast by their lanterns. Ahead lay a field of broken trees and chunks of packed snow the size of boulders. To the left, the white mass swept up the steep side of the mountain. Somewhere to the right, lost in the night and sheets of falling snow, the slide broke off, falling into the Nason Creek basin. Dougherty pulled Clary to his side and stopped to get his bearings.

"Better regroup here," Dougherty gasped, now completely out of breath. "Gotta be careful. Walk right off. Fall into the creek."

Clary was doubled over, his hands on his knees.

Within a few minutes, the rest of the men had caught up. Gathered in a tight circle, the combined force of their lanterns shed enough light for Harrington to get an accurate head count.

"You about done in, Al?" Harrington asked. "I can go on ahead."

"I'll get us down to the Berne depot," Dougherty replied.

"Speak for yourself, Al," Clary said, still out of breath.

"Let's go, Ira. You'll be a better man for it." Dougherty picked up his lamp and began to pick his way across the face of the slide. He was enjoying pulling Clary along—a man who was his superior.

Eyes wide with surprise, the telegraphers at Berne stood aside as Dougherty led the exhausted men into the small depot.

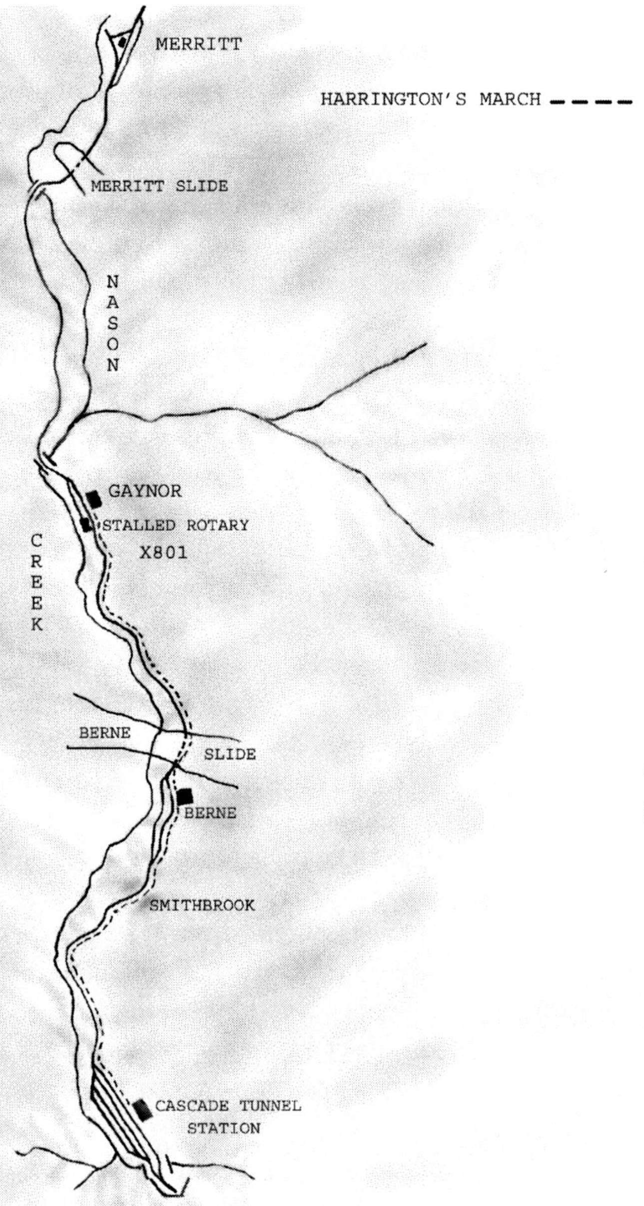
MERRITT
HARRINGTON'S MARCH
MERRITT SLIDE
NASON
CREEK
GAYNOR
STALLED ROTARY
X801
BERNE
SLIDE
BERNE
SMITHBROOK
CASCADE TUNNEL
STATION

"You boys better bundle up and head out with us," Harrington told the three men. "You've dodged a bullet twice, might not be as lucky next time."

"We're not going out there tonight," stated one man with slicked back hair and thick glasses. "We've talked about it. We plan to keep the station open, sir."

"Suit yourselves," said Harrington, shrugging his shoulders. "Let's go, boys."

There were no protests, no complaints as they left the tiny outpost behind. The merciless wind sliced at the men, sending cold daggers into exposed faces and ears. Pulling down their hats and turning up their coat collars, bent against the force of their relentless enemy, the men marched on.

Less than a half mile from the station, the increasing depth of the snow slowly bogged the party down. Loose and unpacked, with each step their feet broke through the thin crust. For men already dulled from the fatigue of countless hours on duty, the march west became a battle of will.

"Like wading through deep water," Dougherty remarked to no one particular.

"Agin the current at that," added Dupy, who had now taken the lead, breaking the trail.

Further west, deeper the snow, Dougherty thought. *To my knees now. Bury poor Ira before we make Cascade. Keep an eye on the boys. I can make it. Make sure the others keep up.*

Ahead, Dougherty saw Dupy's lantern suddenly fall into the snow. Dupy's partner, Stan Meredith stopped.

"Need some help, mates!" Meredith called out. "Archie's collapsed!"

Thrashing through snow, Dougherty came to Meredith's aid. Motionless, Dupy was sprawled face first in a small drift. Each grabbing a shoulder, Meredith and Dougherty lifted Dupy's limp form up and began to shake him.

"Come on, Arch!" Dougherty yelled into his ear. "Wake up!"

He grabbed a handful of snow and rubbed it in Dupy's face.

"Arch!" he hollered, "Arch!"

"Oh God, oh God," Dupy kept repeating, slowly moving his head around.

"You okay, old boy?" Meredith asked, helping to steady the still-weak man.

"Don't know what happened. Just felt like I fell off a cliff or some damned thang," Dupy said, still trying to clear his head.

"Head to the back of the line, Arch, you did your part," Harrington directed. "Al, Ira, stay with him and help him along. Make sure no one falls behind."

The men were walking in single file. The flame in Clary's lantern flickered and went out. Furious, he flung it into the woods lining the snow-choked right of way.

"Mr. Hill ain't gonna take kindly to you tossing railroad property into the woods, Ira," commented Dougherty.

"Right now, Mr. Hill and this railroad can go straight to hell," Clary growled.

Too dark. Too much snow falling. Don't know where we are, Dougherty thought. *Cut at Smithbrook. Should be close. Gonna be hell getting through it.*

Stan Meredith fell in behind Dougherty, Clary and Dupy.

"Just getting too deep," gasped Meredith. "Couldn't go another step. Sorry chaps, didn't pull my weight."

"Who's up front now?" Dougherty asked.

"Charlie Baker's breaking trail," Meredith answered. "Almost up to his waist in places."

"You boys keeping up back there?" Harrington hollered, above the rush of the wind whipping through trees rendered invisible by the darkness.

"I'm herding them along, Bill," Dougherty shouted back.

Like chasing in the cows from pasture, Dougherty realized. *Warm. Summer mornings before sunrise. Get milking done early so could bind oats. Take a lantern, go out. Call the cows. Come boss! Come boss! Never knew if I had them all until I got to the barn. Cows always walked one behind the other. Just like us. Warm summer mornings.*

The deep cut at Smithbrook was completely filled with drifts. Again, stronger men stomped a trail across the snow-choked passage through the rock outcropping. Dougherty remained in the rear, helping the weaker men who had fallen behind. Clear of the cut, the party found themselves wading in snow nearly to their waists.

"How long we been out here?" Dougherty asked Clary. "Cascade's gotta be just around the bend."

"Hell if I know," Clary said, his voice weak. "Hours, days, I don't know. What the hell difference does it make?"

"Just asking, that's all," Dougherty mumbled.

Keep walking. Help Bill keep the rest walking. So goddamned cold. Ears hurt. Can't feel my fingers. Feet quit hurting. Can't feel my toes. Just want to lie down and get some sleep. Keep talking to yourself. Gotta stay awake. Don't close your eyes for a second. Wonder if the rest of the boys feel like this?

As more men took their turn clearing the way through the deep snow, each soon fell to the rear, exhausted. Dougherty continued to remain behind, at times shouldering the panting men in an effort to keep them moving.

"You want me to take a turn up front, Bill?" Dougherty offered at one point.

"Keep them moving, Al," came Harrington's voice through the driving snow. "It's widening out, we're coming into the yard!"

"You hear that, Ira, we're about there," Dougherty said, trying to contain his relief. "We're about there, Arch. Just keep walking. 'Nother half hour."

Through the snow, faint lights could be seen. The dark forms of the snowbound section crew cars loomed to the right, and the deep cut left by the passes of their plow the day before hemmed them in on the left. Onward Dougherty walked, his head down. He focused on his feet, secretly urging himself to keep putting one foot in front on the other.

And then Harrington shouted out the words Dougherty and the rest of the men had been longing to hear.

"Station's just ahead boys! We made it!"

Keep walking, Dougherty told himself. *Hundred steps and I'll be there, maybe less. Left foot, right foot, left foot, right foot.*

A soft thud brought Dougherty out of his trance. He looked around.

Arch's on ahead, so's Stan. Dulled by fatigue, Dougherty kept walking. *Ira! Where's Ira?*

Dougherty spun around and retraced his steps, shining his lantern side to side.

"Ira! Ira!" he called out.

"What's going on back there?" Harrington shouted back.

"Ira's fallen behind. Can't find him." Dougherty hollered, his voice choked with fear.

Dupy and Meredith came to Dougherty's side, aiding in the search with the light from their lanterns. Spread out a few feet apart, they continued to slowly backtrack. They went only a few paces before they stumbled on Clary's motionless form, already being covered by the storm's deadly blanket.

"Found him!" Dougherty shouted.

With a reserve of strength he did not know he had, Dougherty set down his lantern and lifted Clary up. Wrapping his long right arm around Clary's waist, Dougherty half carried, half dragged him the final quarter mile to the station.

The door to the depot was jammed with men anxious to get inside. Dougherty could feel his strength faltering.

Twenty-five feet, he thought. Made it this far. Can make it. Gotta make it.

Harrington was standing outside, counting heads. He saw Dougherty approach, staggering, with Clary still on his shoulder.

"Clear the way, boys!' he shouted. "Let Al get Ira inside!"

Like the parting of the Red Sea, those still gathered on the station's porch stepped aside. Dougherty, his knees shaking, made his way through. Inside, with a final burst of strength, he gently let Clary slide to the floor near the stove. Relieved to see that he was breathing, Dougherty stood up and looked around. The rest of the men were filing inside and finding places to sit.

Harrington walked over to Dougherty. He grabbed the big brakeman's shoulders with both hands and squeezed hard.

"I can't thank ya enough for what you did tonight, Al. We'd still be out there if it wasn't for you." He released his grip, and then, to Dougherty's surprise, Harrington's strong arms embraced him. There was a moment of silence, and Harrington backed away.

"I cuss your ass out this afternoon on the plow and then you save all our bacon tonight. I ain't going to forget this, Al." Harrington took off his hat and sat on the edge of the desk. He ran his gloved hand through his wet, matted hair and yawned. "I tell ya. As long as I live, I ain't gonna forget this."

"Just doing what needed to be done, Bill. That's all."

Exhaustion and relief finally overtook both men. Harrington nodded but said nothing. He wandered back to his office at the rear of the station. Dougherty slumped down, his back against the wall next to Clary. All around him sat men, their clothes soaking wet, their breathing heavy. Most were asleep.

Dougherty looked up at the clock over the operator's desk. *Four in the morning. Got here just in time to head out and bring in the cows.*

Dougherty finally let his eyes close. In an instant, visions of warm summer days on the farm back home drifted into his mind and became his dreams.

Sunday, February 27, 1910, 5:30 a.m.
James Henry O'Neill, Superintendent

O'Neill barely noticed the falling snow. Indeed, the only way he might have paid any attention to the weather was if the wind died down and the snow finally stopped. He finished his coffee, staring blankly out the window of his car.

Never been in a jam this tight. Got to figure a way out, he pondered. *Get a plow coming west from Spokane. Try and get one from the NP to help out Dowling.*

"Don't like the idea of you going down that mountainside alone, sir," Lewis Walker, O'Neill's steward, worried aloud. He reached across O'Neill and refilled his coffee cup.

"Not to worry, Lewis," O'Neill answered. "When I get out to the plows, I'll grab a couple of the biggest brakemen I can find and have them go with. How's that?"

"You sure you don't want me to find something for you to take along to eat? Just don't seem right, me sending you back out in this storm on an empty belly," Lewis fretted.

"I'm fine, Lewis. Running low on stores all around, from what I hear. Save what you got. I told Mr. Blackburn last night he can sleep in my bed. I want you to take care of him almost as good as you take care of me," instructed O'Neill.

Walker, having returned to the kitchen, poked his head into the room where O'Neill was sitting.

"Almost, sir?" he inquired, confused.

"Well, yes, don't want you to baby him like you baby me. I'll never live it down if the men find out how much you spoil me." O'Neill looked away from the window and gave Walker a wink and a smile.

"I swear, Mr. O'Neill, I'm never gonna know when you are telling it straight and when you're just a pullin' my leg." Walker ducked back into the kitchen, laughing.

Earl Longcoy, hair combed, freshly shaved, walked out from the front of the car. Walker handed him a steaming cup of coffee as he shuffled past the kitchen compartment. O'Neill motioned to him to sit.

"Sorry sir, meant to get up earlier," Longcoy mumbled, trying to suppress a yawn. "Did you sleep well?"

"Barely slept a wink, if you want the truth, Earl. Too tired to sleep. Too much on my mind," O'Neill admitted. "But good to get a fresh change of clothes and warmed up a bit. Now then, I'm leaving for Scenic. Keep a watch for Harrington. As soon as he gets back with that coal from Merritt, have the Wellington operator send him west. We have to start bucking out that slide."

"Understood, sir," Longcoy acknowledged between sips of coffee.

"I'll try and track down Pettit before I leave. If you're asked by anyone from that train when the line will be open, just tell them we are doing what we can to get through the slides to the west, and that I've gone to Scenic to wire for more help. Anything beyond that is either none of their damned business or beyond your authority to comment. Understand?" O'Neill lectured.

"I'll keep a closed lip, sir. No sense in generating any undue anxiety," Longcoy promised. "The passengers have been asking about you attending a meeting with them. I've been putting them off. Told them last night you were too exhausted."

"Good. I'll keep Pettit informed and let him handle the folks on the train. I've heard bits and pieces of the demands from their so-called committee. Just a bunch of business types trying to throw their weight around." O'Neill put on his coat and hat. "All the more reason not to tell those people any more than they need to know. Oh, and keep a close watch on the key. As soon as service is restored up here, have them get word to me. If I'm not at Scenic, I'll be with Mr. Dowling's outfit to the east."

"Very good, sir." Longcoy rose as well and extended his hand. "Be careful, sir."

O'Neill grasped the boy's thin, clammy hand and shook it.

"Not to worry, Earl, I'll probably stay the night with Dowling out on the plow, but come back up tomorrow or the day after at the latest."

O'Neill turned for the rear door of his car.

"You stay out of Bailets' whiskey, Lewis!" he hollered over his shoulder. "The last time you were up here for a week I had to pay your bar tab out of my own pocket. Caught hell for it at home!"

Walker rushed out from the front compartments of the car. He had a small parcel in his hands.

"Now you know I believe whiskey is the devil's work, Mr. O'Neill. You don't need to be a spreadin' around such stories. Now you take this, you're gonna need it." Walker pressed the package into O'Neill's hands.

"What the hell you got here, Lewis?" O'Neill asked.

"Dry socks. Bring me back some stores so I can start cookin' proper, you hear me, sir?" Walker ordered.

"Earl, do me a favor. While I'm gone, try and explain to Lewis I'm not operating this railroad just so he can practice his cooking." O'Neill pulled his hat down and headed out into the dark morning.

Need to find Pettit. Get in and out without getting mobbed by that damned committee, O'Neill thought. *Unless I miss my guess, he's probably sleeping in a forward seat in the day coach.*

Once he located an open vestibule between the day coach and first sleeper, O'Neill quietly climbed aboard. Weaving through the narrow passage, he spotted Pettit stretched out in a seat near the front of the car. The passengers not privy to the berths in the sleeper cars were wrapped in brown-checked blankets, sound asleep.

Warm. Folks seem comfortable, O'Neill observed. *Keep the engine steamed up. Pack in some food. Another couple of days up here ain't going to hurt a thing. Best just to wait it out.*

O'Neill slipped into the seat across the aisle from the snoozing conductor. He gently shook his shoulder. Pettit's eyes blinked a few times, then focused on O'Neill's face.

"Mr. O'Neill," he whispered, sitting upright. "How can I help?"

"I'm hiking down to Scenic, Mr. Pettit. I need to wire out and get more help on the way. The double rotary is stalled west of town. It's blocked off by a slide full of trees. Harrington is plowing east. I plan on packing in food if necessary. Best to keep your people near the train," O'Neill quietly explained.

"You know there's talk among some of the men about hiking out. Once they find out you have, I don't think I'll be able to stop them from following, sir," Pettit warned.

"You're right, we can't stop them. Just make it very clear, once they leave this train, they are on their own. The railroad has no responsibility or liability. Beyond that there's not much you can do. Make sure they realize how dangerous the slide down from Windy Point is," O'Neill advised.

"I'll do what I can to discourage them if they decide to go, sir."

"Can't image why anyone would want to leave this nice warm train and brave this damned storm," O'Neill said standing up. "Safe and sound right here. Damned fools."

"All the snow has got a few of them scared, that's all," Pettit said quietly. In his usual manner, he tipped his hat, then settled back into his seat.

Making his way out, O'Neill winked at a small child who had woken and was staring at him. He patted her on the head, held his index finger to his lips then pulled the blanket up over her shoulders.

"Too early," he whispered. "Go back to sleep."

Thoughts of his wife and baby at home rushed through O'Neill's head. He held the image for an instant as he looked at the child, and then drove the picture from his mind.

See them soon enough.

Wading through knee-deep snow, crawling over two massive slides, O'Neill was tired by the time he arrived at the stalled plows. Wisps of steam floated from their boilers, white wood smoke from their stacks. Men with lanterns were scattered out across the avalanche and on the hill above, chopping wood and shoveling snow into the tenders. Irving

Tegtmeier stood on the tender of the X-802, shining his lamp down into the water tank.

"Have you seen Mr. Blackburn?" O'Neill called out.

"Shoveling snow into the tender of the trailing plow," Tegtmeier answered, never looking up from his work.

The quiet seemed odd to O'Neill. His giant snow plows and locomotives sat in silence, slowly being subdued by the grip of the storm. It was the ringing of the axes on the hill above and across the face of the slide to the east that O'Neill heard, rather than the roar of the machines in which he had placed his faith.

Never thought I'd live to see the day couldn't buck a slide with a rotary and a couple of pushers.

Blackburn was manning the steam hose running from the boiler back to the water tank on the X-800's tender. Three others beside him shoveled snow down into the hatch. A cloud of steam drifted from its interior.

"Mr. Blackburn, a word, if you please," O'Neill said.

Handing the hose to one of the men, Blackburn leaped off the tender and onto the snow bank, landing beside O'Neill. Face drawn, nose and ears red, eyes set deep into his head, he too had aged over the past week.

"Can you spare a man or two, Art?" asked O'Neill. "I'm going to Scenic and wire out for more help. Be good if I could take a couple of boys along to help break a trail."

"Sure." Blackburn turned towards the tender and pointed to two of the men shoveling snow. "You and you, come here! Mr. O'Neill needs you two to go with him to Scenic."

The two men, one large and strongly built, the other shorter, stocky, and muscular, laid down their shovels. Like Blackburn, they made a slight running start across the back of the tender and jumped onto the adjacent snow bank, joining the two officials.

"Any sign of Harrington? Was out here all night, never made it back to the depot." Blackburn explained.

"No, nothing. I'm going to wire both Brown and Gruber. I want plows coming each way and at least 300 men rounded up. Hope to have them here by tomorrow. Trying to open this railroad by ourselves is bullshit," O'Neill exclaimed. "I'll find out where Dowling is and check his progress while I'm at it. Will spend tonight at Scenic, not sure about tomorrow. You're in charge up here."

"I understand, sir," answered Blackburn. "I'm going to try and get a big crew out here today. Want to have enough firewood cut and stacked down here so we can get back to working on chopping out that slide," Blackburn informed O'Neill. "Wood in the slide is too green to burn. Hoped to be able to kill two birds with one stone, chop out the slide, burn the wood, but that ain't working out."

"Whatever you think's best," O'Neill said. He turned to the two brakemen, Wickham and Churchill. "Gentlemen, let's get going. By the way, Mr. Blackburn, Lewis is expecting you tonight for sure. Feel free to sleep in my car while I'm gone."

"Thank you, sir." Blackburn jumped back onto the tender. "Glad I'm staying up here," he called out to O'Neill. "Goddamned dangerous out on that trail west."

With strength proportional to his size, Wickham plowed a trail through the snow drifted across the tracks—tracks that should have long ago carried trains 25 and 27 out of the mountains. After nearly an hour of hard going, the little party scaled the troublesome slide blocking the east portal of Shed 3.3. The three men wormed their way through the narrow opening between the top of the snow and the roof of the shed. They slid feet first into the dark interior. Passing through the shed, Wickham clawed partway up the snow bank blocking the opposite end. Stopping, he reached down and pulled Churchill and O'Neill up with him. The grip of his giant hands was like a mechanical claw.

Hate to get in a barroom brawl with this man, O'Neill thought.

As they hiked downgrade, the closer they got to Windy Point, the harder the wind blew. Churchill took the lead once they passed through the shed, falling back after a half mile. O'Neill was next and vowed to make a good showing. Waist deep at times, he continued to press forward.

I can make it to Shed 4. Keep moving forward. It's just up ahead, he thought.

Clear of the final snow shed, Wickham bounded into the lead. The howl of the wind and the exertion required just to walk prevented the men from saying a word to each other. As they worked their way around the narrow precipice leading to Windy Point, sudden gusts rose violently from the Scenic Basin, seven hundred feet below. Twice the men were driven backward by the wind's sudden and unseen fury.

"Watch your step!" O'Neill yelled at Wickham, but the brakeman kept walking.

A long ways down if we slip. O'Neill and Churchill moved closer to the rocky upward slope of the mountain.

O'Neill cupped his hands and shouted once more. "Move in! Move in! Too close to the edge!"

His words barely left his mouth when a small slide cascaded down from above. It knocked Wickham off balance. For in instant he teetered, fighting against the force of the snow. Then suddenly he was gone.

Churchill tried to bound past to see what had happened to Wickham but O'Neill grabbed him and pulled him back.

"He's gone! Nothing we can do! Get too close you'll go over!" shouted O'Neill.

"But what if he's hung up? Needs our help?" Churchill protested.

"Hung up on what? It's straight down right here. We need to keep going. We'll look for him when we get to the bottom." O'Neill, struggling to curb his own fear did not let go of the shaken Churchill.

That's three men we've lost. Wonder how many more before this is over?

Pulling the scared man along, O'Neill battled his way around Windy Point, finally stopping at the top of "Old Glory." For a moment, O'Neill just stared down the steep, snow- covered rock fall. He knew better than to be fooled by the smooth layer of white. Underneath, in some cases mere inches, were any number of sharp, jagged boulders.

"Be best to stay out of the middle," O'Neill told Churchill. "Stick to the edge where the smaller rocks are—snow'll be deeper. Pull the tail of your coat under your ass and try and ride down on it as much as you can. Don't try and stop yourself with your hands, you'll shred 'em to pieces. I'll go first."

Sitting on his coat tails, O'Neill took a final look down. He took off his hat and stuffed it down the front of his coat.

Pick a good line. Once I get going, no stopping, O'Neill thought.

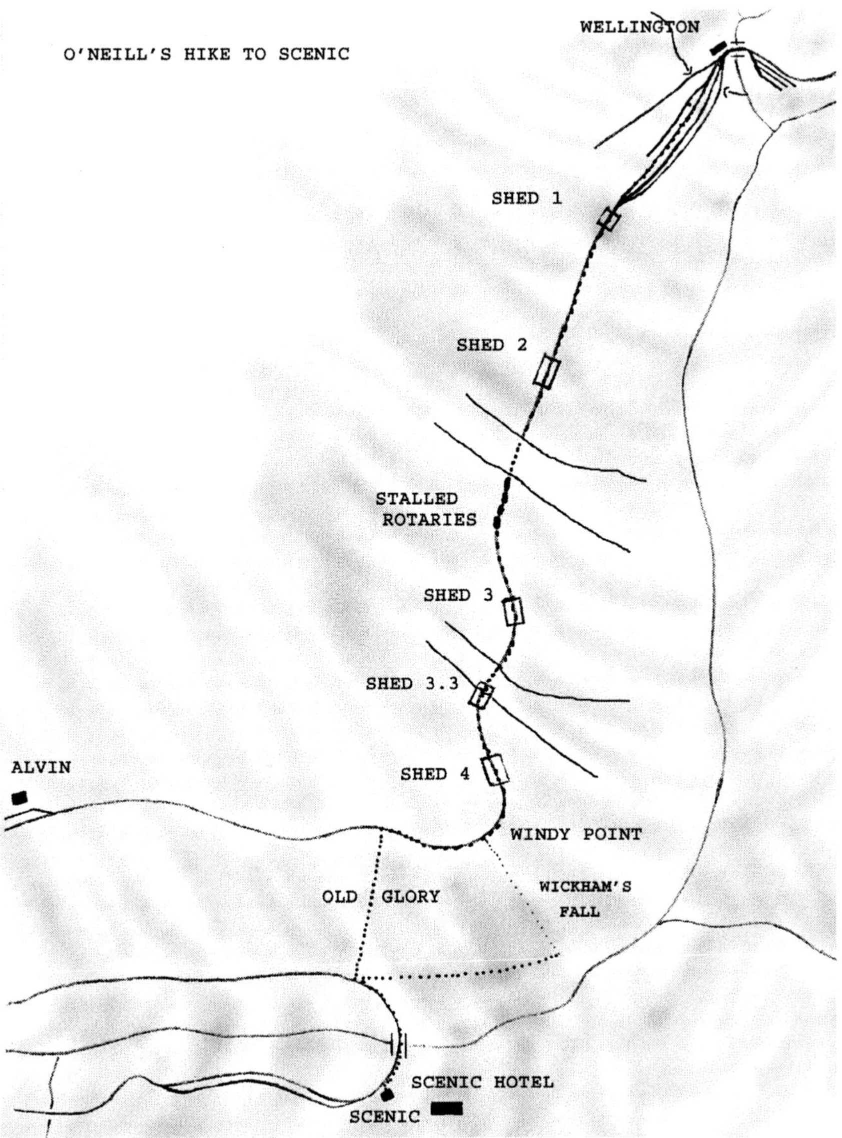
O'NEILL'S HIKE TO SCENIC
WELLINGTON
SHED 1
SHED 2
STALLED
ROTARIES
SHED 3
SHED 3.3
ALVIN
SHED 4
WINDY POINT
OLD GLORY
WICKHAM'S
FALL
SCENIC HOTEL
SCENIC

"Guess it's a good thing I've got one child and another on the way," O'Neill quipped with a straight face. "You have children, Mr. Churchill?"

"No sir," Churchill answered, now sitting beside O'Neill.

"Pick the wrong route down and you'll never sire offspring, Mr. Churchill. Follow me!"

With that, O'Neill scooted himself over the edge. Try as he might to watch where he was going, his eyes closed as he gained speed. He kept his hands between his legs, holding onto his coattail as if it would somehow guide him safely down the steep hill. Shoulders hunched, he leaned back slightly. He could feel the rough edges of the rocks hidden by the snow trying to scrape at his hind side. Suddenly, he lost his balance. No longer sliding, he was rolling, over and over, and then he was still.

"Make way!" came a shout.

Instinctively O'Neill rolled to his left. He propped himself up in time to see Churchill roll past and come to rest a few yards from a downed log. Both men rose, staggering, brushing off snow like it was dust.

"You alright, sir?" Churchill asked.

"Seem to be. How about you?" O'Neill inquired.

"No worse for wear, I guess."

"Hell of a ride," O'Neill admitted. He looked around and got his bearings. "Well, let's see if we can locate Wickham."

O'Neill pulled out his crumpled hat and placed it down hard on his head. They tumbled down the last few paces off the slide and onto the clogged lower level of track. The rails were covered with snow, making it obvious to O'Neill it had been sometime since Dowling had passed through with the X-808. A well-used trail had been packed down.

Dowling's east. Must be cut off. Men walking back and forth to Scenic, he surmised.

Rather than follow the line around the bend to the station at Scenic, the two men veered off to the left and made their way along the banks of the Tye River. They headed into the woods at the base of the mountain estimating where Wickham had fallen. Once under the towering firs, they were finally sheltered from the wind and falling snow.

They had not traveled far before they stopped in their tracks.

"Would you look at that," Churchill gasped.

"Hey boys, made it down I see," Wickham greeted the two stunned men, wiping blood from his forehead. "Took one hell of a tumble myself."

"How the hell …?" O'Neill's voice trailed off.

"Don't know myself, sir," Wickham admitted. "Was in the middle of the slide. Snow all around. Guess the snow bounced off the rocks more than me."

The stacks of telegrams received at Scenic and the stacks O'Neill sent did nothing to ease his mind. A relief train was coming east from Skykomish with more workers, but what he really needed were more mechanical plows, not hand shovels. He wired both his superiors, Gruber in Spokane and Brown in Seattle, asking for additional rotaries. Not until the operator reminded him did O'Neill realize it was Sunday, so he opted not to wait for confirmations. Instead, he left the station and began the walk out to the X-808.

Get a plow started west from Spokane, be in Leavenworth by late tonight, early tomorrow, O'Neill calculated. *Hope to hell someone gets that message under his nose today. Brown'll have to get me help from the NP. They're probably as stuck as I am.*

O'Neill followed the trail from Scenic along the low line that climbed the base of Windy Mountain. Although engrossed in thought, still he missed familiar sounds of a working steam plow.

God, hope they're not stuck too, O'Neill worried. The information contained in the messages he had just read did nothing to improve his mood. A relief train was stuck down in the Tumwater Canyon. Any plow coming west was going to have to break it loose first.

Damned fool thing Devery tried to do, come west with no rotary escort. Buggering things up but good.

He kicked at the snow as he walked. Pausing, he surveyed the hillside above and studied the pack.

Gotta be five, six feet on the level. Already crawled over two slides. Can't get relief up to Wellington by train until we get this plowed back out. Got supplies up the ass sitting down at Sky. Not a goddamned way to get them here. Pack stores into Wellington. Only way I can figure. Line's plugged tighter than I thought.

Ahead, O'Neill saw the rear of a parked coal hopper, part of Dowling's plow train. Realizing the risk of being cut off to the west by slides, Dowling had wisely taken two full hopper cars with him, one trailing the two pusher engines, the other sandwiched between the locomotives and the tender of the snow plow. Men were on top of the latter, transferring coal into the plow's bin.

"What's got you stopped?" O'Neill asked the men shoveling. To his surprise, he recognized two of the men as ones who had quit the day before up at Wellington.

"Damned plow's broke down, I guess," one answered.

O'Neill continued up onto the plow's fire deck.

"What the hell's going on here?" he asked the startled fireman.

"Broken flue, sir. Mr. Dowling's working on it right now."

O'Neill could hear pounding coming from inside the boiler as he made his way forward along the narrow, wood gangway. Passing into the cab, he saw that the back wall had been partially torn out, the smoke box door open. Inside, J.J. Dowling and Will Mackey were sprawled out, working by the light of two lanterns.

"What goes here, J.J.?" O'Neill asked as he leaned against the top of the smoke box, poking his head inside.

"Mr. O'Neill! Didn't expect to see you here!" Dowling exclaimed. "Popped a flue on this damned old teapot. Will and I are trying to bolt a saddle patch around it. On a lower coil, mostly water, so need to patch it. If it was just a steam leak I'd say to hell with it."

"Need an extra hand?" O'Neill offered.

"Sure, crawl on in," Dowling replied, wiping sweat from his face.

O'Neill shed himself of his hat and coat. On all fours, he carefully worked his way into the smoke box and then alongside the jacket of the boiler. Mackey had crawled in backwards and was now face to face with the superintendent. Dowling was astride Mackey's back.

"Not exactly the easiest place to work," Mackey said.

"Okay, Will, grab the bottom of that saddle, I'll hold the top. Give Mr. O'Neill a couple of bolts. When we get the bottom and top halves of the saddle sandwiched over that leaky pipe, try and get the holes lined up and get a couple of bolts through and nuts started. Understand, sir?" Dowling instructed.

"Understood." O'Neill held out his hand. Rolling onto his side, Mackey dug four bolts and nuts from the pocket of his overalls. Cramped, O'Neill carefully clenched them in his hand.

"Don't worry if you drop a couple, sir," Mackey said. "I've got more. Been dropping more bolts around here than cuss words, truth be known."

Dowling slipped the top half of the patch over the ruptured pipe. His arm and wrist bent like a circus contortionist, Mackey worked to get the lower half to fit on the underside.

"That's all I can do." Mackey gritted his teeth, his voice strained.

O'Neill took a deep breath. Threading his fingers and wrist through the maze of pipes, he worked slowly but deliberately.

Don't get in a damned big hurry.

With his fingers as a guide he felt the depression of the hole. He worked the first bolt out of the palm of his hand. By carefully nudging it with his fingers, he stood it upright and it slipped into the hole. Still not lined up with the hole on the lower half, he and Mackey worked the lower portion of the patch back and forth until the bolt fell through.

"Hold her steady, boys. Let me get a nut started," O'Neill whispered.

His wrist hurt. His fingers were growing numb, their circulation being cut off by the awkward position they were in. He fumbled for a nut. Just as he worked one out to the tip of his thumb and index finger, he lost his grip and it fell to the bottom of the boiler.

"Goddamn it!" he shouted.

"Got the language of a master mechanic," Dowling joked.

O'Neill slowly worked another nut into place. He tried to thread it onto the bolt. With each attempt, the bolt would move with the upward pressure he was placing on the nut.

Gotta steady the top of that damned bolt, he thought. Working his other hand over the pipes, he held down the head of the bolt with his right index finger while trying to start the nut with his left hand. On the third attempt he felt the threads catch.

"Got her, by damned!" he exclaimed.

The second bolt went easier. By the time all six were in place and the nuts cinched finger tight, the patch was secure. Taking a break, all three men pulled their tired arms and hands out from the maze of boiler flues.

"That's the hard part. Rest will go easy," Dowling said. "Nice work, Mr. O'Neill. Will, crawl out and get those wrenches. We'll tighten her down and be ready to put the water back to her. Be going before you know it, Mr. O'Neill."

O'Neill worked his way back out of the smoke box and into the cab. He stretched his back and shook his hands, trying to restore blood flow. Mackey was gathering the wrenches spread out on the floor.

"Heard anything from my dear brother Jimbo?" he asked O'Neill.

"Wish I had, Will," O'Neill answered. "He's gone east with Harrington after the coal at Merritt. Haven't heard from them in a couple of days."

Mackey crawled headfirst back into the smoke box with the wrenches.

"Jimbo and Bill. Now there's a combination," Mackey said, his voice echoing from the narrow confines of the boiler. "If those two can't get a plow down to Merritt and back, nobody can."

"He took a tumble off one of the tenders the other night. Knocked the wind out him, but he seems fine now." O'Neill squatted down, peering back inside at the men working.

"The hell you say," Mackey answered. "There, J.J., I got a wrench on the lower back corner. Doesn't surprise me—Jimbo was always the one falling out of trees back home. Best to keep him on level ground."

The men fell silent. Only an occasional grunt from Dowling or Mackey, and the clang of wrenches slamming against the boiler pipes, resonated from inside.

"That should do it," Dowling finally said. "Mr. O'Neill, can you crawl in a ways and help grab these wrenches and lanterns?"

"I don't know, Mr. O'Neill. Ol' J.J. here's been ordering you around pretty good ever since you showed up," Mackey said, handing him a large monkey wrench. "I'd say he's bucking for your job."

"Oh, for Christ sakes, Will," Dowling groaned.

"Mr. Mackey, right now J.J. can have my job."

Sunday, February 27, 1910, 10:30 a.m.
John Robert Meath, Engineer

"You know, Pete, this ain't exactly what I had in mind when Blackburn said we could head back to Wellington," Meath told Peter Imberg, as he threw a shovelful of snow to the side.

"Should be sleeping somewhere in a warm bed instead of shoveling more damned snow," Imberg complained.

"All thanks to those fine gentlemen on the work crews quitting in a huff, Peter old boy." His head down, Meath scraped at the deep snow with his shovel, trying to outwork the wind.

Having finally been relieved from tending the stalled plows all Saturday night, Meath, Imberg and the others walked back to Wellington in hopes of eating a meal and getting a few hours of restful sleep. Hiking through the storm and over the slides blocking the line, they joked of how it might feel to actually sleep in a bed, rather than the fire deck or cab of a plow.

The men had not gotten past the stalled trains. Ed Sweeney, engineer of the mail train, hailed them and motioned the men to come over by his engine.

"I need your help boys—in some deep shit here," he told the men. "I'm about out of water on my engine, and the engine on the passenger is about out of coal. Make matters worse, my injectors are clogging.

Need to get my engine shoveled out and pulled up alongside of the 1418. I'll get water from him, he'll get coal from me."

With little choice, Meath and the rest grabbed the shovels collected by Sweeney and Frank Martin, the engineer of the 1418. They split up, with one crew working at digging out engine 1032, while Meath and the others tried to clear away the seventy-five-foot section of track that kept the two locomotives from standing abreast.

Bat Nelson soon joined the group, his pants legs soaking wet.

"So, you and Archie figure out what's wrong?" Meath asked.

"Same old problem," Nelson said, stopping to lean on his shovel. "Fir needles have got the screens plugged. Water's so low and there's been so much shit shoveled in, gonna need to try and get enough good water in there so all the crap floats on top, above the screens."

"How the hell they gonna do that?" Imberg asked. He, too, stopped shoveling.

"Come on, boys, we can bullshit and shovel at the same time," ordered Meath. "Standing around here like those good-for-nothings Harley had up here."

"Up yours, Bobby," Imberg scowled, returning to work.

"Soon as they get the 1032 off the mail train and next to the 1418, Frank and Ed are gonna try and run a siphon from one to the other. Pull the clean water out of one to fill the other. They're scaring up a hose right now," Nelson explained.

"I know a gal down on Market that can suck hard enough to get that siphon going, now that you mention it," said Meath in his dry, expressionless tone.

"You're going straight to hell, Bobby, you know that," Nelson responded. "Talking like that on the Sabbath."

"By God, I see Harley finally found a crew dumber than that last bunch," came a familiar voice.

Meath looked up and could not suppress the smile that immediately broke across his face.

"Al! Where the hell did you come from?" he shouted. He immediately wrinkled his eyebrows and started turning his head, looking to his side and then behind. "Say, didn't you forget to bring something with you?"

"Like what?" Dougherty asked, grabbing a shovel.

"Well, let's start with a snow plow and coal, then we can finish with a certain Snow King," replied Meath.

"Let me tell you, boys, we had one hell of a night last night," Dougherty began.

The men continued to work as Dougherty regaled them with the epic hike back from Gaynor. Not to be outdone, Meath filled Dougherty in on the problems they were having to the west.

"So nothing's moving right now?" Dougherty asked.

"Just Dowling," Meath answered.

Like kids who had run out of things to say, the men fell silent, intent on their work. They would clear out a ten-foot section of track, then fall back to skim off the snow the wind had deposited on what they had already cleaned. For all their effort, working as hard as their beleaguered bodies would allow, they were barely staying ahead of the wind.

"That looks pretty good, boys," Sweeney stated some three hours later. "Should be able to get a good-enough run to buck through the rest."

Martin grabbed a coiled section of hose and climbed into his engine. Meath and the rest of the men threw a few last shovelfuls of snow off the track. They were about to move off the tracks, allowing Sweeney to move his engine, when a stranger approached the group.

"Good morning, gentlemen," he said in a cheery voice. "Name's Chantrell—H.D. Chantrell. I've been asked by the Reverend James Thomson to spread the word he is conducting Sunday services in the observation car in a few minutes. If you have the time to spend, you're welcome to attend."

"Well now," Nelson said, "That's mighty kind of the Reverend."

"Remember the Sabbath day to keep it holy, it says in the Good Book," Imberg added.

"My good Mr. Chantrell, as you can see, we're a little tied up at the moment," Meath chimed in, "but we truly appreciate his concern for our spiritual well-being."

"Well, if you have time, you're all welcome," Chantrell repeated. He turned to leave.

"You know, Mr. Chantrell, there is one theological issue that has been on my mind. If you could, you might take it up with the good Reverend on my behalf," teased Meath.

"I'll certainly try. What do you want me to ask him?" Chantrell asked, not knowing he was being set up.

"Well, Mr. Chantrell, it's like Mr. Imberg here said, you know, remember the Sabbath day to keep it holy?" led Meath.

"Well, yes sir. That is exactly why the Reverend Thomson is holding services," Chantrell offered.

"Exactly," agreed Meath. He looked into the sky and held out his hands, catching the falling snow. "Ask the good Reverend, why it is the Almighty doesn't see fit to follow his own rules?"

Without breaking a grin, Meath threw a shovel over his shoulder and walked away from the stammering Chantrell and smiling men.

"Hey, Mister," Martin hailed the retreating Chantrell, "you might have the Reverend give a prayer that we get some water in the boiler of Ed's engine while you're at it. You folks are gonna get mighty cold if we don't."

Some skillful throttle work on the part of Sweeney soon had his engine alongside the passenger train's locomotive. By then, most of Harrington's crew arrived. A group of them climbed aboard the tender of the 1032 and began transferring coal. Partridge and Christian, the firemen off the engines, worked with Martin and Sweeney getting the siphon hose rigged between the tender tanks. It took a number of attempts at filling the hose before the water began to flow between the engines.

"The good reverend must be a pretty good at praying," Martin said, once the siphon began to work. He crossed himself.

"You know Al, a little churching up might not be a bad idea," Meath suggested. "Let's head on up and see what the Reverend's got to say about us poor trapped sinners."

"You go on, Bobby, you're off. I need to get on down to the slide with the rest of the boys and start chopping," replied Dougherty.

"Suit yourself, Al," shrugged Meath. "I expect a nice pile of dry wood neatly stacked on the 802's fire deck. It's up to you to keep me and ol' Bat here warm and dry tonight."

"Now if a bottle of Bailets' finest were to show up in the tool box tomorrow, we just might make that happen," added Ira Clary who had now joined the group.

"Meath! I might have known!" bellowed Harrington appearing from the storm. "Come on boys, quit hanging around this bastard. We better get down to that slide. Give ol' Blackburn one hell of a surprise. Time for Mr. Meath and this sorry bunch to get some rest."

"He's going to church, Bill," Nelson said. "There's a preacher on the passenger train."

"Church? Not a bad idea. Tell the Almighty if he ends this damned snow I'll quit cussing," Harrington said. "I'm serious. The rest of you, let's get going."

Shovels on their shoulders, Harrington's crew filed off. Heads against the wind, they looked like a prison chain gang marching off to another day in a life sentence of hard labor. For a moment, Dougherty stayed back. He grabbed Meath by the arm and pulled him aside.

"I was there when they found Johnny," Dougherty told Meath in a whisper. "Was really bad. Damned near got sick. Wood splinters in his body. Bloody snow everywhere. Ever see a dead man before, Bobby?"

"Not like that, Al," Meath admitted.

"His eyes were open. Just staring," continued Dougherty. "I think he saw it. Was alive when he got buried. Maybe tried to save himself."

"You don't know that for certain, Al," Meath said, trying to console his friend. "If he did, it was quick. That's for certain."

"God, I hope so, Bobby," Dougherty sighed. "Just can't get it outta my head."

"You will. It'll pass." Meath draped his arm across Dougherty's broad shoulders. "There's demons floating around here, Al. I'm feeling them too. Don't let them get to you."

"Guess you're right about that. Never thought of it that way." Dougherty paused. He gave his friend a pat on the back. "Guess I'll see you around, Bobby. You know, Sherlock's just sitting up there with nothing to do. He's prime for a prank."

"I'll work on it, Al. Give me a couple of days and we'll get him good." Meath returned the casual pat on the back. As Dougherty trudged off into the snow with Harrington and the rest of his crew, he turned and gave Meath a quick wave.

A large crowd was gathered into the rear of the observation car. The women were seated at the front, wearing their best. The men had put on suits, their hair combed, faces cleanly shaven. Most of them stood with their heads bowed and hands folded.

Meath quietly took a place in the back corner of the compartment, his filthy hat in hand. He was acutely aware of the grime and stench he carried. He was surprised to find Ben Jarnigan, Ed Lindsay, and Dan Gilmore standing opposite him, along with a few of Harley's Italians. They quietly acknowledged Meath's glance and returned to their private meditation.

Reverend Thomson was preaching about the importance of prayer in times of peril, and having the patience to await God's answer. It made little sense to the cynical Meath.

Why pray to you God? Wait forever. Answer that never comes, Meath pondered. *Been praying for three days for You to end this storm. Everyone else praying the same damned thing. Ain't done us a lick of good has it, Lord.*

The reverend concluded his sermon and led the gathering in the words of Psalm 27. Meath listened closely to the words.

"Though a host encamp against me, my heart shall not fear …"

When's the last time you slammed into a slide in the middle of the night, Lord? I'll show you fear.

"Though a war rise against me, yet I will be confident …"

Confident that it's gonna be a month before we get this railroad running again thanks to You and Your storm, Meath thought.

"For he will hide me in his shelter in the day of trouble …"

You keep these days of trouble coming Lord. The only shelter I'll get to hide in is the cab of a plow.

"He will conceal me in the cover of his tent, he will set me on a rock."

More like bury me under a mountain of snow. You're not going to end this storm. Even I've got that figured out. You want a prayer? I'll give you one. Do what you're gonna do, Lord. No one stopping You. But watch over the boys. You've taken Bjerenson and Elerker, that's enough. Just watch over us Lord. Keep Ira, Bill, Benny over there, all of us. Watch over Al, conceal him in your tent, Lord. Just keep all of us safe. Amen.

Meath crossed himself and raised his head. Reverend Thomson

was still offering petitions in his flowing language. The rest of the congregation had their heads bowed. All but the children had their eyes closed.

Slipping unnoticed out of the car, Meath stepped off into the snow. He ambled toward the bunkhouse, still thinking about whether or not he really believed in God. Raised Catholic, he went through catechism and still occasionally attended confession and Mass. It was more out of habit than a strong sense of faith in God, he decided.

All during that short service, rage began building inside of him. His demons returned with a vengeance. Dougherty describing the body of Bjerenson did not help. While inside the observation car, with people around, Meath managed to keep the demons in check. Once outside, alone, he could not contain them any longer. Not knowing what else to do, he stared into the snow-choked sky. Clenching his fists, he hollered.

"I mean it, Lord! Keep the boys safe!"

Sunday, February 27, 1910, 2nd Trick Wellington
Basil Sherlock, Telegrapher

Sherlock slumped at the operator's desk. His hands were folded, his chin supported by his thumbs, and his elbows propped on the smooth wooden arms of the chair. His eyes were fixed on the silent telegraph key as if he were expecting it to come back to life at any moment. A feeling of isolation came over him like never before.

Remember when we first came here last summer. Knew the snow would keep us from doing much. Never dreamed it would cut us completely off from the rest of the world, Sherlock pondered.

Could be worse. Could be stuck up here alone like Avery or Flannery. Lonesome growing up. Father making me work in his damned doctor's office. Not lonely anymore. Althea ended that. Folks around home still can't figure why she married me. Not sure myself. Cut off and isolated up here in these god-forsaken mountains, but not alone.

The sudden ringing of the phone startled Sherlock.

"Scenic here, you're back on line to the west. Phone and telegraph. Tell Mr. Blackburn."

"Copy tha ..."

A low rumble and gentle vibrating of the windows stopped Sherlock mid-sentence. It was if is a train were approaching the depot. He rocked forward in his chair and peered anxiously outside, but saw nothing except the mix of rain and snow falling in the last light of day.

Even before Sherlock could go outside to investigate, the sound and mild shaking was over.

A small earthquake? he wondered.

"Leave the line open, if you please. There's something going on outside."

Stepping out on the platform, Sherlock looked past the station at the Bailets Hotel. A group of men stood on its porch, pointing across the flats to the mountains behind the small town. Curious, Sherlock walked beyond the end of the station and looked in the direction the men were gazing.

"My God," he gasped.

Through the clouds he could see that a large section of snow broke loose from near the top of one of the peaks. The avalanche had roared down a narrow gully, snapping off trees and carrying the debris out across the flats behind the station, on the opposite side of Haskell Creek. Shaken by the sight, Sherlock hustled back inside.

This is insanity, Sherlock fretted, his fear fast getting the better of him.

He stood in front of the bay window studying the mountain directly across the deep ravine. To his horror, Sherlock could see where another slide had just thundered down its flank, cascading over the remains of the abandoned switchback route over the summit.

Sherlock, hands shaking, sat back down.

Got to get word out. Someone in charge needs to know what's happening up here.

He put the headset on and pulled the mouthpiece to his face. To his relief, he could hear the faint static that told him the line was still open. He pressed the foot treadle.

"Dispatcher. Wellington."

"Dispatcher. Good to hear from you. What goes up there, Sherlock?"

"The snow is sliding. A small slide has come down behind town and a larger one across the canyon from the depot. No one else is here. Mr. Blackburn is down with the plows—they're stuck west of town. I haven't seen Mr. Harrington …"

"Slow down, Sherlock. You say slides are coming down around town?"

"Yes. I'm worried about the passenger trains."

"Hold the line, Sherlock. I'll tell the chief."

To Sherlock, it felt as if hours were passing. *Come on. Hurry up. Line could go dead any second.*

"I've got a message from the chief," Johnson finally said, after what seemed an eternity. "I'll key it out on line so Mr. O'Neill gets a copy down at Scenic."

The key rattled to life, the dots and dashes clear and crisp. Sherlock grabbed a pad and began to write: "Pettit: Use every precaution necessary for safety of passengers and if necessary back trains into tunnel. G.W. Turner."

Sherlock keyed his confirmation. He ripped the master copy off the pad and grabbed his coat. *Got to get this to Pettit.*

Conductor Pettit was trying to calm a group of passengers when Sherlock boarded his train. Sensing the telegraph operator's anxiety, Pettit quickly excused himself. Now he stood with Sherlock outside the nearly-buried coaches of Train 25. They gazed up at the white hillside looming above the tracks. Pettit took another look at the message Sherlock had delivered.

"So it's left to me, is it," Pettit sighed. He looked at the snow drifts blocking the line that lead to the tunnel nearly half mile away. "Leave the trains here and a slide hits, I'll be damned. Getting back to the tunnel … line plugged, no shovelers, no coal for the engines …"

His voice trailed off.

"I don't know what to tell you, Mr. Pettit. I just thought the officials in Everett needed to be advised, and this is the message they sent," Sherlock stammered.

"For all the good this order does. Right now, this train is my responsibility, Mr. Sherlock. You did you job, Turner did his. Puts it right back to me." Pettit tipped his hat and returned to the coach.

Back in the depot, Sherlock threw a shovel of coal into the stove. He stood with his back to its radiating heat, drying off.

Snow keeps sliding, packing up Althea and running for the tunnel. Insanity. Did my part. Glad I told Johnson and Pettit.

Outside, men were walking past the station.

Changing shifts. Men coming back from the west, Sherlock realized. *Hope Blackburn is with them. Need to get word to him of the slide danger. Wall of snow could come crashing down from behind me. End up like Bjerenson and Elerker.*

The stomping of boots out on the platform gave Sherlock a jolt. Eyes wide, he leaped from his chair just in time for the door to open.

"Jesus, Sherlock, looks like you just saw a ghost." To Sherlock's relief, it was Blackburn.

"The telegraph and phones are back on line, sir," Sherlock reported. "There's been slides coming down. I reported that to Mr. Johnson in Everett. Was sent this message from Chief Dispatcher Turner. I delivered it to Pettit."

Blackburn read the station copy of the message.

"Back the train into the tunnel? Jesus Christ!" exclaimed Blackburn, obviously agitated. "And how does the almighty Turner propose we do that? Ignorant ass. Harrington says the tunnel cut is so goddamned plugged it's going to take us half a day of bucking to clear the goddamned thing out! If I didn't know any better, I'd say you and those jackasses in Everett are getting a little spooked."

"Not at all, Mr. Blackburn. I just feel it's my duty to keep a close watch on anything that might be of importance, that's all," defended Sherlock. "My concern right now is with the safety of the passengers."

Blackburn threw the message pad on the desk. His eyes fixed on Sherlock.

"Your concern is with the safety of the passengers!" he shouted. "Your concern! Like all of us out there busting our asses don't care? Is that what you are telling me?"

"M-M-Mr. Blackburn, p-please," stuttered Sherlock. "I meant n-n-no such thing. A n-n-number of the passengers have been coming in and expressing concern with the heavy snow on the steep mountainside. Th-that's all. A few have told me they want us to organize some of our men to help them hike out. I heard others talk about wanting to move the train back to the tunnel."

Towering over the seated Sherlock, Blackburn took off his gloves, exposing his dirty hands. He glared at the young telegrapher, pointing an index finger just under Sherlock's nose.

"Now you listen to me, Sherlock," he said, slowly and distinctly. "That train is safe right where it's at. Those passengers could not ask for a safer place to stay. You don't know shit about this mountain. You hear me? You don't know shit!"

"Yes sir," Sherlock mumbled.

"Now ring up Scenic. Let's hope O'Neill is there."

To Sherlock's relief, the operator at Scenic was able to locate the superintendent. Vacating the chair, Sherlock gladly went to the far side of the operator's room while Blackburn conferred with his boss.

Be good to know what's being said, Sherlock thought. *Better to stay out of Blackburn's way.*

Their conversation complete, Blackburn went over to the stove. He poured himself a cup of coffee. He took a drink and wrinkled his nose.

"Running low on coffee, are we, Sherlock?" he asked, having regained his composure.

"Running low on everything," Sherlock muttered now back at the desk.

"Mr. O'Neill and I agree. 25 stays where it's at," Blackburn told Sherlock. "Help's coming. More men have already arrived and we're hoping to get a couple more plows coming this way. God knows we need them."

Blackburn finished his coffee in silence.

"I'll be in Mr. O'Neill's car for a few hours. If anything important comes in, get me." Blackburn grabbed the door and then paused. "Don't let those slides across the valley spook ya, Sherlock. They come down across there all the time. That's why the railroad is over here now and not on the side of that damned mountain."

With that, Blackburn left the station. His head was down, his shoulders hunched, and his hands thrust into his coat pockets.

O'Neill gone, beat down. Now Blackburn. No one knows what to do. Isolated. As trapped as those poor passengers.

Monday, February 28, 1910, 11:00 a.m.
William Harrington, Assistant Trainmaster

"Would you look at that, Ed," Harrington whistled, leaning on his shovel.

Ed Lindsay was working with an ax alongside Harrington. He stopped chopping long enough to look up. Out of the fog came five railroad men, trudging along the trail across the slide. Squinting, Lindsay tried to make out the faces, but they were hidden under the drooping brims of foul-weather hats.

"Looks like Sweeney for sure," Lindsay observed. "That Irv next to him?"

"Yeah, him and Blomeke. Might be Walt Vogel and maybe Huff bringing up the rear," decided Harrington.

As the men approached, Harrington called out, "To what do we owe the honor, gentlemen? Here to lend a hand?"

Gathering around Harrington and Lindsay, Irving Tegtmeier stripped off his hat and undid the metal latches of the heavy rain slicker.

"Can't believe I let you talk me into wearing this goddamned thing, Sweeney. Wetter from sweating in this thing than if I was just walking in this goddamned rain," Irving Tegtmeier complained.

"Hey Dunc!" Lindsay yelled, "Your cousin from the better-bred side of the family's here to pay you a visit."

"Tell him to go to hell!" Duncan Tegtmeier hollered back. Standing on the hillside above the plow, he waved at the group then continued pitching snow into the lead plow's tender.

"He's never gotten over the fact my old man was the tougher of the two brothers. Used to kick the shit outta his old man when they were growing up back in the old country, from what we've been told," Irving Tegtmeier related.

"You seen Mr. Blackburn?" Walter Vogel, conductor of Train 27, asked. "We're headed down to Scenic. At least we want to. Figured we'd better check in with him first."

"Here he comes now," said Lindsay nodding to his right.

"What goes here, boys?" Blackburn asked, joining the group, ax in hand.

"Well, that poor brakemen that came stumbling by an hour or so ago, you see him?" Sweeney began.

Blackburn looked at Harrington and Lindsay. All three men shrugged their shoulders.

"Anyway, he came up from the 808. Guess they need a little help. Me and Irv thought we'd go on down and do what we can, if that's alright by you, Mr. Blackburn," explained Sweeney.

"All right, I see no reason why not," said Blackburn. "What about Jim Mackey? Heard he made it back from Gaynor. He might be able to help as well."

"Oh God, no, Mr. Blackburn!" Irving Tegtmeier exclaimed. "Will Mackey's engineering the 808 from what we hear. You remember the last time those two got paired up on a plow?"

"No," Lindsay interrupted, "what the hell happened?"

"That's right, forgot about that," Blackburn recalled. "All those two bastards did was sneak drinks and fight about goddamned everything. That must've been one happy house when those two were growing up. Worst plow run I ever made."

"Those two assholes would fight over whistle signals. Jimbo would be up front and call for one thing, Will was the wheelman, he'd whistle off for something else 'cause he figured Jim didn't know shit what he was doing. I didn't know whether to go forward, back up, stop or just say to hell with the both of them." Irving Tegtmeier laughed with the rest of the group, shaking his head.

"We vowed right then and there never to pair those two up again," concluded Blackburn, himself chuckling. "Now, Mr. Vogel, how can I help you?"

"Well, sir, since those boys were heading down, I thought I'd try and get word out about the mail. Find out what kind of help Mr. O'Neill has coming. If things work out, weather turning and all, might try and organize a pack crew to haul it out," Vogel answered. "I asked Mr. Blomeke and Mr. Huff to come along and help break the trail."

"We could come back up or go out to the 808, sir," Blomeke interjected.

"That sounds fine," Blackburn quickly decided. "You men report to Mr. O'Neill. Might be good to get some experienced plowmen out on the 808 for relief. Not sure, but if Mr. O'Neill was able to get a plow from the NP coming east, we'll need more men down there to crew it up. Sky call board has to be getting low on plow crews."

"Let's mush onward, boys," Sweeney said. "You blokes take care. See ya when we get up here with the 808."

The men split up and returned to work. Harrington cleared the snow from another large limb. Together with Lindsay, they would either cast it aside or, if too large, Lindsay would chop it into manageable lengths while Harrington continued to pitch the snow away.

"What's with Blackburn, lately?" Lindsay asked between swings of his ax. "Ain't near the asshole he usually is."

"Couldn't tell you, Ed," answered Harrington. "Probably like the rest of us. Too damned tired and discouraged to put up a fight anymore."

"In that case, be good if he just stayed tired and discouraged." Lindsay grabbed a chunk of the limb he was been cutting. Breaking off the final thread of wood, he tossed it over the bank. Head down, he resumed a rhythmic swinging of his ax on the next log uncovered by Harrington's shovel.

"Well, he can't stay this way," Harrington said. "Gotta be an ass most the time to be a good trainmaster."

"You ain't an ass, Bill," said Lindsay. "Least not all the time."

"Yeah, well I ain't a full-time trainmaster either," Harrington scowled. "And I don't intend on becoming one."

"Hell, Bill, word is you're next in line. Blackburn ain't gonna be here forever. Most of us figure O'Neill's grooming you up for the job." Lindsay stopped chopping and wiped the rain from his face.

"Not me, Ed. Not me," Harrington replied. As he shook his head, drops of water fell from the brim of his tattered black felt hat and the ends of his moustache.

The two men fell silent. A cold wind whipped past. Large wet snowflakes began to fall with the rain.

Worst kind of weather. Hate rain-snow mix, Harrington thought. *Colder than just rain, wetter than just snow. Trainmaster Harrington. Thought about it. Lil isn't hearing any of it. Weren't for the extra money, wouldn't have taken the Snow King job. Should never have let O'Neill talk me into it. Him and his goddamned mail trains. Be personally grateful. Can't believe I fell for that.*

Harrington sank his shovel into the packed snow. Prying with the handle, he was able to break free another chunk of the near-glacial ice entombing another large tree. In heaving the heavy mass aside, a dull ache burned through his shoulders and back.

Getting old. Can't take another winter like this. Lil's right. Time to get off the hill. Need to be home more. Kids getting old.

Harrington could not understand why they were even attempting to dig out the huge slide that separated the plow train from Wellington. Blackburn ordered it, probably on the insistence of O'Neill, Harrington surmised. To chop wood and keep the boilers hot, that he could comprehend, but to try and whittle away at a glacier eight hundred feet long and thirty feet deep with hand tools and a few exhausted trainmen seemed a complete folly. Since arriving the previous afternoon, he and about thirty men had worked steadily, save for a meal break, and managed to dig away less than fifty feet.

The stalling of his plow train at Gaynor set Harrington's spirits on a tailspin that even the occasional light-hearted talk amongst the crew had yet to stop. He had heard about people going mad with depression. He was beginning to believe he was walking that dark path.

Getting the trains dug out. Should be up at Wellington working on that, not here. Have to get back to Gaynor. Get my outfit going again. Damned fool thing to do. Just leaving it. Christ, be up here another month before getting this mess straightened out. Be April, damned springtime before I get home.

Harrington paused and looked around. Lindsay was chopping on the opposite side of a tree trunk lying across where the tracks were buried. He recognized the big frame of Al Dougherty up on the hill, swinging a double-bit ax like an experienced logger. Ira Clary and Homer Purcell were next to Dougherty, loading up armloads of freshly-split firewood and carrying it down the steep hillside to the plows and pusher engines.

Wonder if they feel like me? Single, no wife, no kids. Probably don't care if they're here or chasing some red stocking up and down Market Street. God, I miss Lil. Little Bernice and Donnie. Probably driving her mad right now. Dorothy's off at school. Can't wait just to sit in my chair in the front room. Not even think about this goddamned railroad. Good thing Lil's not the worrying kind. Be beside herself by now. Railroading's no way to treat a woman.

"Looks like the damned circus is coming to town, Bill."

Lindsay's voice broke through Harrington's quiet turmoil.

"What'd you say, Ed? Wasn't listening," Harrington said.

"I say, it looks like a damned circus parade." Lindsay was once again looking upgrade.

"What the hell," Harrington's voice trailed off as he stood next to Lindsay.

A group of men walked by in single file. None looked their way. No greetings, just silence as they struggled through the slushy surface of the slide. Most kept their heads down against the wind and pelting rain and snow. Bringing up the rear was Conductor Pettit. He smiled and waved, but made no attempt to come over and speak.

"Passengers off the train, Ed," Harrington observed.

"Wait til Blackburn notices. He'll have Pettit's ass in a sling in no time," Lindsay predicted.

Both men scanned the hill, finally fixing their eyes on Blackburn. He, too, was watching the parade, but made no movement toward the group. Seeing Harrington and Lindsay, he waved a hand in disgust and went back to chopping firewood.

"Blackburn's lost his mind, Bill. He's gone completely mad," mumbled Lindsay. "Why, if Pettit tried to pull a stunt like this yesterday, Art would have chewed all of them up and spit 'em out over the side of the mountain."

Bet Art's feeling like me. Just saying to hell with it all, Harrington realized. *He's just as beat as I am. Biggest goddamned machines on earth just sitting here. We're down to axes and shovels. Hell yes, let those bastards go. Be that much more for us to eat. Damned sure we're going nowhere fast. More food for us and …*

Harrington stopped shoveling. He watched the party slowly disappear into the fog.

"You know, Ed, them business types, I'd put money they all have berths in that back sleeper, you know, the one coupled to the observation car," Harrington thought aloud.

"Yeah, so?" Lindsay replied.

"Feel like sleeping in a nice warm bed tonight?" Harrington asked.

"Oh, I see what you're getting at. Hell, yes, I do!" Lindsay replied with an excited gleam in his eyes. "Give me a soft bed, a pillow, a nice cozy car, and I'll guarantee you I'll sleep like the dead."

Monday, February 28, 1910, 6:00 p.m.
James Henry O'Neill, Superintendent

O'Neill and Master Mechanic J.J. Dowling walked side by side in silence, backtracking to Scenic. Each man was lost in his thoughts. Dowling, having been aboard the X-808 since it left Everett on the twenty-fourth, was on his last legs. The machine had not performed well, and demanded his constant attention just to keep the steam up and the fan spinning. It had drained the energy from Dowling like water from the tender's tank. Progress opening the line from Scenic to the stalled plows west of Wellington had slowed to a crawl, a situation Dowling took as a personal challenge.

For O'Neill, a quick flash of optimism had become a source of pessimism and worry. The arrival of the men from Wellington earlier was welcome relief for Dowling's weary crew. But hope quickly turned to despair when Tegtmeier relayed Harrington's account of the condition of the right-of-way to the east and the large slide at Berne.

"The way Harrington talked, even if they get a plow coming west out of Leavenworth, they've got three, maybe even four days worth of work before they make Wellington," Tegtmeier told O'Neill.

Walking head down, O'Neill finally came to grips with the facts. If the mail on Train 27 was to be delivered anytime soon, and if the passengers onboard Train 25 were to arrive in Seattle before the spring melt, a means other than his snow plows and locomotives would have to be found.

Can't bring passengers down the old construction trail. Snow's too unstable, O'Neill silently reasoned. *Old folks, women, the children. Never make it. Damned near killed a man walking out yesterday.*

"You come sliding down the hill here on your ass yesterday morning, Mr. O'Neill?" Dowling asked. He was looking above at the long snow covered slope to his left. In the last light of day, he could see a number of gouges in the snow.

"Myself and a little brakeman, can't recall his name right now," O'Neill answered.

"Looks to me you must've had some company. Look at all those marks on the hillside," Dowling pointed out. "Army of foot prints down here in the snow too. I'd say a pretty fair bunch of folks slid down here today sometime."

"You're right. Could've been some more of those worthless shovelers I sacked, leaving Wellington," O'Neill allowed.

Quickest way down, damned certain of that, O'Neill thought. He stopped walking and stared up the hillside. Turning, he looked closely at the large trees along the snow-covered tracks.

"J.J., how much rope do we have at Scenic, you know?" asked O'Neill.

"Rope, sir? Can't say as I know. Might have some cable in the tool house," Dowling answered.

"Look up that hill," O'Neill said. "What's the chances of rigging up some kind of line so we could haul the mail out, maybe even the passengers?"

Squinting, Dowling took a long look.

"You might be onto something. Be best if we rigged a couple of blocks. You know, like a clothesline."

"Exactly!" said O'Neill with some excitement returning to his voice. "So we'd need what, a couple thousand feet of rope?"

"If not a little more," Dowling calculated. "A full spool would about do it, I should think. We've got blocks here at Scenic, that I know."

"A line down 'Old Glory.' Got the men to do it. Might be the only way out of this, J.J.," O'Neill admitted.

It was pitch dark when O'Neill and Dowling walked across the

Tye River trestle just east of the depot at Scenic. Nightfall had come quickly. Thick, menacing clouds had suddenly moved in, dumping heavy showers of alternating rain and snow. As the two weary men approached the bridge, the roar of the river gave O'Neill cause for additional worry.

"From the sounds of things the river's already coming up," observed Dowling. "Heavy rain, quick thaw, this fight might just be beginning, Mr. O'Neill."

"Beginning to feel like Pharaoh and the damned plagues," muttered O'Neill. "Last thing we need right now, J.J, is a damned Chinook. A couple days of sun and twenty degree nights would suit me just fine."

"Wind's warming up. River's coming up. Can hear it. It don't lie. We're in for a Chinook. Trust me," predicted Dowling.

The two men walked into the station. Dowling immediately dragged a chair over to the stove and sat down, his long legs sprawled out in front of him. Hat still on, coat still buttoned, his head bobbed as he tried to keep from falling asleep.

"Glad you're here, Mr. O'Neill," the operator said. "Have a number of messages. This one from Leavenworth you might want to read right off."

O'Neill took the thin sheet of near-tissue paper used to type copies of orders. Rubbing his chin, he carefully read the short telegram.

"Mr. Dowling, you still awake over there?" asked O'Neill.

"Barely sir, what is it?" yawned Dowling.

"Message from Leavenworth. Says here a plow left westbound about two this afternoon. Says here it's the 807. Christ that's can't be right. Must mean the 809, wouldn't you say?" asked O'Neill.

"809. Let's see. That's that piece of junk they hold in reserve over in Spokane," said Dowling, still slumped in his chair. "We've had it over here a time or two. I've patched her up and sent 'er on back. About like the 808."

"So it's going to be slow going with that machine?" O'Neill surmised.

"If they have heavy work up the Tumwater, and if that slide at Berne's as big as they say it is." Dowling paused, "Well, let's just say it'll be tough to figure who'll get to Wellington first, us or them. Either way, you're talking three days easy, maybe more. Storm ain't broke yet, you know."

"Any word about a plow coming from the NP?" O'Neill asked the telegrapher.

"There's a message from Brown about that. Guess they're having fits too," responded the operator. "They might be able to free up a plow in a couple of days."

O'Neill took off his hat and coat. Messages in hand, he found another chair and joined Dowling next to the stove. Try as he might to concentrate on the information the telegrams contained, his mind kept going back to the snow-covered slope separating the high line to Wellington and the stranded passengers from the comforts of the Hot Springs Hotel down below at Scenic.

Rigging a line's the easy part. How the hell can we lower people down without killing more folks than we save? O' Neill wondered. *Got to get them over the line to "Old Glory" to begin with.*

"By the way, sir, I have a hand-written note from Conductor Pettit. Sorry for not telling you sooner." The operator rummaged around the top of his desk, eventually producing a water-stained scrap of paper. "Pettit led a group of men off the passenger train. They showed up an hour or so ago. Had this note with them. They wanted me to wire Wellington to tell folks not to try and come over the trail, but the line is down again."

O'Neill grabbed the hand-written note, glanced at the contents and placed it in his shirt pocket. As if suddenly reminded, he pulled out a tin box from the same pocket and produced a cigar and match.

"How many passengers were there?" he asked, trying to light his smoke.

"Maybe nine or ten. Guess Pettit got them down 'Old Glory' and then went back to Wellington," the operator informed O'Neill. "They're all over at the hotel right now."

"Pettit went back, you say? Man deserves a damned metal," O'Neill said, amid puffs of smoke.

"They got a pot of stew boiling over at the section house there, young fella? I could eat a Texas steer right now." Dowling rose from his chair. He let out a long yawn and stretched.

"Believe so," replied the operator.

"Think I'll get a bite and bed down over there. You coming with me, Mr. O'Neill?"

"I might be over later, I've got some business to attend to here," O'Neill said, himself getting up from his chair.

For the next few hours, O'Neill worked with the telegrapher. Messages were sent requesting additional manpower and supplies. Sectionmen were to scour the area for spools of rope. If none could be found or purchased, instructions were sent for agents to buy what was available from the local logging camps.

Too tired to eat, O'Neill finally excused himself to one of the back rooms of the depot, where a small cot had been set up. He knew it was there for Dowling.

Old J.J. Damned nice of him just to head over to the section house. Left me his bed. A good man, O'Neill thought.

Sitting on the edge of the thin mattress, O'Neill unlaced his boots and kicked them off. He pulled out the package of dry socks given to him by Lewis Walker. O'Neill smiled while unwrapping the brown paper. He pulled off the wet, dirty pair he had been wearing since leaving his car the previous day.

Something about dry socks. Makes a man feel a little better no matter what. Leave it to Lewis to think of that. Give him a bonus when this is all over. Give all the boys bonuses. Hill and his bean counters be damned. Make sure my boys are taken care of.

O'Neill stripped off his tweed jacket and dropped it on the floor. Snubbing out the last of a cigar, he spun himself around and unfolded the blanket at the foot of the little bed. His nest made, he finally stretched out, pulling the cover up to his chin. He lay on his back staring up at the ceiling. Tiny streams of light from the operator's room snuck through the cracks around the doorjamb, but were quickly devoured by the darkness.

"Have the third trick operator wake me at four!" O'Neill called out.

"Four, f-o-u-r, it is, Mr. O'Neill," the operator called back. "Good night, sir."

What a day. A few passengers made it out. The rest ain't going to get out anytime soon. Manpower will help. Snow pack needs to set up before we dare bring women and children across. Ropes will help—lower down the mail that way. Be one hell of a hill to run with a toboggan. Toboggan. Sleds!

Sled them out. No reason that won't work. Bundle them up, tie them in. Lower them down in a sled. Once again he pulled the blanket up over his shoulders. *Those folks up there can hang tough for a few more days. We get those sleds, the line rigged up, be one less thing to worry about. Wire for them first thing in the morning.*

O'Neill closed his eyes. He let his muscles relax. Waves of chills went up and down his body. "Keep us this night, oh Lord," he mumbled. "Look over the men. Watch over Berenice and little Peggy."

Miss them. Need to get home soon. Start work tomorrow on a safety line. Finally getting something done.

James Henry O'Neill drifted into a deep sleep.

Monday, February 28, 1910, 9:00 p.m.
Arthur Reed Blackburn, Trainmaster

Earl Longcoy pushed his way through the rear door of O'Neill's private car. In a rage, he slammed it behind him. His face was red, flushed with anger. He took off his coat and threw it across the room.

"You should've never sent me over to meet with those people, Mr. Blackburn," Longcoy complained in an unusually stern voice. "They wanted me to sign a paper."

Blackburn, coffee cup in hand, turned in his chair. He had just arrived back at Wellington from the stalled plows. Soaking wet, his body sore from ax work, he was hoping to finally spend a night in a bed.

"Sign what paper?" he asked. "That ridiculous petition about meeting with O'Neill?"

"No sir. They wanted me to put in writing that I would not send men up from Scenic to take them out across the trail," related Longcoy. "A few of the men are pretty mad about the whole business."

"They what?" asked Blackburn in disbelief.

"They want us to bring the crew up from Scenic with ropes and haul them all out across the trail. I told them that wasn't possible. That's when they wanted me to sign a paper stating I said the railroad was not going to help remove the passengers," Longcoy explained.

"Jesus, this is getting out of hand. Can't Pettit control that mob?" Blackburn was becoming agitated.

"They also want the train backed into the tunnel. They think it's safer," added Longcoy.

"Goes to show you how much sense they have. Hear tell they were complaining about smoke in the tunnel, back when we moved them in so Sweeney could water his engine over at Cascade. Dumb bastards, the lot of them." Blackburn returned to his coffee.

"There's one more thing, sir." Longcoy paused.

"Oh, let me guess, they want motorized coaches up here tomorrow to drive them all to Seattle," Blackburn mumbled sarcastically.

"Well, no sir." Longcoy stared at the floor. "They want someone with authority to come speak with them. I said I did not have the ability to make any decisions. I'm afraid I said you were the man in charge here during Mr. O'Neill's absence. Sorry, Mr. Blackburn. I guess I didn't handle the situation all that well."

Blackburn took a final slurp from his coffee. A long sigh escaped through his nostrils. Tired, he yawned and rubbed his face.

"You did what you could," said Blackburn. "Sounds like they had you backed in a corner. So now the wolf pack over there is waiting to chew on my carcass, is that the plan?"

"I told them I'd speak with you as soon as you got in, and left it at that," informed Longcoy.

Rising from the table, Blackburn took his coat from the back of the chair and put it on. He slowly buttoned the front. He grabbed his hat from a small end table near the door and carefully reshaped it before placing it on his head.

"There, do I look like someone with authority, Mr. Longcoy?" he asked.

"Indeed you do, sir," agreed the young secretary.

Last thing I want to do is meet with a scared mob, Blackburn thought as he made his way through the rain and down the embankment towards Train 25. *Just want a meal. A good night's sleep. Grown men acting like women for Christ sakes.*

As Blackburn walked below the window of the observation car, he could see a large gathering of men in its parlor. He paused for a moment and studied the group. A few were smoking. Those speaking were waving their hands first one way and then another. All seemed to be engrossed in a serious discussion.

Jumping into a real hornets' nest, Blackburn thought. He began walking alongside the coaches. Pettit had closed the majority of the vestibules for the night. The only access to the train was between the smoker and day coach near the front.

Goddamned O'Neill. Never says a word to these poor folks. Goddamned piss poor way to treat people. Don't care who he thinks he is. Going to hear about this. The lot of a trainmaster. Always stuck holding the shitty end of the stick.

The smell of raw sewage caused Blackburn to wrinkle his nose. He could see where sectionmen had shoveled snow away from the underside of the cars during the day. They had wallowed in the filth trying to build ditches to direct the stench over the hillside.

Our boys out here in this weather digging so their goddamned shitters work, and they're still not happy. Acting like a bunch of old women, Blackburn fumed.

Aboard the train, Blackburn took purposeful strides down the aisle. A few women looked at him as he stormed through the day coach but none made an attempt to speak. Passing through the first of the two sleeper cars, he sidestepped a Negro porter, preparing the berths.

"Have you seen Conductor Pettit?" Blackburn asked the man.

"No, sir. He was here, then went to the station. Believe he still be there, sir," the man answered.

Pettit gone too. Nobody wants to deal with these bastards. Goddamned O'Neill. Leaves the shit jobs to me. Blackburn passed across the vestibule and entered the observation car. *Guess it's up to this bastard to deal with those bastards. Get this over with so I can get some sleep.*

His jaw set, his resolve firm, Blackburn walked into the room and immediately confronted the group of men.

"I'm Arthur Blackburn, Trainmaster. Now what's all this fuss about?"

The emphatic tone to his voice and stern stance produced the effect Blackburn had hoped. The room immediately became silent, the group of men staring at him, obviously taken off guard. There was a nervous clearing of throats before a stocky man in a clean suit spoke.

"My name is Edgar Lemman, I'm an attorney. This is Mr. White and Mr. Bethel. The rest of the gentlemen here have asked that we speak on their behalf."

"Very well, speak your piece. I'm here to listen and do what I can," Blackburn replied, keeping his voice level but firm.

Don't lose your temper. Make'em harder to deal with. O'Neill would be tough, but with a quiet voice. Do the same damned thing, Blackburn coached himself.

"We are in agreement that this train is in an extremely dangerous position. Furthermore, we are also in agreement that the railroad's primary responsibility is removing us from this precarious position," Lemman said.

"First, I don't agree that this train is in a dangerous position, sir, and second, the railroad is doing nothing else but working towards getting you folks on your way," Blackburn countered.

Damned lawyer. Fancy talk.

"Mr. Blackburn," interjected White. "What we mean to say is we do not wish to remain here any longer. Others have gotten out over the trail. We expect you to provide us with the manpower and tools necessary to take all of us out."

"It is, after all, the railroad's legal responsibility," Lemman added.

Damned fools. Haven't been out in this storm, don't know what they're talking about. Pick your words carefully, Blackburn thought.

"Gentlemen, this train is by far a safer place than that trail to Scenic. Our own men are out there right now shoveling, unprotected, in areas prone to slide. That is our responsibility. What is not our responsibility is to knowingly expose you folks to undue risk, like that trail," reasoned Blackburn.

"But the snow cap on top of the mountain right above us," protested White. "Certainly you've seen it."

"You cannot deny the danger it represents. It has to be a far worse peril than the trail," argued Lemman.

"We know there is a large work force at Scenic. Mr. Pettit told us as much when he returned this evening. We demand that those men be brought up here immediately and be directed to break the trail and help us out of here!" White said emphatically.

"You can demand all you want, sir, but I will not take men away from the job of opening this line in order to coddle a group of able-bodied men!" snapped Blackburn. "If you wish to leave, fine, but you are on your own. Once you leave this train the Great Northern Railway will not accept responsibility for your fate."

"We're not asking that your men help us, Mr. Blackburn," White said, his voice once again controlled. "We want you to supply the men so that the women, the children and the invalids can be safely removed as well. Use whatever tools are at your disposal. Us men can fend for ourselves."

Toss them a little peace offering. See if I can get them off my back, Blackburn considered. *A few men to guide them out. Stay calm, reason with them.*

"The best I can do in all good faith is to release a half dozen or so men to guide you able-bodied men out. But that's it. Women, children, anyone not in the best of shape must stay here!" Blackburn could hear is own voice rising; he could feel his temper slipping away. He sighed. "Gentlemen, you haven't been out there. You haven't seen the conditions. Snow is sliding down the chutes. No number of men on earth could stop a slide from coming down on top of you out there along that trail. The snow doesn't slide here; there are no gullies, no chutes. It's not like out on that trail. I will not allow innocent people to be put in harm's way based on your panic. You try to move the women and children, I will stop you, rest assured of that."

The room fell silent. The men looked at each other.

Maybe I finally took the wind out of their sails, Blackburn hoped.

"Well, that being the case, then we demand this train be moved into the safety of the tunnel," White proclaimed.

"What?" asked Blackburn in disbelief.

"Do we have to spell it out for you?" Lemman said dryly. "We feel this place is unsafe and that the tunnel will offer us protection from slides. It would seem logical, then, that you immediately move us into the tunnel."

Goddamned twelve feet of snow on the tracks out there. Not a plow to be had. Stupid sons of bitches.

"That, sir, is impossible," Blackburn stated. "Completely out of the question."

"Does the engine have enough coal to back us up to the tunnel?" White asked.

"Probably does, but that makes no difference. All of you have been to Bailets, and most of you have been up to the depot. You know good and well that there's twelve damned feet of snow drifted over the tracks. How the hell are we supposed to get the train through that?"

"You have men—they can shovel the line clear," stated Lemman in a matter of fact manner.

"Shovel a half mile of track covered with twelve feet of snow. You've all gone mad," Blackburn muttered. "Two days ago it took half a day, two engines and a rotary plow to do exactly what you're telling me you want done by hand! Ridiculous, absolutely ridiculous."

"If you were to bring that crew up from Scenic, 150 of them, I should think it could be done in a matter of hours," White said.

Blackburn raised his hand and began counting with his fingers.

"First off, I've heard nothing about one hundred and fifty men down at Scenic. Second, even if there were, it would take away from getting the line open. Third, even if they magically cleared the line to the tunnel, that single engine could not back this train up the grade, and the others here are out of commission. Fourth, even if it could move, the snow would drift in before we reached the tunnel, and if we tried to push these coaches through the drifts, they would splinter and derail all to hell and back. Fifth, if we did make it to the tunnel, there would be no fuel left to burn for heat, and sixth, even if there was fuel left, the fumes from the engine would kill all of you in a matter of hours stuffed in that tunnel. How would you get to the hotel for food or water? While you're stopped in the tunnel you wouldn't dare use the onboard toilets. And let's talk about the wind drifting snow into the cut leading to the tunnel and sealing you off. Have any of you thought about any of this?"

Again the room fell silent, as the men considered what they had just been told.

"You could burn wood in the engine to generate heat if it ran low on coal," argued Lemman.

"You would not even have to provide men. We would gladly chop firewood," added White.

"Didn't you hear a damned word I said?" Blackburn asked, nearly exasperated. "You can chop all the wood you want. This train is not moving an inch towards that tunnel. The tunnel is too dangerous; the track is too choked with snow. We can't move upgrade, period. None of you have a damned notion of what it takes to clear a section of track by hand in this storm. The snow blows in faster than we can shovel it out. Why can't you understand that? For such smart men you're all acting like a bunch of damned fools."

"Now see here, Mr. Blackburn, we will not be addressed in that tone," complained Lemman.

"I'll address you as I deem fit, sir," Blackburn snapped.

"Then what of the sanitary conditions?" Lemmen pressed. "The longer the cars stay stationary, the worse the conditions become."

"The smell from under the coaches is becoming very offensive," White added. "We also hear snow is being melted for our drinking water."

"First you want our men to build you a road in the snow so you can hike out like it's a Sunday walk in the park. Then you want us to clear more snow by hand than we can with our plows. Now you want us to clean your shitters! When you make up your goddamned minds about what you want done, let me know." Blackburn turned to leave.

"Now see here! Your crude language will get you nowhere with us!" Lemman, his face red, shook his finger at Blackburn.

"Just one moment, sir," White said. "Then, as a representative of the railroad, you refuse to take any immediate action upon our requests?"

"No sir. I told you I would supply a half dozen men tomorrow to break the trail for any able-bodied men who wish to leave, provided they are clear on one point: the Great Northern carries no liability or responsibility for anything that might happen. Travel at your own risk," repeated Blackburn.

Lemman produced a sheet of stationary and a fountain pen.

"That being the case, I demand that you sign this paper stating that, as a representative of the Great Northern Railway, you are refusing to authorize any immediate and additional assistance in the safe removal of all passengers from this train," the lawyer stated.

They can pull this shit on poor Longcoy, but it's not going to scour with me, Blackburn smirked.

"You can take your paper and toss it in the sewer ditches under this car, sir," Blackburn said. "I will have men outside of this car at first light tomorrow to assist any of you so-called able-bodied men out over the trail. Good night."

Blackburn turned and walked out of the parlor, leaving the men standing, Lemmen with paper and pen still in his hand. A wave of exhaustion ran over the trainmaster. His legs began to shake and he could feel his lips quivering.

Handled that all wrong, he thought. *Wasn't going to holler or cuss. Be the calm voice of reason. Bastard lawyer trying to push me around. The rest of those idiots believing him.*

His head pounding, Blackburn took a deep breath when he stepped off the stuffy train. It was snowing hard again.

Wind feels warm, Blackburn noticed, as he hiked back towards O'Neill's car. *Odd, snow being driven by a warm wind. Must be me.*

He scurried up the bank to the rear of the A-16. Fatigue overcame Blackburn's body and mind. He consciously blinked his eyes to keep them from glazing over as he walked the final few feet to the car's rear platform steps.

Fighting a loudmouthed lawyer. Takes more out of a man than fighting a snowstorm. Blackburn pulled himself onto the porch and entered the car. *O'Neill and his calm voice of reason be damned. I held my ground.*

Monday, February 28, 1910, 10:00 p.m.
Anthony John Dougherty, Brakeman

Dougherty leaned his ax against the wheel set of the second-class mail car on Train 27. He blew out his lantern and rapped hard on the sliding door. A chain rattled and then the door rolled aside on its track, sending a stream of light out into the night.

"Got room for a wet and tired traveler?" Dougherty asked, tossing his lantern inside.

"Sure, come on up," the clerk said, extending his hand. "A few of your mates are already in here."

"Yeah, they told me this is where all the drunks are," quipped Dougherty.

Through his wet gloves, Dougherty could feel the cold steel of the grab iron he grasped with his left hand. The man grabbed Dougherty's other wrist with both of his hands, and in a swift movement mastered by jumping on and off countless moving freight cars, Dougherty vaulted himself upward, caught his left foot into the lower rung of the side ladder, and landed gracefully into the car.

"Close the damned door," shouted Ira Clary. "Got a winning hand here and the damned wind's gonna blow the deck all over hell!"

Together, Dougherty and the mail clerk slid the door shut.

"Leave her unlocked," Dougherty told the sorter. "I'm heading back out in a bit."

Without saying another word, the postman wandered to the rear of the car and bedded back down amongst the parcels and sacks of mail.

"Evening, boys," Dougherty greeted the group. Homer Purcell, Ira Clary, John Finn and Sam Duncan were sitting around a crude card table made from a mail-sorting tray, stacks of packages and chairs stolen from the depot. A lantern dangled from the ceiling directly over the men. Their soaked coats were hung on mail sack hooks near the coal stove in the front corner of the car. Next to them on the floor were their work boots. The smell of wet wool, combined with men long overdue for a change of clothes and a bath, was thick in the air. It mingled with the unmistakable odor of whiskey.

"Where the hell you been, Al?" asked Clary, discarding a three of hearts.

"Just what the doctor ordered," Purcell said, picking up the three and discarding a seven of clubs.

"Goddamn you, Homer! Been picking up every card I need and throwing down shit," complained Finn, taking a swig out of a half-empty communal bottle of whiskey. Picking a card from the deck, Finn gave it a glance, then threw it half way across the table.

"So where ya been, Al?" Clary repeated, placing his cards face down on the table. He reached across the table and grabbed the bottle. "Need a nip to warm up?"

"Naah, not right now, Ira. Stayed down on the plows and finished splitting a bolt I was working on. Hoped to catch up with Bobby. Maybe figure out a hot one to pull on Sherlock, since we're all here," explained Dougherty.

"You know, Finn, best thing I ever done was sit next to you. Been giving me good cards all night." Duncan picked up the discarded jack of hearts and laid down his hand. "Just read 'em and weep and pay the man his money. That's a rummy, boys!"

"Lemme see that!" Finn shouted.

"Jacks and sixes, they're all there," Duncan jeered, a grin on his face.

A general groan went around the table as the losers counted their points and tossed their hands to the middle. Duncan gathered up the cards and began to shuffle.

"Two bits a hand. You in, Al?" Finn inquired.

"Naah, too broke, too tired. You assholes would clean me out quicker than you're cleaning out Finn," Dougherty replied.

"Go to hell, Al," snarled Finn.

"Too broke, hell. You're saving your money for one hell of a night down on Market," Purcell claimed. "You know boys, every time I walk into the Crescent, the first thing that little French gal wants to know is if Al's with me."

"I've heard the same thing, now that you mention it," Duncan chimed in. "They say you can even out-love a sailor, Al."

"Would you just shut up and deal, Sam?" interrupted Finn.

"Now you boys need to quit this kinda talk. Poor mailman back there's gonna think bad of all of us," Dougherty answered, his face growing red.

"So what's this about you having a birthday in a few weeks, Al?" Duncan asked, dealing out the cards.

"Yep. One year shy of turning into an old man," Dougherty admitted.

"I got news for you, Al, this goddamned storm has already turned all of us into old men," said Clary, as he sorted his cards.

"So, Ira, what card do you want me to turn over?" Duncan asked, slamming the remainder of the deck onto the table.

"I think Al wants to see a queen," joked Finn. A loud laugh erupted from the men.

"Give me an eight," Clary ordered Duncan.

"Give me drink and I'll see what I can do," responded Duncan. The bottle passed, a gulp taken, and Duncan turned over the eight of diamonds. Clary promptly gathered up the card and threw down a three of clubs.

"You cheatin' sons of bitches!" bellowed Finn.

"Calm down, John. Here, take another hit off the jug." Purcell drew a card, kept it, and discarded the three of diamonds. "Now see there, Finn. If you start saving threes, you just might win this hand."

"If I have any say, every one of you assholes are going to end up in hell," growled Finn as he picked up the three. He studied his hand, his eyes shifting over to Duncan. "What the hell you saving, Sam?"

"Aces and kings, John. I'm going for the big money," Duncan nonchalantly replied.

"Not only are you a cheat, but you're a damned liar. You ain't saving no aces." Finn threw down the ace of diamonds.

"Hurts me to hear that, Finn." Duncan calmly picked up the ace and discarded the three of spades. "Now unless I miss my count, you've got two threes in your hand there, Finn, and now there's two more gonna get buried in the pile. You got a few up your sleeve? So, Al, you and Bobby get something cooked up tonight?"

"You dirty bastards. I'm gonna sic Bobby on your asses one of these days," Finn threatened.

"Never did meet up with him," Dougherty interjected. "He had to be down there somewhere. So damned dark, wind blowing so damned hard I didn't look much beyond the 802 and the 1128. I guess he must be in the trailing plow tonight for some reason. I'll catch up with him when we change shifts in the morning."

"Hear tell Bobby's gonna throw you one hell of a birthday wingding soon as we all get the hell outta here," Clary idly mentioned as he picked a card from the deck and promptly set it on the discard pile.

"That'll be the day," Purcell said, drawing a card and keeping it. "Damned Meath's pretty tight with his brass."

"You gonna discard, Homer, or just sit there and stare all night?" challenged Finn. "Bobby'll buy a round every now and then when he wants us to help him in a scheme."

Purcell threw a ten that was promptly taken by Finn.

"Now we're getting somewhere." Finn rearranged his cards.

"Toss that one, John," Dougherty said, leaning over Finn's shoulder.

"Now Al, don't you be helping out ol' John here," Clary protested. "How can we clean him out if someone with a few brains starts helping him?"

"I swear to God, Ira, if the worst goddamned storm of the century wasn't blowin' out there tonight, I'd take you outside right now and we'd settle this thing!" threatened Finn. "So I should throw this one, Al?"

"Yep."

Finn did as Dougherty said, casting aside one of his threes.

"Well that don't do me no damned good," whined Duncan, taking a fresh card from the pile. He looked it over and tossed it down. "Never can get Bobby into a card game. Ever notice that? He don't like doing anything he can't control, the way I see it."

"He's like that," Clary admitted. He drew a card and studied his hand, then eyed Finn. "Best thing I could do is hold my tens."

"Why don't I just give you every cent I got right now, Ira. Save us one hell of a lot of time," complained Finn, taking another drink from the bottle. "Then we can just sit here and get roaring drunk. Hell, go up to O'Neill's car and tell that asshole Blackburn we're moving in with him."

Another loud round of laughter filled the room.

"Would it be possible for you gentlemen to hold it down?" asked the clerk. "I'm trying to sleep back here."

"Sorry, we'll tell our drunk friend Mr. Finn to quiet down," Duncan said, winking.

"Anyway, so you and Bobby going after Sherlock again?" Purcell asked. "That turkey caper, now that was your best ever. Goddamn, even Bobby's gonna have to work to top that one."

"That was a dandy," Dougherty agreed. "You know that Bailets still thinks Sherlock was somehow in on it? Heard him just the other day complaining to one of the passengers how the night operator had his turkey stolen. Ya know, Mr. Snow King Harrington was the one that really set the noose on Sherlock."

"Ain't really talked to Bill since you boys hiked in. How's he doing?" Finn turned and showed his hand to Dougherty.

"Pull from the pile. See if you can make a run out of your first three cards," Dougherty advised. "He took getting stuck down at Gaynor real hard. He still thinks we're balled up here because we didn't get the plow and coal back from Gaynor."

"Was nothing we could do. Biggest damned slide I ever seen over at Berne," Clary admitted. "Al here saved my bacon the other night, John, you hear about that?"

"Keep what you drew, discard that one," Dougherty whispered.

"I heard you were the hero, Al. Too bad, you should've left that little bastard in the snow. I'd be a rich man tonight if you had." Finn's deadpan sarcastic air had the men in stitches once again. Purcell, leaning back in his chair taking a swig from the near empty bottle, rocked forward, choking on the whiskey as he laughed.

"Jesus, Finn," he gasped, coughing and laughing at the same time.

"That was a tough night. Don't need anymore like that, that's God's truth," admitted Dougherty. "Don't know about you boys, but it's tough to keep going back out there. Without the plows, well, just seems we ain't doing a damned bit of good."

There was no immediate response. The bottle was passed around the table a final time as the men continued to play their hands. All of them glanced towards the roof of the car when they heard a portion of accumulated snow slide off. Again there was silence; then, the muted patter of rain drops.

"Warming up," Duncan observed. "We get a quick thaw and we all could be up here another month digging out slides."

"I got a feeling I ain't gonna turn twenty-nine down on Market," lamented Dougherty. "I'll put money I'll be right here buried in this damned snow."

"Nonsense, Al. Dowling will be up here in a day or two to get us going." Clary drew a card, cracked a smile, and fanned his hand across the table. "Finn, I'd say you're about broke. Rummy."

"I'm going back to whist," groaned Finn, tossing his cards down. "At least with that game it takes all night for you bastards to clean me out."

"Sorry, John, couldn't do much with that hand," Dougherty said. "Guess Dowling's outfit's been having trouble, too. Irv went down there to try and help out. That damned 808's a piece of junk."

"Don't be so melancholy, Al," Purcell said. "We'll get you outta here in time for your birthday even if we have to pack you out over our shoulders. So we done playing cards?"

Clary took a fifty-cent piece and tossed it over to Finn.

"I tell ya what, John. You head up to town and find us another bottle, and I'll spot you a few hands. Let you win some of your money back. Hate to have you broke for Al's big birthday down at the joy house of his choice."

"Go out in this?" complained Finn.

"How bad do you want to get laid?" Clary asked.

"Alright," Finn sighed. He looked at his pocket watch. "Bailets is shut down. Gonna have to settle for that rot gut that the Foggs sell."

"Booze be booze on a night like this," shrugged Duncan.

Getting up from his chair, Finn went over and lifted his hat and coat off a mail hook. He sat back down, he pulled on his boots, and laced them up. "Alright, I'll be back in a half hour or so. Don't none of you snakes take off. I'm going to get my money back," warned Finn.

"We'll be here. Take your coat off, Al. You can have Finn's chair while he's gone," invited Purcell.

"Oh no, boys. I've seen you play. Bobby's right. Don't want to gamble on something I can't control. Need my money for that little French gal," Dougherty said, walking with Finn toward the door. "Besides, I'm beat. Bill snuck onto the passenger train. Took one of the berths left by those passengers that left today. Says he's got one for me. Think of that—sleep in a bed tonight."

"That don't sound half bad, Al," admitted Clary. "Well, suit yourself. See ya in the morning."

Finn and Dougherty slid the door open a crack. Outside, the wind was howling between the cars on the adjacent track. Large rain drops were being driven nearly parallel to the ground.

"One hell of a night to go fetch a bottle, Al," Finn said. He jumped from the car, holding on to his hat. Dougherty hit the ground right behind him. Together, they struggled to roll the door shut.

"Jesus, I think I'll duck into a mail car and say to hell with that bed," Dougherty told Finn. "Gotta walk clear around the end of the passenger train and down the other side just to get on."

"I saw Benny Jarnigan and a few of the boys packing blankets into the next car back," Finn told Dougherty. "Here, I'll boost you in."

"You just want me to sleep in that damned mail car so you can steal that bed I was talking about," Dougherty joked.

"Gonna take me the rest of the night to get my money back. Hell, by that time the four of us will be so drunk we won't be able to fall down straight," replied Finn, rain already dripping from his hat.

Arm in arm, wading through the deep, slushy snow, they worked their way back to the next mail car on Train 27. They managed to slide the unlocked door open a crack. Quietly Finn boosted Dougherty up and through the doorway.

"Thanks, John. See ya tomorrow," Dougherty said softly. "Don't worry. If those cheats clean you out, I'll fix you up down on Market."

"I might have to hold you to it," Finn replied. He gave Dougherty a wave. Bent against the wind, he trudged off towards town.

Dougherty smiled as he watched Finn disappear around the observation car of Train 25.

God, I love being up here with the boys.

Tuesday March 1, 1910 1:42 a.m.
Arthur Reed Blackburn, Trainmaster

For a long while, Blackburn sat alone in the parlor of O'Neill's car, playing solitaire. Earl Longcoy had gone to bed hours earlier. Twice, Blackburn's concentration was broken by the distant sound of snapping trees and the muted roar of sliding snow. He paid it little mind once realizing what the noise represented.

Lewis Walker continued to fuss about the car for another hour. He made Blackburn a cup of tea and a ham sandwich, readied O'Neill's bed, and then asked when Blackburn wanted to be awakened. His chores done, Walker excused himself with his usual wide grin and turned in for the night.

O'Neill talks highly of him, Blackburn thought. *Never been around Negroes much. Not sure why folks hate them if they're all like him.*

It was nearly 1:00 a.m. when Blackburn finally made his way into O'Neill's stateroom. A large bed was against the wall next to the window. Blackburn gladly stripped out of his wet, filthy clothes. Down to his long johns, he slipped between the crisp sheets. He rolled on his right side facing the window, curled his legs up, and pulled the blanket up to his neck. The pillow made it feel as if his head was floating on air, yet he lay there wide awake. Finally beginning to feel warm, the chapped, wind-burned skin on his face stung as if he were still facing the elements.

Stomach still churning thanks to those damned passengers, Blackburn fumed. *Should've told them …*

Blackburn forced himself to stop thinking about the meeting.

Getting yourself riled up again. Never get to sleep, he reasoned. *Plan out tomorrow. Find some men to lead passengers out. Go out myself. Find O'Neill. Can't just leave people up here until it thaws. Damn it. Quit thinking. Get to sleep.*

Blackburn nestled his head further into the soft pillow.

Wonder how Rosie is doing? Wonder if she's worried about me? Do anything to have her next to me in this nice big old bed.

Visions of summer days spent on the beach along Puget Sound floated into Blackburn's mind.

Rosie sitting on that big blanket. Picnic lunch, deviled eggs. Holding hands with little Grace. Pants rolled up, wading in the cold water with her. Felt good on a hot afternoon. Three of us combing the beach. Could always find good skipping rocks. Sending them across those blue waters.. Nice, warm evening. Sun setting behind the Olympics. Loved the trolley ride home. Grace asleep on my shoulder. Arm in arm with Rosie. Put little Grace to bed when we got home. Rosie and me …

He began to relax. The nervous energy that had been driving him for days slowly began to leave his body. His eyes finally became heavy, his breathing slow and methodical. The vision of his family was still in his mind.

Large drops of rain, driven in sheets by the warm wind, bounced off the window near Blackburn's head. He paid it no mind. He was exhausted and finally close to sleep.

On the mountainside, far above the car, heavy rain slammed into the snow pack. When massed together, the drops began to form a dark conspiracy. They used their cumulative weight and the warm air propelling them to overcome, to have their way, and alter the defenseless mountain of snow. Deep inside the smooth field of white blanketing Windy Mountain, powdered-sugar ice crystals, long covered by the mass of the week's storms, tried desperately to support the increasing weight. Giving up, being squashed, they slowly, ever so slowly lost their grip on each other and to their more recent counterparts on top.

High above Blackburn, high above the rail sidings at Wellington, a tiny fissure began to make its way laterally across the face of the slope.

Its jagged hairline appeared like a cracked window in the pack's icy glaze. It dodged between the burned snags protruding from the snow. It worked its way down into the pack until it met up with the weakest layer. It worked its way from one end of the siding to the other. It was not satisfied until it spread its danger equally over both trains parked below.

A flash of lightning and a crack of thunder did not rouse the sleeping Blackburn, but it did disturb the snow pack. It might have been the reverberations of the thunder, or a fir bough snapped off by the wind falling to ground, but something caused the weakened snow crystals to finally lose their tenuous grip. The fissure widened. The hillside began to move, slowly, silently, but powerful, so powerful. At first, only small balls of snow rolled off the bank and harmlessly struck the side of O'Neill's car. But in seconds, large chunks pinned the car into place. An instant later, the power of nature's force tore off the car's roof. Thousands of tons of snow poured inside.

It was like a cold, violent slap in the face. Blackburn knew he was awake, but for the life of him, he could not get his bearings. He was suddenly cold. He felt bound. Out of instinct he tried to move his arms to clear his nose and eyes. He could not move. He struggled to breathe. His eyes were open, but it was pitch black. Something kept getting into his eyes, he kept blinking. He gasped for air, but his mouth filled with snow.

Covered with snow. Dig my way out. Can't move my arms.

Panic began to consume Blackburn. Flushed with fear, he felt hot and sweaty. Using all his strength, he tried to free his arms and legs. For all of his effort, he could only move his fingers.

Walker. Longcoy. Need help. Slide?

"Help! Help!"

Blackburn listened. He thought he heard a muffled reply.

"Here! Hey!!"

Blackburn gasped for air. His mouth filled with snow.

Got to dig out. Slide must have hit.

Again he tried to free his arms.

"Help!"

Again his mouth filled with snow. He spat. Using his tongue, he thrust out the melting ice only to have it slowly refreeze around his face.

Going to die. Got to get out.

Blackburn tried to kick his legs, grab handfuls of snow with his hands. His strength began to fail. The effort left him panting, unable to fulfill his need for air.

Can't die here. Rosie. Grace. Got to keep trying.

Barely able to open his mouth, he tried to voice another cry for help. He could tell it was a barely audible whimper. The heat of his initial panic had worn off. Chills racked his body. He tried again to free himself, hoping if nothing else, the effort would fend off the cold. It did little good.

Rest a minute. Cold. Tired.

He listened, hoping to hear the sounds of rescue. There was complete silence. He had no sense of time.

He saw Rosie's face and then the shy smile of his little Grace. He blinked his eyes, trying to fend off his sudden need for sleep.

The beach. Rosie, Grace. Want to be with you. I love you.

Clinching his teeth, in a fit of rage he worked his hands and feet. When the desire to give up was at its peak, he tried even harder to free himself. He worked for what seemed an hour. He could move his right arm a little. He tried to grab handfuls of snow and push it to the side. In the pitch black, he could not tell if he was doing any good. He wasn't even sure which way was up or down. His fingers and toes were devoid of feeling.

No air. Can't breathe. Can't die. Not here.

Blackburn allowed himself to close his eyes.

Rest a minute. Get strength. Dig out before I smother. Help's here by now.

Strangely, Blackburn could feel the weight that had been binding him slowly ease. He thought the hard-packed snow was slowly melting away.

Rosie, Grace. They're coming for me. Be with you soon.

The chills stopped. A sense of calm came over Blackburn.

Be with you soon. Rosie, Grace …

Tuesday, March 1, 1910, 1:43 a.m.
Anthony John Dougherty, Brakeman

Dougherty shifted his weight and rewrapped himself in his blanket. He had pulled two from a heap in the corner of the mail car—one to lie on and one to cover himself. The blanket did little to insulate him from the hard, cold floor.

Should've bedded down on the passenger train, Dougherty thought. *Harrington's probably sleeping snug as a bug.*

Between the stove-oil lamps and the coal-fired heating stove, fumes hung heavy in the air of the buttoned-up car. Musty steam rose from a half dozen soaked work coats hanging near the pot-bellied stove.

Dougherty repositioned the mail sack he was using for a pillow. He had taken off his wet socks and had his feet up against the stove, trying to get some feeling back in his toes. The rest of the men in the car had the same idea. They were fanned out from the car's source of heat in a semi-circle, like the rays of the sun.

Clutching at the blanket, Dougherty tried to suppress the chills that racked his body.

No damned way gonna get warm here. Need a good belt from Finn's bottle. Should've gone with him. Poor Finn. Ira and Homer, biggest card sharks around. Another grin came across Dougherty's face. *Funny, watching them take poor old Finn.*

Ben Jarnigan was on Dougherty's right. On his back, his head also propped against a mailbag, the exhausted engineer was sound asleep.

Jesus, listen to Benny snore. Wish I could just sleep anywhere like him. Dougherty closed his eyes. *Hot bath. Get off this mountain, hot bath first order of business. Sit in that tub for an hour. Be ready for a good bottle and a bad woman.*

Fellow brakeman Archie Dupy was lying on the other side of Dougherty. He snorted and rolled onto his side. Dupy threw his arm across Dougherty's chest. Startled, Dougherty's eyes popped open.

Damn, Arch, was just about asleep. Scared the hell outta me. Dougherty listened to the rain intensify. His mind continued to wander. *Wonder if Bobby's really gonna throw me a big birthday party? Never had one before. Wish Bobby was here. Poor bastard, stuck out on that plow on a night like tonight. Would loved to have seen O'Neill and Brown throw his ass off the 800. Stubborn little shit. Thinks he can work forever. Be with Bobby tonight, Lord. Keep him safe. Best friend a guy could have. Love him like a brother, Lord.*

Dougherty felt his body grow heavier, his head lighter. A slight dizziness came over him.

Finally…going to sleep. Bill says be two weeks before we get the road open. Never seen Bill so beat down. Give Bill strength, Lord. Give us all strength. Says he's gonna tell O'Neill to shove the Snow King job up his ass. Like to be around for that …

Quit thinking about the railroad. Think about warm stuff. Can't get warm …

Still cold …

Back home …

Hot in that old house …

Warm woman …

French gal …

Warm wind blowing through the wheat back home …

Look over all of us, Lord …

Keep us all …

Sleep finally overtook the shivering body of Al Dougherty.

The wall of snow gathered speed. It gained more power sweeping across the main line, and slammed against Train 25. Now, intent on its purpose, its destination, the bottom of the canyon in sight, it moved with a single-minded force and energy. The day coach from Train 25 was lifted off the rails and tossed with cruel intent against the mail car where Dougherty and the others slept. The snow, like a giant swinging a maul and striking a wedge, split all of the wooden cars wide open, not content until the two trains were rolled together in a single mass of debris. Making quick work of the attack, the first wave continued its relentless course to the bottom of the canyon.

Smothering.

Can't move.

Can't breathe.

Cold, dark.

Snow everywhere.

Terrible pain.

Can't stand the pain.

Cold, side, head, can't stand the pain..

Giant logs, daggers of glass, spears of splintered car decking tumbled through the mass like so many leaves in the rapids of the Wenatchee River. Dougherty, Jarnigan, Dupy, and the others, content just to be protected from the storm, were captured, bound tight by the snow and then heartlessly hurled against the far wall of the car as it, too, was being shattered into kindling. As if the solid barrier of moving snow was not enough, the slide seemed to take great joy in using the men as battering rams, crashing all of them through what was left of the car's wall. Their clothes were ripped and cast aside like snow going through the fan of the rotary plows. Their flesh exposed, a splintered fir log slid across their mangled bodies and rolled them down into the canyon. Buried deep, their limbs partially sheared off, their bodies were first tangled with each other, then cruelly spread across the hillside. Only their mingled blood slowly found its way to the surface.

Finally getting warm.

Pain's gone.

Warm, fresh air.

Being carried out of the cold.

Carried out of the snow by strong arms.

The sun was shining bright. A warm breeze touched the face of Al Dougherty. Before him stretched the golden wheat fields surrounding his home in Waverly, Minnesota.

Tuesday, March 1, 1910, 1:44 a.m.
William Harrington, Assistant Trainmaster

It felt good to get out of his wet, filthy clothes. In a warm berth, wearing a clean nightshirt, Harrington tried to block out the past week. Earlier in the evening, he grabbed his grip from the depot when he had gotten back from working the slide to the west. Along with Ed Lindsay, he ate a bowl of watered-down stew in the sectionmens' cookhouse, and promptly headed for Train 25.

"Going up for a night cap at Bailets?" Lindsay had called out.

"Not tonight, Ed," Harrington had replied. "I'll save a bed for you, though."

"Be down in an hour or so, Bill," Lindsay replied. "Ya know, Bill, none of this is your doing. Just remember that."

"I'll try, Ed. See ya in the morning."

As Harrington worked his way back through the coaches, a porter greeted him saying that berth number four, the lower bunk on the first sleeper to the rear, was available, and to make himself at home.

"I've kept the curtains drawn back on the other empty berths as well," the man added. "If a few more of your crew show up, Mr. Pettit says they're free to sleep in them."

Good sort, that Pettit, Harrington thought, as he lay on his back. *Wouldn't mind getting out of the freight chain gang and pull a passenger assignment. Make Lil happy.*

He pulled the blanket over his shoulders.

Getting warmed up. Should've hauled the 807 with me. Knew we'd need all the coal we could take. Leaving it here. Dumb damned thing to do. Need the 801 over here bucking out that slide, agonized Harrington. *Should've known better. Get the damned thing stalled clear across the damned mountain. Piss poor railroading. My fault.*

Harrington closed his eyes and tried to calm himself.

What's done is done. We all agreed. Blackburn, O'Neill. We all agreed I needed to go east. Should've doubled with the 807. Damn it to hell, anyway. Be back here right now boring out that slide.

Rolling on his side, Harrington faced the wall of the car.

Miss Lil. The kids. Little Donnie. Raising hell for certain. Dorothy, spitting image of her mother. Bessie, sweet little Bessie, my little pumpkin face. Hate being here. Need to be home. I miss them all. Settled into my chair.

It was that smile. The one that sent William Harrington head over heels in love with Lillian. That "I'm taking no nonsense from you, Mr. Harrington" smile is what flashed through Harrington's mind as he drifted off to sleep.

Something woke him.

Glass breaking. Loud roar! What the hell?

Moving. Sliding. Snow everywhere.

Tumbling.

Back twisting.

Snow in my mouth and eyes.

My head.

Goddamn, thrown around.

My side! Oh God, my side! Hurts. Hurts like hell!

Hard to breathe.

Rolling over and over.

Goddamn hurt like hell!

Where am I?

Harrington lay still. He lifted his head. A bolt of lightning flashed, its light piercing through the vision of the dazed man. A peal of thunder shook the ground.

"Where the hell am I?" he said aloud. Still disoriented, he peered through the dark. He thought he saw the outline of another man.

"What happened? Where are we?" he called to the figure.

Another flash of lightning lit up the hillside. A second roll of thunder caused the ground to quake. The ghostly figure was gone.

Outside? Below the bank. Raining. Trains gone? God help us! Oh God! Slide rolled us over the bank. No cars, no nothing. All buried. Dear God, no!

Gotta get help.

Harrington tried to stand up. A pain shot through his side and right knee, so intense he promptly fell back down onto the hard snow pack. He saw blood splattered on the white surface.

Bleeding. Can't feel it. Don't know where. In my eyes.

Harrington pulled up the tail of his nightshirt and wiped his face. The cloth instantly became crimson.

Gotta try to get outta here. Barefoot. Gonna freeze to death if I don't. Quiet. No one hollering. Strange.

"Help!" Harrington hollered. Again he winced in pain.

Ribs must be broke. Hard to breathe. Can't holler. Gotta get outta here.

His senses slowly returning, Harrington carefully rose to his feet. He wiped the blood from his eyes and tried to focus on the slope. He saw what he thought were the lights of the Bailets Hotel nearly three hundred feet above him. Scanning the snowfield, he saw again what he thought was another person. Harrington tried to focus, tried to yell something at the figure. Pain shot through his body, dropping him to his knees. He looked again. The form was gone.

Seeing things. Nobody there. Hear hollering from down below. Gotta help my boys.

Gathering what strength he had, ignoring the burning pain shooting through his body Harrington got to his feet. Gritting his teeth, he began to climb upward. The snow was hard. He stepped on a jagged piece of wood jutting from the surface, cutting his foot.

"Goddamn it!" he muttered. His feet were so frozen he felt nothing. Only the bloody footprint he left each step told him his foot had been injured.

The bank grew steeper as he neared the point where the trains had stood. He felt himself falling. He clutched his side with one arm and tried to catch himself with his other. He came down hard on his right hand and wrist. He felt it pop.

Get up. Wrist will swell. Never be able to get up. Need to lay down. Rest a minute. Can't. Get up, keep moving.

A few yards shy of the top of the bank, Harrington could finally focus on the lights of the station. He angled across the slope towards its safety. He paused to catch his breath one more time.

Hollering. Can really hear my boys. Still alive. Buried in snow. Trapped in the trains. Gotta get 'em out. Freeze to death if we don't. Where is everybody?

With new resolve, Harrington hobbled as fast as he could. Blood was still streaming into his eyes, blurring his vision.

Almost there.

"Help!" he shouted ignoring the pain in his side. "Help!"

A few men came out of the Bailets Hotel.

"A slide hit the trains!" Harrington yelled again. "For God's sake! My boys are dying down there!"

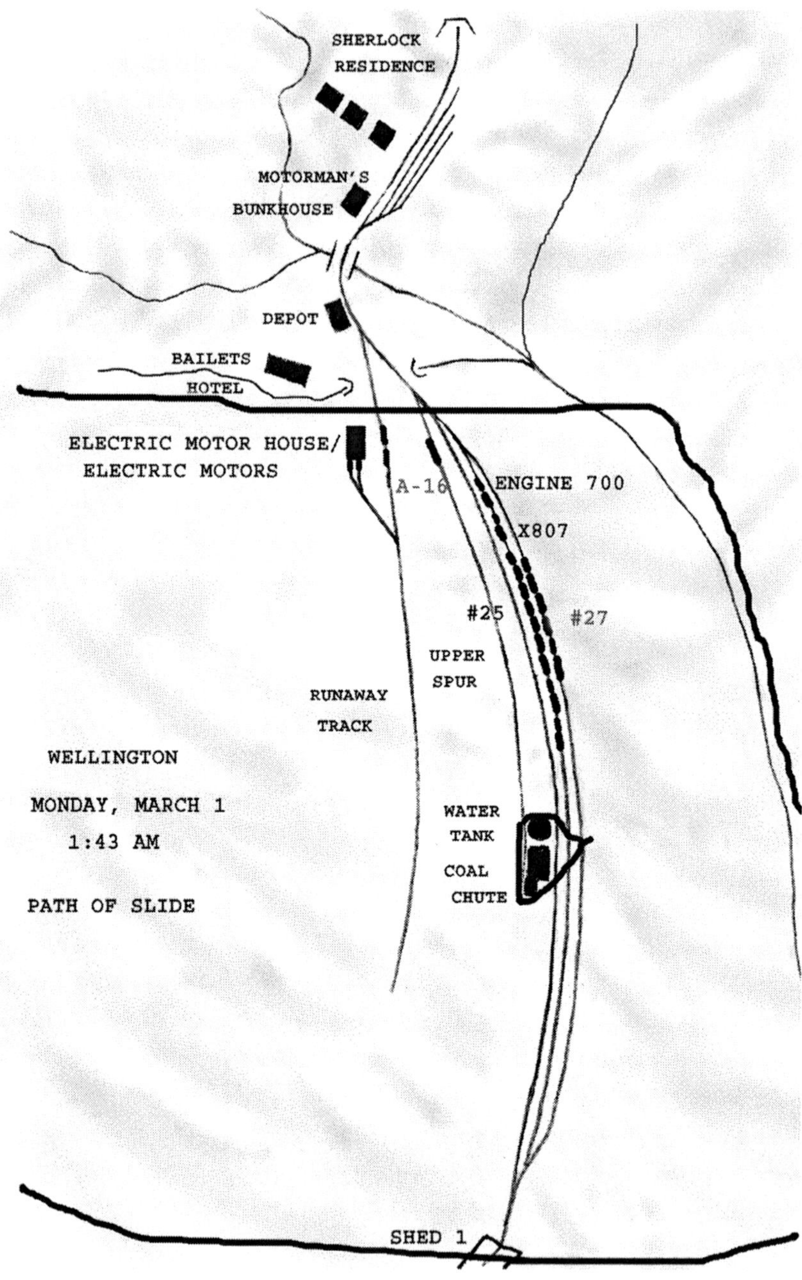
SHERLOCK
RESIDENCE
MOTORMAN'S
BUNKHOUSE
DEPOT
BAILETS
HOTEL
ELECTRIC MOTOR HOUSE/
ELECTRIC MOTORS
A-16
ENGINE 700
X807
#25
#27
UPPER
SPUR
RUNAWAY
TRACK
WELLINGTON
MONDAY, MARCH 1
1:43 AM
PATH OF SLIDE
WATER
TANK
COAL
CHUTE
SHED 1

Tuesday, March 1, 1910, 2:15 a.m.
Basil Sherlock, Telegrapher

Sherlock's nerves were wearing thin. There was nothing for him to do during his shift. The rain was keeping passengers and railroaders inside the hotel, bunkhouse, or the trains. The lines were down again. Even the telephone through the tunnel had gone dead. Flannery walked into the depot a little after 10:00 p.m., and told him he might just as well go home. The men working the day shift out on the stalled plows had returned to town. Those not sleeping in the motormen's bunkhouse had bedded down onboard trains 27 and 25. The station was empty.

"I'll leave the place unlocked. Not like there's any bums sneaking around town on a night like this," Flannery had said.

While walking home, Sherlock twice heard a dull roar and the sound of snapping trees coming from the mountain across the canyon. His heart was pounding in his throat when he finally reached his little cottage on a knoll above the upper yard. He quickly passed through the trench dug in the snowdrifts in front of the house, and ducked inside.

A lamp sat in the middle of the kitchen table, its low flame casting an orange glow in the room. Althea had gone to bed. Sherlock heard another slide thunder down the steep hillside across the canyon. Worried, he stared out the small front-room window but saw nothing. Even with the sheen of the snow, the black night yielded no clues of landforms.

Slides, one after the other. If the snow slides off our roof, grabbing Althea. Head for the tunnel, Sherlock decided. *Just like her. Sound asleep on a night like this. The Second Coming could happen in this very room. Sleep right through it.*

Sherlock let the lamp burn, just in case. He stoked the heating stove with coal, then retired to their bedroom. Quietly taking off his shirt and trousers, trying not to disturb his wife, he slipped into bed. Althea turned facing him, but did not wake up.

How can anyone sleep? Sherlock wondered. *Rain, wind. What next, an earthquake?*

Sherlock bolted upright. He was surprised that he had even fallen asleep. His sudden jolt was even enough to wake his wife.

"Is that you, Basil?"

"Of course it's me, silly. Who else would it be?" Sherlock snapped.

"Anything the matter? What time is it?" Althea was now sitting up as well, yawning.

"Snow's sliding off the mountains everywhere, has been all night," Sherlock told his wife. "If I hear the snow slide off our roof, we're going to gather everything we can and run for the tunnel. Understand?"

"Whatever you say, dear." Althea flopped back down with her head buried in her pillow.

Sherlock remained restless. Tossing and turning, he could not calm himself. At every little creak and groan the house made, he sat up, held his breath, and listened.

"For Pete's sake, Basil, if you can't sleep, just get up. At least let me sleep," Althea scolded him.

A sudden flash of lightning lit their room immediately followed by a loud clap of thunder. He rose from bed and went to the front room to peer out the window. Althea said nothing. Sherlock could tell she had fallen back asleep.

A second flash streaked across the black sky to the south, with the thunder arriving so quickly it seemed to Sherlock the sky was still lit when the house shook with the reverberations.

"Did you see that? You must have heard that!" he called out to his wife.

"Yes, dear, now come back to bed. It'll pass over soon enough," Althea answered in a groggy tone.

Sherlock had no sooner settled back in bed when there was a loud rap at the door. Deep inside he knew something was very wrong. He threw back the blankets and bolted into the front room.

"What's the matter?' he called out, even before he had the door open.

A man was already turning away and hustling back down the path.

"Everybody up!" he hollered. "The trains are down in the ditch!"

Sherlock stood for a moment, stunned.

So the nightmare's happened.

Althea wandered barefoot out of the bedroom. She was about to speak, but as she saw the expression on Sherlock's face, words failed her.

"A slide hit the trains. They need all the help they can get," blurted Sherlock. "I need to get dressed and down to the depot."

"I'll come too. If there's passengers injured, I'll need to be there," Althea stated, already walking back into their room. "Well, don't just stand there, Basil, get your clothes on!"

Bundled in their coats, arm in arm, Sherlock and Althea hurried down the path leading to the depot. He could see lights coming on over at the Bailets Hotel. Squinting through the wind-driven rain, he tried to spot where the slide had come down, to estimate what portions of the trains had been hit. Where once had shone the dull lights of the coaches, he could only see the black of the night.

Althea was tugging at his arm.

"Let's get the bunkhouse set up for a hospital. It's a new building and in a safe place. Lots of beds."

Before Sherlock could speak, Althea had elbowed her way past a few men staggering outside and bolted through the door.

"All of you, out!" she shouted. "Everyone, get up! The trains are wrecked!"

"Geeze lady," a sleepy man called out. "At least let us put on our drawers."

Sherlock stepped in and ushered his wife back outside.

"Just stay put and let them get dressed," he advised his wife.

Leave it to Althea. Go busting into a men's bunkhouse, Sherlock thought, going back into the building.

The men had the lamps turned up and were slowly putting on their clothes.

"Didn't you hear?" Sherlock asked. "Someone came by our house. A slide has hit the trains. They're gone!"

"You sure, Sherlock?" asked Pete Imberg, walking out the door.

"Yes, I tell you there has been a terrible wreck. We need to set this bunkhouse up for a hospital!" Sherlock asserted.

"Can't be that bad," Rich Chambers said, following Imberg. "Come on Pete, let's take a quick look see. Don't get too carried away Sherlock. Be back asleep before you know it."

Althea elbowed her way past Chambers and Imberg.

"I can hear shouts down in the canyon below the hotel," she claimed. "Be quick now. Help those poor people! Get them up here!"

The men had not yet vacated the building before Althea was making up the beds.

"This will never do, Basil. Get over to the hotel and tell Mr. Bailets we need clean linens for the beds. Tell him we are setting up a hospital," she ordered.

"How many sheets and blankets ..."

"Just get as many as he has available. Some material for bandages while you're at it. Now get a move on!"

She turned and hustled into the smaller back room. Surveying the room, she quickly reappeared in the doorway.

"If you see anyone helping any women, tell them they will be put in this room back here. Get some coal while you're at it, Basil. People will be near froze. We'll have to keep this building warm. Now go!"

Head down against the rain and wind, Sherlock glanced up. He was startled to see a man staggering towards him. Barefoot, his nightshirt was soaked in blood. There was a long, deep cut over his right eye. Blood still flowed down the side of his face and dripped off the side of his matted moustache.

"Good God, Mr. Harrington!" Sherlock ran forward.

"Ribs broke, Sherlock. Go easy," Harrington muttered.

Cautiously, Sherlock offered a shoulder for Harrington to lean against. It took all of his strength to support the weight of the barrel-chested Harrington and not cause both of them to fall into a heap.

"What happened out there?" Sherlock asked. "How bad is it?"

"Gone. Everything gone. Buried. Didn't see anybody."

Sherlock guided Harrington through the bunkhouse door.

"Get your feet under the stove, Mr. Harrington. I'll get you a chair," Sherlock told the injured man. "Althea! Come out here! Quickly!"

"Oh dear, you poor man." Althea hustled to his side and helped Harrington into the chair Sherlock slid across the room. She grabbed a blanket from one of the bunks and threw it over his shoulders. "Get your feet near that stove. We have to thaw them out before we can wrap them."

"My foot's bleeding on the floor," Harrington protested.

"Never mind that, get them next to that stove!" snapped Althea. "Basil, get over to the cookhouse and get some hot water. Tell them to keep a kettle on at all times!"

For the second time, Sherlock hustled back outside under strict orders from his wife. Harrington's words, "everything gone," haunted him. He could not imagine how snow, no matter how deep, could simply wipe away two trains.

"Mr. Sherlock, what can I do to help?"

"Oh Mrs. Miles, yes, well, we need hot water at the motormen's bunkhouse, and fresh linens and bandage material from Bailets," Sherlock answered. "Setting up a hospital of sorts there. Mrs. Sherlock is there now. Mr. Harrington is there. Banged up pretty good. Have you heard any news from the trains?"

It was then he saw the stocky woman wiping away tears.

"It's just horrible, Mr. Sherlock. The trains are *gone.* All those poor people have been wiped down into the canyon," she reported. She took a deep breath. "Must not worry about ourselves. I'll get the hot water."

Must not worry about ourselves, Sherlock repeated. *She's right. Need to get bedding and bandages from Bailets. Face him. Had nothing to do with that turkey. Silliness to stay mad over such things. People dying. Shouldn't be worrying about such myself.*

Taking the porch steps two at a time, Sherlock bounded into the saloon. Mrs. Bailets was tending the fire in the warm, well-lit barroom. She turned, wiping her hands on her apron.

"Is Mr. Bailets about?" Sherlock asked.

"He's gone down to help dig people out," she answered.

"We've got a hospital set up in the new bunkhouse. We need fresh linen and bandage material," Sherlock explained. "Can you help us?'

Mrs. Bailets did not immediately answer. To Sherlock, it looked as though she did not trust him.

She can't deny me, she can't. Sherlock worked to hold his temper in check.

"Mr. Bailets was thinking people might wish to take up here," she began. "He chased off some others trying to take things from the store."

"We have an injured man there already. Railroad men for certain will be in the bunkhouse. We're in dire need, madam," Sherlock countered.

"Well, of course, let me see what we can do." She hustled up the stairs leading into the hotel.

"Keep track of what you give us, Mrs. Bailets. I'm sure the railroad will stand for it," added Sherlock.

Loaded with sheets, a bolt of muslin, even a few spare clothes, Sherlock, buffeted by the wind and rain, walked quickly for the bunkhouse. To his right, down in the canyon, he could see specks of light moving across the snowfield. A voice would call from somewhere in the dark, and the lights would rush to converge on the spot.

Must have people dug out by now. Waiting in the hospital, Sherlock hoped.

The near-empty main room in the bunkhouse surprised Sherlock. Althea had cleaned Harrington up and dressed his head wound as best she could. He was lying in a bunk clutching his ribs. His eyes were closed. Sherlock wondered if he had lost consciousness.

"Here're your supplies, Althea," Sherlock called.

Both his wife and Mrs. Miles appeared from the back room.

"Have any more injured been brought in?" he asked.

"Not yet," Althea answered.

"Bob said all the tools, the shovels, axes, all went down with the trains," Mrs. Miles added. "He sent a man over to Cascade Tunnel Station to get men and shovels."

"I'm going to try and find Flannery. Mr. O'Neill has to be notified," Sherlock told his wife. Now with a purpose, he hustled from the bunkhouse intent on aiding the lights moving in the canyon below.

Barely reaching the edge of the slide, he met others struggling out. Some were climbing under their own power; others were supported on the shoulders of the railroaders who had come to their rescue.

"Take all injured to the bunkhouse. I have a hospital set up," Sherlock told all those he met.

"Sherlock!" a voice called. "Over here! Quick!"

The light of a lantern over the bank caught Sherlock's eye. It was waving wildly, as if it was suspended on the limb of a tree being blown in the storm.

"Down here, Sherlock! I need your help!"

In the light of the lantern his stomach turned. Cradled in William Bailets' arms was a small boy. Conscious, the child looked like a terrified animal cornered by a hunter's dogs. His eyes were wide and darting about. He said nothing; only an occasional whimper escaped his lips. Approaching, Sherlock finally saw the splinter of wood piercing the boy's forehead.

"Sherlock, help me get this boy up to the hotel," Bailets asked, panting hard. "Can you take him? I'm about done in."

Without saying a word, Sherlock extended his arms and gently took the boy. He stared at the wood sliver. The force of the snow slide had driven the wooden fragment laterally into the boy's forehead. Blood dripped from the length of the wound and stained the brown-checked blanket in which he was wrapped.

Poor kid. Probably an orphan now. Doesn't even know it, Sherlock thought.

Reaching the hotel, Sherlock laid the child on a dining table. One hand over her mouth, Mrs. Bailets helped Sherlock tuck the boy in.

"That splinter needs to come out and the wound cleaned," Sherlock told Mr. Bailets.

"Not with my hands," Bailets replied, alarmed.

"My father was a doctor. I've seen these kinds of wounds before," explained Sherlock. "Farmers would come in with infected slivers. Can turn to blood poisoning if they're left in."

"That might be true, but I ain't touching that kid and neither is the missus," asserted Bailets.

"Get me a new razor blade and run the edge under a flame. Also a bottle of whiskey," Sherlock ordered. "I'm sure I can do it."

"Suit yourself." Bailets hustled from the room, reappearing in a matter of minutes with the razor, a bottle, a towel, and a clean strip of muslin for a bandage.

"Close your eyes, son," Sherlock said softly. "This might hurt some. Be brave."

The boy shut his eyes, but his body was still tense. Sherlock poured whiskey on the towel and used it to clean the area around the wound. Twice the boy flinched, but made no sound.

Razor in hand, Sherlock took a deep breath. For a moment, he closed his eyes. He could hear his father. "Cut quick and clean."

Not giving himself time to think, Sherlock made a quick, long incision the length of the stick. His hands shaking, he gently pulled the splinter free in one piece. Blood dripped from the boy's forehead and down his cheeks.

"This is going to sting," Sherlock warned. He again cleaned the wound with whiskey. The boy remained silent, tears emerging from his closed eyelids.

Sherlock ripped off a strip of the towel and placed it across the wound. The bleeding had begun to slow. Using the strips of muslin, he wrapped the boy's head, gently holding him slightly upright while he worked. He could feel the small body finally relax.

Inspecting the sliver, Sherlock wrapped it and placed it next to the boy.

"You might want to keep this, son," Sherlock said. "Something to show your grandchildren."

Mrs. Bailets bustled into the room. She replaced the blood-stained wrapping with a clean blanket. Lovingly, she covered the boy.

"My, that looks much better," she exclaimed.

"Hope it doesn't scar," Sherlock said, wiping his hands. "Probably best to keep him here, Mrs. Bailets, if you don't mind."

"Not at all. We'll take good care of this brave little soldier," she agreed, already fussing over the boy.

Sherlock strolled out of the dining hall, through the tavern and back into the storm. Only then did his legs become weak, his head light. Stopping for a moment, he bent over, his hands on his knees. Regaining his composure, Sherlock continued towards the bunkhouse. It was at that point he realized he had performed the operation still wearing his hat and heavy winter coat.

The old man would've chewed my ass for that, Sherlock thought.

Tuesday, March 1, 1910, 3:00 a.m.
John Robert Meath, Engineer

Meath pulled the curtain back around the fire deck of the X-802. He opened the fire box door and worked the fire with his poker, trying to get the green wood to burn down so the ash would fall through the grates and not build up inside. Sparks flew everywhere as he scattered the burning embers evenly across the surface. He threw in another half dozen pieces of split cedar and fir, and slammed the lid closed.

John Pettit was watching the 1128, coupled directly behind Meath's plow. Fires tended for the moment, he joined Meath and they huddled together close to the boiler head in an attempt to stay warm.

"Looks like that storm finally passed," Pettit said. "Can't say as I've ever seen lightning and thunder like that up here. At least this time of year."

"Last time I went through a storm like that was back home," remembered Meath. "A damned tornado ripped through our field and scattered wheat shocks all over the county."

The men fell silent.

"Kinda wish I was with my cousin right now, bundled up all nice and warm on 25," Pettit admitted.

"Conductor of 25's your cousin?" asked Meath.

"Yeah, distant cousin of some sort," Pettit admitted.

"Is anybody there?" came a panic yell from outside.

"Christ, who'd be out in this weather?" Meath got up and poked his head through the curtain. Holding a lantern, drenched to skin, stood James Mackey.

"What the hell you doing here, Jimbo?" inquired Meath. "Get in here before you catch a chill!"

"Can't. Gotta get to Scenic! The trains are gone, Bobby. Get some shovels. Get up to Wellington!" Mackey was nearly in tears.

Meath threw back the curtain and sprang from the plow to the shaken man's side.

"What the hell you talking about?"

Mackey took a breath. He wiped the rain from his face. In the light of the lantern Meath could see his pale skin and the fear in his eyes. It was contagious; a sense of fear began to well deep inside Meath as well.

"Was sleeping in the bunkhouse. Got rousted out. A slide come down. Took out everything. The trains, both of them are over the bank. Covered. They're gone. I gotta get to Scenic to get help. Get O'Neill."

"What goes out there, Bobby?" Pettit was standing on the fire deck. "Jimbo, looks like you've seen a ghost."

Meath spun around to face Pettit.

"A slide's hit Wellington. Took out the trains, I guess," Meath repeated. "Now Jim, you sure the trains are *gone*, not just a car or two shoved over the bank?"

"I gotta get going, Bobby. The goddamned trains are gone. Believe me. Keep a guy here if you have to, but get shovels, axes, anything you got around here. Get tools up to Wellington. Our boys are buried down in the canyon."

With that, Mackey turned and continued towards Windy Point, his head lowered against the driving rain. He hollered at Brown and Ford as he walked past the trailing set, simply telling them go and talk to Meath. Still stunned, Meath silently watched Mackey disappear into the gloom.

"What's Jim babbling about?" Bob Ford asked, joining Meath and Pettit.

"I don't know for sure," is all Meath could muster.

"He says a slide come down. Took out both trains," Pettit answered.

"That's impossible!" Ford snorted. "You know Jimbo. Can't keep two points straight."

"Bob, you and Tom hold the fort here," Meath said. "John and I'll grab a few axes and shovels and head up. Find out what this is all about."

Meath and Pettit were barely out of sight of the stalled plows when another form stumbled over the slide and came into the halo of light produced by their lanterns. Panting, he bent over, trying to catch his breath.

"Wentzel, sectionman," he gasped. "Got a note from the Wellington station agent. Going to Scenic. Get O'Neill. Trains gone. Folks dying."

"Let me see that note," Meath said, holding out his hand.

Taking the slip of paper, Meath unfolded the message. He held it near Pettit's lantern.

Get to the bottom of this. Can't be that bad, Meath thought.

The note was short and corroborated what Mackey and Wentzel had said. It was signed by Will Flannery. Meath handed the paper to Pettit. For a moment Meath closed his eyes. He felt weak in the knees.

"God help them," whispered Pettit. "God help all of them."

"I need that note back. I need to get going," Wentzel shouted.

Meath gave the man the scrap of paper. "Mackey's not far ahead. If you catch him, give him the note. He'll know where to find O'Neill."

Lost in thought, driven by anxious fear, Meath and Pettit hiked along the trail in the snow beat down by the crews tending the stalled plows. Each carried an ax and a shovel over their shoulders.

Can't figure where a slide could've come from, Meath pondered. *No gully above the sidings. Flannery's note. No details. Stretching things. Make sure O'Neill sends some help. Everything can't be gone. Jesus, wonder where Al and the boys were bedded down?*

They rounded the last bend in the right-of-way. The snow shed just west of the yard was partially collapsed. They worked around its edge. The dark form of the coal chute loomed on the hillside. Beyond it a wall of snow blocked the men's view towards the sidings and Wellington.

Coal chute's still here, Meath thought as he and Pettit climbed the snow bank.

"Oh, dear God," Pettit moaned. He stood still, scanning the scene before him. Where there had been sidings occupied two trains, there was nothing but a field of snow.

Lord, no. Can't be. Meath stared into the ravine watching the men with lanterns searching for evidence of the buried trains.

"God, where do you even begin?" Pettit asked, dumbfounded by the sight.

Hope Al and the boys aren't down there, Meath prayed.

Meath handed his ax to the first man he met.

"Here, you can have this, I've got a shovel. Where do you need me?"

"Over by the engines, somebody's trapped there but still alive," the man said. "I'm headed further down."

A wave of relief came over Meath as he approached the scene. He recognized John Finn and Sam Duncan digging with their hands just below the two overturned locomotives. Fog rose from their boilers, which were still hot. Around the engines, pools of near-scalding water simmered, produced from snow melted by the escaping steam.

"John! Sam! I've got a shovel!" Meath hollered.

"Bobby! Watch yourself. Don't fall through into that hot water! Curly's trapped!" Finn called back.

The tender of the 1032 was ripped from the locomotive and cast to one side. The engine had rolled over, and while sliding down the bank on its side, the cab filled tight with snow. John Kerlee, in trying to escape, became wedged solid against the rear portion doorway and the cab's roof. Heat from the boiler had melted a pocket from which only his head could be seen.

Adrenalin seizing control, Meath began to dig furiously at the hard-packed snow.

"We'll have you out real quick, Curly," Meath said.

"I can't goddamned move," Kerlee complained. "Ain't hurtin' bad. Just can't move."

"We got Charlie Smart out already," Finn said, still scraping snow by hand from around the trapped brakeman. "Shook up good, but I think he'll be fine."

"I went down with Homer and Ira," Duncan said as he worked by hand as well.

"You went down?" Meath asked, in disbelief.

"Me, Ira, and Homer. Homer got burned by that water. Ira's beat up some. They're up at the motormen's bunkhouse," told Duncan. "Hurting some myself. Get Curly out and I'll take him on up."

Gotta calm down, Meath cautioned himself. *Try and work the shovel alongside him.*

"Can you feel your arms?" Meath asked Kerlee. "They next to your body or stretched out some?"

"I can't tell, Bobby. Cold. Can't feel."

Meath was on his stomach carefully pulling shovel fulls back, tossing each aside. To free the man, he had to first dig his way inside the cab. It was slow, arduous work, taking hours to accomplish little.

"You're jammed so hard against the roof, I'm gonna have to try and dig out from under you," Meath finally decided.

With new purpose, all three men began to scoop away the packed snow from beneath Kerlee's prone body. Meath, back on his stomach, burrowed his way under the overhang of the cab's roof. He cast the shovel aside and began pulling out snow from alongside and under the man's torso by hand. Kerlee's left arm was finally freed. As more snow was taken from below, Kerlee, wincing in pain, began to wiggle his way out. While Duncan and Finn maintained a steady pull on his shoulders, Meath kept pawing at the snow. With a final effort by Kerlee to kick his legs loose, he was free.

Crawling out from under the overturned cab, Meath straightened up. A gray dawn had broken. Rain mixed with snow continued to pelt down. For the first time he took a look around. There was nothing to see but snow. No evidence of the passenger cars—only scattered pockets of men digging in almost vain hope.

Kerlee tried to stand, but his numb legs would not hold his weight. Meath and Finn knelt down beside him and rubbed his legs, while Duncan kept him propped up.

"Al was with us for awhile last night, Bobby," Finn admitted. "I went up town to fetch a bottle. Helped him climb onto a car on 27's train. I'm afraid we don't know where it's at. Think there was a bunch of boys on it sleeping." Finn's voice trailed off.

Meath's hands and arms went limp. His strength was suddenly robbed from him.

Gone. Al's gone, Meath thought. *Damn it to hell, he's gone.*

"I can't get up," Kerlee blurted. "Give me a hand."

Together Duncan and Kerlee began to pick their way up the smooth bank of snow. Staggering at times, they kept a steady course. Through the gloomy light of dawn Meath watched them until they had come upon another group of workers who threw blankets over their shoulders and led them toward the bunkhouse.

"He's dead, ain't he," Meath said to Finn.

"Don't be thinking that way, Bobby, you of all people," lectured Finn. "We'll find 'em alive and dig'em out."

"We could use a couple of hands down here," came a cry from a man standing near the bottom of the ravine.

Running and sliding, Meath and Finn careened down the hill. Rich Chambers, a shovel in his hand, was with a group of three others digging. They had a large hole opened up in the snow bank, but nothing resembling a car had yet to be uncovered.

"Wait. Quiet," Chambers told the men. He dropped to his knees and put his ear to the snow.

"Can you hear me!" he bellowed.

A muffled shout could be heard, coming from beneath their feet.

"They're down there, boys. Right below us," Chambers said.

Maybe it's the car Al and the rest were in, Meath silently wished. *Worst day of my life. Worst damned day of my life.*

As much as Meath wanted to find anyone alive, the hope that one of the men trapped somewhere below was Al Dougherty drove him to work far beyond what he could normally accomplish. There was no pain in his back, no stiffness in his shoulders. He did not notice the passing of time. The hole became wider, deeper; each shovel of snow was thrown harder and higher to clear; yet it made no difference. Driven by fear, driven by love for their mates, Meath and the others worked.

The hole was nearly six feet deep when the tips of their shovels struck something solid. Using the sides of the spades, they scraped away the last few inches of snow, revealing the roof of a mail car turned on its side. They could clearly hear fists pounding against the wood from within.

"Hand me an ax!" Meath hollered to another group of men who had just arrived.

Chambers and Finn finished clearing off a large section of the car's side.

Meath rapped the ax handle hard against the siding.

"Stand clear in there!" he shouted. "I'm gonna chop you out!"

The pent-up frustration of a week of labor in vain traveled from Meath's shoulders and arms to the sharp bit of the ax. Rapid swings shattered the tongue and groove siding. Winding up like a big-league pitcher, he threw his entire body into the effort, grunting out loud each time the head struck home.

Within minutes, Meath had a gaping hole opened in the side of the car. He threw his ax to the side, slipped his feet into the gash, and jumped inside.

"God bless you, Bobby! We thought we were done for!" Martin White, bloodied, limping, came from the corner of the car into the light streaming from the hole above.

Bat Nelson was at White's side. Holding his arm, dried blood across his face, he managed a grin.

"I knew you boys would come for us."

"Get us to hell outta here," came another voice from the dark corner of the car.

"Duncan?" Meath asked.

Chambers poked his head down through the hole.

"Who you got, Bobby?"

"Bat, Marty White, for sure," Meath answered.

"Ross Philips and 'Dunc' Tegtmeier are here too," Bat called up. "They're against the wall. Pretty banged up."

"Need to find something to help get you boys outta here," Meath realized.

"Back two-thirds of the car is collapsed. Might find something back there a ways," White suggested.

Meath stared into the recesses of the car, waiting for his eyes to adjust to the darkness. He saw what looked to be a sorting table that had been torn from the floor, jammed under part of the caved-in rear portion of the car. He crawled on his knees to retrieve it. Pulling on it, he lost his grip. In an awkward position, his whole body fell flat. Raising himself back up, he could feel a sticky substance clinging to his gloves and coat sleeves. He looked closer and nearly gagged. It was coagulated blood.

"Jesus, give me strength," he mumbled.

The table free, he backed out, still on his hands and knees, pulling it along until he could finally stand up. He approached Nelson and White.

"What the hell's on your …" Nelson was suddenly quiet. "Oh God. There were a couple of the mail sorters in the rear of the car. Oh God forgive me, forgot all about those poor men."

Meath said nothing. He put his mind to setting the table firm under the escape hole. Chambers jumped in and helped boost Nelson and White to freedom. Tegtmeier and Phillips were weak and could do little to help. Hands from the men who had gathered above, and the strong hands of Meath and Chambers below, lifted the injured men to safety.

As Tegtmeier was hauled from the car, he glanced back down.

"God bless you," he whispered.

"Light a lantern and pass it down," Meath called up.

Lamp in hand, Meath ventured into the collapsed the rear of the car, while Chambers scrambled out. The sides were completely crushed. A log was laid across the middle portion of the car. Blood seeped from under the burned snag. Holding his breath, Meath listened.

"Is anybody there?" he called out. Again he stood in breathless silence. He heard nothing.

"Get outta there, Bobby. Nothing says this whole damned thing couldn't come down on you," Chambers warned.

All dead. God have mercy on them. All dead. Just like Al.

Meath blew out the lantern and climbed out of the car.

Tuesday, March 1, 1910, 8:30 a.m.
James Henry O'Neill, Superintendent

For the first time in nearly a week, O'Neill felt rested. A good night's sleep under his belt, and acknowledgement from Everett that the supplies he had ordered would be on their way, put him in a positive mood. Despite the pouring rain, he even allowed a sliver of optimism to slip into his mind as he hiked east to join Dowling on the X-808.

String a line up Old Glory, today. Can pack food in. Snow settles, bring the mail and passengers out. Coming out of the worst of it. Get a plow coming east from Sky. NP my best bet. Relief train and plow out of Leavenworth. Help coming.

The reality of the situation returned in force when O'Neill came upon the X-808. Once again, the plow was not working. While bucking at the packed drifts, one of the extra coal cars had derailed, forcing them to stop. Adding to the woes was the continuing problem of fir needles. Mixed in with the snow being shoveled for water, they had clogged the boiler's water injectors.

Roadmaster Thomas McIntyre was directing his crew of sectionmen, who were cleaning the snow away from the damaged wheels and track. Through the fog, O'Neill could see Will Mackey and Irving Tegtmeier unloading blocks, heavy chains, and the re-railers from the toolbox of the X-808.

"What goes here, Mr. McIntyre?" O'Neill asked as he approached.

"See for yourself, sir." McIntyre snapped, his patience already wearing thin. "Taking all the coal out of this car. Getting too light to be sandwiched between an engine and the plow. Shoved the bastard right off the rail."

"I'll go help bring down the blocking," O'Neill said, crawling out from under the car. "Doesn't look that bad. An easy pull backwards with the re-railers and she should pop right back on."

Damned nuisance. Nothing we haven't handled a million times, O'Neill told himself.

"Mr. Mackey. How can I help?" O'Neill called out.

"Sorry to have you come up on a mess first thing, sir," Mackey apologized, shouldering a heavy linked logging chain. "Just happened, if you must know. So how did you sleep? One hell of a thunderstorm rolled through here last night. You hear it?"

"Slept well, thank you. Heard talk of the storm at Scenic. Never heard a thing. They could've shot cannons off in my ears last night and it wouldn't have woken me up."

Irving Tegtmeier, carrying a re-railer wedge, greeted O'Neill with a slight nod of his head and walked on past. Squatting down, O'Neill picked up an armload of blocking and followed the men back to the derailed car. There he let the blocks tumble into the wet snow, and flexed his arms, which had become cramped with the load.

Seeing the crowd, J.J. Dowling came down off the plow's tender. His pants soaking wet from working inside the plow's tank, he joined the effort to rerail the car.

"Mr. O'Neill! Mr. O'Neill!"

A sectionman, red-faced from running through the slush forming on the top of the snowdrifts, stumbled and nearly fell at the feet of the men working around the car.

"Can I help you?" inquired O'Neill, puzzled by the man's frantic look.

"Wellington. Slide. Just heard about it," the man panted. "Need you at Scenic."

"Slow down. A slide? Where?" O'Neill asked the man.

"What'd he say?" Tegtmeier and the rest of the crew gathered in a tight circle.

"Man just came down from Wellington," the laborer repeated. "A slide hit last night. They say the trains are down over the bank. Got a note from station agent in Wellington. You have to get back to Scenic, sir."

"Oh God," sighed Will Mackey. "Jimbo's up there."

"So's Duncan," added Tegtmeier.

For a moment O'Neill's mind went blank. He was aware all eyes were on him. Every man was listening for what he would say next.

Can't be that bad. Think clear, O'Neill told himself.

"Mr. McIntyre, finish clearing away the snow so this car can be re-railed, then report back to me with as many men as can be spared and still keep this plow running," O'Neill began. "Mr. Dowling, once you are up and running, turn things over to Mr. Tegtmeier and Mr. Mackey. You report back to me. I'll head back to Scenic and see what this is all about."

"My brother is up there, Mr. O'Neill. I want to go up there!" Mackey protested.

"Feeling the same way about Cousin Duncan," Tegtmeier mumbled.

"I need you down here. We have to keep plowing east. The sooner we get up there with our plows, the better off your kin is gonna be. I'll send word down about them as soon as I know what's going on up there," O'Neill promised.

"Note says the trains are gone sir! Not a trace of them!" the messenger interrupted.

"That's enough from you!" O'Neill roared. "All we know right now is based on a note, scribbled in the black of night. Not exactly the most reliable of information. Now let's get to work. Get this plow up and running. I'll see you, Mr. McIntyre, and you, Mr. Dowling, back at Scenic."

The circle of men parted, allowing O'Neill to leave for Scenic. Pausing, he turned. "Thank you, young man, for coming right out with the message. You might just as well stay here, get warmed up, and help however you can."

O'Neill's mind was racing. He had an unsettled feeling that the news was indeed as bad as it sounded, but he did not let his anxiety overpower his mind.

Still dark. Impossible to assess the damage, he reasoned. *Part of the bank could have slid. Knock a few cars sideways. 27 would have kept the coaches from going over unless it hit to the rear. All gone. Hard to believe that.*

What did he mean by "all gone?" O'Neill's thoughts took a dark turn. *What if that's what happened? God, how do I handle that? People trapped. Low on stores. Section crews all down here. Pray to God it's not that bad.*

Hands in his coat pockets, facing the biting wind, he hustled along the trail worn in the snow blocking his railroad. A half hour later, O'Neill strode into the station at Scenic.

"Where's the man from Wellington?" he asked the operator.

"Here, sir," came a voice from the back of the room.

James Mackey rose from a chair next to the stove. His wet clothes appeared to be two sizes too big and hung from his gaunt frame. O'Neill saw his fear and instantly knew the initial reports were not exaggerations.

"You sit for just a moment, Mr. Mackey. Gather yourself." O'Neill turned his attention back to the operator.

Get as clear a view as you can from this man, O'Neill cautioned himself.

"Here's the note from Flannery up at Wellington, Mr. O'Neill," offered the operator. "Mackey showed up first. Sectionman came in right after with this note. He took off for Sky."

"I read the note. It's all true," Mackey interrupted.

"Sit down, Mr. Mackey. I repeat, gather your thoughts," O'Neill told the shaken man in a calm, firm voice.

"Yes sir. It's terrible up there. We have to get help …"

"Mr. Mackey! Calm yourself! I'll hear you out," scolded O'Neill.

He took the folded scrap of paper from the corner of the desk. The note was wet, the writing smudged. The information O'Neill could decipher from the scribbled lines caused him to sit down hard on the edge of the telegrapher's desk. Flannery's handwriting confirmed O'Neill's worst thoughts.

Calm yourself.

O'Neill let go a deep breath. He grabbed a pencil and Western Union pad. Pulling another chair alongside the stove, he sat down.

"Now, Mr. Mackey, tell me exactly what has happened up there," he said.

"I don't know exactly when, maybe half past one, or two this morning, the whole bank above the trains kicked loose. Sent everything over the bank. Can't see a trace of anything," Mackey began.

"What do you mean by 'sent everything'," O'Neill interrupted. "Is the motorhouse gone?"

"Yes sir, and the motors that were standing on the coal track," Mackey answered.

Oh God. O'Neill's stomach became sick. *My car. Blackburn, Earl, and Lewis.*

"What about my car, you know the one I mean?"

Mackey could not look O'Neill in the eye. He turned away, rubbing his red chapped hands across his eyes. His lower lip quivered.

"Gone sir, buried in snow. I ain't making none of this up. Sir, the plow, the dead engine, both trains. You have to believe me, they're over the bank and buried." Mackey was fighting back tears.

"Any sign of life?"

"Didn't stick around very long. Can't say. I heard tell Mr. Harrington was hurt bad, but got out, maybe a few others. That's all I know."

"Any idea how many men are up there now searching for survivors?"

"Hard to say, maybe thirty or thirty-five," Mackey guessed.

O'Neill rose from his chair and glanced at the clock.

Half past ten. Eight hours ago. People still buried. Not much hope of them being alive. Froze to death by now. Goddamn it.

"Mr. Mackey, you walked across the slide to get here, how long is it?"

"Well sir, it crushed that little Shed One. Goes from about Shed 2 all the way up to the east siding switches. Must be about half a mile, I'd say. Goddamned big, and deep. Went around the coal chute. It's still standing. I think the water tank is still there too, not sure," replied Mackey.

"You did just fine. I'm going to send a crew up there with Mr. Dowling and Mr. McIntyre when they arrive. You might just as well go back up with them if you feel up to it."

"My brother, Will. He's with Dowling. Can you get word out to him I'm okay?"

"I'll see to it." O'Neill rose and patted the shaken man on his shoulders.

"How far east from Sky can a train get without rotary protection?" O'Neill asked the operator.

"Wire's down again, but last report Nippon had about three feet on the rail," he replied.

O'Neill lit a cigar and stared out the window. Snowflakes were beginning to mix with the rain.

Need to get up there. Can't. Have to go to Nippon. Get word out. Have to keep the plow moving. Try and get a plow from the NP. Get a relief party on the way. Telegraph Brown and probably Watrous. God, I need to get up there.

Dowling stomped the snow from his boots and came inside.

"So how bad is it?" Dowling asked.

"Bad as it can get," O'Neill answered. He told Dowling what he knew. By then, McIntyre had arrived with a crew of nearly 30 men from the plow crew.

"Mr. Dowling, I want you to make a careful assessment of the situation and get back down here. Don't send a messenger. I need your eyes and your words. Understood?" O'Neill's voice was emphatic. "How soon before the 808 can get back underway?"

"Should be going in an hour or so, I would think," Dowling replied. "You coming up?"

"No. Line's down. I'm going to hike to Nippon and wire for help. Now get going, but for God's sakes keep a level head."

"There's a pair of snowshoes in the tool house," McIntyre called over his shoulder as he left.

It took O'Neill the better part of two hours to reach the station at Nippon. Not used to walking in snowshoes, in his haste he found himself taking long, awkward steps. In his mind he was trying to picture, to grasp the severity of the avalanche. A part of him knew the situation was bad, even worse than what was reported, while another tried to cajole him into believing it was not.

Have to stay at Nippon. Stay with the key. Coordinate relief. Need to get up there somehow.

Arriving at the station, O'Neill ripped off the leather straps binding the snowshoes to his boots. Leaving them where they lay, he burst in the door.

"Your wire up?" he demanded.

"Yes sir," answered the startled operator.

O'Neill grabbed a pad of paper and a copy of the 1910 Great Northern Railway Telegraph Code Book. He sat for a moment, the pencil poised.

Better jumble up the words good. Make sure just G.N. people know. Forgot what time he told me the slide hit. Oh well …

He began to write:

March 1, 1910

"4AM large snow slide extending one-half mile in length came down at Wellington extending from snow shed No. 2 west of Wellington to east passing track switch …"

He paused and began to look up words in the book. He copied down those he wanted to use, then returned to his writing.

" …scrip gay water tank No. 25 and 27's train car A-16 four motors, motor shed, rotary X807 engines 700, 1032, and 1418 all plug 25's train paying or less money. Cannot say to what haul until can ivory them placer care down alarm 100 feet. All guard badly endow. It is thought perhaps by equip we can be able to ditch all plug. Have about 35 men ivory guard and plug placer. Have sent to more men from Scenic and have arranged for rough sling out of hurgle with gash to attend money. Stiles and Dowling on the ground. Understand Harrington and Blackburn bold slightly money. Gash will have to spank from Nippon to Wellington. Track covered with heavy wet snow 3 feet deep east of Nippon.

J.H. O'Neill"

"Send that out to F.B. Brown in Seattle, he can file it and send it to whoever he wants," O'Neill instructed the operator.

O'Neill pulled out a cigar and tried to will away a splitting headache.

Whole damned world's about to find out what happened on my goddamned watch.

Part Three

"I considered the location we had the train in as absolutely safe,"—
James Henry O'Neill

March 2, 1910, 8:00 a.m.
James Henry O'Neill, Superintendent

O'Neill was a relieved to be outside, climbing the trail to Wellington. It was a relief to be out in the open air, dealing with the elements. It was a relief to see the wind finally die down, even if the rain had turned back to snow. It was a relief to be away from the constant ticking of the telegraph key and the ringing of the phone. It was a relief to be away from the need to make decisions not based on first-hand information.

Being a man who prided himself on being able to bring any situation under control in a short period of time, the past twenty-four hours had worn on O'Neill. The very things that were most familiar to him, over which he felt he could exercise control—the opening of the line, the operation of his division—had suddenly become secondary. Railroading was no longer his principle responsibility.

The telegrams arriving from Everett and the main office in St. Paul made no mention of the steps being taken to help him raise the blockade. Instead, O'Neill was told to make sure no one representing the railroad spoke of fault or liability. Other messages outlined the importance of the proper identification of the dead before any names were released, and that no bodies be removed from Wellington until the King County Coroner had arrived. There was even talk of finding a panel of "clear thinking" men to sit on the inevitable Inquest Jury.

Part of being a superintendent was dealing with the occasional wreck.

The damage of property, the deaths of railroaders, even the occasional passenger injured or killed were all part of the job. O'Neill had handled such situations a number of times. This was vastly different, however. The reports of widespread destruction, wholesale loss of life, and the lack of anyone who could identify the dead—particularly among the passengers, had O'Neill reeling.

Passengers living are the ones that walked out, O'Neill reasoned. *Can't ask them to go back up to identify corpses.*

O'Neill was told to try and control the newspaper reporters who were sure to find a way to the scene. There was even a message telling him of the importance of salvaging the First Class mail now covered by the slide. "All efforts must be made" to recover the sacks, is how the message read.

Letter is worth more than a body, O'Neill thought when he first read the telegram.

He felt indignant by the notion that saving the mail was more important than the recovery of the dead. Still, he understood. The dead were a liability, while the mail was an asset.

Liability. All I hear about.

O'Neill spent much of the night on the key and on the phone, convincing his bosses he could do nothing pacing the floor at Nippon. With Harrington injured and Blackburn still missing, no one with authority was currently at the scene, he argued. When General Superintendent Brown wired that he was on his way east from Seattle, and that another band of workers were at Scenic getting ready to hike into Wellington, O'Neill saw his chance to finally get away.

Can't make decisions down here, O'Neill fumed. *Have to get up there with the boys.*

By the time O'Neill and the fifty or so men he was leading headed out, a well-packed trail had been formed in the deep drifts. Climbing the steep slope of "Old Glory" they passed a team of carpenters erecting "A" frames at its base and summit. For a brief moment, O'Neill recalled his optimism the morning before.

Sleds arriving tomorrow. Haul out the passengers all right.

O'Neill, like the rest, had strapped a pack of supplies on his back. His was a couple of bundles of blankets tied together. Bulky rather than heavy, the pack suited his frame.

Out along the trail east of Windy Point, they walked single file. In the lead, O'Neill kept a brisk pace. Where he, Churchill, and Wickam had crawled between the tops of the drifts and the roofs of the snow sheds three days earlier, access holes had now been dug.

They hiked in silence. Visions of the men he left behind flashed through O'Neill's mind as he walked.

Kept looking for Earl to dig me out from under all the paperwork last night, O'Neill thought. *Dig me out. Funny I'd think that at a time like this. Lewis. Never be another like him. Will never replace him.*

He barely noticed the double rotary set. It was nearly completely snowed over. Only the warm boiler jackets were exposed. Wisps of steam escaped through the packed snow. A lazy white haze of strong-smelling wood smoke floated from the stacks of the two plows and two pusher engines. A small crew of men was still on the hillside, chopping wood for their fireboxes and shoveling snow into the tenders for water.

Shedding his pack, O'Neill hopped onto the trailing X-802 and made his way back to the fire deck. James Mackey was tossing wood into the firebox. He stood up with a start.

"Mr. O'Neill. Goddamn, it's good to see you, sir," he said.

"Mr. Mackey, how goes it?" asked O'Neill.

Mackey looked towards the top of the boiler head. O'Neill was not sure if he was looking at the steam gauge, or merely trying to compose himself.

"It's bad, sir. I mean real bad." He looked away again, his eyes watering.

"Who's in charge of the crews out here today?" O'Neill inquired.

"I reckon I'm the boss. Purcell, Clary, White, Harrington, they're all down. Hurt. Ed Lindsay," Mackey paused his lower lip quivering. "Found him earlier this morning. Took a couple of us to identify him. Haven't even found Johnny Parzybok yet."

"What about Duncan Tegtmeier?"

"He's banged up too. Not sure how bad," Mackey answered. "We've got things figured out to keep the plows breathing, sir. You get on your way. We need you up here, sir. I mean it. We need you here."

O'Neill leaped off the plow onto the snow. He squatted down, slipping his arms through the rope loops he had fashioned in his bundles of blankets. Giving a heavy heave he both vaulted himself into a standing position and pulled the bundles onto his back.

"I'll get word to your brother, Jim," he hollered as he hiked past.

"Gonna need those blankets," Mackey called back. "Wrapping the dead folks in them."

The blankets on O'Neill's back suddenly doubled in weight. In the back of his mind he knew there were dead bodies. He knew in Wellington he would come face to face with the death brought on by the slide. But it never occurred to him that when the blankets on his back went back down the mountain, they could very well be serving as the funeral shroud for a man he knew as a friend.

Every one of my rotary conductors hurt or dead, O'Neill pondered. *One of my trainmasters missing, dead by now, the other banged up.*

O'Neill looked up at the snow falling from the sky.

You wiped out my whole command.

All the scraps of information received by O'Neill the previous day did little to prepare him for what he saw when he reached Wellington. Nearly five hundred feet up on the hillside, above where the trains had stood, was a sharp line in the snow. It stretched nearly one-half mile from Shed 1 west of the coal chute to the bend in the hill just west of Bailets Hotel. An even slope of snow extended from that point nearly one thousand feet down to the bottom of the canyon. Even Tye Creek had been partially dammed by the mass of snow and jumbled timber, its course altered. The entire hillside had sloughed off in one massive slide.

Across the face of the slide, pockets of workers were digging large holes and chopping at the exposed timber. Other than the now-cold boilers of the overturned locomotives and the smashed fan of the X-807, there was no sign of any railroad equipment.

O'Neill took his time and carefully surveyed the scene. He sighted along where the engines rested. In his mind, he tried to reconstruct where the trains had stood. To his eye, it appeared the slide had not come straight down the mountain.

Got going up by the motor house first. Came down at an angle. Pushed everything my way. Can tell by how that timber is laying. Some crews are digging too far east. Won't find a car, O'Neill calculated.

Tracing where he believed the main line and sidings were buried, he made his way eastward, sighting on the depot. For a long while he attempted to visualize exactly where his private car had stood. With the usual landmarks gone, O'Neill soon learned he did not know Wellington, or his division, as well as he thought.

My car got hit first, thought O'Neill. He scanned the slope directly below. *Got hit first. Slide wouldn't have been moving fast. Might not be far down the canyon. Gone now.*

The party O'Neill led was already fanned out. Some were taking packs of food up to the hotel or the company cookhouse. Others were making their way further upgrade toward the motormens' bunkhouse with the supplies they packed in. Still others, bearing axes and shovels, were already picking their way down into the canyon to join those digging.

"Let me take that, sir," a man offered as O'Neill approached the depot. "Gonna need these up at the bunkhouse."

Rid of his pack, O'Neill walked into the depot. It was as if nothing of significance had happened. The coffee pot was on the stove. His china cup, the one brought over from his car the day he arrived, hung on one of the hooks. A few men were gathered around, warming themselves. Flannery was manning the desk just as he had been all the days prior.

O'Neill nodded to the men around the stove, and then turned his attention to the work at hand. Personal thoughts of his own loss drifted away. Single-minded concentration on doing what needed to be done took control.

"Do we have any kind of a head count of our own men?" O'Neill asked Flannery.

"Not really," Flannery admitted. "I've got a list of the injured in the hospital and the dead as far as we've been able to identify."

"For now we'll just worry about trying to identify our own boys. Is there a passenger or two that are able to help with the other bodies?" O'Neill did not relish the idea of trying to convince an injured passenger to stare at the faces of the dead. "If not, we'll leave the passengers to the coroner."

"Been steering clear of the hurt passengers, sir. Thought it best to leave them alone," Flannery admitted. "Sherlock and his missus have been tending to them. Mrs. Miles, too."

"But we have no idea who or how many are still missing, correct?" O'Neill pressed.

"No, not really."

"I want you to get over to the hospital and talk to the plow conductors. I need to know who was on those trains," O'Neill ordered. "Going to need to do the same with the passengers, but we'll have to be careful there. Get a list of our men for now, Mr. Flannery."

"Have any sacks of mail been recovered?" O'Neill continued, not letting Flannery leave.

"Two, sir. They're right here under the desk where we can watch them." Flannery motioned to where they were stacked.

"Very good. I understand some post office officials are on their way up here. I want to make sure they are given everything they need to salvage the mail."

"How many injured men are there?" O'Neill inquired next.

"Hold on," Flannery answered, shuffling through his papers. "Here's the list—believe there are fourteen, sir."

"And injured passengers?" O'Neill added, taking the paper from Flannery.

"They're listed there as well, sir," Flannery said. "Eight if I remember right."

God, less than two dozen alive. No hope of finding anymore survivors, that's for damned sure.

He unbuttoned his overcoat and reached inside for a cigar. Placing it to his lips, he realized he had forgotten his matches down at Scenic.

"Damn it," he muttered. He turned to the men still at the stove. "Any of you boys got a light?"

Back out in the falling snow, O'Neill went directly to where the men were digging. He carefully surveyed the hillside, and for a second time, tried to imagine how the slide hit, where the cars might have landed.

Impossible to coordinate an organized effort, O'Neill thought. *Trying to find a needle in a haystack.*

He came upon the men working in a large hole. With shovels and axes, they were removing what appeared to be portions of the motor house.

"Any sign of bodies here?" O'Neill asked.

"Not yet, sir," a section man answered.

"I want you men to fan out further west and down the hill. I doubt there is anything here," claimed O'Neill.

"If you say so, sir. It's just, well, sir, we were thinking your car might be buried near here," the man replied, trying to justify the actions of his men.

"I understand. Right now we need to concentrate on locating the passenger and mail cars," O'Neill countered.

Poor Earl, Lewis and Art. Gonna have to wait to be found. Gotta dig out that goddamned mail. They'd probably understand, O'Neill silently lamented.

He continued down the slope to a large group of men. As he neared, he began to recognize a few of the faces: Rich Chambers, Bob Meath, and Pete Imberg, among others. O'Neill reached for a shovel stuck in the snow and pulled it out.

"Hold on!" Meath shouted. "Put that shovel back right where it was!"

Confused, O'Neill did as he was told. He slid his way down and joined the men.

"Oh, it's you, Mr. O'Neill," Meath said. "Sorry, didn't mean to holler at you. We need to keep those shovels out there where they're at. Using them for markers, sir."

"I see, portions of a car exposed, I assume?" O'Neill replied.

"Not exactly," Imberg mumbled. The rest of the crew had stopped work.

"We sunk poles, shovels, whatever we could find, anyplace there was blood on the snow," Meath explained, his voice somber and quiet. "When it started snowing again we worked the night marking the spots before they got covered up."

So that's how they are doing it. Following a trail of blood into the side of the hill. O'Neill suddenly had to sit down.

"It's tough business, Mr. O'Neill. Tough business," Meath admitted.

Get your mind clear, O'Neill told himself. *Get to work.*

"I'm assuming you're following a blood trail here?" O'Neill asked, trying to be as matter-of-fact as possible.

"Yes sir," Imberg replied, having gone back to digging.

"Any sign of the mail train?" O'Neill continued, now swinging an ax at a large partially- exposed fir log.

"Not yet," Meath admitted. "Mostly we're finding parts of the passenger coaches, the sleepers. We're figuring the passenger train landed on top of the mail train. I'm afraid it's smashed at the bottom of the heap."

Two sacks up at the station. Came off 25's first-class car, O'Neill reckoned.

An hour's worth of hard chopping on the part of O'Neill and Chambers allowed the men to roll aside a large portion of the log blocking their way. The snow had become packed so hard, O'Neill continued to swing his ax to loosen it up for the shovelers.

Once again the snow turned red.

"Jesus, go easy with those axes," Chambers warned.

Carefully the red snow was scraped away. Splinters of wood began to show.

Car decking, O'Neill realized.

What began as a tiny spot was now becoming a frozen sea of red. O'Neill's stomach was turning. He looked at the other men, all the while scraping away the crimson snow with the bit of his ax. They seemed to be blinded to the sight.

It was Meath who reached behind a log and produced a bottle of whiskey.

"Here, sir, take a good hard drink," he offered. "You can sack us all if you want, but this is the only way we've been able to face it."

Standing in snow, red with the blood of their brothers, the men passed the bottle. They gave O'Neill the honor of taking the first drink.

"Better have another," Imberg advised.

Light-headed from the quick, hard drinks, O'Neill went back to work. The sleeve of a work coat emerged, a frozen, purple hand jutting from its cuff. Slowly, more snow was removed. The body was lying face down, the torso bent over what appeared to be another log below. The side of the man was impaled with splinters of wood from the car.

Meath took another drink, then climbed alongside the corpse. One by one, he removed the wood daggers.

Car must be further up the hill, O'Neill thought, trying to occupy his mind with something other than the gruesome sight in front of him. *Poor fellow, slide sent him right out the side. God be with his soul.*

"Can you tell who it is, Bobby?" Chambers asked.

"Give me a hand. We'll lift him out. Froze stiff," Meath replied.

It was awkward. The men were crowded into the small hole dug out around the corpse. They tried to be gentle at first, but the body would not yield. The slide seemed intent on not giving up its dead easily.

"I guess there's no point in treating him like he's alive," O'Neill finally said.

The men said nothing, but with the next effort, each pulled up as hard as they could. The doubled-over remains came free. Placing the body on its side, they were able to look at the face.

His eyes were closed. His lips were drawn. It was as if he were sound asleep. It was John Paryzbok.

"Oh Johnny, Johnny," Imberg moaned, brushing away a tear. "God be with you, my friend."

"He never woke up," Meath observed. "Lucky that way, I guess."

Chambers scrambled out of the hole. He grabbed a blanket and laid it out on the snow. The men boosted the body out, and with some difficulty, managed to stretch the torso flat. His watch, with the initials "J. P." engraved, dangled from his pocket, the hands forever frozen at 1:43.

Parzybok was wrapped in the blanket and tied up in a neat bundle. Imberg produced a scrap of paper and a pencil and wrote "John Paryzbok" in bold letters, slipping it under one of the ropes. Three section men tied another length of rope to the corpse, and then around their waists. Leaning hard into the slope of the hill, they pulled him away.

The crew seemed at a loss as to what needed to be done next. O'Neill himself was unsure.

"Keep digging here?" he finally asked.

"Either that or start tunneling in where we've got another spot marked," Chambers suggested.

"You men pick the next spot and start working," O'Neill ordered, trying to shake off the image of Parzybok. "I'm going to organize some crews to come in behind and continue working these spots where bodies have already found. Eventually all these holes everybody's digging will open up together. Should be able to start seeing what's laying where."

For the rest of the day, O'Neill roamed the hillside, organizing the men into crews. Each crew was given a specific area in which to work, with a specific job to perform. Roadmaster McIntyre and his crew bosses, Harley and Bergstrom, oversaw the progress and kept the men on task. The work was slow and yielded few results, but as night began to fall, O'Neill felt satisfied that progress was being made.

It was nearly dark when O'Neill returned to the depot. He swallowed hard and walked past the station to the section house. Inside were rows of bodies, each wrapped in a blanket, some soaked with blood. He did not count.

"Make way!" someone shouted.

O'Neill stepped aside and allowed three men to pull another body inside. They left the body next to that of Parzybok. O'Neill knelt down and looked at the name written on a Western Union form. "J. L. Pettit."

"Poor Pettit. Faithful to his charges to the very end."

O'Neill rose back up. He took off his hat and crossed himself.

March 3, 1910, 12:30 p.m.
William Harrington, Assistant Trainmaster

Tumbling! Over and over! Snow. Everywhere, snow! Noise. Wood shattering. Loud roar! Quiet. Oh God, screams! My boys!

"Help! Help! We're trapped!"

Gotta help my boys! Can't move!

"Help, Bill! For God sakes! Help us, Bill!"

Can seem them. Benny, Lou, Al! Can't move! Can't help!

"Can't you see us, Bill? We're dying!"

See them. Their eyes! Wide open! Got to move! Got to get to my boys! Legs, arms! Won't move! Got to try!

Harrington's head jerked up from his pillow. He was wrapped tight in his blanket. A sense of panic was racing through his body. His side was throbbing. Beads of sweat dripped from his forehead, his body felt hot and sticky. Blinking his eyes, it took a moment to gather his wits. Dropping back down onto the pillow, he tried to calm himself.

Just a dream. That damned dream again. The same damned dream. My boys. Dying. And I just stand there.

The first light of morning was coming through the window. It would be a while yet before the doctors and nurses would be stirring. Harrington lay on his back, not allowing himself to fall back asleep.

Later in the day, the sight of men bringing stacks of clothes and pairs of shoes into the bunkhouse was the incentive Harrington needed to sit up in his bed. Apart from a few painful trips to the privy, he had stayed flat on his back for the last two days. He did not want to see anyone. He did not want to talk.

Try as he might, he remembered little about what happened. He could remember the lightning. He was not sure if it was the roar of the thunder he recalled, or the roar of the slide the moment it hit his car. It all blurred together.

He remembered gentle hands cleaning his face and wrapping his cut head, but he wasn't sure who it was. He recalled waking up after the first of the nightmares, in severe pain. Ira Clary and Sam Duncan were at his side.

"Easy, Bill, easy," Clary was saying.

Each time he woke, Harrington would look around the room, taking stock of the men who were lying about injured. Each time another person was brought in, he would try to focus his eyes and see who it was that had survived. By the end of the first day, when no others arrived, he knew the loss of life was far worse than he had prayed.

Harrington fell back into a restless sleep that first night, waking up in pain whenever he moved. Two days slipped by and Harrington was not sure where they had gone. When Clary, Nelson or any of the other less injured would come his way, Harrington would close his eyes and pretend he was asleep.

What's there to say? What's to talk about? We're alive. The rest are dead. That's that.

Al, Benny, Arch, even Art, all gone. Never really made peace with Blackburn. Now he's gone. Was a good man, goddamn it. Treated him like shit. All were good men. Now they're goddamned dead.

Sherlock's wife Althea had forced Harrington to eat a bowl of stew the night before. Twice she had changed the dressings on his head and foot. It occurred to him that the gentle hands he recalled cleaning him up were probably hers. Even Sherlock seemed to be making himself useful, Harrington noticed. He was continually running errands, keeping the stove hot, and helping his wife and the doctors.

Might have to change my mind about him, too, Harrington decided.

"Finally sitting up, Mr. Harrington, that's good to see." Once again the petite form of Althea Sherlock was next to his bed. "You need to eat some lunch. They somehow managed to pack in eggs without breaking them. We'll have plates of fried eggs and bacon as soon as Mr. Sherlock brings them up from the cookhouse."

"Are those clothes for us?" Harrington asked.

"Why, yes, they are. Donated by the good people in Everett, I believe," Mrs. Sherlock answered. "Tell me your sizes and I'll see if I can find you something to wear."

Somehow Harrington had been shed of his bloodied nightshirt and was wearing a clean one that obviously belonged to someone else. It was another of the details of the past two days Harrington could not recall.

Need to put on just regular clothes, Harrington decided.

A small dressing room had been partitioned off from the main dormitory using ropes and blankets. Stiff from being in bed so long, Harrington struggled to move. His ribs were now tightly wrapped, making him continually short of breath. He hobbled across the room, careful not to put his full weight on his cut foot. Clary and Purcell were sitting on the edges of their cots, watching him inch across the room.

"Good to see you up and about, Bill," Purcell finally said.

"How you boys doing?" is all Harrington could muster.

"Tolerable, Bill," Purcell answered.

"Alive, Bill, I'm goddamned alive," Clary chimed in.

"Take more than a damned slide to take me out," added Nelson, getting up from his bed.

Duncan Tegtmeier was laying on his side. Obviously in pain, he motioned to Harrington, and slowly sat up.

"Can you get word to Irv that I'm okay? Can you do that for me, Bill?" he whispered.

"Sure Dunc, sure, I'll get it done," Harrington replied. He gently patted his shoulder.

"Here you go, Mr. Harrington, these should do the trick. You can change behind those blankets," Mrs. Sherlock directed him.

A fresh set of clothes on his back, his sore feet in an oversized pair of shoes, and a platter of eggs under his belt, Harrington began to feel a little of his energy return. He waited for the doctors to go into the back room where the injured women were recovering.

"I'm headed out," he told the men. "Anyone want to come with?"

"Been banging around a little too much today, Bill. My back

and leg are starting to hurt. Best stay here a bit longer," Purcell told Harrington.

"I'll come with you," Clary volunteered.

The two men limped out the door. The wind had died down, but wet snow was still falling.

So sick of snow, Harrington thought.

"Finally blew itself out, Bill," Clary said. "Snow and no wind. A week ago today we were over at Cascade busting the trains loose in that damnable blizzard. Figured we had her licked. Remember that, Bill?"

"God, what a mess," is all Harrington could say.

He was looking at the hill the slide had come down. Panning his eyes across the white field, he watched the army of workers digging in the canyon below. For the first time, he saw the aftermath, and he stood staring at the scene almost in awe.

"Not a goddamned sign of them is there, Ira. It's like the goddamned trains were never there. Like the whole railroad was never even here. Look at that, Ira. We plowed night and day for a week and it's like we were never even here."

"Guess the road's shut down clear to Nippon. Heard tell Dowling ain't even this side of the loop yet," Clary added.

The two men limped along the path worn into the deep drifts. Harrington could not take his eyes off the field of snow stretching down the mountainside.

"How is it we lived, Ira? Can you answer me that?" he asked.

"Don't know, Bill, just care that I did. Just wasn't our time." Clary snapped. "You gotta quit thinking about such. You'll go stark raving mad."

It was the sight of the bodies, neatly tied in bundles, laying side by side under the eaves of the station that finally drove the scope of the tragedy deep into Harrington's mind. He wanted to read the names on those that had been identified, but he knew his body could not perform the simple task of bending over. For a long time he stared at the lifeless figures.

"They keeping a list, Ira?" Harrington finally asked.

"Will's got one inside, so I've been told. Ain't seen it," admitted Clary.

"I need to see it. I gotta know."

Harrington walked around the bodies. Both men helped each other step over two corpses that were near the station door.

Gotta find out what's happened to my boys. Harrington could feel himself slowly choking with emotion and guilt. He turned his head away and followed Clary into the depot.

"Bill! Good to see you up and about." O'Neill was standing over Flannery, a slight smile on his lips. "You're just in time. We've got a wire up. I need you and Clary there to help me. Brown wants to know the position of the plows. Sent a message earlier, but I think I got it all wrong. Getting too damned tired to think straight. Now you had the double over at Gaynor?"

"No, I left the single, the 801, over at Gaynor," Harrington told O'Neill, a little surprised by the confusion. "Had two pushers, but just the 801."

"The double is out west here. Damn it I knew that! Stupid mistake on my part. Told Brown the double was at Gaynor stalled. No matter. Flannery, we on line?"

"Appear to be, sir," Flannery answered.

"Good, hang on and we'll get a status report out right away. We'll call it a supplement to the one I sent along to Scenic with that sectionman earlier," O'Neill told Flannery.

"Mr. Harrington, here's a list of the bodies we've identified." O'Neill handed him a sheet of paper. He grabbed another from the desk. "And this is a list of men we know are missing. Finally, here is a sheet of all the men we know to be safe, injured or otherwise. I need you and Mr. Clary to look over each list and see if there are any names of men you knew were here that haven't been accounted for, yet."

"Yes sir," they answered.

Both men sat in chairs near the stove. Harrington gave Clary the list of the injured and those who were safe. It was the death list he had to see.

Pettit, Lindsay, Parzybok, Dan Gilman, Ben Jarnigan—Harrington put the list on his lap. *Not Ben, not Benny.*

The next name nearly brought Harrington to tears. Lou Ross. *Benny and Lou, both gone. Dupy and Dougherty not listed. Neither are Patty Kelly or Bill Kenzal.*

"They got Al and Arch down as missing?" Harrington asked, his voice barely audible.

Clary looked over his list.

"Yeah, Al's here. God, both Dupy and MacDonald are still missing. So's Frank Martin," Clary said. "Art's still missing, so is Longcoy."

"You'll be interested to know, Bill, the eastside rotary is west of Merritt, but they've hit a huge slide," O'Neill interrupted, reading a message that had just come across the wire. "Even if you had made Merritt, you couldn't have bucked that slide and gotten back here in time. The trains would have stayed right where they were no matter."

O'Neill put down the messages and looked straight at Harrington.

"Do you understand what I'm saying? All of us did everything we possibly could have."

Harrington looked back at the list of the dead. He felt alone, guilty for living. *Just want to get outta Wellington. Out of these damned mountains for good.*

"Can't think of anyone else that you haven't got written down on one of these lists," Harrington finally said. He handed the sheets to Clary. "How about you, Ira?"

Clary looked at the names of the dead. Harrington could tell the tough little Irishman was shaken as well.

"Guess not," Clary mumbled.

Harrington struggled to rise from his chair. Flannery sprinted from his desk. He rummaged around in the back room and produced a cane and handed it Harrington.

"Here you go, Bill. If you're going to be walking around, use this." Flannery smiled and gave the men a wink.

Using the cane, Harrington limped across the room, Clary following behind. They paused at the desk.

"Duncan Tegtmeier asked if you could somehow tell Irving he's alright, Mr. O'Neill. Wondering if you could get word down to Everett that I'm alright, long as you're at it. My wife, she can work herself into a fret at times."

"It's been taken care of, Bill," O'Neill reassured him between puffs of his cigar. "You look tired, both of you. Appreciate your help. You'd better get on back before those doctors have my ass in a sling."

Outside, men were pulling Alaskan dog sleds into town. Harrington overheard them discussing how many men it would take to load a single body and trail it out to Windy Point.

"They'll get the dead outta here before the living," Harrington dryly commented to Clary.

"More of them than us," Clary answered.

Harrington stopped and looked back at the slide.

"Having the same bad dream each night," Harrington confessed, his voice cracking with emotion. "I can see the boys trapped, calling for help. I can't move. Can't do nothing to help. They're screaming, dying, and *I can't do a damned thing!*"

"We all got the melancholy, Bill," Clary replied. "I ain't slept worth a shit either. You got to believe it'll pass. If you don't, it'll drive you mad, Bill. Let it pass."

"Just want to get out of here," Ira. Get back home, see Lil and the kids. Just want all of this behind me."

Clary had no answer, no words of encouragement. The two men walked back to the bunkhouse in silence.

A plate of hot ham and potatoes was waiting for him when he sat back down on his bed. Duncan Tegtmeier caught his attention, and Harrington nodded. Relieved, the injured man laid back down.

Guess I did one good deed today, Harrington thought as he ate.

Supper eaten, Harrington pulled off the borrowed shoes and stretched out on the bed. His back against the wall, he took a close look around the room. The two Negro porters were off by themselves, segregated in the far corner of the room. They were in temporary bunks set up the furthest from the heating stove. Even the male passengers were separated from the railroad men. At different times, Harrington caught them looking his way. Whether it was true or not he convinced himself the survivors of Train 25 were staring at him. *Bastards. Blaming me and the boys for all of this.*

Bored and lonesome, Harrington slid down in his bed. For a long time he stared at the ceiling. One of the nurses from the Scenic Hotel came around and checked the dressing on his head.

"How are you feeling this evening?" she asked, her voice bright and cheery. "You want that bandage changed before you nod off?"

"Fine, everything's fine," Harrington mumbled. Thinking he was unduly short with the woman, he added, "Thank you, ma'am. But I am fine."

He watched the room slowly grow dark as evening overtook the mountains. It was the prospect of another long night he dreaded the most.

I can see their faces. Al, that derby he was so proud of. Big dumb farm-boy grin. Oh Lord, do you know how much I'm going to miss all of them? Dupy, always with a plug in his cheek. Spitting everywhere. A bittersweet smile crossed his lips.

They're gone. I'm here. Cuss you Lord. Do nothing but take your name in vain. Hate going to church and here I am. The dark shadows crossing the room entered Harrington's thoughts. *I'm still here. Let me sleep Lord. Just let me sleep in peace.*

Sleep came to Harrington, but he did not rest.

March 4, 1910, 4:00 a.m.
John Robert Meath, Engineer

Meath settled into the familiar seat box of the X-800. He had just finished making his rounds, checking the fire and water level on the 1128 and the plow where he now sat dozing. Since the slide, the crews had divided the responsibility of tending the stalled double set. Each crew of two put in a twelve-hour shift. Tonight, Pete Imberg had come out with Meath to watch over the trailing plow and its pusher.

In order to keep helping with the digging, Meath volunteered to handle the night shifts. Each night he would take an alarm clock out with him. Setting it every two hours, he would try and sleep in-between tending the fires.

It was raining again. His legs stretched out, his arms folded on his chest, he listened to the drops strike the plow's window. The noise brought to mind the showers sweeping across the fields back home, drumming against the window of the bedroom he shared with his brothers.

Old-timer back home. Fought in the Civil War. Tell us stories about the battles, Meath remembered. *What I've seen, not much different from the stories he told trying to scare us. Now I can scare the hell out of him.*

He tried to erase from his mind the gore they had been uncovering. Opening his eyes, he shook his head in a vain attempt to clear his mind. Even in sleep, he was being tormented by the sites he had witnessed.

The day before, he had walked by a group of men as they uncovered the body of the interurban motorman Meath had spoken to at Bailets. The man was kind to him, Meath recalled. He told the diggers the man had a daughter. Her body had to be close by. He joined the crew searching for the girl. The child's broken body was found an hour later, not far from where her father had come to rest.

"You keep these two together," Meath ordered the men as they wrapped the bodies. "Can't remember the man's name, but the little girl is his daughter. Her name's Thelma."

It was no secret that Meath was not going to rest until Al Dougherty had been found. By the end of the first day, Meath knew that Dougherty was not alive. By the end of the second day, he only hoped that his friend's death had been swift and painless. He prayed the body was not ripped and broken like so many they were finding.

I know he's gone, Meath thought. *Ain't going to give up looking until I know he's heading home.*

The nights out on the plow were hard for Meath. He was torn between wanting to get away from the carnage, and the desire to locate his friend. He wanted to be the one to find Dougherty, yet he thought it might be best to see only a tag of paper on a brown-checkered blanket.

Bob Ford was shaking Meath's shoulder.

"Wake up, Bobby. Me and Will Courtney will take over."

Yawning and stretching, Meath rose from the seat box.

"Still raining, Bob?" Meath asked.

"Like a bastard. Diggers didn't do much last night. Afraid of another slide with all this rain. O'Neill and McIntrye decided to pay them twenty cents an hour plus give them their board, just so they'll go back to work this morning," Ford reported.

Meath joined Imberg and began the hike back up to Wellington. The two men had little to say.

"Wonder when we'll get 'em all out?" Imberg finally asked.

"Don't know. Still haven't got our way down to 27. Snow's settling and melting some. Helps," Meath answered.

"You going up for a bite of breakfast?" Imberg questioned.

"Maybe later. Going down to see how the digging is going first," Meath decided out loud.

Before leaving for plow duty the day before, Meath thought he saw the remains of a mail car's sliding door underneath some timber he was chopping. He returned to the same spot. Men were just arriving from breakfast and beginning to work. Once again Rich Chambers and John Pettit were at his side, swinging axes and shoveling snow.

"Heard they found your cousin, John," Meath said. "Sorry to hear he died."

"Joe was a good man," Pettit remarked. "Has a fair-sized family he's leaving behind. Gonna make it tough."

"Newspaper guys are making him out to be a real hero," Chambers added. "He deserves it. He did one hell of a job with those passengers, from what I hear."

The men spent a couple of hours hacking through two more large logs. With the help of the section men, Meath and Chambers rolled sections of the timber aside. A tangled mat of broken tree limbs still covered what appeared to be a portion of the side of a mail car. Meath climbed down below the bucked logs, chopping at the tree limbs and handing the pieces up to the others.

"It's definitely a mail car door," Meath called up as he worked. "Can't tell if there's anything under it."

Meath pulled at a few more limbs, cracking them off by hand. His heart in his throat, he reached down and pulled at the door. Pettit jumped down and pried with his shovel. Squatting down, Meath got his hands underneath and held it long enough for Pettit to do likewise.

"On three, John," Meath puffed. "One. Two. Three!"

The men lifted with all their strength. The door broke free of the remaining limbs and snow. In a swift, continuous movement, they lifted the door over their heads and cast it aside. Then they turned to see what was underneath.

In the snow was a crushed derby. There was a sudden silence. Squatting down, Meath carefully picked up the hat.

"Is it Al's?" Pettit asked nearly in a whisper.

Meath knew that Dougherty kept his home address tucked in the inner band. "Now you'll know where to send me in case I get killed," Dougherty often joked. He would periodically write it out on a new piece of paper, if the other was getting faded and smudged from sweat. Reshaping the hat, Meath ran his finger under the worn leather. A slip of paper fell out. On it, "A.J. Dougherty, Waverly, Minn." was written.

"Yeah, it's Al's," Meath answered.

"Don't mean shit though," Pettit replied. "Slide could have taken it anywhere. No telling where Al is."

Here. Close by. Can feel it, Meath thought. *Found your hat. Where the hell are you?*

"Want to keep digging here, Bobby?" Chambers asked.

Meath poked at the packed snow that was beneath the door. He felt his shovel hit something pliable. "There's something under here," he called out.

Working together, Meath and Pettit scraped away the dirty snow.

Go slow, Meath cautioned himself.

"Whatever it is, sure is soft," Pettit noticed.

A final swipe with their shovels revealed two mail sacks. Still intact, their drawstrings closed, they appeared to be undamaged.

"Mail sacks." Meath called out. "Give us a hand and we'll boost them out."

They began to shovel away the remainder of the snow entombing the sacks. Meath sunk his shovel under one of the canvas bags to pry it free. Pulling his shovel out to get another bite, he saw a tattletale covering of red snow on the tip of the spade.

"There's bodies under there, John," Meath warned.

Each man grabbed onto the drawstring of a bag and wiggled it free. Underneath it they could see scraps of clothing. Hands shaking, Meath and Pettit pitched the second sack aside.

It was Pettit who saw it first. He pushed Meath back, trying to block his view.

"Don't look, Bobby!" he hollered.

Meath ignored the warning and stepped around Pettit. At his feet, face down, was the crushed skull of a man. Meath dropped to his knees and slowly began to brush the blood soaked snow from the rest of the body. The man's coat and shirt were in shreds. Like so many of the bodies Meath had seen in the last few days, this man had been impaled multiple times as the walls of the car in which he slept exploded when struck by the weight of the snow. His left arm was badly broken, twisted behind his back at a grotesque angle. Another log was across the back of his legs, preventing the men from turning the body over.

"Give me that ax, John," Meath ordered.

On his knees, he straddled the dead man's legs and began to carefully whittle at the log.

"It's Al, ain't it, Bobby," Pettit said, his voice cracking.

"We found him," is all Meath could say, his back to the men. If he had turned to face them, they would have seen the rain falling from the sky mixing with the sweat from his forehead and tears from his eyes. His rhythmic swings of his ax were all that kept sobbing spasms from overpowering him.

Up at the depot. Me the judge, you the prosecutor. Springing that turkey caper on Sherlock and Bailets. Remember that Al? That shit-eating grin of yours. Love ya like a brother. Gonna miss ya, brother.

Meath continued to chop at the logs binding his friend.

If you're in your heaven God, please, please have his eyes closed when we roll him over, Meath silently prayed.

The last fir limb chopped free, Meath threw the ax aside.

"Okay, Johnny, let's roll him over and lift him outta here," Meath sighed, wiping his face.

They carefully lifted the body from the snow and laid it on its back. The face was badly disfigured with cuts and from the fierce blow that the dead man had taken to the head. The man's mouth was closed. It looked to Meath as if his lips were in a slight, even peaceful smile. The man's eyes were shut.

"Let's get him out of here," Meath said, his voice quivering. "Time to take Al home."

March 5, 1910, 11:00 a.m.
Basil Sherlock, Telegrapher

A sheet of paper on the kitchen table and fountain pen in hand, Sherlock sat gazing out the small front window of his cottage. The sun would break through the clouds, if only for fleeting moments, sending shafts of light into the room. Althea was back in their bedroom, sound asleep. The doctors and nurses from Everett had taken over the responsibilities of caring for the injured in the bunkhouse, finally allowing Sherlock and his wife to go home. Althea, who had been working night and day, was exhausted.

Sherlock yawned. With the telegraph wire back up, he had returned to his usual four-to-midnight shift. O'Neill had been battling with the news reporters who were trying to send their accounts over the line, claiming the telegraph line was tenuous at best and needed to be kept clear for railroad messages. Compromising, he agreed to give the newspapermen a block of time in the evening to send out their stories. That job fell on Sherlock and third trick man, "Mississippi" Avery.

"I've had it with this place," he had told Althea when he arrived home from his shift the previous night. "When I get up tomorrow, I'm writing my letter of resignation."

"Sleep on it, dear," is all his wife said. She pulled the quilt over her shoulders and went to sleep.

No telling when we'll be able to get out of this hell, Sherlock realized, *but by damned I'm going to get a replacement coming.*

For Sherlock, the last straw was the bodies lined up across the front of the station. Just to get into the depot, he had to make his way around the wrapped corpses. The previous night, a small bundle had been placed directly in front of the door. It was obviously the body of a child. The sight convinced Sherlock he had to leave.

He penned the date across the head of the page, paused, then simply wrote:

"To: Mr. James O'Neill, Supt. Cascade Division

Sir,

I, Basil J. Sherlock, am hereby notifying you of my intent to resign the position of 2nd trick operator Wellington, Washington, effective immediately."

Sherlock reread the simple note.

Can't just up and leave. No way out of here. Might throw us out of our house. Say good riddance, Sherlock concluded. *Best to soften the blow a bit.*

He added the line, "I will perform my duties until such time a replacement can found."

Sherlock signed the letter.

Althea came from their room. She poured herself a cup of hot water out of the pot Sherlock had simmering on their cook stove. She brushed back her hair and sat opposite her husband. She quietly stared at the steaming cup, steeping a blend of tea.

"Wrote your letter, I see," she commented, sipping at her tea. "Guess I need to start packing our things."

"No real hurry, we're not going anywhere soon, that's for certain," Sherlock replied.

"So where are you taking me next?" she asked.

"Let's go back home, Althea. Iowa, maybe Illinois would suit me just fine. Some place where there are no mountains and the snow doesn't slide," Sherlock said.

"A different kind of place up here. We never really fit in, did we, Basil. Tight circles of people, hard to break in and be a part. You understand, Basil?"

"Those men gave me nothing but grief down at the depot," Sherlock replied. He paused and looked at his wife. Once again the vision of the bodies flashed through his mind. "They gave me grief, but they were good-enough sorts. I won't miss this place, but I'll miss of few of the men."

Althea, tea cup in hand, walked across the room and stared across the canyon.

"These mountains can be beautiful. Christmas this year was lonely, but it was beautiful. Remember how it was, Basil? Clear, cold, the snow, those mountains," her voice trailed off.

"Those God-forsaken mountains are damned ugly now though, aren't they," snapped Sherlock.

"It's not the mountains that's ugly right now. God's the one who's ugly."

"Althea! That's blasphemy." Sherlock scolded.

It was as if she had not heard him. Althea turned and calmly strolled back to the table. She set her cup down. Circling behind Sherlock, she flopped her arms over his shoulders and leaned forward, reading the short letter.

"You're right, Mr. Sherlock," she admitted. "We need to get out of here. I want to go someplace that God hasn't forsaken."

His letter of resignation neatly folded and tucked in his breast pocket, Sherlock left early for work. Not sure where O'Neill might be, he wanted to make sure the letter was in his hands today.

The sooner I get this behind me the better, Sherlock thought.

The scene around the section house and depot was the same as it had been the past two days. Rows of bodies were still lined across the platform. Workers were loading some onto sleds for the trip west out to Windy Point, where they were lowered to Scenic. The news reporters that Sherlock had quickly come to despise were milling about, trying to get quotes from anyone who would talk. Sherlock had even heard *The Seattle Times* was making Althea out to be somewhat of a heroine.

Hear tell they make it sound like she did it all, Sherlock secretly pouted. *Guess my name isn't even mentioned.*

Sherlock popped his head in the door.

"You're early, Sherlock," Flannery said, somewhat surprised. "Want to get a head start on the newspaper wires?"

"Where's Mr. O'Neill?" Sherlock asked, ignoring Flannery's jibe.

"Out along the slide somewhere, I think," Flannery responded. "Guess they still haven't found his car."

His nerves on edge, Sherlock walked down to the scene. He hadn't really been there since the night it all happened. Cooped up in the bunkhouse, running errands for Althea and the doctors, he hardly had a chance to glance at the aftermath.

Warmer temperatures and the rain triggered a slow melt. A jungle of trees was starting to emerge, as well as bits and pieces of the destroyed cars. Pockets of men were swarming at various points along the hillside like ants attracted to a fallen crumb of a picnic lunch. Sherlock surveyed the scene, finally spotting O'Neill pacing near the spot once occupied by his private car.

Terrible time to talk to him, Sherlock admitted to himself. *Trying to find his own car. Have to tell him my intentions.*

Sherlock pulled the letter out of his pocket. He wanted to have it in hand when he approached the superintendent. As he struggled up the slope, O'Neill turned and watched him approach.

"Good day, Mr. O'Neill. Nice to see a little sun, finally," greeted Sherlock.

"Mr. Sherlock. What brings you out here?" O'Neill asked.

Just tell him, Sherlock coached himself.

"Sir, well, my wife and I have been talking," he began. "And well sir, you know she's not happy here. Has had her fill she tells me. And well, sir, here …"

He held out the letter. O'Neill took the paper but did not unfold it or read its contents.

"It's my letter of resignation, sir."

There, said it, Sherlock thought, relieved.

"I see," is all that O'Neill said. He turned and looked back down into the canyon. "Still can't find my car. You realize that, Sherlock? A damned mystery. Longcoy, his mother and sister are in Everett right now waiting to hear of his fate. Blackburn's wife, Lewis' wife, all waiting and we can't find the damned thing!"

"Terrible sir, truly is." Sherlock looked away, not wanting to see O'Neill's expression.

"I'll wire Everett and get a replacement coming as soon as possible, Sherlock. Understand your missus did one hell of a job in the bunkhouse," O'Neill said, still looking down the slope. "You too, for that matter. I intend on making sure the higher-ups know."

"Thank you, sir. We just did what had to be done, I guess."

Embarrassed that I'm resigning, thought Sherlock. *No matter. Have to get out of here.*

"You will stay on until relieved?" O'Neill asked.

"Yes sir, of course, sir. Duty is duty and I'll do mine. Told the wife we couldn't leave right away," replied Sherlock.

"Very well." O'Neill walked away.

For a long time Sherlock watched him. He had a shovel. Every few steps he would stop and jab it into the snow. Sometimes he would even dig a hole before moving on.

Never find it way up here, Sherlock decided. *Slide took it clear to the bottom.*

Sherlock wandered back to the station. Although glad that O'Neill did not seem bothered by him quitting, deep down he felt guilty placing the reason all on Althea.

Easier just to say Althea wants out, Sherlock told himself, justifying his actions. *Less questions to answer.*

Stepping over the bodies near the door, Sherlock walked back into the depot. Flannery was receiving a message, a grin across his face.

"Good news" he said, as he finished deciphering the dots and dashes clicking from the telegraph.

"Got a report from Leavenworth. They got Harrington's set going. Took it back to Leavenworth. They're refueled and heading this way. Line's open to Gaynor. Bringing up some powder. Gonna blast their way through the slides."

"Any idea when they'll get this far?" Sherlock asked.

"No, not really, but they're on their way," answered Flannery.

On their way. Could be days, could be weeks. Who the hell knows? Sherlock thought.

"So what's doing on this side?" inquired Sherlock, hoping the plows were closer.

"Last I heard, Dowling busted the hell out of the 808. That plow from the NP has things opened up about to Corea, so Dowling took his rig back to Delta to get it fixed. I guess there's talk about bringing up some powder monkeys to do some blasting on this side too," Flannery explained.

"Gonna take forever to get out of here," Sherlock pouted aloud.

"So what's your hurry?" asked Flannery.

"I just handed my resignation to Mr. O'Neill, that's my hurry. Sick of this place, well, my wife certainly is. We want out," admitted Sherlock.

"The hell you say!" Flannery said, somewhat surprised.

"I'll stay on duty until a replacement shows up. Until we can get the hell outta here. But as soon as we can get packed and get out, we are, by damned," asserted Sherlock.

"Well, if the missus ain't happy, guess I can't blame you. Been one hell of a week, that's for certain," Flannery allowed. "Guess none of us will ever forget any of this."

"Might try to forget some of it, but probably won't ever be able to," Sherlock added. "How can you forget having dead bodies laid out in front of the station like stacks of packages needing to be loaded on the next train?"

There was silence in the room. Sherlock wandered over and took his cup off the hook and poured himself a cup of coffee, just as he had done countless times in the past six months.

"Need to get these updates out to O'Neill. You want to, Basil?" Flannery asked.

"Not really. I'll watch the key if you want to," Sherlock offered.

"Good man." Flannery put on his coat and slipped out the door.

Settled into the chair, Sherlock rocked back and drank his coffee.

Was a part of history, he pondered. *The stories we'll tell when we're old.*

Looking around the station he could once again hear the bursts of laughter on those nights when the men were gathered around. He recalled the tense anticipation amongst the men that something was going to happen whenever Meath and Dougherty were in town. The pranks, the jokes—even if they were sometimes aimed at him, Sherlock suddenly looked on them with fondness.

Will never see a crew like that together in one place again, Sherlock quietly reflected. *That's all changed. Dougherty's dead. Kelly, with that beautiful tenor voice, dead. Wonder if it'll ever be the same?*

Flannery came bursting through the door. Out of breath, his face was flushed.

"Found O'Neill's car," he panted.

"Where?" Sherlock asked.

"Funny thing," Flannery replied. "O'Neill told me it was just about where you two were standing. By the way, they've found the mail cars, too. They'll be bringing the sacks in here. Got some post office people here. Want to spread the mail out and dry it. You're gonna have one fun time tonight, Basil."

Sherlock got up from the chair and finished his coffee.

"I guess it could be worse," he told Flannery. "I swear, for as predictable as a railroad is supposed to be, this is the most unpredictable place I have ever been."

"Gonna miss it, ain't ya, Basil," smiled Flannery.

"Not at all. Not one little bit," Sherlock lied.

March 6, 1910, 8:00 p.m.
James Henry O'Neill, Superintendent

O'Neill walked alone, away from Wellington. With his car found, the bodies of Blackburn, Longcoy, and Walker had been recovered. He made sure they were sent out right away for Scenic. Walker never woke up--of that he was certain. It was the haunting faces of Longcoy and Blackburn that O'Neill could not shake from his mind.

They saw death coming, O'Neill thought. *Could see it in their faces. Trying to fight their way out. Horrible way to die. Goddamned reporters right there. Hope they have the good sense to keep that to themselves. Blackburn's wife, Earl's mother don't need to know everything. Need another man to replace Earl. Don't even want to think about replacing Lewis. Was one of a kind. Blackburn too. Harrington's not up to the job, yet.*

O'Neill was tired. He was tired of the circus generated by the press, tired of the demands of the railroad to control the information being reported, tired of the constant talk of liability, tired of seeing the bodies of his men stacked like cord wood around the station. He told Sherlock he was going to walk through the tunnel and sleep at Cascade Tunnel Station. He took a lantern and left.

The cut leading to the tunnel was completely plugged with snow. Driven by the wind, a snow drift nearly covered the portal, extending well inside the confines of the bore. Wading through the unbroken surface, O'Neill began to have second thoughts about the sense in his decision to leave Wellington to rest.

He slid down the back face of the drift into the tunnel, and landed in a pool of water. The snow outside had blocked the drainage ditches; another problem no one had considered.

Gonna be talk about why the train wasn't put here in the tunnel, O'Neill thought. *Second-guessing. Everybody's doing it. Gonna get worse. Putting that passenger train in here. Never crossed my mind. No reason it should have. Now looks damned obvious. Not obvious a week ago. Gonna spend the rest of my life explaining why.*

O'Neill walked in a tiny world of light. Darkness had long since descended on the mountains, turning even the tiny spot of light that normally shone bright at the far end of the tunnel to black. He relished the solitude.

Man needs to be alone sometimes. Time to think. Maybe sending Harrington east alone was a mistake. Could have plowed the upper yard and put the trains there. Could have, but I didn't. Just didn't know. How was I supposed to know?

Deep in the core of the mountain, the light from O'Neill's lantern reflected off icicles that had formed from water running down the soot-coated walls. They glistened briefly as he walked past, their radiance quickly passing into the murk of the tunnel.

Damned papers. Like to run the whole bunch out of town. Lawyers telling me to run information through that Underwood. Make sure he's telling our side of things. Don't trust the bastard. Running a big story on me today. King of the Snow Fighters, he says he's going to call me. Supposed to think it's a big honor. King of the Snow Fighters my ass. Ask Blackburn's or Pettit's widow if I'm the goddamned King of the Snow Fighters. Underwood. Dumb son of a bitch. Doesn't have a goddamned clue what happened up here. What we're going through.

Supposed to gather up all the telegrams. Lawyers want them all. Code book too. Lawyers running the railroad. Just want to get back to what I know. Running trains. Have to be in Seattle in a week. Testify at a coroner's inquest. Be just the start of it. Going to get our asses sued. Goddamned lawyers. Licking their chops.

Take the heat for all this. Keep the boys clear of the lawyers. Just did what they knew how to do. No right or wrong. We all just did what we had to. No choices. What the hell else could I have done?

Hold the trains in Leavenworth. Brown would have been all over my ass for holding the mail for no good reason. Passengers on 25 would have been screaming to high heaven for being stuck. Was no reason to hold them. Had things under control. Four plows running.

Fresh air was streaming into the tunnel. It hit O'Neill's face. He breathed deep, filling his lungs with its crisp newness.

Tunnel would've killed them. Cut was plugged. Train would have been stuck in here in a matter of hours. Couldn't get food to them. Right answer was to hold them just where they were at. Safest place. The only safe place I knew. Didn't know I'd have to hold them there that long. People want to know why this happened. Nothing to do with the passing tracks at Wellington. That hillside above Shed 3.3. No one will understand. That's what killed all those people. That damned hill. Just couldn't keep that section clear long enough to get the trains by.

O'Neill walked out of the east portal of the tunnel. The skies over Cascade Tunnel Station were clear. Stars by the thousands cluttered the sky. He set his lantern down in the snow. Fumbling through his pockets for a cigar, he finally produced one, lighting it by the flame of the lamp. He took a couple of slow puffs, searching the sky for the Big Dipper and North Star, just as he did as a boy out on the Northern Plains.

Be a boy again. No cares. No worries. Be happy to be back on the gang. All you worry about is having enough brass to buy a bottle. Play a hand of cards. Make good money, the Old Billy Goat pays me well. Paying my dues this week.

The snow was loose. O'Neill was quickly up to his knees wading into the dim lights of the station. He could see where Harrington had bucked through the slide. In the muted light being cast off the snow he could see the remains of the cook house.

Slide here and the one that cut us off at Shed 2. Same kind of slide that took out the trains. Maybe I should've known. Just didn't know.

Staring at the remains of the cookhouse, O'Neill suddenly remembered the first of the casualties.

The two cooks. Forgot about those two souls. Must still be here. Need to get them over to Wellington and down the mountain. Terrible just to let them lie here. More death to deal with.

O'Neill paused at the station door, taking the last puffs on his cigar before tossing the still-smoking butt out into the snow. He strolled into the depot. The dozing operator quickly rocked forward in his chair, surprised to see the superintendent.

"Mr. O'Neill, sir," the man stammered, his face red with embarrassment. "Afraid you caught me napping. Quiet around here."

"Well, that's why I'm here. Want to do some napping in the quiet myself," O'Neill replied. "Are the bodies of the two cooks still here?"

"Yes sir," the man answered. "Out back in the snow."

"Your lines west are up, aren't they?" O'Neill quizzed.

"Ever since Wellington got back on line, we've been on line, sir. You need me to send something out?" inquired the operator.

"Yes, get a wire to Everett. We need to know what to do about the two dead men here," O'Neill ordered.

"I'll get right to it, sir. Haven't been over to Wellington. How bad is it, if you don't mind me asking?" the telegrapher wondered. "Been hearing bits and pieces. Sounds terrible."

"It's bad, son. Very bad. You saw what happened here. Multiply that by fifty. You understand what I'm saying. Multiply the two dead men here by fifty."

O'Neill walked into Harrington's office in the back.

"I'm going to bed down back here. Have the third trick man wake me around five. Need to be back at Wellington come first light. Good night, son."

"I'll take care of things, sir. You have yourself a good night's sleep," the young operator answered.

O'Neill set his lamp on the small desk in Harrington's office. The room was bare; the desk showed no signs of ever being used. Harrington was given the space more out of courtesy than necessity. O'Neill never once believed a man like Harrington would need an office, let alone use it. Still, there was a cot set up across the back wall, and it served as a good place to sleep if a person were stuck for a long period of time on the mountain.

Sitting on the edge of the bed, O'Neill kicked off his boots. He took off his suit coat and tossed it over the back of the desk chair.

His shirt collar loosened, O'Neill stretched out on the cot, his hands clasped behind his head. He looked blankly at the ceiling until his eyes became used to the dark. He could see vague details of the tongue-in-groove lumber and the chipped paint.

Was led into a trap, he thought. *You did it, Lord. You led us right into a trap. Ambush. Walked right into it. How do I explain to the widows, mothers, fathers that it was all a trap? Wonder if we'll ever be able to just tell the world what really happened? Did what we knew was right. Guess what was right wasn't enough.*

My fault, or yours, Lord?

Going to take that question with me to my grave.

March 7, 1910, 1:30 p.m.
William Harrington, Assistant Trainmaster

It was a ragtag group, strung out along the trail to Windy Point. Word had been spread among the men in the hospital that anyone able to walk to Scenic would be taken by train to Everett or Seattle that afternoon. A number of the less injured had little problem convincing the attending doctors that they were fit to make the trip. When a doctor balked at releasing Harrington, he rose from his cot and stared the man down. Grabbing his hand-me-down coat and cane, he limped towards the door.

"Like to see you stop me," he snarled.

On his way out of town, Harrington popped his head into the station, where O'Neill was standing over the desk. The railroad lawyer who had arrived earlier was seated next to Flannery, gathering up stacks of telegrams.

"If you have no objections, I'm going home on today's train, Mr. O'Neill," Harrington said.

"Of course not, none at all, Bill. Get yourself healed up as quickly as possible. I'm going to need you. Flannery, send a wire immediately to Everett. Have our office inform Mrs. Harrington that her husband is arriving this evening. Make that Priority," O'Neill ordered.

"I must be going as well," the lawyer said, stuffing the messages into a box. "Catching that same train. We will keep you informed of our plans for the inquest."

Harrington quickly excused himself and left the depot without saying another word.

Damned lawyers. Have no use for any of them, Harrington thought.

The skies had finally cleared and the sun produced a glare off the snow that kept Harrington squinting. By the time the injured reached the stalled plows, most were ready for a rest. Clary, Purcell and Duncan were standing opposite the 1128. Pete Imberg was leaning from the cab. Both Clary and Purcell rented rooms from Imberg and his wife, Gena Marie in Everett.

"Tell Gena I'm alive and I'll be home as soon as I shove Meath's sorry ass into Wellington," he was telling the group.

Boys snapping out of it, Harrington thought. *Maybe Ira's right. Maybe the melancholy will pass in time.*

Harrington was hobbling towards his friends when a familiar voice stopped him.

"Hey sailor, you lookin' for a good time?"

Meath was leaning against the doorway of the X-802. It had been a week since the two men had seen each other. What Harrington saw was a good friend who had gone through hell. Deep down, he knew Meath saw the same in him.

"Up yours, Bobby," Harrington said. "Besides, you're not my type."

With his usual agility, Meath leapt from the plow, landing on his feet next to Harrington.

"Finally heading home to Lil's loving arms, are you, Bill?" Meath asked.

"Headed home to an ass-chewing more like it," replied Harrington, hoping to disguise his longing for his wife and family. "I haven't wired her or anything until today. Have a notion I'm going to hear about it."

"Ah, bullshit. She loves you, Bill, and we both know it," Meath said.

The two men stood side by side in silence. They looked out across the Scenic Basin and scanned the jagged snow-covered peaks. A few stragglers, injured passengers, walked past.

"So when you heading home, Bobby?" Harrington finally asked.

"Oh, I'll stick it out until we get the line open. We seem to be short of crews all of a sudden. It's something I gotta do. See it out to the end. Anyway, ain't got nothing to go home to any more," Meath admitted. "What about you? You coming back or bidding out? Word is you're up to take Blackburn's place."

"I'll probably be back. Done being the 'Snow King.' You can bet your next pay on that," Harrington replied. "Not interested in Art's job, either. Nothing's been said to me and I ain't asking."

"Just ain't gonna be the same, is it, Bill," Meath sighed.

Harrington knew Meath was thinking of Dougherty. He leaned on Meath who in turn draped an arm across the broad shoulders of his friend.

"I got faith in you, Bobby. The day will come when we'll need the services of Judge Grogan. He'll show up again," Harrington predicted. There was another long silence. Each was lost in his own thoughts, bittersweet memories of friends now dead.

"I'd better get a move on, Bobby," Harrington finally said, amidst a long sigh. "Miss my train and Lillian will have my ass in a sling. You take care. Keep a sharp eye. Snow pack's far from set."

Cane in hand, Harrington began to walk away.

"You're the Snow King, Bill. Always will be!" Meath called out.

Without turning back, Harrington waved his cane in the air.

"Up yours, Bobby!" he shouted over his shoulder.

Best wheelman on the railroad, Harrington thought. *God help me, I do love that bastard.*

By the time Harrington arrived at the top of "Old Glory," the bulk of the party was gathered around the ropes strung down its slope. A pulley system had been set up and was being used to raise and lower the sleds bearing supplies and the bodies of the dead. Alongside, a second set of ropes followed the foot trail. Stretched out below, the injured were slowly making their way down, sidestepping and holding onto the line with both hands. Clary and Purcell were about midway down, and Duncan just starting the descent.

"Got an extra empty sled, sir," a man called out to Harrington. "We can lower you down in it, if you want."

Lowered down like a dead man. No goddamned way, Harrington silently fumed. *Roll down this hillside before I'd do that.*

"I'm fine," Harrington answered.

He hooked his cane over his forearm and slowly began to walk down the steep trail. His feet slipped around inside his oversized shoes, making it tough to dig his heels into the snow. Each step was hard and deliberate, jarring his side. With each jolt, pain shot through his ribs. By the time he reached the base of the hill, his lungs were heaving, his arms aching.

A number of the others had gathered to catch their breath. Nearly doubled over from pain, Harrington sat on a downed log next to a man he vaguely recognized.

"You must be Harrington," the man said. "White's my name. Henry White. You don't recognize me, do you."

Still bent over, panting, Harrington turned his head and looked at the man.

"Something tells me … we've met," he gasped. "Can't place it. Saw you in the bunkhouse."

"We met briefly before that. You remember seeing someone out in the snow right after the slide?" White asked.

"Don't remember much of that night at all," replied Harrington, finally catching his wind. "Was pretty dazed. Tough to know what was real. I can't say as I recollect seeing a soul."

"Oh, I was real. Like you. I tried to stand up, then fell down. By the time I got back up, you were gone," White recalled.

"If you say so. I really don't recall much about that night," Harrington insisted.

"Didn't know what happened to you until they hauled me into the bunkhouse," White continued.

"A lot of good men, most of them my friends, got killed that night," Harrington lamented.

"Yes, well, damned terrible. Terrible place to have had those trains," continued White.

So that's it. Give me hell about putting the trains on the sidings. Harrington closely eyed White. *Be careful what you tell this son of a bitch.*

"Had no choice. Looking back, it ended up being one hell of a place. No reason not to at the time, though." Harrington pulled himself up and began to walk towards Scenic before White could reply.

A train consisting of two baggage cars and a single coach was standing in front of the station. Harrington, hoping to have a seat to himself, loitered around the platform while section men loaded the last of the bodies dug out that day into the baggage cars.

Wonder who we're hauling home with us, Harrington pondered. *Best I don't know.*

Harrington followed the last passenger onto the train. Standing at the head of the aisle, he surveyed the coach. The two Negro porters were making the trip. Knowing their place, they sat together in a seat in the far corner. Clary and Purcell were together, and were in a deep conversation with Duncan and Kerlee, sitting across from them.

Slowly walking down the aisle, Harrington spotted an empty seat on the car's right side, near the front. Settling in, he stretched out his leg, trying to rub the pain out of his knee. He took another look around the coach. Henry White was talking to a man he recognized as the Great Northern lawyer who had been up at Wellington most of the day.

Shouldn't have said a goddamned word to that guy, Harrington scolded himself. *Over there spilling his guts to that damned lawyer.*

There was a gentle jolt. As the car began to move, Harrington looked long and hard at Windy Mountain. Far up on the side hill, just shy of "Old Glory," he could see J.J. Dowling's outfit working east. Smoke was shooting skyward from the plow and engines, a plume of white snow gracefully arching over the side.

Never seen that before, Harrington realized. *Always been the poor bastard on the plow. Quite a sight.*

Tired from the hike, Harrington dozed most of the way down the hill to Skykomish. In his half-conscious state, he saw the faces of men now dead. Choking with emotion, he would force himself to come to his senses and try to think of something else for fear the ngithmares would return.

The train pulled into the yard at Skykomish. It came to a stop near the roundhouse, so a fresh locomotive could be coupled for the trip to Everett and Seattle.

"Anyone got the time?" Harrington asked.

"Four-fifteen," answered the lawyer.

Struggling, Harrington stood up and made his way to the front of the coach.

"Where you headed, Bill? Clary inquired.

"I've got some business over at the station," Harrington said.

He dropped off the coach just as the engine that had brought them down from Scenic pulled away. The engineer, waving at Harrington, gave him a short salute with the whistle.

"Don't leave without me," Harrington told the young brakeman.

Cane in hand, Harrington picked his way across the rail yard and into the depot. Second trick operator George Pierce saw Harrington approaching. By the time he limped into the room, the man was digging through the top drawer of his desk. Producing a silver dollar, he slapped it down on the corner.

"Here's your buck, Mr. Harrington," Pierce said. He turned to the mouthpiece and pressed the foot treadle. "Dispatcher, Skykomish. OS Extra …"

"I didn't bring you that lantern back, George," Harrington admitted.

"Hold on a minute, dispatcher." Pierce turned in his chair. "You brought yourself back, Mr. Harrington. If that ain't worth a buck, I'll be goddamned if I know what is. Take it and get outta here, I got work to do."

Pierce smiled and winked, then turned back to resume talking on the phone. Harrington put the coin in his pocket and hobbled back to the train.

As the train made its way out of the mountains and into the lowlands, Harrington was glad to finally see green grass. Seeing color again almost came as shock. The alder trees along the right-of-way were showing signs of budding; the pussy willows out in force.

Spring's just around the corner. Right about one thing. That storm was the last one of the year.

For a large part of the trip, Harrington tried to keep his anticipation of seeing his wife and children in check. He was not sure why; he just felt it was the thing to do. But as the train closed the last miles across the Snohomish Valley flats, he gave in.

Wonder what Lil's wearing? She probably put on her Sunday best. Hope she's there. Could be no one even told her I'm on my way. Told Flannery, but she might not've got the message. God, I hope she's there.

Closing his eyes, Harrington hoped to doze away the last miles to the station. He tried to visualize where the train was without sneaking a peak out the window. It seemed to take an hour to cover the last five miles, before he could feel the car's brakes take hold and the train slow to a stop.

On purpose, Harrington was sitting on the side opposite the platform. He did not try to stand up and look across for Lillian. Clary, Purcell, Duncan and Kerlee were up in a flash, making their way down the aisle.

"Get off your ass, Bill," Clary said, slapping Harrington's shoulder, a grin on his face. "There's a damned good-looking woman out there waiting for you. If you don't get out there and claim her, by God, I will."

Be nice to walk off of here without this damned cane, Harrington decided. He got up awkwardly. *Damned fool. Grab the cane and get the hell off this train.*

The sun was at Harrington's back, setting behind the Olympic Mountains. In the twilight, its rosy glow was cast on the face of Lillian Harrington. The sight nearly brought her husband to tears before he had even gotten off the train. She had on her Sunday dress, her long hair put up under a small hat. He could tell she was trying to smile, all the while wiping tears from her eyes with a lace handkerchief.

She's beautiful, is all Harrington could think.

He limped across the platform. Lillian said nothing at first. Harrington bent forward slightly, allowing his wife to carefully wrap her arms around his neck.

"You need a shave and a bath, Bill. You stink," she whispered in his ear, amid her snuffling.

"Love you too, Lil," Harrington said. He dropped the cane and gathered his wife in his arms.

They stood for a moment, holding each other. Choreographed by years of marriage, both released their grip of the other at the same time. Lillian stepped back. She dried her eyes and smoothed the front of her dress.

"Come along. The railroad sent an automobile to take us home.

Roughest ride I've ever had," she said in her usual matter-of-fact voice. "Alice is watching the children. Ever since I told them you were coming home today, they've been little hellions."

"Can't wait to see them. Missed you. Missed them," Harrington muttered.

"My goodness, Bill. What are you wearing? You look like a hobo!"

"I could still be in my bloody nightshirt, Lil. All my clothes went down in the damned slide." A smile broke across his face and finally a laugh. Each chuckle sent a bolt of pain through his side, but the pure joy of being reunited with Lillian was enough for him to be able to ignore the jabs. "A week ago I came within a gnat's ass of getting killed, and you're wondering why I'm not ready for the society page. I love ya, Lil. By damned, I do love ya."

He tried to give her a quick pat on the behind, but, as usual, was too slow. She batted his hand away.

"William Harrington! Stop that!" she snapped.

Harrington helped his wife into the back seat of the automobile. She was crying again. It took a couple of tries before Harrington was able to negotiate the running board and narrow doorway, sitting hard against his wife in the seat. They rode in silence, shoulder to shoulder, Lillian's arm laced through his. Harrington's ribs felt every pothole the car hit.

"Might work around town, but these damned motor carriages will never replace a train for long trips, " Harrington hollered into Lillian's ear.

The faces of Harrington's children were pressed against the front window when the motor carriage pulled up. It occurred to Harrington that they were more interested in the automobile than they were in him.

Lillian helped her husband up the front steps. By the time Harrington was on the porch, the front door was open and a great cloud of young humanity was circling about his legs. A shrieking chorus of "Poppa!" was filling his ears.

"Children, please, let your father at least get in the house," Lillian scolded. "Remember, be careful. Your father is hurt!"

Handing his cane to son Donald, Harrington bent down and scooped little Bessie into his arms.

"Ah, Pumpkin Face. Give me a kiss," he said, choking back tears of his own.

His youngest daughter rubbed his beard with her soft hand and then planted a wet kiss on his cheek.

"Have you been looking after your mother, Dorothy?" he asked his eldest daughter as he walked into the house.

Dorothy was wiping away tears as well, hardly able to speak.

"Was scared, Poppa. Thought you were dead." She wrapped her arms around Harrington's middle.

"Well, I'm not, so all's well that ends well," Harrington said, rubbing the top of her head.

"What about you, Donnie, been behaving yourself?" asked Harrington.

"Mother got me a baseball, Poppa. We can play later, okay?" blurted his son.

"Sure, let me rest a bit, then I'll teach you to catch," Harrington promised. He reached in his pocket and took out the silver dollar he collected at the Skykomish depot.

"Here Donnie," he said, placing the coin in his hand, "this is for you."

"Wow, Poppa!" he exclaimed.

"I'll get one for you too, Dorothy," Harrington quickly added. "And even you, Pumpkin."

Harrington rubbed his grizzly face against little Bessie, making her laugh.

Walking into the front room, Harrington set Bessie down. He looked around.

"You don't know how many times I thought about this moment, Lillian. Finally home safe, just sitting here." He lowered himself into his overstuffed chair.

Their neighbor came in from the kitchen.

"So glad you're home safe, Bill. We were all worried sick. I left you some supper, Lillian. You don't need to be cooking, tonight of all nights," she said.

"Thank you, Alice. You're a dear." Lillian escorted their neighbor to the front door.

"Here, Poppa, put your feet up." Donald shoved the stool under Harrington's feet and pulled off the borrowed shoes.

"Okay, children, run along and get cleaned up for supper. Dorothy, make sure Donald washes his hands on both sides. Take Pumpkin with you. I want to talk to your father for a few minutes," Lillian instructed.

Gonna catch hell now, Harrington thought, smiling.

Pulling up the footstool that was in front of her chair, Lillian sat at Harrington's side. She grabbed his left hand and squeezed it tight.

"I went to visit Rosie Blackburn yesterday. Went to the station with her to claim the body. It was horrible, but I didn't want her to go alone. Little Grace was with her. She's afraid to let her go. They're completely alone." Lillian paused.

"I'm so sorry ..." Harrington began.

"Let me finish, Bill. There are fathers and mothers grieving because their sons are dead. There are widows all over this city. I came as close as I ever want to come to being one of them, Bill. We got the news of the slide and didn't know. They said you were missing along with Art." Lillian fumbled for her handkerchief.

"I want you off that mountain, Bill. Off those god-awful plows. I don't want to be a widow. I don't want our children to have to go to their father's funeral. You understand?" she pleaded.

Harrington let go of Lillian's hand. With his finger he wiped the tears off her cheeks.

"I don't know what I'm going to do, Lil. I just don't know. I promise I'll never take the Snow King job again. You have my word on that," Harrington said, his voice low. "There's some talk about me taking Art's job. If that happens, it'll only be until O'Neill finds someone permanent, maybe just through the summer."

"What about next winter, Bill? If you're still a conductor, you'll be right back on those plows again and we both know it. You've got the experience and they'll make you go back," Lillian argued.

"Can't win a fight with you, can I, Lil? Been thinking about that. Might take a little time, but I'll use my seniority to take Pettit's place on 25. Get a regular run on a passenger. Regular days off. How's that sound?" Harrington reasoned.

"Mother said never to marry a railroad man," Lillian said, a smile now on her face. "Just stay off those plows, Bill."

Shouts were coming from the back-porch washroom, along with the splashing of water.

"Those children of yours Bill, been hellions all day!" Lillian got up and gave Harrington a soft kiss on the top of his head. "You really do smell, Bill, and yes, I love you too."

With the same grace that had struck Harrington when he first met her, Lillian swept from the room out to the kitchen.

Home. Safe. The nightmares. Maybe they'll go away.

Alone, Harrington tried to relax. Sitting in that familiar, overstuffed chair he closed his eyes. Immediately the faces of the men he knew, those with whom he had formed such strong bonds of friendship, the men he loved, the men now gone; immediately, their faces came clear in his mind.

Harrington put his hands to his face and wept.

March 8, 1910, 5:30 p.m.
John Robert Meath, Engineer

"Fire in the hole!" a voice yelled. "Fire in the hole!"

Meath stopped shoveling coal and watched a group of men scurry from the slide that had been blocking their way to Wellington for over a week. There was a moment of complete silence, then a series of ground-trembling explosions. Large chunks of packed snow and timber flew into the air. When the smoke and ice crystals settled, a team of loggers, brought up from the camps at Skykomish and Index, swarmed over the scene. Within minutes the air rang with the sound of their axes and the rhythm produced by men working the ends of cross-cut saws.

It had been a fine, spring-like day. The sun was out, and the air warm. J.J. Dowling had pulled the X-808 through Shed 3.3 early in the morning and plowed up to the stalled rotaries. The crew of quarry men and loggers with him began blasting through the giant slide that had, in many ways, sealed the fate of nearly one hundred people.

Glad they're blowing that slide all to hell, Meath thought. *That pile of snow killed my best friend.*

The plow crews had begun the task of transferring fuel from the cars Dowling had brought to the empty tenders of the stalled plows and pushers. Carpenters at Scenic had built half a dozen sleds designed to carry coal, accommodating two men pulling and one shoving.

Other men shoveled out the snow frozen around the wheels of the equipment.

"You know Will, been wondering all damned day, why didn't we think of blasting through that slide a long time ago?" Jim Mackey asked his brother.

Will kept pitching coal from the sled to the tender of the X-802.

"Oh sure, that's one hell of a good idea. We don't know shit about blasting. Would have blown up this whole damned railroad," Will said, not breaking stride. "Just get back to work and keep your good ideas to yourself, Jim."

"No, I'm serious, Will." Jim went back to shoveling as well, but pressed his point. "I ain't saying we would have done the blasting. Just should have brought them boys up here right off. When we first started having trouble bucking the drifts."

"You see what I've had to put with all these years, Bobby?" Will said, staring at his brother and shaking his head. "There's no goddamned way those powder monkeys would've come up here in the middle of that goddamned blizzard. Only a bunch of hard-headed railroaders would be so stupid as to try and beat Mother Nature at her own game, and look where it got us."

"Now listen, Bobby, you tell me, wouldn't it have been smart to bring those boys up here right off?" Jim pleaded, ignoring his brother.

"Can you two assholes even agree that you're brothers?" Meath asked.

Good to hear the boys joking around. Been a tough pull, Meath thought. *Need to get my spirits up too. Still expect to see Al. Pop out from inside one of the plows. God help me, I miss him.*

Their sled empty, the three men headed back for another load. It was a good crew that had been assembled to revive the plows. In spite of the hard work and fatigue, Meath was enjoying himself. Bob Ford, Pete Imberg, Rich Chambers, John Pettit, Stan Meredith, Irving Tegtmeier, the Mackey brothers; enough men had been gathered that they could at least partially cover the giant holes left by those who were gone. The men were joking and laughing. Progress was finally being made.

Reason for hope, Meath thought as he watched Tom Brown and Joe Stafford throw coal from the hopper car onto their sled.

"Good to see you high-powered engineers are not too proud to shovel coal," Meath hollered over to the two men.

"Ah, up yours, Bobby," Brown scowled. "Should've never let O'Neill talk me into relieving you that night. You wouldn't be so full of piss and vinegar today."

Again came the cry, "Fire in the hole!" Seconds later, the mountains reverberated with explosions.

"Blasting a trail right through that slide," Stafford said.

"You taking the 802, Bobby?" Brown asked.

"Don't want to be a throttle hog, but yeah, I'd like to be the one," Meath admitted.

"She's all yours," Stafford agreed.

"Besides, we need the best wheelman we got on the point," Jim Mackey said, getting ready to pull the full sled forward. "I got a bottle resting on you, Bobby."

"Now what the hell are you talking about?" Will asked, standing next to his brother. Together the two pulled hard on the sled's rope harness.

Meath fell in behind and began to shove the load towards the tender of his plow.

"Yeah, what are you talking about?" he asked between grunts.

"Hold up a minute," Jim ordered. "You mean you boys ain't heard?"

"Heard what, goddamn it! For once in your life would you just get to the point?" Will shouted in his brother's ear.

"Well, you don't have to holler," Jim pouted.

"Jesus Christ, I pray I'm adopted," Will said gazing at the sky.

"Just tell us what you're yapping about, Jimbo," Meath joined in.

"The bet. There's a bet on. The boys on the eastside plow say they're gonna buck more of the big slide than we are."

Meath thought over the possibilities as they pulled the sled up to the tender of the 802.

Getting back to normal around here, he quietly realized. *Whaddya think Al, should we take'em up on this bet? You always liked this kind of talk.*

Grabbing a shovel, he and the Mackeys began to empty their sled.

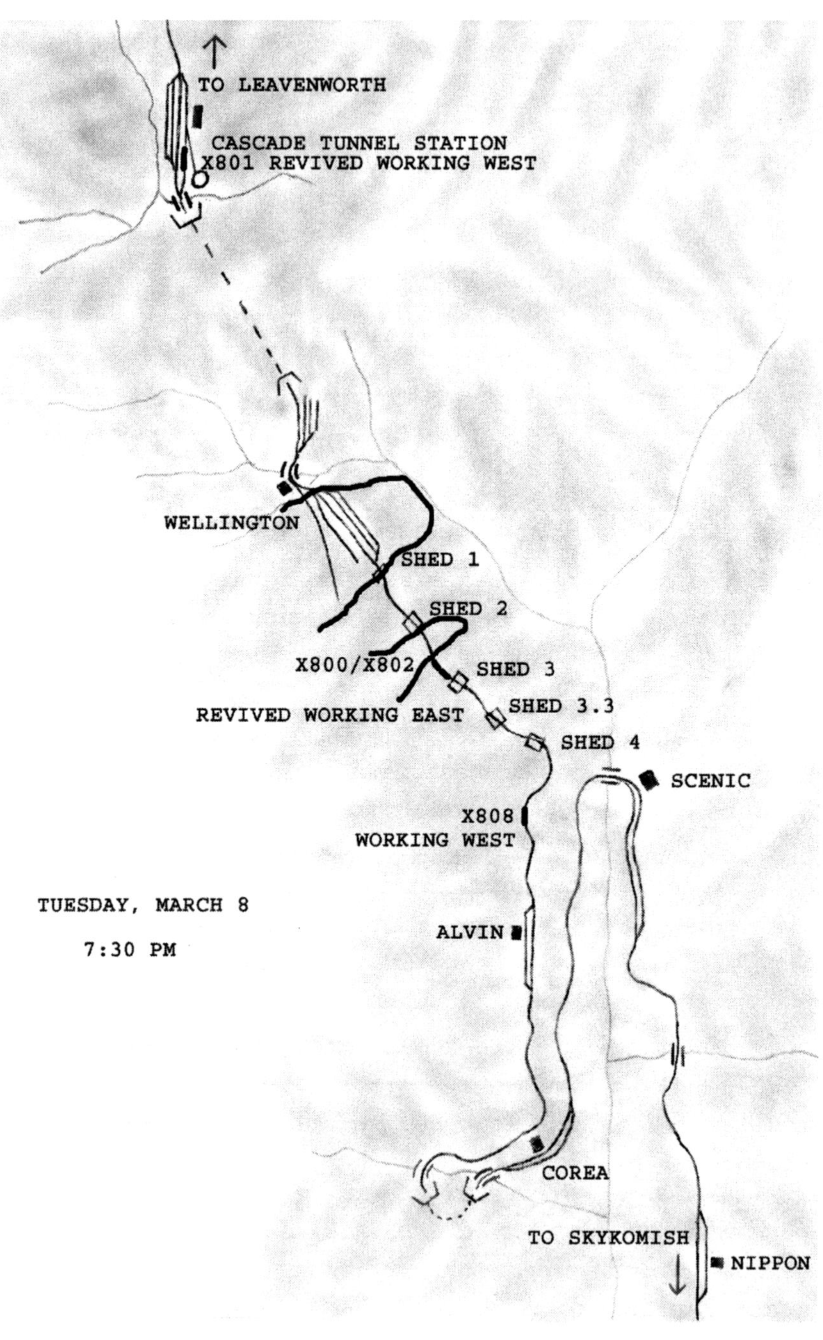
TO LEAVENWORTH
CASCADE TUNNEL STATION
X801 REVIVED WORKING WEST
WELLINGTON
SHED 1
SHED 2
X800/X802
SHED 3
REVIVED WORKING EAST
SHED 3.3
SHED 4
SCENIC
X808
WORKING WEST
TUESDAY, MARCH 8
7:30 PM
ALVIN
COREA
TO SKYKOMISH
NIPPON

"We bore out more of the big slide than they do," Meath pondered aloud. "I don't know about you, Will, but I'm in for a round. Hear tell that plow from the east is a hunk of junk anyway. We can plow more than those assholes."

"Well, they don't exactly have a hunk of junk, Bobby," Jim confessed.

"Alright, Jim, now what aren't you telling us?" Will asked, acting as if he was about to take the flat side of his shovel to his brother's head.

"I hear tell they swapped out. Turned the 801 and are coming west with it. She's a snow-eating son of a bitch, you know," Jim mentioned, as if the information was of little consequence.

"Turn your head, Bobby," Will said. "I'm going to cold-cock him right here and now."

"Ah hell, I'm still in," Meath decided.

Jimbo and Will, Meath chuckled. *About like a bad bottle. A little bit goes a long way, but it's kinda fun drinking out of it.*

J.J. Dowling came off the slide and approached the group.

"Getting pretty dark. Powder boys are going to call it a day. They've got enough blasted to keep you boys going most of the night," Dowling reported. "You got enough coal to run?"

"Hey Stan," Meath called out. "We ready to go?"

"Been holding her back some, if the truth be known. The chaps will have to keep shoveling snow for water, but I'd say the coal pile will hold for a good long bit," Meredith informed the group.

From behind, the whistle of the 1128 suddenly pierced through the twilight. A cheer went up from the men gathered around the engine. Within seconds a second volley erupted from the 1154, answered by the trailing X-800.

"Can't have them stealing all the thunder," Meredith said. He reached for his whistle chord and sent a stream of pressurized steam through the brass whistle of the X-802. It was a symphony that gave Meath goose bumps.

Hear that, Al? We're back in business.

Dowling and Roadmaster McIntyre gathered the crews together and jobs were assigned. A group of section men would stay with the outfit throughout the night, helping on the slide, hauling coal, and shoveling snow into the tenders of the plows and pushers. Dowling was taking his outfit back down to Scenic, hoping to return in the morning with yet another car of coal.

"If you boys are going to win that bet, we'd better keep these tea pots hot," quipped Dowling. "Let's get to it. Irving, you and Jimbo take charge. Will, I'll have you come back with me."

"Thank you, thank you J.J.," Tegtmeier told Dowling. "Those two have been driving us crazy all day."

"Didn't think it was that bad," Jim Mackey mumbled.

"Bad, all you did all day was argue with me," Will Mackey countered.

"Get them outta here!" Tegtmeier screamed.

A loud round of laughter broke out as the group of men broke up. Dowling and Will Mackey headed back to the X-808, with Jim Mackey and Irving Tegtmeier joining Rich Chambers in the cab of the X-802.

Meath hopped onto the fire deck.

"You ready, Stan?" he asked the Welsh fireman.

"That I am, my good fellow," Meredith grinned. "You just try and run me low on steam."

Meath passed through the narrow door and made his way down the gangway alongside the boiler. He knew he was ready. It felt good to sit on the hard, seat box. The smell of hot grease and steam filled his nostrils. His machine was alive. For the first time in a couple of weeks, he felt alive.

Looking forward into the cab, Meath saw Irving Tegtmeier leaning out the door, ready to give everyone the "highball." Closing his eyes, he could see the broad back of Al Dougherty hanging from that door. Instead of Rich Chambers, he saw Archie Dupy on the clutch, a puddle of tobacco juice already at his feet. In his mind, it was Bill Harrington's hand that grabbed the cord and whistled for reverse, and Art Blackburn hanging from the other door. Behind him, Meath wanted to believe it was Bat Nelson firing his plow, with Benny Jarnigan's skilled hands on the throttle of the pusher.

The plow gave a lurch and moved backwards. Meath's heart was in his throat with excitement.

Well, here goes, he thought, pulling his hat down. Gloves on his hands, he grabbed the Johnson Bar and waited.

"Highball!" Tegtmeier hollered. Chambers gave the whistle two short blasts. Meath answered, and each pusher replied.

"Let's wind her up, Bobby!" came the order.

Meath slammed the reverser forward halfway and pulled his throttle out four notches. For the second time in so many hours, he got goose bumps as he heard the steam rush into the pistons, the quarter shafts spinning the pinions, the giant ring gear beginning to turn. The sweet music of exhaust erupting from the plow's stack finally brought tears to Meath's eyes.

The plow moved forward. Meath waited. He heard Chambers engage the clutch. Squeezing the catch, he gave the machine four more notches on the throttle. It sounded right. It felt right.

"Here we go!" Tegtmeier shouted.

Meath pushed the Johnson Bar all the way forward. Releasing the catch on the throttle, he pulled it out to the last notch. The plow rammed into the snow, black from the power blasts.

"She's taking her all, Bobby!" Tegtmeier bellowed in a voice of near triumph.

Meath glanced to his right at the nail where normally his coffee cup swung. On it hung a battered derby hat.

"Got a bottle riding on this. Let's you and me get this railroad running again, Al."

The End

Epilogue

On March 9, 1910, Rotary X-801 rolled through the Cascade Tunnel from the east and began plowing west towards the station at Wellington and the slide beyond. Three days later, on March 12, the two plow trains—the X-802 from the west and the X-801 from the east—met. The following day, March 13, with the line declared open, a large slide struck near Alvin, hitting the X-808, which was assigned to protect the eastbound Oriental Limited. The force of the avalanche carried the plow over the bank, claiming the last victim of the disaster, an Italian section man. The final death toll stood at 100: 96 at Wellington, 2 at Cascade Tunnel Station, 1 at Chiwaukum, and 1 at Alvin. Of the total, 55 were railroaders. The first through-train arrived at Wellington on March 15, 1910. Protected eastward by Rotary X-802, when the plow arrived in Leavenworth, John Robert Meath and others walked to the depot to "sign off." They had put in an incredible 21 days of continuous duty without so much as a hot bath, a change of clothes, or regular sleep and meals.

James Henry O'Neill continued to rise in the ranks of Great Northern Railway management. In 1912, he became the Assistant General Superintendent of the Western Division. Within a year, he was promoted to General Superintendent. During the World War I government takeover of the nation's railroads, O'Neill was the Terminal

Manager of the US Consolidated Lines. Once the railroads were again privatized, O'Neill became the General Manager of the Great Northern Operating Department, Lines West, where he worked until he died suddenly of a heart attack on January 11, 1937, at age 64.

On January 12, 1929, ceremonies were held at Scenic, Washington, officially opening the eight-mile Cascade Tunnel. On that day, the "old high line" to Wellington was abandoned. One of the dignitaries in attendance was James Henry O'Neill.

William Harrington quickly recovered from his injuries. He briefly accepted the position of Trainmaster vacated by the death of Arthur Blackburn. Keeping his promise to Lillian, he gave up the position, to become the conductor on Trains 25/26, the very same passenger run that was destroyed by the Wellington Slide. In a twist of fate, on January 22, 1916, an avalanche struck his train near the siding at Corea. Although Harrington was uninjured, eight passengers on his train died. Shortly after that event, Lillian Harrington got her wish. William Harrington left train service and became a yardmaster at Everett, finally retiring from the Great Northern as a dispatcher.

Basil and Althea Sherlock left Wellington on March 16, 1910. Due to her service in the hospital at Wellington, Althea Sherlock was asked to testify at the coroner's inquest held that same week. The Sherlocks moved to the Midwest and never returned to the mountains of the West. Sherlock worked as a telegrapher and dispatcher in Iowa and Illinois, finally retiring in Willmar, Minnesota, not far from Waverly, the final resting place of Anthony John Dougherty.

John Robert Meath worked his entire career as an engineer on the Cascade Division of the Great Northern. He eventually married Lizzie McCabe, and settled in Everett. They did not have children. Upon retiring, the Meaths moved back to their hometown of Hammond, Wisconsin where they now rest together in the St. Mary's cemetery.

Three years after the disaster, on October 20, 1913, a negligence suit was brought against the Great Northern Railway on behalf of William Topping, the orphaned son of Ned Topping, a passenger killed on Train 25. The case was tried in King County Superior Court. Topping's lawyers successfully kept such railroad witnesses as James O'Neill, William Harrington, Ira Clary, and Robert Meath from clearly telling the story of the blockade by the use of the rules of admissible evidence. Plaintiff attorneys continually voiced objections to the testimony of railroad witnesses, claiming it to be "incompetent, irrelevant and immaterial" even in cases where specific written orders were being recounted. As a result, the jury decided in favor of Topping, convicting the Great Northern Railway of gross negligence.

Arguing on appeal before the Washington State Supreme Court, Great Northern Railway lawyers were able to gain a reversal of the lower court ruling in August, 1914. Chief Justice Herman D. Crow cited "Vis Major," an "act of God," as the legal precedence.

In the course of testifying before the King County Coroner's Inquest, William Harrington was asked if he saw anyone during those first moments after he emerged from the slide. To the jury he said: "I did not see a soul. I heard some of my boys holler way down below … but I did not see them."

Lucius Anderson, Porter	injured
Charles Andrews, Engineer	survived
William Avery, Telegrapher	survived
Samuel Bates, Fireman	injured
Earl Bennington, Fireman	killed
John Bjart, Laborer	killed
John Bjerenson, Cook	killed
Arthur Blackburn, Trainmaster	killed
William Bovee, Brakeman	killed
Alex (Ed) Campbell, Motor Conductor	killed
J.O. Carroll, Engineer	killed
G. Christy, Laborer	killed
Ira Clary, Rotary Conductor	injured
William. Corcoran, Engine Watchman	killed
William Doerty, Brakeman	killed
Anthony John Dougherty, Brakeman	killed
J. J. Dowling, Master Mechanic	survived
E.S. Duncan, Brakeman	injured
William Duncan, Porter	killed
Archie Dupy, Brakeman	killed
Harry Elerker, Cook's helper	killed
Joseph Finn, Engineer	survived
Earl Fisher, Fireman	killed

William Flannery, Telegrapher	survived
Robert Ford, Engineer	survived
Inigi Giammarusti, Laborer	killed
Donald Gilman, Electrician	killed
Mike Guglielmo, Laborer	killed
William Harrington, Asst. Trainmaster	injured
Milton Hicks, Brakeman	killed
Benjamin Jarnigan, Engineer	killed
G.R. Jenks, Fireman	killed
Charles Jennison, Fireman	killed
Sidney Jones, Fireman	killed
John (Pattie) Kelly, Brakeman	killed
William Kenzal, Brakeman	killed
James (Curly) Kerlee, Brakeman	injured
Gus Leibert, Laborer	killed
J. Liberati, Laborer	killed
Steven (Ed) Lindsay, Rotary Conductor	killed
Earl Longcoy, Secretary to Supt. O'Neill	killed
James J. Mackey, Traveling Engineer	survived
Francis Martin, Engineer	killed
Archibald McDonald, Brakeman	killed
John Robert Meath, Engineer	survived
Robert Miles, Engineer	survived
George (Bat) Nelson, Fireman	injured
Peter Nino, Engine Watchman	killed
James Henry O'Neill, Superintendent	survived
T.L. Osborne, Engineer	killed
Harry Partridge, Fireman	killed
John Parzybok, Rotary Conductor	killed
J.L. Pettit, Passenger Conductor	killed
Ross Phillips, Brakeman	injured
Homer Purcell, Rotary Conductor	injured
Antonio Porlowlino, Laborer	killed
William Raycroft, Brakeman	killed
L. Ross, Fireman	killed
John Scott, brakeman	survived
Basil Sherlock, Telegrapher	survived

Charles Smart, Fireman	injured
Adolph Smith, Porter	injured
Carl Smith, Laborer	killed
Andrew Stohmier, Brakeman	killed
Vasily Suterin, Laborer	killed
Edward Sweeney, Engineer	survived
Duncan Tegtmeier, Traveling Engineer	injured
Irving Tegtmeier, Traveling Engineer	survived
Giovanni Tosti, Laborer	killed
Walter Vogel, Conductor	survived
Lewis George Walker, Steward	killed
Julian Wells, Brakeman	killed
M.O. White, Rotary Conductor	injured
G.R. Yerks, Fireman	killed
Unidentified Laborer	killed
Unidentified Laborer	killed
Unidentified Laborer	killed
Unidentified Laborer	killed
Unidentified Laborer	killed
Unidentified Laborer	killed

Acknowledgements

Saying this text represents my life's work would not be an exaggeration; that I did it alone, would. Thus it would be remiss of me not to thank those who have helped.

The pioneer work of Ruby ElHult, author of *Northwest Disaster* is the foundation on which much of the Wellington knowledge is based. In particular, the notes she took during her first hand interviews with Wellington survivors proved to be an amazing treasure trove of information and insights. Sadly, Ruby has gone ahead and has joined the spirits of Wellington.

There is no way I can give enough credit or thanks to Robert Kelly. No one cares more about the history of Stevens Pass and Wellington than Bob, and no one shares his findings more than Bob. Gary Krist, author of *The White Cascade* writes, "Bob has a passion for the subject that proves infectious to all who experience it." To that, I can add no more. Bob is indeed, the spirit of Wellington personified.

The sharp eyes and sharp red pencils of Brian Jennison and Mary Beth Conlee turned my passive verbs into active, and placed commas and dashes where they should. Both asked the questions that needed to be asked, forcing me to turn this jumble of words into a readable story. I am truly thankful that they paid close attention when in grammar class.

To all those I brow-beat into reading and commenting on all the various versions of this book, thank you. My wife Janice, Ted Benson, Greg McDonnell, Donald Gill, Marilyn Proby, Margie Williams-Anderson, Carol Voss, Christine Perkins, Ben Bachman, Ben Krause, and Kern Kemmerer come to mind.

Added to the list is Gary Krist. His meticulous reading of the manuscript and pointed questions asked of me while researching his own book on the event, *The White Cascade*, aided me in bringing the story presented here into clear focus. Gary has, at times been my personal cheerleader, and his knowledge of the publishing industry has been both a help and the inspiration needed to see this project come to fruition.

Finally, I will go out on a limb, but I feel it proper to thank the "boys of Wellington." Clearly, this is their story. For what ever reason, I am simply the portal though which they decided to finally show us all what they endured. Were it not for their regular visits, this text would not exist. To their spirits I owe the greatest debt of gratitude.

CPSIA information can be obtained at www.ICGtesting.com
Printed in the USA
BVOW080528270912

301523BV00001B/6/P

9 781440 161773